A GROOM WORTH WAITING FOR

BY
SOPHIE PEMBROKE

D1137878

MILLS & BOON

Published in Great Britain 2014
by Mills & Boon, an imprint of Harlequin (UK) Limited,
Eton House, 18-24 Paradise Road, Richmond, Surrey, TW9 1SR

© 2014 Sophie Pembroke

ISBN: 978-0-263-91308-8

23-0814

Harlequin (UK) Limited's policy is to use papers that are natural, renewable and recyclable products and made from wood grown in sustainable forests. The logging and manufacturing processes conform to the legal environmental regulations of the country of origin.

Printed and bound in Spain
by Blackprint CPI, Barcelona

Sophie Pembroke has been dreaming, reading and writing romance for years—ever since she first read *The Far Pavilions* under her desk in Chemistry class. She later stayed up all night devouring Mills & Boon® books as part of her English degree at Lancaster University, and promptly gave up any pretext of enjoying tragic novels. After all, what's the point of a book without a happy ending?

She loves to set her novels in the places where she has lived—from the wilds of the Welsh mountains to the genteel humour of an English country village, or the heat and tension of a London summer. She also has a tendency to make her characters kiss in castles.

Currently Sophie makes her home in Hertfordshire, with her scientist husband (who still shakes his head at the reading-in-Chemistry thing) and their four-year-old *Alice-in-Wonderland*-obsessed daughter. She writes her love stories in the study she begrudgingly shares with her husband, while drinking too much tea and eating homemade cakes. Or, when things are looking very bad for her heroes and heroines, white wine and dark chocolate.

Sophie keeps a blog at www.sophiepembroke.com, which should be about romance and writing but is usually about cake and castles instead.

For Emma, Helen & Mary.

CHAPTER ONE

'WHAT DO YOU MEAN, he's coming here?' Thea Morrison clasped her arms around her body, as if the action could somehow hide the fact that she was wearing a ridiculously expensive, pearl-encrusted, embroidered ivory wedding dress, complete with six-foot train. 'He can't!'

Her sister rolled her big blue eyes. 'Oh, calm down. He just told me to tell you that you're late to meet with the wedding planner and if you aren't there in five minutes he'll come and get you,' Helena said.

'Well, stop him!'

No, that wouldn't work. Nothing stopped Flynn Ashton when he really wanted something. He was always polite, but utterly tenacious. That was why his father had appointed him his right-hand man at Morrison-Ashton media. And why she was marrying him in the first place.

'Get me out of this dress before he gets here!'

'I don't know why you care so much,' Helena said, fumbling with the zip at the back of the dress. 'It's not like this is a real wedding anyway.'

'In two days there'll be a priest, a cake, some flowers, and a legally binding pre-nup saying otherwise.' Thea wriggled to try and get the strapless dress down over her hips. 'And everyone knows it's bad luck for the groom to see the bride in the wedding dress before the big day.'

It was more than a superstition, it was a rule. Standard Operating Procedure for weddings. Flynn was not seeing this dress a single moment before she walked down the aisle of the tiny Tuscan church at the bottom of the hill from the villa. Not one second.

'Which is why he sent me instead.'

Thea froze, her blood suddenly solid in her veins. She knew that voice. It might have been eight years since she'd heard it, but she hadn't forgotten. Any of it.

The owner of that voice really shouldn't be seeing her in nothing but her wedding lingerie. Especially since she was marrying his brother in two days.

Yanking the dress back up over her ivory corset, Thea held it tight against her chest and stared at him. 'I thought you weren't coming.' But there he was. Large as life and twice as... Hell, she couldn't even lie in her brain and finish that with *ugly*. He looked...grown up. Not twenty-one and angry at everything any more. More relaxed, more in control.

And every inch as gorgeous as he'd always been. Curse him.

Helena laughed. 'Eight years and that's all you have to say to him?' Skipping across the room, blonde hair bouncing, she wrapped her arms around him and pressed a kiss against his cheek. 'It's good to see you, Zeke.'

'Little Helena, all grown up.' Zeke returned the hug, but his gaze never left Thea's. 'It's good to see you too. And rather more of your sister than I'd bargained on.'

There was a mocking edge in his voice. As if she'd planned for him to walk in on her in her underwear. He wasn't even supposed to be in the country! Flynn had told her he wouldn't come and she'd been flooded with relief— even if she could never explain why to her husband-to-be.

But now here Zeke was, staring at her, and Thea had never felt so exposed.

She clutched the dress tighter—a barrier between them. 'Well, I was expecting your brother.'

'Your fiancé,' Zeke said. 'Of course. Sorry. Seems he thought I should get started with my best man duties a few days early.'

Thea blinked. '*You're* Flynn's best man?'

'Who else would he choose?' He said it as if he hadn't been gone for eight years. As if he'd never taunted Flynn about not being a real Ashton, only an adopted one, a fall-back plan. As if he hadn't sworn that he was never coming back.

'Anyone in the world.' Quite literally. Flynn could have appointed the Russian Prime Minister as his best man and Thea would have been less surprised.

'He chose his brother,' Helena said, giving Thea her usual *are you crazy?* look. She'd perfected it at fifteen and had been employing it with alarming regularity ever since. 'What's so weird about that?'

Helena hadn't been there. She'd been—what? Sixteen? Too young or too self-absorbed to get involved in the situation, or to realise what was going on. Thea had wanted to keep it from her—from everybody—even then. Of course with hindsight even at sixteen Helena had probably had a better idea about men than Thea had at eighteen. Or now, at twenty-six. But Helena had been dealing with her own issues then.

'So, you're here for the wedding?' Thea said.

Zeke raised his eyebrows. 'What else could I possibly be here for?'

She knew what he wanted her to say, or at least to think. That he'd come back for her. To tell her she'd made the wrong decision eight years ago and she was making a worse one now. To stop her making the biggest mistake of her life.

Except Thea knew full well she'd already made that. And it had nothing to do with Zeke Ashton.

No, she had her suspicions about Zeke's return, but she didn't think he was there for her. If he'd come back to the family fold there had to be something much bigger at stake than a teenage rebellion of a relationship that had been dead for almost a decade.

'I need to get changed.'

Keeping the dress clasped tight to her body, Thea stepped off the platform and slipped behind the screen to change back into her sundress from earlier. She could hear Helena and Zeke chatting lightly outside, making out his amused tone more than the words he spoke. That was one thing that hadn't changed. The world was still a joke to him—her family most of all.

Hanging the beautiful wedding dress up carefully on its padded hanger, Thea stepped back and stared at it. Her fairytale dress, all sparkle and shine. The moment she put it on she became a different person. A wife, perhaps. That dress, whatever it had cost, was worth every penny if it made her into that person, made her *fit*.

This time, this dress, this wedding…it had to be the one that stuck. That bought her the place in the world she needed. Nothing else she'd tried had worked.

Shaking her head, Thea tugged the straps of her sundress up over her shoulders, thankful for a moment or two to regroup. To remind herself that this didn't change anything. So Zeke was there, lurking around their Tuscan villa. So what? He wasn't there for *her*. She was still marrying Flynn. She belonged with Flynn. She had the dress; she had the plan. She had Helena at her side to make sure she said, wore and did the right thing at the right time. This was it. This villa, this wedding. This was where she was supposed to be. Everything was in its right place—apart from Zeke Ashton.

Well, he could just stay out of her perfect picture, thank you very much. Besides, the villa was big enough she probably wouldn't even notice he was in residence most of the time. Not a problem.

Sandals on, Thea smoothed down her hair and stepped back out. 'Now, if you'll excuse me, I have a meeting with the wedding planner to attend.'

'Of course,' Zeke said, with that infuriating mocking smile still in place. 'We wouldn't dream of delaying the blushing bride.'

Thea nodded sharply. She was *not* blushing.

She'd made a promise to herself eight years ago. A decision. And part of that decision meant that Zeke Ashton would never be able to make her blush again.

That part of her life was dead and buried.

Just two days until the wedding. Two more days—that was all. Two days until Thea Morrison got her happily-ever-after.

'In fact,' Zeke said, 'why don't I walk you there? We can catch up.'

Thea's jaw clenched. 'That would be lovely,' she lied.

Two days and this miserable week would be over. Thea couldn't wait.

She barely looked like Thea. With her dark hair straightened and pinned back, her slender arms and legs bronzed to the perfect shade of tan…she looked like someone else. Zeke studied her as she walked ahead of him, long strides clearly designed to get her away from his company as soon as physically possible.

Did she even remember the time when that had been

the last thing she'd wanted? When she'd smile and perform her hostess duties at her father's dinner parties and company barbecues, then sneak off to hide out somewhere private, often dark and cosy, with him…? Whoever she'd pretended to be for their parents—the good girl, the dutiful daughter—when they were alone Zeke had seen the real Thea. Seen glimpses of the woman he'd always believed she'd become.

Zeke shook his head. Apparently he'd been wrong. Those times were gone. And as he watched Thea—all high-heeled sandals, sundress and God only knew what underneath, rather than jeans, sneakers and hot pink knickers—he knew the girl he'd loved was gone, too. The Thea he'd fallen in love with would never have agreed to marry his brother, whatever their respective fathers' arguments for why it was a good idea. She'd wanted love—true love. And for a few brief months he'd thought she'd found it.

He'd been wrong again, though.

Lengthening his own stride, he caught up to her easily. She might have long legs, but his were longer. 'So,' he asked casually, 'how many people are coming to this shindig, anyway?'

'Shindig?' Thea stopped walking. 'Did you just call my wedding a *shindig*?'

Zeke shrugged. Nice to know he could still get under her skin so easily. It might make the next couple of days a little more fun. Something had to. 'Sorry. I meant to say your fairytale-worthy perfect day, when thou shalt join your body in heavenly communion with the deepest love of your heart and soul. How many people are coming to *that*?'

Colour rose in her cheeks, filling him with a strange sense of satisfaction. It was childish, maybe. But he wasn't going to let her get away with pretending that this was a real, true love-match. It was business, just like everything else the Morrisons and the Ashtons held dear.

Including him, these days. Even if his business wasn't the family one any more.

'Two hundred and sixty-eight,' Thea said, her tone crisp. 'At the last count.'

'Small and intimate, then?' Zeke said. 'Just how my father likes things. Where are you putting them all up? I mean, I get that this place is enormous, but still…I can't imagine *your* guests doubling up on camp beds on the veranda.'

'We've booked out the hotel down the road. There'll be executive coaches and cabs running back and forth on the day.'

A small line had formed between her eyebrows, highlighting her irritation. That was new, too.

'Why do you care, anyway?'

'I'm the best man,' he reminded her. 'It's my job to know these things.'

That, apparently, was the line that did it. Spinning round to face him straight on, Thea planted her hands on her hips and scowled at him. 'Why are you here, Zeke? And don't give me some line about brotherly duties. I know full well what you think about Flynn.'

Did she? Maybe she could enlighten *him*, then. Zeke had long since given up trying to make sense of his relationship with his adopted brother. After he'd left home he'd spent months lying awake thinking about it. Wondering if he could have changed things if he'd realised sooner, before that last conversation with his father that had driven him away for good… But in the end the past was the past. He'd had to move on. Besides, this wasn't about him and Flynn. It was about Flynn and Thea.

'Well, if you're not going to buy brotherly affection,

I doubt you'll go for family loyalty either.' He shrugged. 'I'm far more interested in what our fathers said to get you to agree to marry the Great Pretender.'

'Don't call him that,' Thea snapped. 'It wasn't funny when we were kids, and it's not funny now. And is it so hard to believe that I might actually *want* to marry Flynn?'

'Yes,' Zeke said automatically. And not just because she wasn't marrying *him*, whatever his business partner, Deb, said.

'Well, I do.' Thea stared at him mulishly, as if she were barely resisting the urge to add, *So there!*

Zeke leant back against the sunny yellow stone of the hallway, staring down through the arches towards the terrace beyond and the green vines snaking up the trellis. Clearly they were no longer in a hurry to get to the meeting, which gave him a chance to find out what had been going on around here lately.

'Really?' he said, folding his arms across his chest. 'So you're saying that the fact that your marriage will merge both sides of the business for all time, and give your heirs total control, hasn't even crossed your mind?'

Thea pulled a face. 'Of course it has.'

'And if it hadn't I'm sure your father would have made it very clear.' Thomas Morrison was always very good about making his daughter understand the implications of her actions, as Zeke remembered it. Especially when they could benefit him—or threatened to inconvenience him.

'But that doesn't mean it wasn't my decision,' Thea said.

And suddenly all Zeke could think about was the last decision Thea had made, right before he'd skipped out on the family, the business and the rest of his life.

'Of course not,' he said, with a sharp, bitter taste in his mouth at the words. 'I know you like to weigh your decisions very carefully. Make sure you're choosing the most beneficial option.'

Thea's jaw dropped slightly. What? Had she expected him not to notice exactly how mercenary her behaviour was? Maybe eight years ago she might have fooled him, but he knew better now. He knew exactly what mattered to her—and it wasn't him.

'What, exactly, are you trying to say?' She bit the words out, as if she were barely holding back a tirade of insulted pride. 'And I'd think very carefully before answering.'

Zeke gave her his most blinding smile. 'Exactly what you think I'm trying to say. That suddenly it makes an awful lot of sense why you chose to stay here instead of coming away with me eight years ago. What was the point once you knew I wasn't the heir any more?' He shrugged, nonchalantly, knowing it would irritate her even more. 'Gotta say, though…I'm surprised it took you this long to bag Flynn.'

She was going to explode. Literally just pop with rage and frustration, spilling bitterness and anger all over the expensively rustic scrubbed walls of this beautiful villa.

Except that would probably make Zeke Ashton smirk even more. So, instead, Thea took a deep breath and prepared to lie.

'As hard as it may be for you to believe, I am in love with your brother.' Her voice came out calm and cool, and Thea felt a small bubble of pride swelling up amongst all the fury. There'd been a time when any words Zeke had spoken to her had provoked an extreme reaction. When they were kids it had usually been annoyance, or anger. Then, when they were teenagers, that annoyance had suddenly become attraction, and then anger, arousal… By the time he'd left… all sorts of other complicated reactions had come into play.

But not any more. Now she was an adult, in control of

her own life and making her own decisions. Zeke Ashton's barbs and comments had no power over her any longer. It felt incredibly freeing.

'Love?' Zeke raised an eyebrow. 'You know, I'm starting to think you've got your definition of that word wrong.'

'Trust me, I know *exactly* what it means.' Love meant the incredible pain of loss when it was gone. Or the uncertainty of never knowing if it was returned. It baffled Thea why so many people thought love was a good thing.

'Really? Well, I'm sure I'm just thrilled that you've finally found true love. Guess I was just a practice run.'

Thea's stomach rolled at the reminder. It wasn't that she'd thought he'd forgotten their teenage fling, or even forgiven her for the way it had ended—he'd made it very clear in the half-hour he'd been in the villa that neither had happened. But she hadn't expected him to want to actually *talk* about it. Weren't men supposed to be strong and silent on matters of the heart? Suffering in silence, and all that?

Except Zeke had always loved the sound of his own voice. Apparently that hadn't changed, even if nearly everything else had.

'That was a long time ago, Zeke. We were kids.' Too far in the past to bring up now, surely? Even for Zeke, with his ridiculous need to *talk* about everything. 'We've both moved on. We're different people now.'

'Want to throw in a few more clichés with that?' Zeke shook his head. 'Look, you can rewrite history any way you like. And, trust me, I'm not here to try and win you back—even to get one over on Flynn. But you're not going to convince me that this is anything but a business deal with rings.'

'You're wrong,' Thea lied. 'And you'll see that. But…'

'But?' Zeke asked, one eyebrow raised again in that mocking expression that drove her crazy. 'But what?'

'Even if it was a business deal…what would be wrong with that? As long as we both know what we're getting into…' She shrugged. 'There are worse reasons to get married.'

'Maybe.' Zeke gave her a slow smile—the one that used to make her insides melt. 'But there are so many better reasons, too.'

'Like love,' Thea said, apparently still determined to stick to her story.

Zeke didn't buy it, and knew he wouldn't, no matter how hard she tried to convince him. He knew what Thea in love looked like, and this wasn't it.

At least not his Thea. The old Thea. He shook his head. He couldn't let doubt in now. The only thing in his life that had never let him down was gut instinct. He had to trust himself, especially since he couldn't trust anyone else. Not even Thea.

'Love's the big one,' Zeke agreed. 'But it's not the only thing that counts. Trust. Respect. Common values—'

'We have those too,' Thea broke in.

'Sexual compatibility,' Zeke finished, smirking when her mouth snapped shut. 'That's always important for long-term happiness, I find.'

Her gaze hardened. 'Really? And how's that working out for you? I can't help but notice you've come to my wedding alone, after all.'

He had a comeback for that somewhere, he was sure. But since Flynn arrived at that moment—cool, collected, and always an inch and a half taller than Zeke—he didn't have to search for it.

'Zeke! You made it.' Flynn stepped up and held out a hand, but before Zeke could even take it Thea had latched on to her fiancé's other arm, smiling up at him in a sickeningly adoring manner.

Keeping the handshake as perfunctory as possible, Zeke moved out of their circle of love and into his own space of scepticism. 'How could I resist the opportunity to be the best man for once? Might be the only chance I get.'

Flynn's smile stiffened a little at that, but he soldiered on regardless. Always so keen to play up the family loyalty—to be a part of the family he'd never really thought he belonged in. Zeke would have thought that their father choosing Flynn over him would have gone a long way to convincing his brother that there was only one golden boy in the family, and that blood didn't matter at all.

'I wouldn't want anyone but my brother beside me on such an important day,' Flynn said.

He didn't even sound as if he was lying, which Zeke thought was quite an accomplishment.

'Really? Because I have to admit I was kind of surprised to be asked.' Zeke glanced at Thea, who gave him an *I knew it!* look. 'Not as surprised as Thea was to see me here, of course,' he added, just because he could. She glared at him, and snuggled closer against Flynn's arm. There was absolutely no chemistry between them at all. And not a chance in hell they'd ever slept together. What on earth was Thea doing with him?

'You said he wasn't coming,' Thea pointed out—rather accusingly, Zeke thought.

'I wasn't sure he would,' Flynn admitted, glancing down at Thea with an apologetic smile.

Zeke wasn't sure he liked the idea of them talking about him in his absence. What had she said? How much had she told him?

'But, Zeke, you were the one who left us, remember? Not the other way round. Of course I asked you. You're my brother.'

'And that's the only reason?' Zeke asked. An uncomfortable feeling wriggled in his chest at the reminder of his disappearance, but he pushed it aside. He hadn't had a choice. His father had made his position very clear, and that position had taken any other options Zeke might have had off the table. He'd only hung around long enough to waste his time talking to Thea that same night, then he'd been gone. And nobody looking at Zeke now, at how far he'd come and how much he'd achieved, could say that he'd made a mistake by leaving.

Flynn didn't answer his question. With a sigh, he said, 'Dad's got a dinner planned for tonight, by the way. To welcome you home.'

Zeke appreciated the warning too much to point out that a luxury Tuscan villa belonging to some client or another wasn't actually 'home', no matter how many swimming pools it had. 'A prodigal son type thing? Hope he's found a suitably fatted calf.'

'I'm sure there was some poor animal just *begging* to be sacrificed on your behalf,' Thea said. 'But before then don't we have a meeting with the wedding planner to get to, darling?'

The endearment sounded unnatural on her tongue, and Flynn actually looked uncomfortable as she said it. Nobody would ever believe these two actually loved each other or wanted to see each other naked. Watching them, Zeke couldn't even see that they'd ever met before, let alone been childhood friends. He could imagine them on their wedding night—all unnatural politeness and a wall of pillows down the middle of the bed. If it wasn't Thea doing the marrying, it would be hilarious.

'She had to leave,' Flynn said. 'But I think we sorted out all the last-minute details. I said you'd call her later if there was anything you were concerned about.'

'I'm sure it's all fine,' Thea said, smiling serenely.

Even that seemed false. Shouldn't a woman getting married in two days be a little bit more involved in the details?

A door opened somewhere, slamming shut again as Hurricane Helena came blowing through.

'Are you guys still here?' she asked, waves of blonde hair bobbing past her shoulders. 'Shouldn't you all be getting ready for dinner? Thea, I had the maid press your dress for tonight. It's hanging in your room. Can I borrow your bronze shoes, though?'

'Of course,' Thea said, just as she always had to Helena, ever since their mother had died.

Zeke wondered if she even realised she did it.

'Come on, I'll find them for you now.'

As the women made their way down the corridor Helena spun round, walking backwards for a moment. 'Hope you brought your dinner jacket, Zeke. Apparently this welcome home bash is a formal affair.'

So his father had been sure he'd come, even if no one else had. Why else would he have set up a formal dinner for his arrival?

Helena turned back, slipping a hand through her sister's arm and giggling. Thea, Zeke couldn't help but notice, didn't look back at all.

Beside him, Flynn gave him an awkward smile. He'd always hated having to wear a bow tie, Zeke remembered suddenly. At least someone else would be miserable that evening.

'I'll see you at dinner,' Flynn said, setting off down another corridor.

'Can't wait.' Zeke's words echoed in the empty hallway. 'Gonna be a blast.'

CHAPTER TWO

THEA SHOULD HAVE known this wasn't just about shoes.

'So…Zeke coming home. Bit of a shock, huh?' Helena said, lounging back on Thea's ridiculously oversized bed.

'Yep.' Thea stuck her head in the closet and tried to find her bronze heels. Had she even packed them?

'Even though old Ezekiel Senior has planned a welcome home dinner?'

'I told you—Flynn didn't think he'd come,' Thea explained. 'So neither did I.'

'So Flynn was just as shocked?' Helena asked, too innocently.

'Probably,' Thea said. 'He just hides it better.'

'He hides *everything* better,' Helena muttered. 'But, to be honest, he didn't seem all that surprised when I told him Zeke had arrived.'

Thea bashed her head on the wardrobe door. Rubbing her hand over the bump, she backed out into the room again. 'Then maybe he just had more faith that his brother would do the right thing than I did. I really don't think I brought those bronze shoes.'

'No? What a shame. I'll just have to wear my pewter ones.' Helena sat up, folding her legs under her. 'Why don't you trust Zeke? I thought you two were pretty close before he left.'

Thea stared at her sister. She'd known all along she didn't have the stupid shoes, hadn't she? She'd just wanted an excuse to quiz her about Zeke. Typical.

'We were friends,' she allowed. 'We all were. Hard not to be when they were over at our house all the time.'

'Or we were there,' Helena agreed. 'Especially after Mum…'

'Yeah.'

Isabella Ashton had quickly taken pity on the poor, motherless Morrison girls. She'd been more than happy to educate fourteen-year-old Thea in the correct way to run her father's household and play the perfect hostess. At least until Thea had proved she wasn't up to the task and Isabella had taken over all together. Thea would have been relived, if she hadn't had to bear the brunt of her father's disappointment ever since.

And been made to feel like an outsider in my own home.

Thea swallowed and batted the thought away. Helena probably didn't remember that part of it. As far as she was concerned Isabella had just made sure they were supplied with any motherly advice they needed. Whether they wanted it or not.

Thea moved over to the dressing table, looking for the necklace Isabella had given her for her eighteenth birthday. The night Zeke had left. She'd wear it tonight, along with her own mother's ring. Isabella always appreciated gestures like that.

'And you've really not spoken to Zeke at all since he left?' Helena asked.

Thea wondered how much her sister suspected about her relationship with Flynn's brother. Too much, it seemed.

'Not once,' she said firmly, picking up Isabella's necklace. 'Not once in eight years.'

'Strange.' Helena slipped off the bed and came up behind her, taking the ends of the chain from her to fasten it behind her neck. 'Do you think that's why he's come back now? Because you're getting married?'

'Well, he was invited, so I'm thinking that was probably the reason.'

'No,' Helena said, and something about her sister's quiet, firm voice made Thea look up and meet her eyes in the mirror. 'I meant because *you're* getting married.'

Thea swallowed. 'He didn't come and visit the last time I almost got married.'

'Or the time before that,' Helena said, cheerfully confirming her view of Thea as a serial fiancée. 'But then, those times you weren't marrying his brother.' The words *And you didn't go through with it...* went unsaid.

Thea dropped down onto the dressing table stool. Wouldn't that be just like Zeke—not to care that she might marry someone else as long as it wasn't a personal slight to him? But did he even know about the others? If he did, she predicted she'd be subjected to any number of comments and jibes on the subject. *Perfect.* Because she hadn't had enough of that at work, or from her friends, or even in the gossip pages.

Only Helena had never said anything about it. Her father had just torn up the pre-nups, asked his secretary to cancel the arrangements, and said, 'Next time, perhaps?' After the last one even Thea had had to admit to herself that she was better off sticking to business than romance.

It was just that each time she'd thought she'd found a place she could belong. Someone to belong to. Until it had turned out that she wasn't what they really wanted after all. She was never quite right—never quite good enough in the end.

Except for Flynn. Flynn knew exactly what he was getting, and why. He'd chosen it, debated it, drawn up a contract detailing exactly what the deal entailed. And that was exactly what Thea needed. No confused expectations, no unspoken agreements—this was love done business-style. It suited her perfectly.

Zeke would think it was ridiculous if he knew. But she was pretty sure that Zeke had a better reason for returning than just mocking her love life.

'That's not why he's back.'

'Are you sure?' Helena asked. 'Maybe this is just the first time he thought you might actually go through with it.'

'You make me sound like a complete flake.' Which was fair, probably. Except she'd always been so sure… until it had become clear that the men she was supposed to marry weren't.

Helena sighed and picked up a hairbrush from the dressing table, running it through her soft golden waves. Thea had given up wishing she had hair like that years ago. Boring brown worked fine for her.

'Not a flake,' Helena said, teasing out a slight tangle. 'Just…uncertain.'

'"Decisionally challenged", Dad says.'

Helena laughed. 'That's not true. You had a perfectly good reason not to marry those guys.'

'Because it turned out one was an idiot who wanted my money and the other was cheating on me?' And she hadn't seen it, either time, until it had been almost too late. Hadn't realised until it had been right in front of her that she couldn't be enough of a lover or a woman for one of them, or human enough to be worth more than hard cash to the other. Never valuable enough in her own right just to be loved.

'Because you didn't love them.' Helena put down the

brush. 'Which makes me wonder again why exactly you're marrying Flynn.'

Thea looked away from the mirror. 'We'll be good together. He's steady, sensible, gentle. He'll make a great husband and father. Our families will finally be one, just like everyone always wanted them to be. It's good for the business, good for our parents, and good for us. This time I know exactly what I'm signing up for. That's how I know that I've made the right decision.'

This time. This one time. After a lifetime of bad ones, Thea knew that this decision had to stick. This was the one that would give her a proper family again, and a place within it. Flynn needed her—needed the legitimacy she gave him. Thea was well aware of the irony: he needed her Morrison bloodline to cement his chances of inheriting the company, while she needed him, the adopted Ashton son, to earn back her place in her own family.

It was messed up, yes. But at least they'd get to be messed up together.

Helena didn't say anything for a long moment. Was she thinking about all the other times Thea had got it wrong? Not just with men, but with everything…with Helena. That one bad decision that Helena still had to live with the memory of every day?

But when she glanced back at her sister's reflection Helena gave her a bright smile and said, 'You'd better get downstairs for cocktails. And I'd better go and find my pewter shoes. I'll meet you down there, okay?'

Thea nodded, and Helena paused in the doorway.

'Thea? Maybe he just wanted to see you again. Get some closure—that sort of thing.'

As the door swung shut behind her sister Thea wished she was right. That Zeke was ready to move on, at last, from all the slights and the bitterness that had driven him away and kept him gone for so long. Maybe things would never be as they were when they were kids, but perhaps they could find a new family dynamic—one that suited them all.

And it all started with her wedding.

Taking a deep breath, Thea headed down to face her family, old and new, and welcome the prodigal son home again. Whether he liked it or not.

It was far too hot to be wearing a dinner jacket. Whose stupid idea was this, anyway? Oh, that was right. His father's.

Figured.

Zeke made his way down the stairs towards the front lounge and, hopefully, alcohol, torn between the impulse to rush and get it over with, or hold back and put it off for as long as possible. What exactly was his father hoping to prove by this dinner?

Zeke couldn't shake the feeling that Flynn's sudden burst of brotherly love might not be the only reason he'd been invited back to the fold for the occasion. Perhaps he'd better stick to just the one cocktail. If his father had an ulterior motive for wanting him there, Zeke needed to be sober when he found out what it was. Then he could merrily thwart whatever plan his dad had cooked up, stand up beside Flynn at this ridiculously fake wedding, and head off into the sunset again. Easy.

He hadn't rushed, but Zeke was still only the second person to make it to the cocktail cabinet. The first, perhaps unsurprisingly, was Thomas Morrison. The old man had always liked a martini before dinner, but as his gaze rose to study Zeke his mouth tightened and Zeke got the odd impression that Thea's dad had been waiting for him.

'Zeke.' Thomas held out a filled cocktail glass. 'So you made it, then.'

Wary, Zeke took the drink. 'You sound disappointed by that, sir.'

'I can't be the only person surprised to see you back.'

Zeke thought of Thea, standing in nothing but the underwear she'd bought for his brother, staring at him as if he'd returned from the dead. Was that really how she thought of him? In the back of his mind he supposed he'd always thought he *would* come back. When he was ready. When he'd proved himself. When he was *enough*. The wedding had just forced his hand a bit.

'I like to think I'm a pleasant surprise,' Zeke said.

Thomas sipped his martini and Zeke felt obliged to follow suit. He wished he hadn't; Thomas clearly liked his drinks a certain way—paint-stripper-strong. He put the glass down on the cocktail bar.

'Well, I think that depends,' Thomas said. 'On whether you plan to break your mother's heart again.'

Zeke blinked. 'She didn't seem that heartbroken to me.' In fact when she'd greeted him on his arrival she'd seemed positively unflustered. As if he was just one more guest she had to play the perfect hostess to.

'You never did know your mother.' Thomas shook his head.

'But *you* did.' It wasn't a new thought. The two families had always been a touch too close, lived a little too much in each other's pockets. And after his wife's death…well, it hadn't been just Thomas's daughters that Zeke's mother had seemed to want to look after.

'We're old friends, boy. Just like your father and I.'

Was that all? If it was a lie, it was one they'd all been telling themselves for so long now it almost seemed true.

'And I was there for both of them when you abandoned them. I don't think any of us want to go through that again.'

Maybe eight years had warped the old man's memory.

No way had his father been in the least bit bothered by his disappearing act—hell, it was probably what he'd wanted. Why else would he have picked Flynn over him to take on the role of his right-hand man at Morrison-Ashton? Except Zeke knew why—even if he didn't understand it. He had heard his father's twisted reasoning from the man's own lips. That was why he'd left.

But he couldn't help but wonder if Zeke leaving hadn't been Ezekiel Senior's plan all along. If he'd *wanted* him to go out in the world and make something of himself. If so, that was exactly what Zeke had done.

But not for his father. For himself.

'So, you think I should stick around this time?' Zeke asked, even though he had no intention of doing so. Once he knew what his father was up to he'd be gone again. Back to his own life and his own achievements. Once he'd proved his point.

'I think that if you plan to leave again you don't want to get too close while you're here.'

The old man's steely gaze locked on to Zeke's, and suddenly Zeke knew this wasn't about his father, or even his mother.

This was about Thea.

Right on cue they heard footsteps on the stairs, and Zeke turned to see Thea in the doorway, beautiful in a peacock-blue gown that left her shoulders bare, with her dark hair pinned back from her face and her bright eyes sharp.

Thomas clapped him on the shoulder and said, 'Welcome home, Zeke.' But the look he shot at Thea left Zeke in no doubt of the words he left unsaid. *Just don't stay too long*.

The air in the lounge felt too heavy, too tightly pressed around the stilted conversation between the three of them—until Helena breezed in wearing the beautiful pewter shoes that had been a perfect match for her dress all along. She fixed drinks, chatting and smiling all the way, and as she pressed another martini into their father's hand some of the tension seemed to drop and Thea found she could breathe properly again.

At least until she let her eyes settle on Zeke. Maybe that was the problem. If she could just keep her eyes closed and not see the boy she remembered loving, or the man he'd turned into, she'd be just fine. But the way he stood there, utterly relaxed and unconcerned, his suit outlining a body that had grown up along with the boy, she wanted to know him. Wanted to explore the differences. To find out exactly who he was now, just for this moment in time, before he left again.

Stop it. Engaged to his brother, remember?

Flynn arrived moments later, his mother clutching his arm, and suddenly things felt almost easy. Flynn and Helena both had that way about them; they could step into a room and make it better. They knew how to settle people, how to make them relax and smile even when there were a million things to be fretting about.

Flynn had always been that way, Thea remembered. Always the calm centre of the family, offset by Zeke's spinning wild brilliance—and frustration. For Helena it had come later.

Through their whole childhood Thea had been the responsible eldest child, the sensible one, at least when people were looking. And all the while Helena had thrown tantrums and caused chaos. Until Thea had messed up and resigned her role. Somehow Helena had seemed to grow to fill it, even as Isabella had taken over the job of mother, wife and hostess that Thea had been deemed unsuitable for. If it hadn't been for her role at the company,

Thea wondered sometimes if they'd have bothered keeping her around at all. They certainly hadn't seemed to need her. At least not until Flynn needed a bride with an appropriate bloodline.

'Are we ready to go through for dinner?' Isabella asked the room at large. 'My husband will be joining us shortly. He just has a little business to finish up.'

What business was more important than this? Hadn't Ezekiel insisted on this huge welcome home feast for his prodigal son? The least he could do was show up and be part of it. Thea wanted nothing more than for Zeke to disappear back to wherever he'd been for eight years, and *she* was still there.

Thea glanced up at Zeke and found him already watching her, eyebrows raised and expression amused. He slid in alongside her as they walked through to dinner.

'Offended on my behalf by my father's tardiness?' he asked. 'It's sweet, but quite unnecessary. The whole evening might be a lot more pleasant if he *doesn't* join us.'

'I wasn't…it just seemed a little rude, that's all.'

'Rude. Of course.'

He offered his arm for her to hold, but Thea ignored it. The last thing she needed was to actually touch Zeke in that suit.

'That's why your face was doing that righteously indignant thing.'

Thea stared at him. '"Righteously indignant thing"?'

'Yeah. Where you frown and your nose wrinkles up and your mouth goes all stern and disapproving.'

'I…I didn't know I did that.'

Zeke laughed, and up ahead Helena turned back to look at them. 'You've always done it,' he said. 'Usually when someone's being mean about me. Or Flynn, or Helena. It's cute. But like I said, in this case unnecessary.'

Thea scowled, then tried to make her face look as neutral as possible. Never mind her traitorous thoughts—apparently now she had to worry about unconscious overprotective facial expressions, too.

There were only six of them for dinner—seven if Ezekiel managed to join them—and they clustered around one end of the monstrously large dining table. Her father took the head, with Isabella at his side and Flynn next to her. Which left Thea sandwiched between Zeke and her father, with Helena on Zeke's other side, opposite Flynn. Thea couldn't help but think place cards might have been a good idea. Maybe she could have set hers in the kitchen, away from everybody…

They'd already made it through the starter before Ezekiel finally arrived. Thea bit her lip as he entered. Would he follow the unspoken boy-girl rule and sit next to Helena? But, no, he moved straight to Flynn's side and, with barely an acknowledgement of Zeke's presence in the room, started talking business with his eldest son.

Thea snuck a glance at Zeke, who continued to play with his soup as if he hadn't noticed his father's entrance.

'Did he already welcome you back?' Thea asked. But she knew Ezekiel Senior had been locked in his temporary office all day, so the chances were slim.

Zeke gave her a lopsided smile. 'You know my father. Work first.'

Why was she surprised? Ezekiel Ashton had always been the same.

'Well, if he's not going to ask you, I will.' Shifting in her seat to face him a little, Thea put on her best interested face. 'So, Zeke… What have you been up to the last eight years?'

'You don't know?' Zeke asked, eyebrows raised. 'Aren't you supposed to be in charge of PR and marketing for the company? I'd have thought it was your business to keep on top of what your competitors are up to.'

Too late Thea realised the trap she'd walked straight into. 'Oh, I know about your *business* life,' she said airily. 'Who doesn't? You set up a company purposely to rival the family business—presumably out of spite. It's the kind of thing the media loves to talk about. But, really, compared to Morrison-Ashton This Minute is hardly considered a serious competitor. More a tiny fish.'

'Beside your shark?' Zeke reached for his wine glass. 'I can see that. But This Minute wasn't ever intended to be a massive media conglomerate. Big companies can't move fast enough for me.'

That made sense. Zeke had never been one for sitting in meetings and waiting for approval on things he wanted to get done. But according to industry gossip even his instant response news website and app This Minute wasn't enough to hold his attention any more.

'I heard you were getting ready to sell.'

'Did you, now?' Zeke turned his attention across the table, to where his father and Flynn were still deep in conversation. 'That explains a lot.'

'Like?'

'Like why my father added his own personal request that I attend to my wedding invitation. He wants to talk about This Minute.'

So *that* was why he was back. Nothing to do with her, or Flynn, or the wedding. Not that she'd really thought it was, but still the knowledge sat heavily in her chest. 'You think he wants to buy it?'

'He's *your* CEO. What do you think?'

It would make sense, Thea had to admit. Their own twenty-four-hour news channels couldn't keep up with the fast response times of internet sites. Buying up This

Minute would be cheaper in the long run than developing their own version. And it would bring Zeke back into the family fold...

'Yes, I think he does.'

'Guess we'll find out,' Zeke said. 'If he ever deigns to speak to me.'

'What would you do?' Thea asked as the maid cleared their plates and topped up their wine glasses. 'Would you stay with This Minute?' It was hard to imagine Zeke coming back to work for Morrison-Ashton, even on his own terms. And if he did he'd be there, in her building, every day...

'No.' Zeke's response was firm. 'I'm ready to do something new.' He grinned. 'In fact, I want to do it all over again.'

'Start a new business? Why? Why not just enjoy your success for a while?'

'Like your father?' Zeke nodded at the head of the table, where Thomas was laughing at something Isabella had said.

Thea shook her head. 'My dad was never a businessman—you know that. He provided the money, sat on the board...'

'And left the actual work to my father.' He held up a hand before Thea could object. 'I know, I know. Neither one of them could have done it without the other. Hasn't that always been the legend? They each brought something vital to the table.'

'It worked,' Thea pointed out.

'And now you and Flynn are ready to take it into the next generation. Bring the families together. Spawn the one true heir.'

Thea looked away. 'You need to stop talking about my wedding like this.'

'Why? It's business, isn't it?'

'It's also my future. The rest of my life—and my children's.' That shut him up for a moment, unexpectedly. Thea took advantage of the brief silence to bring the conversation back round to the question he'd so neatly avoided. 'So, you didn't tell me. Why start up another new business?'

Zeke settled back in his chair, the thin stem of his wine glass resting between his fingers. 'I guess it's the challenge. The chance to take something that doesn't even exist yet, build it up and make it fantastic. Make it mine.'

It sounded exciting. Fresh and fun and everything else Zeke seemed to think it would be. But it also sounded to Thea as if Zeke was reaching for something more than just a successful business venture. Something he might never be able to touch, however hard he tried.

'You want to be a success,' she said slowly. 'But, Zeke, you've already succeeded. And you still want more. How will you know when you've done enough?'

Zeke turned to look at her, his dark eyes more serious than she'd ever seen them. 'I'll know it when I get there.'

But Thea was very afraid that he wouldn't.

CHAPTER THREE

So NOW HE KNEW. Had Thea told his dad about the rumours, Zeke wondered, or had the old goat had his own spies on the lookout? Either way, his presence in Italy that week suddenly made a lot more sense. Ezekiel Senior wanted This Minute.

And Zeke had absolutely no intention of giving it to him.

As the rest of the guests enjoyed their dessert Zeke left his spoon on the tablecloth and studied his father across the table. How would he couch it? Would he make it sound as if he was doing Zeke a favour? Or would he—heaven forbid—actually admit that Zeke had achieved something pretty great without the backing of Morrison-Ashton? He'd have to wait to find out.

After dinner, Zeke decided. That would be when his father would finally acknowledge the presence of his youngest son. Probably he'd be summoned to the study. But this time he'd get to go on his own terms. For once Ezekiel wanted something he, Zeke, possessed, rather than the other way round.

That, on its own, made it worth travelling to Flynn and Thea's wedding.

Zeke only realised he was smiling when Flynn suddenly looked up and caught his eye. Zeke widened his grin, raising an eyebrow at his brother. So, had dear old dad just bro-

ken the news to the golden boy? And did that mean Thea
hadn't told her beloved about the rumours she'd heard?

Flynn glanced away again, and Zeke reached for his
spoon. 'You didn't tell Flynn, then?'

Thea's dropped her spoon against the edge of her bowl
with a clatter. 'Tell Flynn what?' she asked, eyes wide.

Interesting. 'Well, I meant about the This Minute sale,'
he said. 'But now I'm wondering what else you've been
keeping from your fiancé.'

Thea rolled her eyes, but it was too late. He'd already
seen her instinctive reaction. She was keeping things from
Flynn. Zeke had absolutely no doubt at all.

'I didn't tell Flynn about the sale because it doesn't directly affect him and it's still only a rumour. If your father decides to make a bid for the company I'm sure he'll
fill Flynn in at the appropriate time.' Thea looked up at
him through her lashes. 'Besides, we don't talk about you.'

'At all?' That hit him somewhere in the middle of his
gut and hit hard. Not that he'd been imagining them sitting around the dining table reminiscing about the good
old days when Zeke had been there, or anything. But still,
despite his initial misgivings over them talking about him
in his absence, he thought this might be worse. They didn't
talk about him *at all*?

'Apart from Flynn telling me you weren't coming to
the wedding? No.' Thea shrugged. 'What would we say?
You left.'

And she'd forgotten all about him. Point made. With a
sharp jab to the heart.

But of course if they didn't talk about him… 'So you
never told Flynn about us, either?'

She didn't look up from her dessert as she answered.
'Why would I? The past is very firmly in the past. And I
had no reason to think you would ever come back at all.'

'And now?'

Raising her head, she met his gaze head-on. 'And now there's simply nothing to say.'

'Zeke.'

The voice sounded a little creakier, but no less familiar. Tearing his gaze away from Thea's face, Zeke turned to see his father standing, waiting for him.

'I'd like a word with you in my office, if you would. After eight years…we have a lot to discuss.'

They had one thing to discuss, as far as Zeke was concerned. But he went anyway. How else would he have the pleasure of turning the old man down?

Ezekiel had chosen a large room at the front of the villa for his office—one Zeke imagined was more usually used for drinks and canapés than for business. The oversized desk in the centre had to have been brought in from elsewhere in the house, because it looked utterly out of place.

Zeke considered the obvious visitor's chair, placed across from it, and settled himself into a leather armchair by the empty fireplace instead. He wasn't a naughty child any more, and that meant he didn't have to stare at his father over a forbidding desk, waiting for judgement to be handed down, ever again.

'Sit,' Ezekiel said, long after Zeke had already done so. 'Whisky or brandy?'

'I'd rather get straight down to business,' Zeke said.

'As you wish.' Ezekiel moved towards the drinks cabinet and poured himself a whisky anyway. Zeke resisted the urge to grind his teeth.

Finally, his father came and settled himself into the armchair opposite, placing his glass on the table between them. 'So. You're selling your business.'

'So the rumour mill tells me,' Zeke replied, leaning back in his chair and resting his ankle on his opposite knee.

'I heard more than rumour,' Ezekiel said. 'I heard you were in negotiations with Glasshouse.'

Zeke's shoulders stiffened. Nobody knew that, except Deb and him at the office, the CEO at Glasshouse and his key team. Which meant one or other of them had a leak. Just what he *didn't* need.

'It's true, then.' Ezekiel shook his head. 'Our biggest competitors, Zeke. Why didn't you just come to me directly? Or is this just another way of trying to get my attention?'

Zeke will never stop trying to best his brother. The words, eight years old, still echoed through Zeke's head, however hard he tried to move past them. But he didn't have time for the memory now.

'I haven't needed your attention for the last eight years, Father. I don't need it now.'

'Really?' Ezekiel reached for his whisky glass. 'Are you sure? Because you could have gone anywhere, done anything. Yet you stayed in the country and set up a company that directly competed with the family business.'

'I stuck to what I knew,' Zeke countered. Because, okay, annoying his father might have been part of his motivation. But only part.

Ezekiel gave him a long, steady look, and when Zeke didn't flinch said, 'Hmm...'

Zeke waited. *Time to make the offer, old man.*

'I'm sure that you understand that to have my son working with Glasshouse is...unacceptable. But we can fix this. Come work with us. We'll pay whatever Glasshouse is paying and you can run your little company under the

Morrison-Ashton umbrella. In fact, you could lead our whole digital division.'

Somewhere in there, under the 'let me fix your mistakes' vibe, was an actual job offer. A good one. Head of Digital… There was a lot Zeke could do there to bring Morrison-Ashton into the twenty-first century. It would give him enough clout in the company in order not to feel as if Flynn was his boss. And he would be working with Thea every day…

'No, thanks.' Zeke stood up. He didn't need this any more. He'd grown up now. He didn't need his father's approval, or a place at the table, or even to be better than Flynn. He was his own man at last. 'I appreciate the offer, but I'm done with This Minute. Once I sell to Glasshouse I'm on to something new. Something exciting.'

Something completely unconnected to his family. Or Thea's.

'Really?'

Ezekiel looked up at him and Zeke recognised the disappointment in his eyes. It wasn't as if he hadn't seen that peculiar mix of being let down and proved right at the same time before.

'And if I appeal to your sense of family loyalty?'

Zeke barked a laugh. 'Why would you? You never showed *me* any. You gave Flynn all the chances, the job, the trust and the confidence. You wanted me to find my own road.' He crossed to the door, yanking it open. 'Well, Dad, I found it. And it doesn't lead to Morrison-Ashton.'

'Well,' Flynn said, dropping to sit beside her on the cushioned swing seat. 'That was a day.'

'Yes. Yes, it was.' Thea took the mug he offered her and breathed in the heavy smell of the coffee. 'Is this—?'

'Decaf,' Flynn assured her. 'You think I don't know what my wife-to-be likes?'

'Less "likes",' Thea said, taking a cautious sip. Everyone knew that on a normal day she'd be on her third double espresso well before lunch. 'More that I don't need anything else keeping me awake at night right now.'

'Hmm…' Flynn settled against the back of the seat and, careful of her coffee cup, wrapped an arm around Thea's shoulders, pulling her against him. 'Want to tell me what's keeping you awake?'

Thea tucked her legs up underneath her, letting Flynn rock the swing seat forward and back, the motion helping to relax the tension in her body.

They didn't share a room yet; it hadn't really seemed necessary, given the agreement between them. So he didn't have to know exactly how many hours she spent staring at the ceiling every night, just waiting for this wedding to be over, for the papers to be signed and for her future to be set and certain. But on the other hand she was marrying the man. He'd be her companion through life from here on in, and she wanted that companionship badly. Which meant telling him at least part of the truth.

'I guess I'm just nervous about the wedding,' she admitted.

'About marrying me?' Flynn asked. 'Or getting through the day itself?'

'Mostly the latter.' Thea rested her head against his comfortable shoulder and sighed. 'I just want it to be done. For everyone else to leave and for us to enjoy our honeymoon here in peace. You know?'

'I really, really do.'

Thea smiled at the heartfelt tone in his voice. This was why a marriage between them would work far better than any of the other relationships she'd fallen into, been passionate about, then had end horribly. They were a fit—a pair. If they actually loved each other it would be a classically perfect match.

But then, love—passion, emotion, pain—would be what drove them apart, too. No, far better this friendship and understanding. It made for a far more peaceful life.

Or it would. Once they got through the wedding.

'Feeling the strain, huh?' Thea patted Flynn's thigh sympathetically. 'Be grateful. At least my sister didn't walk in on you in your wedding lingerie this morning.'

'I don't have any wedding lingerie,' Flynn pointed out. 'I have the same boring black style I wear every day. Hang on. Did Zeke…?'

'Yep. He said you sent him to fetch me to meet with the wedding planner. So you wouldn't see me in my dress before the big day.'

'Sorry,' Flynn said, even though it obviously wasn't really his fault. 'I just know how important the traditions are to you. I didn't want to upset you.'

Thea waved a hand to brush away his apology, and Flynn reached over to take her empty coffee cup and place it safely on the table beside him. 'It's not your fault. Just something else to make this day difficult.'

'That does explain why he was in such an odd mood this afternoon, though,' Flynn mused. 'All those defensive jokes. He always did have a bit of a crush on you, I think. Even when we were kids.'

A bit of a crush. Thea ducked her head against Flynn's chest to hide her reaction. Had there ever been such an understatement? She'd assumed at first that Flynn had known something of her relationship with his brother—despite their attempts at secrecy it seemed that plenty of others had. But it had quickly become clear he'd no idea.

And they'd never talked about him, so she'd been perfectly happy to consign it to the realms of vague memory.

'I don't think that's why,' she said. 'I'm sure it's just being here, seeing everyone again after so long. It must be strange.'

'It was his choice.' Flynn's voice was firm, unforgiving. 'He could have come home at any time.'

'Perhaps.' What had *really* brought Zeke back now? *Was* it his father's summons? Not to satisfy the old man, of course, but to show him how much Zeke no longer needed him. To deny him whatever it was he wanted just out of spite?

The Zeke she'd seen today hadn't seemed spiteful, though. He was no longer the angry boy, lashing out, wanting revenge against his family, his life. Her. So why was he here?

Thea didn't let herself believe Helena's theory for a moment. If Zeke had really wanted to see her he'd had eight years. Even if he hadn't wanted to see his family again he could have found her—made contact somehow. But he hadn't. And by the time Thea had known where he was again any lingering regret or wish to see him had long faded. Or at least become too painful to consider. That wound was healed. No point pulling it open again.

Except now he was here, for her wedding, and she didn't have a choice.

Flynn shifted on the seat, switching legs to keep them swinging. 'Anyway… Talking about my prodigal brother isn't going to help you feel any more relaxed about the wedding. Let's talk about more pleasant things.'

'Like?'

'Our honeymoon,' Flynn said decisively, then faltered. The swing stopped moving and his shoulder grew tense under her cheek. 'I mean… I don't mean…'

Thea smiled against his shirt. He was so *proper*. 'I know what you mean.'

'I was thinking about the day trips we might take—that sort of thing,' Flynn explained unnecessarily. 'There are some very fine vineyards in the region, I believe. I don't want you to think that I'm expecting…well, *anything*. I know that wasn't our agreement.'

Thea pushed herself up to see his face. The agreement. It had been written, signed, notarised months ago—long before the wedding planning had even begun. They both knew what they wanted from this marriage—the business convenience, the companionship, fidelity. The document had addressed the possibility of heirs—and therefore sex—as something to be negotiated in three years' time. That had been Thea's decision. Marriage was one thing. Children were something else altogether. She needed to be sure of her role as a wife first.

But now she wondered if that had been a mistake.

'Maybe we should… I mean, we can talk again about the agreement, if you like?'

Flynn's body stilled further. Then he started the swing moving again, faster than before. 'You've changed your mind?'

'I just…I want our marriage to be solid. I want the companionship, and everything else we discussed, but more than anything I want us to be partners. I don't want doomed passion, or anger and jealousy. I want true friendship and respect, and I know you can give me that.'

'And children?' Flynn asked, and Thea remembered just how important that was to him. How much he needed a family of his own—she suspected not just to make sure there was a legitimate Morrison-Ashton heir for the business.

'In time,' she said, 'yes, I think so. But I'd still like a

little time for us to get to know each other better first. You know…as husband and wife.'

Was that enough? Would he get the hint?

'You want us to sleep together?' Flynn said. 'Sorry to be blunt, but I think it's important we both know what we're saying here.'

Another reason he'd make a good husband. Clarity. She'd never had that with Zeke. Not at all. 'You're right. And, yes, I do.'

'Okay.'

Not exactly the resounding endorsement she'd hoped for. 'Are you all right with that?'

Flynn flashed a smile at her. 'Thea, you're a very beautiful woman and I'm proud that you're going to be my wife. Of course I'm okay with that.'

'You weren't sounding particularly enthusiastic.'

'I am. Really.' He pulled her close again and kissed the top of her head. 'Who knows? Maybe we'll even grow to love each other as more than friends.'

'Perhaps we will,' Thea said. After all, how could she tell her husband-to-be that the last thing she wanted was for either of them to fall in love with each other. Sex, marriage, kids—that was fine. But not love.

Hadn't it been proved, too many times already, that her love wasn't worth enough?

The corridors of the villa were quieter now. Zeke presumed that everyone was lingering over after-dinner drinks in the front parlour or had gone to bed. Either way, he didn't particularly want to join in.

Instead, he made his way to the terrace doors. A little fresh air, a gulp of freedom away from the oppression of family expectation, might do him some good.

Except the terrace was already occupied.

He stood in the doorway for a long moment, watching the couple on the swing. Whatever he'd seen and thought earlier, here—now—they looked like a real couple. Flynn's arm wrapped around Thea's slender shoulders... the kiss he pressed against her head. She had her legs tucked up under her, the way she'd always sat as a teenager, back when they'd spent parties like this hiding out together. The memories were strong: Thea skipping out on her hostessing duties, sipping stolen champagne and talking about the world, confiding in him, telling him her hopes, plans, dreams.

It hurt more than he liked, seeing her share a moment like that with someone else. And for that someone else to be his brother...that burned.

It shouldn't, Zeke knew. He'd moved past the pain of her rejection years ago, and it wasn't as if he hadn't found plenty of solace in other arms. She'd made her choice eight years ago and he'd lived by it. He hadn't called, hadn't visited. Hadn't given her a chance to change her mind, because he didn't want her to.

She'd chosen their families and he'd chosen himself. Different sides. Love had flared into anger, rejection, even hate. But even hate faded over the years, didn't it? He didn't hate her now. He didn't know what he felt. Not love, for certain. Maybe...regret? A faint, lingering thought that things might have been different.

But they weren't, and Zeke wasn't one for living in the past. Especially not now, when he'd finally made the last cut between himself and his father. He'd turned down the one thing he'd have given anything for as a boy—his father's acceptance and approval. He knew now how little that was worth. He was free, at last.

Except for that small thin thread that kept him tied to the woman on the swing before him. And by the end of the week even that would be gone, when she'd tied herself to another.

His new life would start the moment he left this place. And suddenly he wanted to savour the last few moments of the old one.

Zeke stepped out onto the terrace, a small smile on his lips as his brother looked up and spotted him.

'Zeke,' Flynn said, eyes wary, and Thea's head jerked up from his shoulder.

'I wondered where you two had got to,' Zeke lied. He hadn't given it a moment's thought, because he hadn't imagined they could be like this. *Together.* 'Dinner over, then?'

Thea nodded, sitting up and shifting closer to Flynn to make room for Zeke to sit beside them. 'How did things go? With your father?'

'Pretty much as expected.' Zeke eyed the small space on the swing, then perched on the edge of the low table in front of them instead.

'Which was…?' Flynn sounded a little impatient. 'I don't even know what he wanted to talk to you about. Business, I assume?'

'You didn't tell him?' Zeke asked Thea, eyebrow raised.

'We were talking about more important things,' Thea said, which made Flynn smile softly and kiss her hair again.

Zeke's jaw tightened at the sight. He suspected he didn't want to know what those 'more important things' were. 'Your father wanted to try and buy my business,' he told Flynn.

'He's your father too,' Flynn pointed out.

Zeke laughed. 'Possibly not, after tonight.'

'You told him no, then?' Thea guessed. 'Why? To spite him? You've already admitted you want to sell.'

'He wanted me to come and work for Morrison-Ashton.'

'And that would be the worst thing *ever*, of course.' Sarcasm dripped from her voice. 'Are you really still so angry with him?'

Tilting his head back, Zeke stared up through the slats of the terrace roof at the stars twinkling through. 'No,' he answered honestly. 'This isn't... It's not like it was any more, Thea. I'm not trying to spite him, or hurt him, or pay him back for anything. I just want to move on. Sever all ties and start a whole new life. Maybe a new company, a new field. A new me.'

'So we won't be seeing you again after the wedding, then?' Flynn said, and Zeke realised he'd almost forgotten his brother was even there for a moment. He'd spoken to Thea the same way he'd always talked to Thea—with far more honesty than he'd give anyone else. A bad habit to fall back into.

'Maybe you two would be worth a visit,' he said, forcing a smile. 'After all, I'll need to come and be favourite Uncle Zeke to your kids, right?'

At his words Flynn's expression softened, and he gave his fiancée a meaningful look. Thea, for her part, glanced down at her hands, but Zeke thought he saw a matching shy smile on her face.

Realisation slammed into him, hitting him hard in the chest until he almost gasped for breath. *That* was what they'd been talking about—their 'more important things'. Children. He'd been so sure that this marriage was a sham, that there was nothing between them. But he hadn't imagined kids. Even when he'd made the comment he'd expected an evasion, a convenient practised answer. Another sign that this wasn't real.

Not *this*. Not the image in his head of Thea's belly swollen with his brother's child. Not the thought of how much better parents Flynn and Thea would be than his own father. Of a little girl with Thea's dark hair curling around a perfect face.

'Well, you know you'll always be welcome in our home,' Flynn said.

The words were too formal for brothers, too distant for anything he'd ever shared with Thea. And Zeke knew without a doubt that he'd never, ever be taking them up on the offer. Maybe he didn't love Thea any more, but that tightly stitched line of regret inside him still pulled when she tugged on the thread between them.

He couldn't give Thea what she wanted—never had been able to. She'd made that very clear. And in two days she'd be married, that thread would be cut, and he'd never see her again.

'I should get to bed,' Thea said, unfolding her legs from under her. 'Another long day tomorrow.'

Flynn smiled up at her as she stood. 'I'll see you in the morning?'

Thea nodded, then with a quick glance at Zeke bent and kissed Flynn on the lips. It looked soft, but sure, and Zeke got the message—*loud and clear, thanks*. She'd made her choice—again—and she was sticking with it.

Fine. It was her choice to make, after all. But Zeke knew that the scar of regret would never leave him if he wasn't sure she was happy with the choice she was making. If he wanted the freedom of that cut thread, he had to be able to leave her behind entirely. He had to be sure she knew what she was doing.

Zeke got to his feet. 'I'll walk you to your room.'

CHAPTER FOUR

THIS WAS EXACTLY what she didn't want. Which, in fairness, was probably why Zeke was doing it.

It had been too strange, sitting there with the two brothers, talking about her future as if Zeke might be part of it—in a role she'd simply never expected him to take. Hard enough to transition from fiancée to wife to mother with Flynn, without adding in her ex as her brother-in-law. It had all been so much easier when she'd imagined he was out of her life for good. That she'd never have to see him again. She'd got over the hurt of that loss years before.

The villa was in darkness, and their footsteps echoed off the tiled floors and painted stone walls. The place might be luxurious, but in the moonlight Thea couldn't help but find it creepy. From the hanging tapestries to the stone arches looming overhead, the shadows seemed oppressive. And it felt eerily empty; everyone else must have gone to bed hours before.

She'd expected Zeke to talk, to keep up the banter and the cutting comments and the jokes, but to her surprise they walked in a companionable silence. She could feel him beside her, the warmth of his presence a constant reminder of how close he was. If she stretched out a finger she could reach his hand.

But she wouldn't.

As they climbed the stairs, Zeke only ever one step behind her, his hand next to hers on the banister, she catalogued all the questions she wanted to ask.

Why are you back?
Why didn't you call?
Are you really going to stay?
What do you want from me now?

There had to be a rhyme and reason to it all somewhere, but Thea couldn't quite put her finger on it. Maybe he didn't know the answers, either. Maybe that was why he seemed always on the edge of asking a question he wasn't sure he wanted her to answer.

'I'm just down here,' she whispered as they reached the top of the stairs. 'You're over that way, right?'

Zeke nodded, but made no effort to head to his own room. After a moment Thea moved towards her door, very aware of him still behind her.

Hand on the door handle, she stopped again. 'What do you want, Zeke?' she asked, looking at the door in front of her.

She felt his sigh, a warm breath against her neck. 'I want to be sure.'

'Sure of what?'

'Sure that you're…happy. That this is really what you want. Before I leave.'

'You're not going to come and visit again, are you?' She'd known that even as he'd talked about being Uncle Zeke. She'd known the truth of it all along. She already knew the answers to all her questions in her heart.

Zeke was here to say goodbye.

'No.'

She turned at the word, and found herself trapped between Zeke's body and the door. He had one arm braced against the wood above her head, the other at his side, fist clenched.

'Why?' More of a breath than a question.

'I need…I need to move on. Away from my family, from yours. For good.'

'Eight years wasn't long enough for you to stop hating us, then?'

'I didn't—'

He stopped short of the lie, which Thea appreciated even as his meaning stabbed her heart. She'd known he hated her. She couldn't let herself be surprised by the confirmation.

'It's not about that any more,' Zeke said instead. He gave a low chuckle. 'I've spent so long caught up in it, in proving myself to my father even as I hated him. So long living my life because of my past, even if I didn't realise I was doing it. And it's time to stop now. Time to build a life for myself, I guess.'

Without us, Thea finished for him in her head.

'So what I need to know is—*are* you happy? Is this really what you want? Or is it just what you think you're supposed to do?'

Zeke's gaze caught hers as he asked his questions, and Thea knew she couldn't look away from those dark eyes even if she'd wanted to.

Was this what she wanted? She thought about Flynn. About how easy it was with him compared to in her previous disastrous attempts at relationships. About everything she could have with him. This wasn't just for their fathers, this time, or even for Helena. This was for her. To give her security, the safety of knowing her place in the world. Knowing where she belonged.

She blinked, and told Zeke, 'This is what I want.'

Time stretched out between them as he stared into her

eyes as if scanning for truths. Finally his eyelids fluttered down, and Thea snapped her gaze away.

'Okay…' Zeke spoke softly, and she was sure she heard relief in the word. 'Okay.'

When she looked back he lowered his lips and kissed her, soft and sweet, before stepping away.

'I hope to God you're not lying to me this time, Thea,' he said, and he turned and walked away to his room.

Thea stood and watched him go, the wood of the door at her back and her grip on the door handle the only things holding her up.

'So do I,' she whispered when his door had closed behind him.

Loosening his tie, Zeke threw himself onto the bed and pulled out his phone. He'd promised Deb an update when he arrived, but between Thea in her underwear and thwarting his father he hadn't had much of a chance.

He checked his watch; London was behind them anyway. She'd still be up.

'So?' Deb said when she answered. Her usual greetings and pleasantries were apparently not deemed necessary for him. 'How's it going?'

'My father wants to buy This Minute.'

'He heard we were selling to Glasshouse?' Deb asked, but there didn't seem to be much of a question in her words. More of a sense of inevitability.

Suspicion flared up. 'Yeah. Any idea how that might have happened?'

'Not a clue,' she replied easily. 'But it's kind of handy, don't you think?'

'No.' Had she leaked it? Why? He should be mad, he supposed, but he trusted Deb. She always had a perfectly logical reason for her actions, and he was kind of curious to find out what it was this time.

'I do,' she said. 'I mean, with two interested parties the price will go up, for starters. And, more than that, this gives you a chance to decide what you really want.'

'Other than to get out of here?'

'That's one option,' Deb said. 'The other is to return to the family fold.'

Zeke remembered the look on his father's face when he'd turned him down. That had felt good. 'I think I already burnt that bridge tonight.'

'That works too.' Deb sounded philosophical about the whole thing. 'At least it was your choice to make this time.'

Sometimes Zeke really regretted the occasional late-night drinking sessions with his business partner. His tongue got loose after alcohol, and she knew him far too well as a result.

'Anyway, it's done,' he said, steamrollering past any analysis of his relationship with his father that she had planned. 'Now I just need to get through the wedding and then I can get back to my real life again.'

'Ah, yes. "The Wedding".' Her tone made it very clear that it had capital letters.

'That is what I came here for.'

'And how was it? Seeing Thea again?'

A vision of her standing there, wedding dress around her waist, flooded his mind. But Deb really didn't need to know about that. 'Fine.'

'You think she really wants to marry your brother?'

'I do.' He was just unsure about her motives.

'Then do you really have to stay?'

'I'm the best man, Deb. Kinda necessary to the proceedings.'

'Zeke...' Her voice was serious now, and he knew it was time to stop joking.

'It's fine. It's just a couple of days and I can put it all behind me.'

'You don't have to put yourself through this, you know. If you're satisfied that she's not being coerced into this by your father—'

'Oh, I'm pretty sure she is.'

'But you said—'

'Which doesn't mean she doesn't want to go through with it.' He sighed. Explaining the peculiarities of the Morrison and Ashton families to outsiders was never easy. 'Look, I need to stay. I need to see this through. It's the only way I'm ever going to...I don't know.'

'Have closure?' Deb said, knowing his own thoughts better than himself as usual. That was always disturbing. 'Fine. But if you need me to manufacture a work emergency to get you out of there...'

'I know where you are. Thanks, Deb.'

'Any time.' She paused, and he got the impression she wasn't quite done with him yet. 'Just...don't stay just to punish yourself, okay?'

'Punish myself for what?'

'Leaving her in the first place.'

The phone went dead in his hand. Apparently goodbyes were no longer necessary, either. He tossed it onto the bedside table and flopped back onto the bed.

This time Deb didn't know what she was talking about. Zeke had absolutely nothing to feel sorry for.

He just hoped Thea knew that, too.

Thea didn't sleep.

She dotted concealer under her eyes the next morning, knowing that Helena would spot the dark shadows anyway.

She'd just have to tell her that it was pre-wedding nerves. Which would no doubt lead to another rousing rendition of the *'It's not too late to back out'* chorus. Still, that had to be better than telling her sister the truth.

The truth about the past, that was. Thea wasn't even sure if *she* understood the truth of her and Zeke in the present.

Helena had laid out her chosen outfit for Thea to wear the day before her wedding and Thea slipped into the pale linen dress without question. One of the advantages of having a younger sister with an eye for style, colour and fashion was never having to worry if she'd chosen the right outfit for an occasion. This week, more than ever, she needed the boost to her confidence of knowing she looked good.

She appreciated it even more when, as she reached the bottom of the stairs, she was accosted by Ezekiel Ashton, Senior.

'Thea! Excellent. I just need a little word with you, if you wouldn't mind.'

Whether she minded or not, Ezekiel ushered Thea into his temporary office—away from the tempting smells of hot coffee and pastries.

Ezekiel's desk was covered in papers and files, his laptop pushed away to the corner, precariously balanced on a stack of books. Thea cleared a ream of paper covered in numbers from the visitor's chair and sat down. His office at the company headquarters was usually neat to the point of anal. Had he been up all night working after his meeting with Zeke? Or was he just missing his terrifyingly efficient PA Dorothy? And, either way, what exactly did he think he needed Thea for?

What if this wasn't business? What if this was some sort of *'welcome to the family, don't hurt my son'* talk? And, if so, how could she be sure which son? Because he was a little late for one of them…

Laughter bubbled up in her chest and Thea swallowed it down as Ezekiel creakily lowered himself into his chair. This was Ezekiel Ashton. Of course it was going to be about business.

'Now, Thea. I appreciate that work might not be your highest priority today, given your imminent nuptials. But this wedding has given us a unique opportunity. One I need you to take full advantage of.'

He gave her a meaningful look across the desk, and Thea's heart sank. This was business, yes, but it was personal, too. This was about Zeke.

'What are you hoping I'll be able to do?' Thea crossed her legs and stared back at her father-in-law-to-be. She couldn't promise anything when it came to Zeke. She'd burnt that bridge long ago. But how to explain that to Ezekiel without telling the whole miserable story?

Ezekiel leant back in his chair, studying her. 'Zeke has always been…fond of you.'

He waited, as if for confirmation, and Thea forced a nod.

'We were friends. When we were younger.'

'I'm hoping you might be able to utilise that friendship.'

No sugarcoating it, then. Not that she'd really expected any such thing from Ezekiel.

'We haven't seen each other in eight years,' Thea pointed out. 'And we didn't…we weren't on the best of terms when he left.'

A slightly raised eyebrow was the only hint that this came as a surprise to Zeke's father. 'Still. After all this time I'm sure you can both forgive and forget.'

Forgive? Thea thought she'd managed that years ago, until Zeke had shown up and reminded her of all the reasons she had to be angry with him. Almost as many as he had to be angry with her.

Forget? Never.

Thea took a breath. Time to refocus the conversation. 'This is about This Minute, right?'

Ezekiel gave a sharp nod. 'I'm sure you can understand the value to Morrison-Ashton of bringing Zeke's little business under the company umbrella.'

'I'd hardly call it a "little business",' Thea said. Its turnover figures for last year had been astronomical. Far higher than their own digital news arm. 'And I think the detrimental effect of *not* buying This Minute is of far higher importance to you.'

'True.'

His gaze held a hint of grudging appreciation. *Good.* In her five years working her way up to running the PR department of Morrison-Ashton Ezekiel had never given her a single sign that he appreciated the work she did, or believed it really added value to the company. It was about time he realised she brought more than a name and some money to the table. She wasn't her father, after all.

'Which is why I need you to persuade him to sell This Minute to us,' Ezekiel finished.

Any satisfaction Thea had felt flew away. *Why did he have to choose this day to suddenly have faith in my abilities?*

'I was under the impression that Zeke had already declined your offer.' And he would continue to do so. She might not have seen him in eight years, but she knew Zeke. He'd never give his father what he wanted without a fight.

'Of course he has,' Ezekiel said, impatiently. 'Otherwise why would I need you? Zeke's letting his pride get in the way, as usual. He knows that the best thing for him and This Minute is to become part of Morrison-Ashton, and for him to take up his rightful role here.'

The role you refused to give him eight years ago. 'He seems very set on moving on to something new.'

'And selling This Minute to Glasshouse.'

'Glasshouse?'

That would be a disaster. For Morrison-Ashton, at least. This Minute would give their main competitor a huge advantage in the digital arena, and the PR fallout from Zeke Ashton defecting to Glasshouse would run and run. It would certainly eclipse any positive coverage her wedding to Flynn was likely to garner.

'Precisely,' Ezekiel said, as if he'd heard every one of her thoughts. 'We need Zeke to sell to Morrison-Ashton. For the family as much as the business. So, you'll do it?'

Could she? Would Zeke listen to her? Would he care? Or would he go out of his way to do the opposite of anything she asked, just as he did with his father? If she could make him see reason…if she could win this for them… This wouldn't just be a business victory. This would assure her place in the Ashton family more than marrying Flynn could achieve.

But even if he did listen…could she ask this of him? Could she choose the business and the family over Zeke all over again, knowing it would hurt him?

Only one way to find out.

'I'll do it.'

Zeke had never given very much thought to weddings beyond showing up in an appropriate suit and whether or not there'd be a free bar. But sitting at a small wrought-iron table at the edge of the villa's huge entrance hall, taking his time over coffee, he had to conclude that, really, weddings were a whole lot of palaver.

The villa had been humming with activity since dawn, as far as he could tell. Before he'd even made it downstairs garlands of flowers and vines had been twisted round the banisters of the staircase, the floors had been polished, and potted trees with ribbons tied around their trunks had been placed at the base of each arch that spanned the hall.

He had no doubt that every other room in the villa would be receiving similar treatment over the next twenty-four hours, but they'd started with the area most likely to be seen by the greatest number of people that day.

And, boy, were there a lot of people. Guests had started arriving very early that morning, flying in from all over the world. From his chosen seat he had a great view of the front door, through a large arch that opened onto the hallway. Clearly not everyone was staying at the hotel down the road, as several couples and families with suitcases had pitched up already and been shown to their rooms. Family, Zeke supposed. He recognised some and recognised the looks he received even better. First the double-take, checking that it really was him. Then the raised eyebrows. Then a whisper to a companion and the whole thing started over again.

Zeke had seriously considered, more than once, taking a pen to the linen napkin he'd been given and fashioning some sort of sign.

Yes, it would say, *it really is me. Zeke Ashton Junior, black sheep, passed-over heir, broke his mother's heart and had the cheek to come back for his brother's wedding. And, no, I'm not selling my father my company, either. Shocking, isn't it?*

The only thing that stopped him was that, even if he managed to fit all that on a napkin, no one would be able to read it from the sort of distance they were keeping. So instead he smiled politely, raised his coffee cup, and refused point-blank to leave his table. People wanted to stare? Let them.

As the hour became more reasonable other people started to stop by, ostensibly to drop off presents but probably to gawp at the villa and try and catch a glimpse of the bride. Zeke wished them luck; he hadn't seen hide nor hair of her since he'd said goodnight the evening before.

That, Zeke thought ruefully, had been a mistake. Swilling the dregs of his coffee around at the bottom of his cup, he tried not to remember the way Thea had smelled, so close in the darkness, and failed. Just as he'd failed to forget every moment of that last night he'd spent with her before he left.

The way she'd smiled at him before the party. The way she'd kissed him and sworn that it didn't matter when he told her about Flynn taking his job. The way she'd supported him when he'd decided to go and face his father, tell him what he really thought of him.

How his rage had bubbled to the surface as he'd approached his father's office. How unprepared he'd been for what he'd heard there.

Mostly he remembered the moment he'd known he had to leave. Right then—that night. He remembered climbing up to Thea's window to ask her to come with him, and her tears as she told him she couldn't. Wouldn't. The way his heart had stung as he'd realised she really meant it.

Eight years and he couldn't shake that memory.

Couldn't shake the hurt, either.

Catching the eye of the maid, Zeke gave her his most charming smile. She frowned, but headed off to fetch the coffee carafe anyway. Zeke supposed she had other things she was supposed to be doing today, and he was stopping her. But no one had told *him* what to do. He might be the best man, but it seemed the title was wholly ceremonial.

Flynn had disappeared out earlier with one of their cousins, apparently not even spotting Zeke at his table. Whatever tasks there were to be performed today, Flynn seemed to have plenty of help.

Which left him here, drinking too much coffee, and overthinking things. Not ideal.

Across the wide hallway he heard heels clicking on stone and looked up, already knowing somehow who it was.

Thea looked tired, Zeke thought. Was that his fault? Had she been kept awake thinking about exactly where everything had gone wrong between them as he had? He motioned to the maid for a second coffee cup and waited for Thea to cross the hall and sit down at his table. Even if she wanted to avoid him he knew the lure of coffee would be too strong for her.

It took her a while, because another crowd of people had arrived with gifts wrapped in silver paper and too much ribbon and she'd got caught up playing hostess. Zeke watched her smiling and welcoming and thanking and thought she looked even less like the girl he remembered than she had in her wedding dress. The Thea he'd known had hated this—all the fake smiles and pretending to be delighted by the third set of champagne flutes to arrive in the last half-hour. She'd played the part well enough after her mother died, at her father's insistence, the same way she'd acted as a mother to Helena and run the Morrison household for the three of them. But she'd always escaped away upstairs at Morrison-Ashton company parties, as soon as it was at all polite. These days it seemed she relished playing the part.

Eventually Isabella arrived, her smiles and gestures even bigger than Thea's. As his mother took over the meet-and-greet, Thea stepped back from her guests, a slightly disappointed frown settling onto her forehead, looking suddenly out of place. After a moment she moved across the hallway towards him. And the coffee. Zeke had no doubt that the caffeine was more appealing to her than his presence.

'Good morning, Zeke.' Thea swept her skirt under her as she sat, and smiled her thanks at the maid as she poured the coffee. 'Did you sleep well?'

'Like a baby,' Zeke lied. 'And yourself?'

'Fine, thank you.'

'Up early on wedding business?' he asked, waving his coffee cup in the direction of the new arrivals.

'Actually, I was just catching up on a few work things before tomorrow.' Thea picked up her cup and blew across the surface. 'I'll be off for almost a month for the honeymoon, so I'm trying to make sure everything is properly handed over.'

'I'd have thought you'd have more important things to do today than work. Wedding things,' he added when she looked confused.

Thea glanced down at her coffee cup again. 'To be honest, I've been able to leave most of that to the wedding planner. And Helena and Flynn.'

'Most brides *want* to be involved in their wedding plans, you know.' At least, the ones who wanted to get married. Who were marrying a man they loved. And Zeke was beginning to think that Thea didn't fall into *either* of those categories, whatever she said.

'I didn't say I haven't been involved,' Thea said, her voice sharp. 'But at this point it's all the last-minute details and fiddly bits, and Helena is much better at making things look good than I am.'

'So, what *are* you doing today, then?' Zeke asked.

'Actually, I do have one very important wedding-related task to do,' Thea said. 'And I could really use your help.'

Zeke raised his eyebrows. 'Oh?'

Thea nodded. 'I need to buy Flynn a groom's gift. I thought you might be able to help me find something he'd like.'

He hadn't seen his brother in eight years, and he'd had precious little clue what the man liked before then. But if this was the excuse Thea needed to talk to him about whatever was really on her mind, he'd play along. It might even be fun.

'Okay,' he said, draining his coffee. 'I'll bring my car round while you get ready to go.'

But Thea shook her head. 'Oh, no. *I'm* driving.'

CHAPTER FIVE

THE MORE SHE thought about it, the more Thea was convinced that this was a brilliant idea. She could use the shopping trip to sound Zeke out on his plans for This Minute before she approached the more difficult task of convincing him to sell it to Morrison-Ashton. And at the same time she could prove exactly how happy she was to be marrying Flynn by choosing her husband-to-be the perfect wedding gift.

Plus, it got her out of the villa—*and* she got to drive. That was almost enough to assuage the twinges of guilt that still plagued her about her mission that morning.

'Why am I not surprised?' Zeke asked as she pulled up outside the front door in her little red convertible.

'I like to drive.' Thea shrugged, her hands never leaving the wheel as Zeke opened the passenger door and lowered himself into the seat. 'It was an engagement present from Flynn.'

Well, he'd given it to her anyway. She rather suspected that Helena had helped him choose it. Flynn's idea of appropriate gifts tended to be more along the line of whatever the jeweller recommended.

'Of course it was.' Zeke buckled up his seat belt and rested his arm along the side of the door.

He looked casual enough, but Thea knew he was gripping the seat with his other hand. He'd complained regularly about her driving in the eleven months between her passing her test and him leaving.

'So, where are we going?'

'There's a small town just twenty minutes' drive or so away.' Smoothly, Thea pulled away from the villa and headed down the driveway, picking up speed as they passed another load of guests coming up. She'd just have to pretend she hadn't seen them later. 'It has some nice little shops, and there's a wonderful trattoria where we can stop for lunch.'

'Sounds nice. And I'm honoured that you're choosing to spend your last day of single life with me. Really.'

Thea rolled her eyes and ignored him. There was plenty of time to deal with Zeke and his terrible sense of what counted as funny once they reached the town. For now, she just wanted to enjoy the drive.

Zeke fiddled with the car stereo as Thea turned off onto the main road, and soon they were flying through the gentle hills and green and yellow fields of the Tuscan countryside to the sound of the classic rock music he'd always insisted on.

'I *know* I don't own this CD,' Thea said—not that she cared. Somehow it sounded right. As if they'd fallen back in time to the day she'd passed her driving test, just a few weeks after her seventeenth birthday, and Zeke had let her drive his car for the first time.

Zeke held up his phone, connected to the stereo by a lead she hadn't known existed. 'You know me. I never travel without a proper soundtrack.'

The summer sun beamed down on them as they drove along the winding road, past farms and other villas and the occasional vineyard. She'd have two weeks to explore this land with Flynn, Thea thought. Two whole weeks to get used to the idea of being his wife, to get to know him as her husband, before they headed back to London to set up their new home together. It would be perfect.

The heat on her shoulders relaxed her muscles and she realised that Zeke was blissfully silent beside her, not even commenting on her speed, as any other passenger might have done. Maybe he was remembering that first trip out, too. Maybe he was remembering what had happened afterwards, when they'd found a ruined barn on the edge of a nearby farm and he'd spread his jacket out over the hay as he laid her down and kissed her...

Thea glanced at the speedometer and relaxed her foot off the accelerator just a touch.

Time to think of calmer things. Like Flynn, and their honeymoon.

Eventually she slowed down to something approaching the speed limit as they passed rows of stone houses on the outskirts and joined the other traffic heading over the bridge into the town. Thea pulled into the same parking space she'd used the last time she'd visited, just outside the main *piazza*. She grabbed her handbag, waiting for Zeke to get out before she locked the car.

'So,' he asked, pushing his sunglasses up onto his head as he stepped into the shade of the nearest building, 'where first?'

Thea stared down the street, through its red stone arches and paving, and realised she hadn't a clue. What *did* you buy your future husband as a wedding gift, anyway? Especially one who, even after decades of friendship, you didn't actually know all that well?

Glinting glass caught her eye, and she remembered the jeweller's and watch shop she and Helena had found down a winding side street off the *piazza*. Surely there'd be something there?

'This way,' she said, striding in what she hoped was the right direction through the crowds gathered to watch a street entertainer in the *piazza*.

'Where you lead…' Zeke said easily, letting her pass before falling into step with her.

Thea's stride faltered just for a moment. He didn't mean anything by it, she was sure—probably didn't even remember the song. But at his words a half-forgotten melody lodged in her head, playing over and over. A promise to always follow, no matter what.

Her mum had sung it often, before she died. And Thea remembered singing along. The tune was as much a part of her childhood as bickering with Helena over hairbands and party shoes. But more than that she remembered singing it to Zeke, late at night, after half a bottle of champagne smuggled upstairs from the party below. Remembered believing, for a time, that it was true. That she'd follow him anywhere.

Until he'd actually asked her to leave with him.

Shaking her head to try and dislodge the memory, she realised they were there and pushed open the shop door. There was no time for dwelling on ancient history now. She was getting married tomorrow.

And she still needed to find her groom the perfect gift.

'Right,' she said. 'Let's see what this place has that screams *Flynn*.'

The answer, Zeke decided pretty quickly, was not much.

While Thea examined racks of expensive watches and too flashy cufflinks he trailed his fingers over the glass cases and looked around at the other stuff. Flynn wasn't a flashy cufflinks kind of guy, as far as he remembered. But maybe Thea knew better these days.

He glanced over and she held up a gold watch, its oversized face flashing in the bright overhead lights. 'What about this?'

'Flynn has a watch,' Zeke pointed out.

'Yeah, but maybe he'd like a new one. From his wife.'

'Wife-to-be. And I doubt it. The one he wears was Grandad's.' He'd spotted it on his brother's wrist the night before, at dinner, and stamped down on the memory of the day their father had given it to him.

'Oh.' Thea handed the watch back to the assistant. 'Maybe we'll look at the cufflinks instead, then.'

With a sigh, Zeke turned back to the other cases, filled with precious gems and metals. Maybe he should get something for his mother. Something sparkly would probably be enough to make up for any of the apparent pain Thomas had said she'd felt at his departure. Not that Zeke had seen any actual evidence of that pain.

Maybe she was just too caught up in the wedding festivities to remember that she'd missed him. It wouldn't be the first time that other people, other events, had taken precedence over her own sons.

A necklace caught Zeke's eye: pale gold with a bright blue sapphire at the centre. The same colour as Thea's dress the night before. He could almost imagine himself fastening it around her neck as they stood outside her room—a sign that he still…what? Cared? Remembered what they'd had? Regretted how things had ended? Wanted her to be happy? Knew that even though they'd both moved on they'd always be part of each other's past?

That was the hardest thing, he decided. Not even knowing what he wanted to tell Thea, what he needed her to understand. It wasn't as simple as hating her—it never could be, with Thea. But it wasn't as if he'd shown up here this weekend to tell her not to marry Flynn, to run away with him at last instead. As they should have done eight years ago.

No, what he felt for Thea was infinitely more complicated. And if there was a single piece of jewellery that could convey it to her, without him having to find the words, he'd buy it for her in a heartbeat—no matter the cost. But there wasn't.

With a sigh, Zeke dragged his gaze to the next case, only to find tray after tray of sparkling diamond solitaires glinting up at him.

Engagement rings. *Not helpful, universe. And why choose now to get a sense of humour, huh?*

Besides, she already had one of those. He'd glimpsed it flashing in the candlelight at dinner, recognising it as his grandmother's, and had barely even managed to muster any surprise about it. What else would the favoured Ashton heir give to his fiancé-cum-business partner? They were building an empire together, based on their joint family history.

A history Zeke had all but been written out of eight years ago.

'I'm going to have to think about it,' Thea told the shop assistant apologetically, and Zeke, realising he was still staring at the engagement rings, spun round to face her.

'We're leaving?'

'For now,' Thea said.

Zeke followed her out of the shop, letting the door swing shut behind him. 'Nothing that screamed *Flynn*, huh?'

'Not really. He's not really a flashy cufflinks kind of guy, is he?'

Something tightened in Zeke's chest, hearing her echo his thoughts, but he couldn't say if it was because she knew Flynn better than he'd thought or because her thought processes still so closely resembled his.

'So, where next?' he asked, trying to ignore the feeling.

'Um, there's a leather shop down here somewhere.' She waved her hand into an arcade of small, dark but probably insanely expensive shops, hidden under the arched stone roof. She hadn't even let Helena explore them properly last time. 'Do you think Flynn needs a new briefcase?'

'I think Flynn will love whatever you buy him, because it's from you.'

Thea gave him a look. One that suggested she was trying to evaluate if he might have been taken over by aliens recently. 'Seriously?'

'Okay, I think he'll pretend to love it, whatever it is, because that's the appropriate thing to do.'

'And Flynn *does* like appropriate.' She sighed and headed towards the leather shop anyway. 'Do you remember the hideous tie you bought him that last summer?'

'He wore it for his first day at work,' Zeke said, relishing the thought all over again. It had been the most truly horrendous tie he'd been able to find anywhere. Expensive, of course, so that his mother couldn't object. But hugely inappropriate for the serious workplace with its neon tartan. The perfect graduation gift for the perfect brother. Zeke had known Flynn would wear it just so as not to offend him. And that Flynn would never realise it was a joke gift.

'He changed it on the train before going into the office,' Thea told him, thus ruining a perfect memory.

'Seriously? That's a shame. I did love thinking of him sitting in meetings with the board wearing that tie,' Zeke said wistfully.

'He's probably still got it somewhere,' Thea said. 'He might not be stupid enough to wear it for work, but he's definitely sentimental enough that he won't have thrown it away. After all, it was the last thing you gave him before…'

'Before I left,' Zeke finished for her. 'Yeah, I don't think he was as bothered by that as you think.' Seemed like nobody had been.

She gave him a small sad smile. 'Then maybe I do know your brother better than you, after all.'

Did she? She should—she was marrying the guy. But the very fact she'd admitted she wasn't sure that she did… The contradictions buzzed around Zeke's brain, and at the heart of them was the disturbing thought that maybe Flynn *had* cared after all.

And another question. Had Thea?

The problem, Thea decided, wasn't that she didn't *know* what sort of things Flynn liked. It was just that he knew them better and had, in pretty much every case, provided them for himself. He already had the perfect briefcase, his grandfather's watch and a reliable pair of cufflinks. Whatever the item, he'd have researched it, chosen the best-quality one he required, and been satisfied with his purchase. Whatever she bought would be used a few times, to show his appreciation, then shoved to the back of a cupboard like that hideous neon tartan joke tie.

This whole trip had been a mistake. She'd wanted to show Zeke that she knew her fiancé, that they were in tune as a couple. Instead all she seemed to be proving was that whatever she brought to the marriage wasn't really required.

No. This wasn't about briefcases and watches. She brought a lot more to the table than material goods. She wasn't her father, just providing the money and then sitting back to watch the tide of success come rolling in. She was part of the company, part of Flynn's life, and part of their future together.

Which was great as a pep talk, but rubbish at helping her find a wedding present for her husband-to-be.

'What about this one?' Zeke held up a tan leather handbag. 'It's a man bag!'

'I'm pretty sure it's not,' Thea said. 'It has flowers decorating the strap.'

'Flynn's secure enough in his masculinity to carry it off,' Zeke argued, slinging the bag over his shoulder and pouting like a male model.

'I am *not* buying him the wedding present equivalent of a neon tartan tie, Zeke.' Thea turned back to the briefcases and heard him sigh behind her.

'Then what *are* you going to buy him?' Zeke picked up a black briefcase and flipped the latch open. 'Hasn't he already got one of these?'

'Yes.'

'So does he need a new one?'

'No.'

'Then can we go for lunch?'

Thea sighed. He did have a point, and she *was* hungry. She'd missed breakfast, thanks to Ezekiel Senior and his request.

She tensed at the memory. Never mind the perfect wedding gift, she had another job to do today. And lunch would be the perfect time to broach the subject. Preferably after Zeke had enjoyed a glass or two of wine. Or three. Three might be the magic number.

'Come on, then,' she said, opening the door and preparing to leave the cool shadows of the shopping arcade behind and step back out into the piazza. She waved a hand in the direction of a familiar-looking dark alleyway. 'The little trattoria I was talking about is down here somewhere.'

It wasn't fancy, but Zeke had never been one for the expensive restaurants and big-name places. He'd used to prefer hidden gems and secret spots that were just their own. She was always surprised, even after so long, when she caught a magazine photo of him at some celebrity chef's opening night at a new restaurant, or on the red carpet with some actress or another. That wasn't the Zeke she remembered. And now, spending time with him again, she wondered if it was even the Zeke he'd become. Was it just that being seen was the only way he had to let his father know that he was a success now, in his own right?

Maybe she'd ask him. After the wedding. And after she'd persuaded him to sell This Minute to his father.

So probably never, then.

Thea pushed open the heavy painted wood door under a sign that just read 'Trattoria' and let Zeke in first. He smiled at the nearest waitress and she found them a table next to the window without hesitation; only a few other tables were occupied. Thea couldn't help but think this was probably a good thing. If Zeke threw pasta all over her when she tried to talk to him about his father at least there wouldn't be too many witnesses. Helena would be cross about the dress, though…

'Can I get you some drinks?' the waitress asked, her English clearly far better than Thea's Italian had ever been. She let Zeke order a local beer before she asked for a soft drink. Alcohol really wasn't going to help the conversation they needed to have.

'So, you've been here before?' Zeke asked, looking around him at the faded pictures on the stone walls and the bare wooden tables.

The small windows had all been thrown open to let in air, but the heat of the day and the lack of breeze meant that not much coolness was moving around, save from the lazy spin of the lone ceiling fan. Thea's dress had started to stick to her back already, and she longed for that soft drink.

'I came here with Helena last week,' she said. 'Just

after we arrived. I can recommend the *pappardelle* with wild boar sauce.'

'With Helena? Not Flynn?' Zeke pressed.

Thea wondered why he cared anyway. He'd left, and had every intention of leaving again, without even the faint hope that he might return this time. What did he care if she married Flynn or not? Besides not letting his brother win, of course.

Maybe that was what this came down to. All Zeke wanted was to prove a point and then he'd move on. In which case she had pretty much no chance of talking him into selling them This Minute.

But she still had to try.

'No, not with Flynn. He didn't fly in until a couple of days ago. They needed him in the office.'

'But they didn't need you?'

Dammit. Why did Zeke always know exactly what niggled at her? And why did he always have to push at that point?

'My planning for the wedding kind of *is* part of my job at the moment.' Thea toyed with the menu in her hand so she didn't have to see his reaction to that.

'Of course,' Zeke said. 'The final union of the two biggest families in media. It's quite the PR stunt.'

'It's also my life,' Thea snapped back.

'Yeah, but after the last twenty-four hours I still can't tell which of those is more important to you.'

Thea looked up, searching for a response to that one, and gave an inward sigh of relief when she saw the waitress coming over with their drinks.

'Are you ready to order?' she asked, placing the glasses on the table.

Zeke smiled at her—that charming, happy-go-lucky

smile he never gave Thea any more. 'I'll have the wild boar *pappardelle*, please. I hear it's excellent.'

'The same, please,' Thea said. But she wasn't thinking about food. She was thinking about how she'd let her work become her life, and let her life drift away entirely.

Zeke sipped his beer and watched Thea, lost in thought across the table. He'd thought it would be fun, needling her about how her wedding was actually work. He'd had a run of honeymoon jokes lined up in his head—ones he knew she'd hate. But now…well, the humour had gone.

'I'm sorry,' he said, even though he wasn't sure he was, really. He'd only told the truth, after all. Something that happened far too little in their families.

'You're *sorry*?' Thea asked disbelievingly.

Zeke shrugged. 'Not really the done thing, is it? Upsetting the bride the day before her wedding.'

'I'm not upset.'

'Are you sure? Because you look a little…blotchy.' The way she always had moments before she started crying.

But Thea shook her head, reaching for her glass with a steady hand. 'I'm fine. Like you say, you've been back less than twenty-four hours. I don't expect you to understand the relationship and the agreement that Flynn and I have developed and nurtured over the past two years.'

'Two years? You've been with him that long?'

'Yes. You don't think marriage is something I'd rush into, do you?'

Actually, he'd assumed that the idea had come up in a board meeting, that their respective fathers had put forward a proposal document to each of them and they'd weighed up the pros and cons before booking the church. But Zeke didn't think she'd appreciate *that* analysis.

'You did last time,' he said instead. 'With What's-his-name.'

'Cameron,' she supplied. 'And how did you know about him?'

'I wasn't thinking about him.' How many guys *had* she almost married since he'd left? 'I meant the Canadian.'

'Scott.'

'Yeah. I read about him on our Canadian news site. Hockey player, right?'

'Right.'

'Whirlwind engagement, I heard.'

'And he was equally quick with the cheating, as it turned out.'

'Ah.' He hadn't known that. All that had been reported was that the wedding had been called off with hours to spare. So like Thea to protect the guy's reputation even as he was hurting her. 'So who was this Cameron guy, then?'

'A business associate. Turned out he loved my business, and my money, a lot more than he loved me.'

'Never mix business with pleasure, huh?' Zeke said, before remembering that that was exactly what she was doing with Flynn. 'I mean…'

Thea sighed. 'Don't worry. I am well aware of the disastrous reputation of my love-life. You can't say anything I haven't heard before.'

He hated seeing her like this. So certain she would make a mistake. Was that why she was marrying Flynn? The safest bet in a world full of potential mistakes?

Sometimes a woman has to choose the safest road, Zeke. We can't all afford to hike the harder trails if we want to arrive safely.' The words were his mother's, eight years old now, but he could see their truth in Thea's face. For the first time he wondered who Thea would have become if her own mother had lived. Or if Thomas Morrison had never met Ezekiel Ashton. Would she be happier? Probably, he decided.

'You weren't always rubbish at love,' Zeke said, the words coming out soft and low.

Her gaze flashed up to meet him, as if she was looking for a hidden jibe or more mockery. He tried to keep his expression clear, to show her that all he meant was the words he'd said.

Clearly he failed. 'Yeah, right. Funny man. Of course you know *exactly* how early my failure at love started.'

'I didn't mean—' he started, but she cut him off.

'My first love—you—climbed out of a window to escape from me on my eighteenth birthday, Zeke. I think we can all see where the pattern started.' Bitterness oozed out of her voice, but all Zeke could hear was her saying, *'No, Zeke. I can't.'* Eight years and the sound had never left him.

Hang on. 'Wait. Are you blaming *me* for your unlucky love-life?' Because as far as he was concerned he was the one who should be assigning blame here.

'No. Yes. Maybe.' She twisted her napkin in her hands, wrapping it round her fingers then letting it go again.

'I feel much better for that clarification.'

'I don't want to talk about this any more.'

She might not, but after eight years Zeke had some things he wanted to say. And she was bloody well going to listen. 'And, in the name of accuracy, I wasn't trying to escape you. In fact you might recall me begging you to come with me.' Standing on that stupid wobbly trellis, wrecking whatever that purple flower had been, clinging onto the windowsill. She'd looked out at him, all dark hair and big eyes, and broken his heart.

'I wouldn't call it begging,' Thea said, but even she didn't sound convinced.

'You said no. You chose to stay. You can't blame me for

that.' That moment—that one moment—had changed his entire life. Made him the person he was today. She could at least *try* to remember it right.

'You chose to leave me. So why can't I blame you? You're still blaming me. Isn't that why you're here? To make my life miserable because I made the right decision eight years ago and you hate that I was right for once?'

No. That wasn't it. That wasn't what he was doing. He was here to draw a line under everything there had ever been between them, under his bitter resentment of his family that had ruled his life for too long. Zeke was moving on.

But sometimes moving on required looking backwards. Closure—that was what this was.

'The right decision,' she'd said. 'You never once imagined what life might have been like if you' d left with me that night?' Because he had driven himself crazy with it even when he'd known it was pointless. Self-destructive, even. Had she been spared that?

Apparently not. 'Of course I did, Zeke! Endlessly, and a thousand different ways. But it doesn't change the fact that I was needed at home. That I was right to stay.'

And suddenly Zeke knew what it was he needed to move on. What it would take to get the closure he craved.

So he looked up at her and asked the question.

'Why?'

CHAPTER SIX

WHY?

As if that wasn't a question she'd asked herself a million times over the past eight years.

She knew the answer, of course. Helena. She'd needed a big sister right then, more than ever. Thea couldn't have left her, and she didn't regret staying for her for one moment.

But if she was honest that wasn't the only answer. And it wasn't the one she wanted to give Zeke. It wasn't her secret to tell, apart from anything else.

'Because we were too young. Too stupid. Zeke, I was barely eighteen, and you were asking me to leave my whole life behind. My family, my future, my plans and dreams. My place in the world. Everything.'

'I'd have been your family. Your place. Your future.'

Zeke stared at her, his face open and honest. For the first time since he'd come back Thea thought she might be seeing the boy she'd known behind the man he'd become.

'You know I'd have moved mountains to give you anything you wanted. To make every dream you had come true.'

The worst part was she did know that. Had known it even then. But she hadn't been able to take the risk.

'Perhaps. But, successful as you are now, I bet it wasn't like that to start with. You'd have had to struggle, work every hour there was, take risks with your money, your reputation.' She could see from his face it was true. 'And what did you think I'd be doing while you were doing that? I wanted to go to university, Zeke. I had my place—all ready and waiting. I didn't want to give that up to keep house for you while you chased your dream.'

'I wouldn't... It wouldn't have been like that.'

'Wouldn't it?'

'No.' He sounded firmer this time. 'Look, I can't change the past, and I can't say what would have happened. But, Thea, you know me. *Knew* me, at least. And you have to know I would never have asked you to give up your dreams for mine.'

'Sorry...' the waitress said, lowering their plates to the table. 'I didn't mean to... Enjoy!'

She scampered off towards the kitchen and Thea wondered how much she'd heard. How much she was now re-telling to the restaurant staff.

Zeke hadn't even looked at his lunch. 'Tell me you know that, Thea. I wouldn't have done that.'

Thea loaded pasta onto her fork. 'Maybe you wouldn't. Not intentionally. But it happens.' She'd seen it happen to too many friends, after they got married or when they started a family. At eighteen, she didn't think she'd have had the self-awareness to fight it.

'What about now, then?' Zeke asked, still looking a little shaken. 'Do you really think it will be different with Flynn?'

'Yes,' Thea said, without hesitation. She knew about business—knew what she needed to do there. Her marriage with Flynn would only enhance that. She wouldn't give it up just to be someone's wife. 'We've talked about it. About our future. We both know what we're getting into.'

Had it all written down in legalese, ready to be signed along with the marriage register.

Their conversation on the terrace the night before came back to her and she felt a jangle of nerves and excitement when she thought about what she'd agreed to now. Maybe that—a family—would be what she needed to make the whole thing feel real. She knew it was what Flynn wanted, after all. She frowned. But they hadn't spoken yet about what would happen then. Would he expect her to stay at home and look after the kids? If so, they had a problem.

Mentally, she added the topic to the list of honeymoon discussions to have. They had time. They hadn't even had sex yet, for heaven's sake.

The thought was almost amusing—especially sitting here with her fiancé's brother, a guy she had actually slept with. Lost her virginity to, in fact. *Along with my heart.*

Was that why none of the others had stuck? She had wondered sometimes, usually late at night, if Zeke had broken something inside her. If, when he'd left, he'd taken something with him she could never get back. But now he was here and she'd decided she was better off without whatever it was he'd taken. Better off choosing a sensible, planned sort of relationship. Maybe it didn't burn with the same intensity, but she stood a better chance of making it out without injury.

She might not have been able to fulfil the role her father had hoped she would, after her mother's death. Maybe she hadn't been a great hostess or housekeeper, or able to help Helena in the way a mother would have. But those were never supposed to be her roles, anyway. Not in her father's household. This time she'd found her own role. Her own place in her own new family. And she wasn't giving that up.

She couldn't. Not when she risked returning to that

empty, yawning loneliness that had followed Zeke's departure. With Zeke gone, Helena sent away for months, her father locked in his study and Isabella taking over everything Thea had thought was her responsibility…the isolation had been unbearable. As if the world had shifted in the wake of that horrible night and when it had settled there'd been no room for Thea any more. Nowhere she felt comfortable, at home.

And she'd been looking for it ever since. University hadn't provided it, and the holidays at home, with Helena floating around the huge house like a ghost, certainly hadn't. Working her way up at Morrison-Ashton, proving she wasn't just there because of her father, that had helped. But a corner office wasn't a home, however hard she worked.

Flynn…their marriage, their family…he could be. And Thea couldn't let Zeke, or anyone, make her question that.

She watched Zeke, digging into his *pappardelle* and wondered why it was he'd really come back. Not for her—he'd made that much clear. So what was he trying to achieve?

'Zeke?'

He looked up from his bowl, eyes still unhappy. 'Yeah?'

'Why did you come back? Really? I mean, I know it wasn't just for my wedding. So why now?'

With a sigh, Zeke dropped his fork into his bowl and sat back. 'Because…because it was time. Because I'm done trying to win against my father. I'm done caring what he thinks or expects or wants. I'm ready to move on from everything that happened eight years ago.'

'Including me?'

'Including you.'

Thea took a breath, held it, and let it out. After this week they'd be done with each other for good. She'd be married, and the past wouldn't matter any more. It felt…strange. Like an ache in a phantom limb. But she felt lighter, too, at the idea that everything could be put behind them at last.

Except, of course, she had one more thing to do before she could let him go.

Her gaze dropped down to her bowl as guilt pinged in her middle. This might be the one thing she could do to make sure Zeke never came back. But it was also one more step towards earning her place as an Ashton. And that meant it was worth it.

The way Thea's body relaxed visibly at his words left Zeke tenser than ever. Was she that relieved to be finally rid of even the memory of him? Or, like him, was she just so tired of lugging it all around every day? Was she happy to have the path clear for her happy-ever-after with Flynn? Or just settling for the safety of a sensible business marriage?

He'd ask…except those kind of questions—and caring about the answers—didn't exactly sound like leaving her behind.

One more day. He'd make sure she got down the aisle, said 'I do', and rode off into the sunset. Then his new life, whatever it turned out to be, could begin.

'Before you leave us all behind completely, though…' Thea said.

Zeke's jaw clenched. There was always one more thing with Thea.

'I need to talk to you about something.'

A hollow opened up inside him. This was it. Whatever reason Thea had for dragging him out to buy a stupid gift for his brother, he was about to find it out. And suddenly he didn't want to know. If he had to leave her behind for ever he wanted to have this last day. Wanted to leave believing that she'd honestly wanted to spend time with him before he went. For the sake of everything they'd had once and knew they could never have again. Was that so much to ask?

Apparently so.

'I spoke to your father this morning,' Thea said, and Zeke's happy bubble of obliviousness popped.

'Did you, now?' He should have known that. Should have guessed, at least. He'd let himself get side-tracked by the experience of being with Thea again, and now he was about to get blindsided. Another reason why being around Thea Morrison was bad for his wellbeing.

'He wanted me to talk to you about—'

'About me selling This Minute to Morrison-Ashton,' Zeke finished for her. It wasn't as if his father had any other thoughts in relation to him.

'Yes.'

One simple word and the hollow inside him collapsed in on itself, like a punch to the gut folding him over.

'No,' he said, and let the anger start to fill him out again.

How could she ask? After everything they'd been to each other, everything they'd once had…how did she even dare?

His skin felt too hot and his head pounded with the betrayal. He knew exactly why she was doing it. To make sure he left. To make sure her perfect world went back to the way she thought it should be. To buy her place in his family, at his brother's side.

Because Morrison-Ashton and their families had always mattered more to her than he had. And he should have remembered that.

Thea pulled the face she'd always used to pull when he'd been annoying her by being deliberately difficult. He'd missed that face until now. Now it just reminded him how little his feelings mattered to her.

'Zeke—'

'I'm not selling you my company, Thea.' He bit the words out, holding in the ones he really wanted to say. He wasn't that boy any more—the one who lost control from just being near her. This was business, not love. Not any more.

'Your father is willing to match whatever Glasshouse are offering…'

'I don't care.' *Just business*, he reminded himself.

'And even if you don't want to take up a position within Morrison-Ashton we could still look at share options.'

'I said no.' The rage built again, and he flexed his hand against his thigh to keep it from shaking.

'Our digital media team are putting together a—'

'Dammit, Thea!' Plates rattled as Zeke slammed his fist down on the table and the restaurant fell silent. 'Will you just listen to me for once?'

'Don't shout, Zeke,' Thea said, suddenly pale. 'People are looking.'

'Let them look.' He didn't care. Why should he? He'd be out of here tomorrow. 'Because I'm going to shout until you start listening to me.'

Thea's face turned stony. Dropping her fork into her bowl, she pulled out her purse and left several notes on the table. Then she stood, picked up her bag, and walked out of the restaurant.

The rage faded the moment she was out of his sight and he was Zeke Ashton the adult again. The man he'd worked so hard to become, only to lose him the moment she prodded at a sore spot.

Picking up his bottle of beer, Zeke considered his options. Then he drained the beer, dropped another couple of notes onto the stack and followed her, as he'd always known he would.

So had she known, it seemed, which irritated him more than it should have. Thea stood leaning against the wall of the restaurant, waiting for him.

'I left a very decent tip,' he said, watching her, waiting to see which way she'd jump. 'It seemed only fair since we walked out without finishing our meals.'

'Yelling suppresses the appetite.' Thea pushed away from the wall.

'It seemed the only way to get you to listen to me.'

Turning to face him, she smiled with obviously feigned interest. 'I'm listening.'

Suddenly his words felt petty, unnecessary. But he said them anyway. 'I will not sell This Minute to Morrison-Ashton.'

She gave a sharp nod. 'So you've mentioned. Now, if that's all, I want to go back to the villa.'

'What about Flynn's present?' Zeke asked, matching her stride as she headed for the car at speed.

'It can wait.'

'The wedding's tomorrow. I think you're pretty much out of time on this one.'

Thea opened the car door and slid into her seat. 'So I'll give him a spectacular honeymoon present instead.'

Zeke didn't want to think about what she might come up with for that. Except he already had a pretty good idea.

'Like the present you gave me for my twenty-first?' he asked, and watched Thea flush the same bright red as her car as she started the engine.

'You have to stop that,' she said, pulling away from the kerb.

'Stop what?' he asked, just to make her say it.

She glared at him. 'Look. I'm getting married tomorrow. So all this reminiscing about the good old days is getting kind of inappropriate, don't you think?'

'Oh, I don't know.' Zeke watched her as she drove, hands firm on the wheel, shoulders far more tense than they had been on the drive in. He was getting to her. And for some reason he really didn't want to stop. 'I think the question is whether Flynn thinks it's inappropriate.'

'Flynn doesn't know.'

'You mean you're not going to tell him about our shopping trip?'

'I mean he doesn't know about us at all. That we were ever…anything to each other.'

Thea took the last turning out of the town and suddenly their speed rocketed. Plastered back against his seat, Zeke tried to process the new reality she'd just confronted him with. She'd said they didn't talk about him, but he hadn't realised it extended this far. She'd written him out of their history completely, and the pain of that cut through his simmering anger for a moment.

'But…how?' How could anyone who knew them, who had seen them together back then, not known what they were to each other? They had been seventeen and twenty-one. *Subtle* hadn't really been in their vocabulary, despite Thea's requests to keep things secret. He hadn't cared who knew. Certainly their parents had known. How could Flynn have missed it?

'He was away at university, remember?' Thea said. 'And not just round the corner, like you. He was all the way up in Scotland. I guess he just…he was living his own life. I didn't realise at first, when we…started this. But it became clear pretty quickly. He just…didn't know.'

'And you didn't think it was important enough to tell him about?' Didn't think *he* was important enough. Suddenly Zeke wanted nothing more than to remind her just how important he'd been to her once.

'Why would I? You were gone. You were never com-

ing back as far as I was concerned. And even if you did…
even now you have…'

'Even now I have, what?'

'It doesn't change anything. You and I are ancient history, remember? What difference does it make now what we might have had eight years ago?'

But it did make a difference. Zeke couldn't say how, but it did. And suddenly he wanted her to admit that.

Thea tried to focus on the road, but her gaze kept slipping to the side, watching Zeke's reactions. It wasn't a test, wasn't as if she'd said anything untrue, but he wasn't reacting quite the way she'd expected.

She knew Zeke—had always known Zeke, it seemed. She knew that for him to come back now, into this situation…whatever his reasons…he wouldn't pass up the opportunity to drag up the past. He'd want his brother to feel uncomfortable, to know that he'd had her first. Punishment, she supposed. Partly for her, for not leaving with him, for breaking their deal. And partly for Flynn, for taking everything Zeke had always assumed was his.

Not telling Flynn… It had seemed like the best idea at the time. And when Zeke had returned she'd been so relieved that she hadn't. One less thing to drive her crazy this week. Her relationship with Flynn might not be the most conventional, but their marriage agreement did have a fidelity clause, and she really didn't want to have an excruciatingly awkward conversation with her fiancé and probably their lawyers, maybe even their fathers, about whether Zeke's return would have any effect on that.

Of course it didn't. They'd both moved on. But Flynn liked to be thorough about these things.

'It makes a difference,' Zeke said suddenly, and Thea

tried to tune herself back into the conversation, 'because you're lying to your fiancé. My brother.'

Thea gave a harsh laugh. 'Seriously? You're going to try and play the loving brother card? Now? It's a little late, Zeke.'

'I'm the best man at your wedding, Thea. Someone tomorrow is going to ask me if I know of any reason why you shouldn't get married.'

'You don't! Me sleeping with you eight years ago is not a reason for me not to get married tomorrow.'

Zeke raised an eyebrow. 'No? Then how about you lying to your fiancé? Or the fact you left your last two fiancés practically at the altar?'

'Why were you reading up on my love-life anyway?' She hadn't thought to ask when he mentioned Scott before. She'd been more concerned with getting the conversation away from her past romantic disasters. 'I don't believe for a second you just happened to stumble across that information on your site.'

'Did you think I hadn't kept up with you? Kept track of what was going on in your life?'

'Yes,' Thea said. 'That's exactly what I thought. I thought you left and forgot all about the people you left behind.'

'I didn't leave you behind.'

The countryside sped past faster than ever, but Thea couldn't bring herself to slow down. 'Zeke, you left and you didn't look back.'

'I asked you to come with me.' His mulish expression told her that even eight years couldn't change the fact that she'd said no. Too late now, anyway.

'And I told you I couldn't.'

Zeke shook his head. 'Not couldn't. Wouldn't.'

'It was eight years ago, Zeke! Does it really matter which now?'

'Yes!'

'For the love of God, why?'

'Because I've spent eight years obsessing about it and I need closure now, dammit! Preferably before you marry my brother and send me away again.'

Thea's head buzzed with the enormity of the idea. Eight years of obsession, and now he wanted closure. Fine. She'd give him his closure.

Slamming on the brakes, Thea pulled over to the side of the road, half into a field of sunflowers, and stopped the engine. Opening the door, she stepped out onto the dusty verge at the edge of the road, waiting for Zeke to follow. He did, after a moment, walking slowly around to where she leant against the car. She waited until he stopped, his body next to hers against the warm metal.

'You want closure?' she said.

'Yes.'

He wasn't looking at her—was choosing to stare out at the bright flowers swaying in the breeze instead. Somehow that made it all a little easier.

'Fine. What do you need to know to move on?'

Now he turned, his smile too knowing. 'I need to know that *you've* moved on. That you're not still making the same bad choices you made then for the same bad reasons.'

'I made the right choice,' Thea said, quietly. 'I chose to stay for a reason.'

'For Helena. For your father.'

'Yes.'

'You were living your life for other people to avoid upsetting your family, just like you are now.'

'No. I'm living my life for me.' And making the right

decisions for the future she wanted. She had to hang on to that.

'Really? Whose idea was it for you to marry Flynn?'

'What difference does it make? I'm the one who chose to do it.'

'It makes a difference,' Zeke pressed.

Did the man not know how to just let go of something? Just once in his intense life? Was it too much to ask?

'Fine. It was your father's idea,' Thea said, bracing herself for the inevitable smugness. Lord, Zeke did love being right.

'Of course it was.' But he didn't sound smug. Didn't sound vindicated. If anything, he sounded a little sad.

Thea turned to look at him. 'Why did you ask if you already knew?'

'Because I need you to see it. I need you to see what you're doing.'

His words were intense, but his eyes were worse. They pressed her, demanded that she look the truth in the face, that she open herself up to every single possibility and weigh them all.

Thea looked away, letting her hair fall in front of her face. 'I know what I'm doing.'

Zeke shook his head. 'No, Thea. I don't think you do. So, tell me. Why did you stay when I left?'

'Why do you think? We were too young, Zeke. And besides, my family needed me. Helena needed me.' More than ever right then.

'Why?'

'Oh, I don't know, Zeke. Why do you think? Why would a motherless teenage girl *possibly* need her big sister around to look out for her?' That wasn't the whole reason, of course, but the rest of it was Helena's secret to tell.

'She had your father. And my mother.'

A bitter laugh bubbled up in her throat. 'As much as she might pretend otherwise, your mother is not actually *our* mother.'

'Just as well, really,' Zeke said, his voice low, and she knew without asking that he wasn't thinking about her marrying Flynn. He was thinking about all the things they'd done in dark corners at parties, about his twenty-first birthday, about every single time his skin had been pressed against hers.

And, curse him, so was she.

'I had to stay, Zeke,' she said.

'Give me one true reason.'

Thea clenched her hand against her thigh. Did the man simply not listen? Or just not hear anything he didn't like? 'I've given you plenty.'

'Those weren't reasons—they were excuses.'

'Excuses? My family, my future—they're excuses?' Thea glared at him. 'Nice to know you hold my existence in such high esteem.'

'That's not what this is about.'

'Then what *is* it about, Zeke?' Thea asked, exasperated. 'If you don't believe me—fine. Tell me why *you* think I stayed.'

'Because you were scared,' he said, without missing a beat.

'Ha!'

'You stayed because other people told you it was the right thing to do. Because you knew it was what your father would want and you've always, *always* done what he wanted. Because you've never been able to say no to Helena ever since your mother died.' He took a breath. 'But mostly you stayed because you were too scared to trust your own desires. To trust what was between us. To trust *me*.'

The air whooshed out of Thea's lungs. 'That's what you believe?'

'That's what I know.'

When had he got so close? The warm metal of the car at her back had nothing on the heat of his body beside her.

'You're wrong,' she said, shifting slightly away from him.

He raised an eyebrow. 'Am I?' Angling his body towards her, Zeke placed one hand on her hip, bringing him closer than they'd been in eight long years. 'Prove it.'

'How?' Thea asked, mentally chastising her body for reacting to him. This was over!

'Tell me you don't still think about us. Miss us being together. Tell me you don't still want this.'

Thea started to shake her head, to try and deny it, but Zeke lowered his mouth to hers and suddenly all she could feel was the tide of relief swelling inside her. His kiss, still so familiar after so long, consumed her, and she wondered how she'd even pretended she didn't remember how it felt to be the centre of Zeke Ashton's world.

Except she wasn't any more. This wasn't about her— not really. This was Zeke proving a point, showing himself *and* her that he could still have her if he wanted. And he'd made it very clear that he didn't—not for anything more than showing his father and his brother who had the power here. She was just another way for him to get one over on the family business.

And she had a little bit more self-respect than that, thank you.

'Thea,' Zeke murmured between kisses, his arm slipping further around her waist to haul her closer.

'No.' The word came out muffled against his mouth, so she put her hands against his chest and pushed. Hard.

Zeke stumbled back against the car, his hands abandoning her body to stop himself falling. 'What—?' He stopped, gave her one of those ironic, mocking looks she hated.

'I said no.' Thea sucked in a breath and lied. 'I *don't* still think about us. I *don't* miss what we had. It was a childish relationship that ran its course. I was ready for my own life, not just to hang on to the edges of yours. That's why I didn't come with you.' She swallowed. 'And I certainly don't want *that*. Especially not when I'm marrying your brother tomorrow.'

For once in his life Zeke was blessedly silent. Thea took advantage of the miracle by turning and getting back into the car. She focussed on her breathing…in and out, even and slow. Strapped herself in, started the engine. Familiar, easy, well-known actions.

And then she said, 'Goodbye, Zeke,' and gave him three seconds to clear the car before she screeched off back to the villa.

CHAPTER SEVEN

ZEKE STARED AFTER the cherry-red sports car kicking up dust as it sped away from him. Thea's dark hair blew behind her in the breeze, and he could still smell her shampoo, still feel her body in his arms.

He was an idiot. An idiot who was now stranded in the middle of nowhere.

Pushing his fingers through his hair, Zeke started the long trudge up the path towards the villa. At least Thea had driven him most of the way home before kicking him out.

Not that he could really blame her. He knew better than to ambush her like that. He'd just been so desperate to hear her admit it, to hear her say that she'd made a mistake not going with him that night.

That she still thought about him sometimes.

But clearly she didn't. She stood by her decision. And he had to live with that. At least for the next couple of days. Then he'd be gone, ready to start his own life for once, without the memories and the baggage of trying to prove his family wrong.

He'd told Thea he wanted closure, and she'd given it to him. In spades.

It was a long, hot, depressing walk back to the villa. By the time he got there, dusty and sweaty, the only thing he wanted in the world was a shower. It was nice, in a way, to have his desires pared down to the basics. Simpler, anyway.

Of course just because he only wanted one thing, it didn't mean he was going to get it. Really, he should have known that by now.

'Zeke!' Helena jumped up from her seat in the entrance hall, blonde waves bouncing. 'You're back! Great. I wanted to— What happened to you?'

'Your sister,' Zeke said, not slowing his stride as he headed straight for the stairs. 'She's trying to destroy my life, I think.'

'Oh,' Helena said, closer than he'd thought. Was she going to follow him all the way to his room?

'Don't worry,' Zeke told her. 'I know how to thwart her.' All he had to do was not sell his company to Morrison-Ashton—which he had no intention of doing regardless— and let her marry Flynn—which he appeared to have no choice in anyway.

Even if both things still made him want to punch some poor defenceless wall.

'Right…'

Helena sounded confused, but she was still following him. Clearly he needed to address whatever her problem was if he were to have any hope of getting his shower before the rehearsal dinner.

Sighing, Zeke stopped at the top of the stairs and leant against the cool, stone wall for a moment. 'You wanted to…?'

Helena blinked. 'Sorry?'

'You said you wanted to…'

'Talk to you!' Helena flashed him a smile. 'Yes. I did. I mean, I do.'

'Can it wait until after I've had a shower?'

She glanced down at the elegant gold watch on her slender wrist. 'Um…no. Not really.'

'Then I hope you can talk louder than the water pressure in this place.' Zeke pushed off the wall and continued towards his room. 'So, what's up, kid?'

'I'm hardly a kid any more, Zeke,' Helena said.

'I suppose not.' She had been when he'd left. Barely sixteen, and all big blue eyes and blonde curls. Actually, she was still the last two, but there was something in those big eyes. Little Helena had grown up, and he wondered how much he'd missed while he'd been gone. What had growing up in this family, this business, done to her? Because he already knew what it had done to Thea, and he wouldn't wish that on anyone.

'In fact I'm the maid of honour tomorrow. And you're the best man.'

Zeke froze outside his bedroom door. What on earth was she suggesting?

Helena's tinkling laugh echoed off the painted stone of the hallway. 'Zeke, you should see your face! Don't worry—I'm not propositioning you or anything.'

Letting his breath out slowly, so she wouldn't suspect he'd been holding it, Zeke turned the door handle. 'Never thought you were.'

'Yes, you did,' Helena said, brimming with confidence. It was nice to see, in a way. At least that hadn't been drummed out of her, the way it had Thea.

'So, what are you saying?' Zeke kicked his shoes to the corner of the room, where they landed in a puff of road dust.

'We have responsibilities. We should co-ordinate them.' Letting the door swing shut behind her, Helena dropped down to sit on the edge of his bed, folding her legs up under her.

'As far as I can tell, other than an amusing yet inoffensive speech, I'm mostly superfluous to the proceedings.' Not that he cared. He knew his role here—show up and prove a point on behalf of the family that he was still a part of Morrison-Ashton. And he'd give them that for Flynn and Thea's wedding day. Not least because he knew it would be the last thing he ever had to give them. After tomorrow he'd be free.

'You're the best man, Zeke. It takes a little more than that.'

'Like dancing with you at the reception?' Stripping off his socks, Zeke padded barefoot into the bathroom to set the shower running. It took time to warm up, and maybe Helena would take the hint by the time it was at the right temperature.

'Like making sure the groom shows up.'

Zeke stopped. 'Why wouldn't he?' Did Helena know something he didn't? That *Thea* didn't?

'Because… Well…' Helena gave a dramatic sigh and fell back to lean against the headboard. 'Oh, I don't know. Because this isn't exactly a normal wedding, is it?'

That's what he'd been saying. Not that anyone—or at least not Thea—was listening. 'I'm given to understand that this is something they both want,' he said, as neutrally as he could.

Helena gave him a lopsided smile. 'She's been giving you the same line, huh? I thought maybe she'd admit the truth to *you*, at least.'

'The truth?' Zeke asked, when really what he wanted to say was, *Why me, 'at least'?*

'I know she thinks this is what she should do,' Helena said slowly. 'That it's the right thing for the company and our families. She wouldn't want to let anyone down—least of all Isabella or Dad.'

'But…?'

Tipping her head back against the headboard, Helena was silent for a long moment. Then she said, 'But…I think she's hoping this wedding will give her something it can't. And I don't think it's the right thing for her, even if she won't admit it.'

A warm burst of vindication bloomed in Zeke's chest. It wasn't just him. Her own sister, the one she'd stayed for eight years ago, could see the mistake Thea was making. But his triumph was short-lived. There was still nothing he could do to change her decision.

Zeke sank down onto the edge of the bed. 'If you want to ask me to talk to her about it…you're about two hours too late. And, as you can see, it didn't go particularly well.' He waved a hand up and down to indicate the state of him after his long, hot, cross walk home.

Helena winced. 'What did she do? Leave you on the side of the road somewhere?'

'Pretty much.'

'Dammit. I really thought…'

'What?' Suddenly, and maybe for the first time ever, he really wanted to know what Helena thought. Just in case there was a sliver of a chance of it making a difference to how tomorrow went.

Helena gave a little one-shouldered shrug. 'I don't know. I guess I thought that maybe she'd talk to you. Open up. There was always something between you two, wasn't there? I mean, she never talked about it, but it was kind of obvious. So I thought…well, I hoped… But she's so scared of giving Dad and Isabella something else to use against her, to push her out…'

'That's what I told her,' Zeke said, but then something in Helena's words registered. 'What do you mean, push her out? And what was the first thing they used against her?'

She stared at him as if it wasn't possible he didn't already know. But then she blinked. 'Of course,' she murmured. 'It was the night you left. I told her... I told her right before her eighteenth birthday party—talk about insensitive. But I guess she never told you...'

Zeke was losing patience now. He felt as if there was a bell clanging in his head, telling him to pay attention, that this was important, but Helena kept prattling on and he *needed to know*.

'What, Helena? What did you tell her?' And, for the love of God, could this finally be the explanation he'd waited eight years for, only to have Thea deny him?

Helena gave him a long look. 'I'll tell you,' she said, her tongue darting out to moisten her lips. 'But it's kind of a long story. A long, painful story. So you go and have that shower, and I'll go and fetch some wine to make it slightly more bearable. I'll meet you back here in a little bit, yeah?'

Zeke wanted to argue—wanted to demand that she just *tell* him, already—but Helena had already slipped off the bed towards the door, and it looked as if once again he wasn't being given an option by a Morrison woman.

'Fine,' he said with a sigh, and headed for the shower.

At least he wouldn't stink of sweat and sun and roads when he finally got his closure.

She had her wedding rehearsal dinner in two hours. She should be soaking in the bath with a glass of something bubbly, mentally preparing herself for the next thirty-six hours or so. She needed to touch up a chip in her manicure, straighten her hair, check that her dress for the evening had been pressed. There were wedding presents to open, lists of thank-you notes to make, a fiancé to check in with, since she hadn't seen him all day... And at some point she should probably check with Housekeeping that

Zeke had made it home alive—if only so she could slap him again later, or something.

But Thea wasn't doing any of those things. Instead she sat in Ezekiel Ashton's office, waiting for him to get off the phone with London. Just as she had been for the last forty minutes.

'Well, that's one way of looking at it, I suppose,' Ezekiel said into the receiver, and Thea barely contained her frustrated sigh.

Dragging a folder out of her bag she flipped through the contents, wishing she could pretend even to herself that they were in any way urgent or important. At least then she wouldn't feel as if she was wasting her time so utterly.

'The thing is, Quentin...'

Thea closed the folder. He could have asked her to come back later. He could have cut short his call. He could have looked in some way apologetic. But all Ezekiel had done was wave her into the visitor's chair and cover the receiver long enough to tell her he'd be with her shortly. Which had been a blatant lie.

She'd leave, just to prove a point, except he was almost her father-in-law and he already wasn't going to like the news she was bringing.

She sighed again, not bothering to hide it this time, and realised she was tapping her pen against the side of the folder. Glancing up at the desk, she saw Ezekiel raising his eyebrows at her.

Oops. Busted.

'I think I'm going to have to get back to you on that, Quentin,' he said, in his usual calm, smooth voice. The one that let everyone else know that as far as he was concerned he was the only person in the room that mattered. Zeke had always called it his father's 'Zeus the All-Powerful' voice. 'It seems that something urgent has come up at this end.'

Like the existence of his PR Director and soon-to-be daughter-in-law. Or perhaps the possibility of buying This Minute. Thea didn't kid herself about which of those was more important to the man across the desk.

'So, Thea.' Ezekiel hung up the phone. It was a proper old-fashioned one, with a handset attached by a cord and everything. 'Dare I hope that you're here with good news about my youngest son?'

Thea winced. 'Not…exactly.'

'Ah.' Leaning back in his seat, the old man steepled his fingers over his chest. 'So Zeke is still refusing to consider selling This Minute to Morrison Ashton?'

'I'm afraid so,' Thea said. 'He…he seems quite set on his decision, I'm afraid. And he says he's ready to move on from This Minute, so even offering him positions within the company didn't seem to help. He's looking for a new challenge.'

Ezekiel shook his head. 'That boy is always looking for an impossible challenge.'

He was wrong, Thea thought. Apart from anything else, Zeke was certainly no longer a boy. He'd grown up, and even if he'd always be twenty-one and reckless in the eyes of his family, *she* could see it. Had felt it in the way he'd kissed her, held her. Had known it when he'd told her the real reasons she hadn't left with him. He saw the truth even if she didn't want to face it. She *had* been scared. Even if in the end the choice had been taken away from her, and she'd had to stay for Helena, she knew deep down she'd never really thought she'd go. Hadn't been able to imagine a future in which she climbed out of that window and followed him.

Which was strange, because it was growing easier by the hour for her to imagine running out on this wedding and chasing after him. Not that she would, of course.

And not that he'd asked.

He'd wanted her to admit her mistake, had wanted to prove a point. But, kiss aside, there'd been no real thought or mention of wanting *her*.

Maybe Ezekiel was right. Maybe she was just his latest impossible challenge.

'Well, I can't say I'm not disappointed,' Ezekiel said, straightening in his chair. 'Still, I'm glad that you tried to convince him. That tells me a lot.'

Thea blinked at him. 'Tells you what, exactly?'

'It speaks to your commitment to the company—and to Flynn, of course. And it tells me that both you and Zeke have moved past your...youthful indiscretion.'

Heat flared in Thea's cheeks at his words. *Youthful indiscretion*. As if her history with Zeke was something to be swept under the carpet and forgotten about.

But wasn't that what she was doing by not telling Flynn about it?

Thea shook her head. 'I don't think that the childhood friendship Zeke and I shared would influence either of us in the matter of a business decision,' she said, as calmly and flatly as she could manage.

'Thea,' Ezekiel said, his tone mildly chastising. 'My son was in love with you once. He would have done anything for you. That he's said no to you on this matter tells me that he has moved on, that he no longer feels that way about you. And the fact that you asked him in the first place, knowing his...*feelings* for the family business—well, as I say, it's good to know where your loyalties lie.'

Nausea crept up Thea's throat as she listened to the old man talk. She knew he was right. She chosen work and business over a man she'd once thought hung the moon. Over someone who, whatever she might say to his face, still *mattered* to her. All because the old man across the desk had asked her to.

Worst of all was the sudden and certain knowledge that he'd known exactly what he was doing. This was the only reason Ezekiel had asked her to talk to Zeke about This Minute in the first place. It had been a test. Just like suggesting that she marry Flynn. Just like Zeke asking her for one true reason why she'd stayed. Just like her father, eight years ago, when she'd broken the news to him about Helena. Just like her first two engagements.

It was all a test—a way to find out if she was worthy of being a Morrison or an Ashton. Pushing her and prodding her to see how she'd react, how she'd cope, what decision she'd make, how she'd mess up this time. Her whole life was nothing more than a series of tests.

And the worst thing was she knew she was only ever one wrong answer away from failing. Just as she'd failed Helena.

Slowly, her head still spinning with angry thoughts, Thea got to her feet. 'I'm glad that you're satisfied, sir,' she said. 'Now, if you'll excuse me, I need to go and prepare for the rehearsal dinner.'

'Of course…of course.' Ezekiel waved a hand towards the door. 'After all, your most important role in this company is still to come tomorrow, isn't it?'

Thea barely managed a stiff nod before walking too fast out of the office, racing up the stairs, and throwing up in her bathroom.

When Zeke stepped out of the bathroom, a towel tightly tied around his waist, Helena was already sitting on his bed, halfway through a large glass of wine.

'Hang on.' Grabbing his suit hanger from the front of the wardrobe, he stepped back into the steam-filled bathroom and dressed quickly. At least he'd be ready for the rehearsal dinner early, and he'd feel better having whatever conversation this was fully dressed.

Helena handed him a glass of wine and he sat on the desk chair across the room, watching her, waiting for her to start.

She bit her lip, took another sip of wine, then said, 'Okay, so this isn't a story many people know.'

'Okay…'

'But I think it's important that you know it. It… Well, it might explain a bit about how Thea became…Thea.'

Anything that did that—that could explain how the free and loving girl he'd known had become the woman who'd left him at the side of the road today—had to be some story. 'So tell it.'

Helena's whole upper body rose and fell as she sucked in a breath. 'Right. So, it was a month or so before Thea's birthday. Before you left. I was sixteen. And stupid. That part's quite important.' She dipped her head, gazing down at her hands. 'Thea was babysitting for me one night. Dad was off at some business dinner, I guess. And even though I'd told him a million times that sixteen-year-olds don't need babysitters he was very clear. Thea was in charge. What she said went, and she was responsible for anything that happened while he was out.'

'Sounds like your dad,' Zeke murmured, wondering where this was going. 'I guess something happened that night?'

'I…I wanted to go out. I asked Thea, and she said no, so I nagged and whined until she gave in. I had a date with this guy a couple of years ahead of me in school. I knew Thea didn't like him, so I kinda left that part out when I told her I was going.'

Zeke had a very bad feeling about this story all of a sudden. 'What happened?' he asked, the words coming out raw and hoarse.

'He took me to his friend's house. There was beer, and

some other stuff. And the next thing I knew…' Helena
scrubbed a hand across her eyes. 'Anyway… They told me
it was my own fault—that I'd said yes and I just couldn't
remember. I was so ashamed that I didn't tell anyone. Not
even Thea. Not until six weeks later.'

'The night of her party?' Zeke guessed. She'd been crying, he remembered, when he'd climbed in her window to
tell her he was going and ask if she'd decided to come or
not. He'd thought it had been because she'd decided to stay.

'Yeah. I wouldn't have, but…I was pregnant.'

The air rushed out of Zeke's lungs. 'Oh, Helena…'

'I know. So I told Thea, and she told Dad for me, and then
I got sent away for the summer until the baby was born.'

Helena's voice broke at last. Zeke thought most people
would have given in to tears long before. Happy-go-lucky
Helena hid a core of steel.

'She was adopted, and I never saw her again.'

Zeke crossed the room in a second, wrapping an arm
around her as she cried. 'I should have been here.' Helena
had been a little sister to him in a way Thea never had
been. They'd been more. But Helena… Helena had been
important to him too, and he hadn't even said goodbye.
Hadn't dreamt of what she might be going through.

Helena gave a watery chuckle. 'What could you have
done? Besides, I had Thea.'

This was what she'd meant. Why she'd had to stay.
He'd always thought—believed deep down—that her
words about Helena and her family were excuses. But they
weren't. Helena really *had* needed her. Of course she'd
stayed. But why hadn't she told him?

'But there's a reason I've told you this,' Helena said,
snapping him back to the present. 'You have to understand, Zeke. Things changed after that night, and you
weren't there to see it. You remember how it was—how

Dad pushed her into taking over Mum's role after she died? He expected her to be able to do everything. School, the house, playing hostess for his clients, looking after me…'

'I remember,' Zeke said, bitterness leaking into his voice. She'd hated it so much. 'It was wrong. Hell, she was—what? Fourteen? Nobody should have that kind of responsibility at that age.'

'Well, she thought it *was* her responsibility. And so did he. So when all this happened…' Helena swallowed so hard Zeke could see it. 'He blamed her. Said that if she'd paid more attention it never would have happened. He took it all away from her. And that was when Isabella stepped in.'

'My mum?'

Helena nodded. 'She took over. She ran our house as well as yours. She became part of the family more than ever. She looked after me, played hostess for Dad…'

'She pushed Thea out,' Zeke finished for her. How had he not noticed that? Not noticed how little a place Thea seemed to have, even in her own wedding.

'Yeah. I wasn't here to start with, so I don't really know the whole of it. But ever since it's been like Thea's been trying to find her way back in. Find a place where she belongs.'

'And you think that's why she's marrying Flynn?'

Helena tilted her head to the side. 'I don't know. That's what I… I worry, that's all.'

And she was right to. Of *course* that was what Thea was doing. She'd practically admitted as much to him, even if he hadn't understood her reasoning.

'And the thing is, Zeke,' Helena went on, 'despite everything Thea blames herself for what happened to me and what happened next. She always has. Even though it isn't her fault—of course it isn't. But she was responsible for me that night. That's what Dad told her. And she thinks that if she hadn't let me go out that night everything would have been different.'

'*Her* fault?' Zeke echoed, baffled. 'How can she possibly…?'

'She calls it the biggest mistake she ever made.'

Suddenly Zeke was glad that Helena didn't know what Thea had given up to stay with her. He couldn't blame either of them any more. But could he make Thea see that one mistake didn't mean she had to keep making the same safe decisions her whole life?

'Thank you for telling me this, Helena.'

Helena gave a little shrug. 'Did it help?'

'Yeah. I think so.'

Pulling away, Helena watched his face as she asked, 'So, do you think you can talk Thea out of this wedding?'

'I thought I was supposed to be making sure the groom showed up on time?'

'If she decides to go through with it, yeah. But I want to be very sure that she's doing this for the right reasons. Not just because she's scared of being pushed out again for not doing what the family wants.'

Zeke grinned. 'Looks like we're on the same side, then.'

'Good.' Standing up, Helena smoothed down her dress and wiped her eyes. 'About time I had some help around here. Now, come on, best man. We've got a rehearsal dinner to get to.'

'And a wedding to get called off,' Zeke agreed, following her to the door.

He had his closure now, but he had far more, too. He had the truth. The whole story. And that was what would make all the difference when he confronted Thea this time.

CHAPTER EIGHT

THEA SCANNED THE dining room through the crack of the door, then glanced down at her deep red sheath dress, wondering why she felt as if she was walking into a business dinner. Of all the people she'd recognised in the room, waiting for them to walk in, only three had been family. Everyone else was someone she'd met across a conference table. This time tomorrow she'd be married, and her whole new life would start. But she was very afraid, all of a sudden, that her new life might be a little too much like her old one.

'Ready?' Flynn asked, offering her his arm.

He looked handsome in his suit, Thea thought. All clean-shaven and broad shoulders. Safe. Reliable. Predictable. Exactly what she'd decided she wanted in life.

'Or do you want to sneak into Dad's study for a shot of the good brandy before we face the gathered hordes?'

Thea smiled. 'Tempting, but probably not advisable. Besides, your Dad's almost certainly still working in there.'

'There is that.' Flynn sighed. 'I had hoped he'd see this as more of a family celebration than a networking opportunity.'

Nice to know she wasn't the only one who had noticed that. 'I guess he doesn't see any reason why it can't be both. I mean, he knows our reasons for getting married. He helped put together the contract, for heaven's sake.'

'Yeah, I know,' Flynn said, sounding wistful. 'It's business. I just… It would be nice if we could pretend, just for a couple of days, that there's something that matters more to us.'

Thea stared at him. She was going to marry this man tomorrow, and she'd never once heard him speak so honestly about their life or their relationship.

'Flynn? Are you…?' *Are you what? Getting cold feet? Unhappy with me? Not the time for that conversation, Thea.* 'Did you want to wait? To get married, I mean? To someone you're actually in love with?'

Because it was one thing to marry a man you didn't love because that was the deal. Another to do it when he was secretly holding out for more. She thought back to their conversation on the porch, about kids and the future. How happy he'd been at the idea of a family.

But Flynn shook his head, giving her a self-deprecating smile. 'Don't listen to me,' he said. 'We're doing the right thing here. For us and for the business. And, yeah, the fairytale would be nice, I guess. But it's not all there is. And who knows? Maybe you and I will fall in love one day.'

But they wouldn't, Thea knew, with the kind of sudden, shocking certainty that couldn't be shifted. As much as she liked, respected and was fond of Flynn, and as much as she enjoyed his company, she wasn't ever going to be in love with him. She knew how that felt, and it wasn't anything like this.

Thea tried to smile back, but it felt forced. 'Are you ready to go in?' she asked, wishing she'd just said yes when he'd asked her the same question. The knowledge she'd gained in the last two minutes seemed too much for her body—as if she could barely keep it inside on top of every other thought she'd had and fact she'd learned since Zeke came home.

'As I'll ever be,' Flynn said, flashing her a smile. 'Let's go.'

He pushed the door open and the volume level of conversation in the room dipped, then dropped, then stalled. Everyone stood, beaming at them, waiting for them to walk in and take their seats as if they were some kind of royalty. And all Thea could see was Zeke and Helena, standing together near the head of the huge table, leaning into each other. Helena murmured something Thea couldn't hear, and Zeke's lips quirked up in a mocking grin. Talking about her? Thea didn't care. All she knew was that she wanted to be over there, chatting with them, and not welcoming the fifty-odd other people who had somehow got themselves invited to her rehearsal dinner.

She let Flynn take the lead. His easy way with people meant that all she had to do was smile and nod, shake the occasional hand. She let him lead her to their seats, smiled sweetly at everyone around them as she sat down.

Her father nodded to Flynn, and Isabella said, 'Oh, Thea, you look so beautiful tonight. And those pearls are a perfect match! I'm so glad.'

Thea's hand unconsciously went to the necklace Isabella had given her. The perfectly round pearls were hard and cold under her fingers. You were supposed to wear pearls often, weren't you? To keep them warm and stop them cracking or drying, perhaps?

'Aren't pearls supposed to be bad luck?' Helena asked, topping up her glass of wine from the bottle on the table.

'Oh, I don't think so,' Isabella said, laughing lightly. 'And, besides, who believes those old superstitions, anyway?'

'"Pearls mean tears",' Helena quoted, her voice firm and certain. 'And you're the one who insisted on Thea having all the old, new, borrowed and blue stuff.'

'I like pearls,' Thea said, glancing in surprise at her sister. It wasn't like Helena to antagonise Isabella. For a moment it was almost as if the old teenage Helena was sitting beside her. 'I don't think they mean anything.'

There was silence for a moment, before the doors opened and a fleet of waiters entered, ready to serve the starters. They waited until every bowl was ready and in position, then lowered them all to the table at the same time, before disappearing again as silently as they'd come.

'Saved by the soup,' Zeke murmured from two seats down as he reached for the butter.

Thea studied him as he buttered his roll, and kept watching as Helena topped up his wine, too. He must have walked home, she supposed. His forehead was ever so slightly pink from the sun. But he didn't seem angry, or tense as he had earlier. He seemed calm, relaxed. Even happy.

Maybe he'd got the closure he needed. Maybe he was thinking ahead to leaving the day after tomorrow. To selling This Minute to Glasshouse and moving on to his new life. Thea could see how that might be appealing. Not that she had that option. She didn't want out of this family— she wanted in.

Besides, Zeke had been gone eight years already and still not really moved on. What reason was there to believe he'd be able to put it all behind him for real this time?

Isabella and Flynn kept up the small talk across the table through all three courses. Thea drank her wine too quickly and tried to pretend her head wasn't spinning. And then, as the waiters came round to pour the coffee, her father stood up and clinked his fork against his glass.

'Oh, no,' Thea whispered. 'What's he doing?'

Flynn patted her hand reassuringly, somehow managing to make her even more nervous.

'I know tonight isn't the night for big speeches,' Thomas

Morrison said. 'And, trust me, I'll have the traditional light, adoring and entertaining father of the bride speech for you all tomorrow. But I wanted to say a few words tonight for those of you who've been so close to our family all these years. Who've seen us through our dark times as well as our triumphs.'

'Which explains why almost everyone here is a business associate,' Helena muttered, leaning across towards Thea. 'We've barely seen any family since Mum died.'

'Shh…' Isabella said, without moving her lips or letting her attentive smile slip.

'You all know that getting here, to this happy event, hasn't always been a smooth path. And let me say candidly that I am both delighted and relieved that Thea has finally made a decision in her personal life that's as good as the ones she makes at work!'

The laughter that followed buzzed in Thea's ears, but she barely heard it. Her body felt frozen, stiff and cold and brittle. And she knew, suddenly, that even marrying Flynn wouldn't be enough. To her father she'd still always be a liability. A mistake just waiting to happen.

'And I want to say thank you to the person who has made all this possible,' Thomas went on, waving his arm expansively to include the food, the villa, and presumably, the wedding itself.

Thea held her breath, bracing herself for the blow she instinctively knew was coming next.

'My dear, dear friend, Isabella Ashton.'

More applause—the reverent sort this time. People were nodding their heads along with her father's words, and Isabella was blushing prettily, her smile polite but pleased.

Thea thought she might actually be sick.

'So, let us all raise our glasses to the mother of the

groom and the woman who has been as a mother to the bride for the last twelve years.'

Chairs were scraped back as people stood, and the sound grated in her ears. Wasn't it enough that she'd given them all what they wanted? She was marrying the families together, securing their future, their lineage, and the future of their business. And even today, the night before her wedding, she wasn't worthy of her father's approval, or love.

Thea staggered to her feet, clutching the edge of the table, as the guests lifted their glasses and chanted, 'Isabella!' Even Flynn, next to her, had his wine in the air and was smiling at his mother, utterly unaware of how his fiancée's heart had just been slashed with glass.

It was almost as if she wasn't there at all.

Zeke watched Thea's face grow paler as Thomas wound up his ridiculous speech. Who said something like that about his own daughter the day before her wedding? Especially when that daughter was Thea. He *had* to know how sensitive she was about her perceived mistakes, surely? And then to toast Isabella instead… That had been just cruel and callous.

Maybe he truly didn't care. Not if he could get in a good joke, amuse his business associates… Zeke ground his teeth as he waited for his coffee to cool. He'd never been Thomas Morrison's biggest fan, but right then he loathed the man more than he'd ever thought possible.

Thomas sat down to a round of applause and more laughter, and Zeke saw Thea visibly flinch. Flynn, however, was shaking his father-in-law-to-be's hand and smiling as if nothing had happened. As if he couldn't see how miserable Thea was. He was going to marry her tomorrow and he couldn't even see when her heart was breaking.

Zeke gulped down his rage at his brother along with

his coffee. All that mattered was getting Thea the hell out of there.

Helena appeared over his left shoulder suddenly, pushing something cold and bottle-shaped into his hand. 'Go on,' she said, nodding towards Thea. 'I'll cover for you both here.'

'Thanks,' Zeke murmured, keeping the bottle of champagne below table level as he stood. Catching Thea's eye, he raised his eyebrows and headed for the door, not waiting to see if she followed. Helena would make sure that she did.

Outside on the terrace the air held just a little bite—a contrast to the blazing sun he'd walked back in earlier. Dropping onto the swing seat, Zeke held up the bottle and read the label. The good stuff, of course. Old Thomas wouldn't serve anything less while he was insulting his daughter in front of everyone she'd ever met. Shame Helena hadn't thought to provide glasses… Although, actually, swigging expensive champagne from the bottle with Thea brought back its own collection of memories.

The door to the hallway opened and Thea appeared, her face too pale against her dark hair and blood-red dress. Her skin seemed almost translucent in the moonlight, and suddenly Zeke wanted to touch it so badly he ached.

'Have a seat,' he said, waving the bottle over the empty cushion beside him. 'I think your sister thought you might need this.'

'She was right.' Thea dropped onto the seat next to him, sending the whole frame swinging back and forth. 'Although why she decided I also needed you is beyond me.'

'Ouch.' Unwrapping the wire holding it in place, Zeke eased the cork out of the neck of the bottle. He didn't want the pop, the fizz, the explosion. Just the quiet opening and sharing of champagne with Thea. To show her that *he* knew tonight was about her, even if no one else seemed to.

'Oh, you know what I mean,' Thea said, reaching over to take the bottle from him. 'We're not having the best day, apart from anything else.'

'I don't know what you're complaining about,' Zeke said. 'You weren't the one left in the middle of nowhere in the blazing heat.'

Thea winced, and handed him the bottle back. 'Sorry about that.'

'No, you're not.' Zeke lifted the bottle to his mouth and took a long, sweet drink. The bubbles popped against his throat and he started to relax for the first time that day.

'Well, maybe just a little bit. You deserved it, though.'

'For telling the truth?'

'For kissing me.'

'Ah. That.'

'Yeah, *that*.'

Zeke passed the bottle back and they sat in silence for a long moment, the only sound the occasional wave of laughter from inside or the squeaking of the hinges on the swing.

'I'm not actually all that sorry about that, either,' Zeke said finally.

Thea sighed. 'Yeah. Me neither. Maybe we needed it. You know—for closure, or whatever you were going on about.'

'Actually, your sister helped me with that more than you did.'

Thea swung round to stare at him, eyes wide. 'Tell me you have *not* been kissing my sister this afternoon.'

'Or what?'

'Or I'll drink the rest of this champagne myself.' She took a long swig to prove her point.

Zeke laughed. 'Okay, fine. I have not been kissing Helena. This afternoon or any other.'

'Good.'

'Not that it would be any of your business if I had.'

'She's my sister,' Thea said, handing back the champagne at last. 'She'll always be my business.'

'But not your responsibility,' Zeke said. 'She's an adult now, Thea. She can take care of herself.'

'Perhaps.' Thea studied him carefully. 'When you said that Helena had helped you find closure…what did you mean?'

Zeke tipped his head back against the swing cushion. 'She told me some of what happened. Things I didn't know. About what really happened the night of your eighteenth birthday. Why you didn't come with me. And about what happened next.'

He heard the breath leave Thea's lungs in a rush. 'She told you? About the…?'

'About what happened to her. And about the baby.' He rolled his head to the left to watch her as he added, 'And how it really wasn't your fault.'

Thea looked away. 'That's up for debate.'

'No. It isn't.' No response. 'Thea. Look at me.'

She didn't. 'Why?'

'Because I'm about to say something that matters and I want to be sure that you're listening to me.'

Slowly she lifted her head and her gaze met his. Zeke felt it like a jolt to the heart—the connection he'd thought they'd lost was suddenly *right there*. Part of him again after all these years.

'Whatever mistakes you think you've made in your life, Thea, that wasn't one of them. You cannot make yourself responsible for what those boys did to her.'

'My father did,' Thea whispered. 'I was in charge. I was responsible. And I let her go out.'

'No.' He had to make her understand. Wrapping his arm around her shoulder, he pulled her closer, still keeping them face to face, until she was pressed up against his chest. 'Listen to me, Thea. It wasn't your fault. And you can't live your whole life as if it was.'

Thea stared up into his eyes for a long moment. They were filled with such sincerity, such certainty. Why could she never feel that way about her life? That unshakeable conviction that whatever choice she made was the right one. That fearlessness in the face of mistakes.

Of course in Zeke it also led to occasional unbearable smugness, so maybe she was better off without.

Swallowing, Thea pulled away, and Zeke let her go. 'Is that what you think I'm doing?'

'I know it,' Zeke said, unbearable smugness firmly in place.

'You're wrong, you know,' she said conversationally, looking down at her hands.

Part of her still couldn't believe that Helena had really told him everything. She'd barely discussed it with Thea ever since it happened. As far as she knew Helena had never willingly told anyone else about it—something their father and Isabella had been in full support of. After all, why make a scandal when you can hide one? And coming so soon after Zeke running away... Well, no one wanted to make headlines again. Thea assumed that Ezekiel Senior knew, but maybe not. Isabella had taken care of everything. Maybe she'd never seen the need to brief him on the shocking events.

'Am I? As far as I can see you stayed eight years ago for Helena, and because you were scared. And now—'

'I made the right decision eight years ago,' Thea interrupted. Because if he had to know everything at least she could admit that much. 'And I don't regret it for a moment.'

'Fair enough,' Zeke said, more amicably than she'd expected. 'And we'll never know how things might have worked out if Helena hadn't gone out that night, or if she'd waited one more day to tell you about it. But the point is Helena's all grown up now. She doesn't need you to protect her any more. And yet you're still staying.'

She shook her head. 'My whole life is here. My place is here.'

'Is it?' He gripped her arm, tightly enough that she had to pay attention. 'They pushed you out, Thea.'

The coldness that settled over her was familiar. The same chill she'd felt that whole summer after Zeke had left. 'You don't…you don't know what it was like.'

'Helena told me. She told me everything.'

But that wasn't enough. A description, a few words—it couldn't explain how it felt to have your whole existence peeled away from you. She wasn't sure if even she could explain it to him. But she knew she had to try…had to make him understand somehow.

'It was as if I'd stopped even existing,' she whispered in the end. 'I couldn't be what Dad needed, so there was no place for me any more. I wasn't good enough for him.'

Zeke's grip loosened, but just enough to pull her against his body. She could feel his heart, thumping away in his chest, and the memory of how his arms had always felt like home cut deeper now.

'Then why are you trying so hard to get back in? Surely you can see you're better off without him. Without all of them.'

'You think I should run away, like you?' She pulled back enough to give him a half-smile. 'This is my place. Besides, where else would I go, Zeke?'

'Anywhere! Anywhere you can be yourself. Live your own life. Not make decisions about your personal happiness based on what is best for the family business, or what

our fathers want you to do. Anywhere in the world, Thea.'
He paused, just for a moment, then added, 'You could even
come with me, if you wanted.'

Thea's heart stopped dead in her chest. She couldn't
breathe. She couldn't think. Couldn't process what he was
saying…

'I'm marrying Flynn tomorrow.' The words came out
without her permission, and she watched Zeke's eyes turn
hard as she spoke.

'Why?' he asked. 'Seriously, Thea. Tell me why. I don't
understand.'

'I love him.'

'No, you don't.'

'I might!'

Zeke laughed, but there was no humour in the sound.
'Thea, I'm sure you do love him—in a way. But don't try
and tell me you're in love with him, or vice versa. He didn't
even notice how distressed you were tonight.'

'*You* did.' She could hear the anger in his voice as he
talked about Flynn. Was that for her?

He gave a slight nod. 'Me and Helena. We're your team.'

'And you're leaving me tomorrow.' How could he offer
her a place in the world when he didn't even know where
he'd be tomorrow? Didn't he understand? She needed more
than that. Somewhere she could never be pushed out or
left behind. Somewhere she was enough.

'Yeah.'

'Great teamwork, there.'

Thea stared out into the darkness of the Tuscan hills
beyond. She hadn't answered Zeke's question—something
she knew he was bound to call her on before too long. But
what could she say? Whatever it was, he wouldn't agree or
approve. Should that matter? She didn't want Zeke to leave
hating her. But why not? She would never see him again

once she was married. He'd made that perfectly clear. If all she was protecting was the memory of something already eight years dead, what was the point?

'So?' Zeke asked eventually. 'The truth this time. Why are you so set on marrying Flynn tomorrow?'

'Maybe I think it'll make me happy,' Thea said.

Zeke shifted, turning his body in towards hers, one knee bent to let his leg rest on the seat. 'Do you? Think you'll be happy?'

She considered lying, but there didn't seem much point. Zeke never believed her anyway. 'I think I'll be safe. Secure. I'll have someone to help me make the right decisions. I think I'll have the agreement of all my friends and family that I'm not making a mistake.'

'Not all of them,' Zeke muttered.

'I think I'll have a place here again. A place I've earned…a place I belong. One that's mine by blood and marriage and can never be taken away from me. I'll be content,' Thea finished, ignoring him.

'Content? And is that enough for you?'

Thea shrugged. 'What else is there?' she asked, even though she knew the answer.

'Love. Passion. Happiness. Pleasure.'

'Yeah, you see, that's where I start to make mistakes. I know business. I know sensible, well thought out business plans. I know agreements, contracts, promised deliverables. Pleasure is an unknown quantity.'

Zeke shifted again and he was closer now, his breath warm against her cheek. Thea's skin tingled at the contact.

'You used to know about pleasure,' he said, his voice low.

'That was a long time ago,' Thea replied, the words coming out huskily.

'I remember, though. You used to crave pleasure. And

the freedom to seek it. To do what felt right and good, not what someone said you were supposed to do.'

His words were hypnotising. Thea could feel her body swaying into his as he spoke, but she couldn't do anything to stop the motion. The swing beneath them rocked forwards and back, and with every movement she seemed to fall closer and closer into Zeke. As if gravity was drawing her in. As if nothing she could say or do or think could stop it.

'Don't you miss it?' he whispered, his mouth so close to hers she could feel the words on her own lips.

'Yes,' she murmured, and he kissed her.

CHAPTER NINE

SHE TASTED JUST as Zeke remembered—as if it had been mere moments since his mouth had last touched hers. This wasn't the angry kiss of earlier that day, a kiss that had been more punishment than pleasure. This…this was something more.

Pleasure and pain mingled together. The years fell away and he was twenty-one again, kissing her goodbye even as he hoped against hope that she might leave with him.

Maybe this time it would end differently. Maybe this time he could persuade her. After all, he'd learnt a lot in eight years.

Slipping a hand around her back, he held her close, revelling in the feel of her body against his, back where she belonged. How had he let himself believe, even for a moment, that he could watch her marry someone else and then walk away?

Flynn… The thought of his brother stalled him for a moment, until he remembered him shaking Thomas's hand after that godforsaken speech. He didn't know Thea—didn't know what she needed, let alone what she wanted. He didn't love her any more than Thea loved him. Zeke knew that for sure.

Maybe he'd even understand. And even if he didn't… Zeke was close to the edge of not caring. Flynn didn't deserve her—he'd proved that tonight. And Zeke needed this. Needed her more than ever before.

Zeke ran his palms up Thea's back, deepening the kiss, and felt his heartbeat quicken at the little noises she made. Half moans, half squeaks, they let him know exactly how much more she wanted. And how much he planned to give her...

'Zeke,' Thea murmured, pulling back just a little. 'What about—?'

'Shh...' Zeke trailed his fingers over her neck, feeling her shiver against him. 'Just pleasure, remember?'

Thea gave a little nod, as if she couldn't help but agree, and Zeke took that as permission to kiss her again. First her lips, deep and wanting. Then her jaw, her neck, her collarbone, down into the deep V of her dress and the lacy bra beyond.

'Oh, Zeke.' Thea shuddered again as his hand crept up her thigh, under her skirt, and he smiled against her skin. He remembered this, too. Remembered how natural it felt to have her in his arms, how she responded to his every touch, every kiss. How she arched up against him, her body begging for more. How could she pretend that she wanted anything other than this, than *him*, when her whole body told him otherwise?

He wanted to get her upstairs. Wanted her in his bed, her naked skin against his. But he knew that he had only this moment to convince her, to change her mind, and he couldn't risk the pause being enough to break her out of pleasure's spell. No, he knew Thea. With cold air between them, and a whole staircase to climb to find a bed, she'd start doubting herself. He didn't have time for her to have second thoughts. She was supposed to get married tomorrow, and he couldn't let that happen.

So it would have to be here. He'd seduce her right here

on the terrace. Then she'd see she couldn't marry Flynn. And Flynn would understand that. Wouldn't he?

Tightening his hold on her, Zeke pulled Thea up from the swing across onto his lap, so her knees fell neatly either side of his thighs, all without breaking their kiss. Her body seemed to know exactly what he had planned, moving with his without hesitation. As if it had done it before… Which, of course, it had. Zeke smiled at the memory.

'This remind you of anything?' he murmured, kissing his way back up her throat.

Thea murmured in agreement. 'Your twenty-first birthday party.'

'Out on the balcony…'

'With the party going on right underneath us.'

'That was all *you*, you know.'

Thea pressed against him and he couldn't help but gasp.

'I seem to remember you being there, too.'

'Yeah, but you're the one who dragged me up there.' He could see it now, in his memories. The bright blue dress she'd worn, the naughty look in her eye, the way she'd bitten her lip as she raised her eyebrows and waited for him to follow her into the house…

'I didn't hear you complaining,' Thea said, her hands pushing his shirt up to get to his skin.

Zeke sucked in a breath at the feel of her fingers on his chest. 'I really wasn't.'

She stilled for a moment, and Zeke's hands tightened instinctively on her thighs, keeping her close. 'What is it?' he asked.

'I just… I've never felt that again. What I felt that night, with you…'

The words were a whisper, an ashamed admission, but Zeke's eyelids fluttered closed in relief at the sound of them. 'Me neither. It's never been like it was with you. Not with anyone.' Never felt so much like coming home.

She kissed him then, her hands on his face, deep and loving, and he knew for the first time in eight years that things were going to be okay again.

'Make love to me, Zeke,' Thea whispered, and Zeke looked up into her eyes and smiled.

'Always.'

Thea blinked in the darkness and wondered how it was possible that she'd forgotten this feeling. The sense that her whole body had relaxed into the place where it belonged. That moment of sheer bliss and an empty mind.

Maybe she hadn't forgotten. Maybe, as great as her memories were, it had never been like this for them before. Because, seriously, surely she'd remember something that good.

She breathed in one last breath of satisfaction…pleasure and *home*.

Then she sat up and faced the real world again.

Her senses and thoughts crashed in immediately—a whole parade of them, ranging from her complete idiocy to her goosebumps. It was cold on the terrace…colder than Thea had thought Tuscany could be in the summer. Of course it would probably be warmer if she was still wearing her dress… Beside her Zeke lay on the swing seat, his shirt unbuttoned to reveal a broad expanse of tanned chest.

Somehow this seemed far more dignified for men.

Reaching for her dress and slipping it over her shoulders, Thea tried to stop her mind spinning with the idea of what she'd just done. She'd cheated on her fiancé. She'd become *that* woman—the one who made a stupid mistake that might cost her everything. The night before her own wedding. At her rehearsal dinner! All because Zeke had started talking about pleasure and making her remember how good things had used to be… And hadn't she just finished telling him that wasn't what she wanted any more?

But she couldn't blame Zeke, however manipulated she felt. She'd wanted it. Asked for it, even. All he'd done was give her what she'd craved. What she'd spent eight years trying to forget.

Thea sighed and Zeke stirred at the sound, snaking an arm around her waist to pull her closer. She sank into him as if, having given in once, all her will power had gone.

This was the hardest part. If it was just great sex with Zeke she was giving up it would be easy. Well, maybe not easy, but certainly doable. But that wasn't all it was.

'You're thinking too loudly,' Zeke murmured against her ear, and she sighed again.

It wasn't the sex. It was the way her body felt in tune with his…the way he could anticipate what she needed before she knew she needed it. The way she felt right in his arms. The way she fitted—*they* fitted together. Not just physically, either.

It just felt so natural with Zeke, in a way she knew it never would with Flynn.

But was that enough?

Zeke might know what she needed, but there was no guarantee that he'd give it to her. As much as she'd loved him when they were younger, she knew him, too. Knew what mattered most to him. And while he might have proclaimed from the rafters that the only thing that mattered to him was her, in the end he'd still left her behind when she wouldn't fit in with his plans. Hadn't even listened when she'd tried to explain why she couldn't go.

Sometimes she wondered if it really had been love. It had felt like it, then. But they'd been kids. What had they known?

And even now Zeke didn't understand about doing the careful thing, the *right* thing. About not taking the risk of making things worse. For him, the risk was half the fun—always had been. He'd liked the thought of getting caught at his twenty-first birthday party. And she knew, from watching This Minute grow and develop through the business pages, that half the fun for Zeke was knowing that he was only ever one step, one chance, one risk away from it all coming down. He'd been lucky—brilliant too, of course—but it could have gone either way.

And Thea didn't have room for any more mistakes in her life. Couldn't risk being left with nothing, no place, again.

'Seriously,' Zeke said, shifting to sit up properly, his shirt flapping closed over his chest.

That might make it easier for her to think clearly, at least.

'What's going on in that head of yours?'

Thea sat up. 'I have to go. I need to… My guests are inside.'

Zeke's expression hardened. Reaching over, he picked up her bra and held it out to her, dangling from his fingers. 'You might need this.'

Thea snatched it from him. 'What did you think I was going to do next, Zeke? I'm supposed to be getting married tomorrow, and I'm out here with the best man! That's never a good decision.'

He shook his head ruefully. 'I should have known. You think I'm a mistake.'

'I didn't say that, Zeke.' She never would, knowing how much of his childhood he'd spent thinking that. That his parents would have been happier with just Flynn, their planned and chosen child, rather than the biological one who had come along at exactly the wrong moment. 'I just…

I need to tell Flynn.' That much was a given, surely? 'I need to sort all this out.'

Zeke blew out a breath and settled back against the swing. 'Yeah, okay. I guess disappearing in the middle of the night at some party never was your style, was it?'

'No, that was all you.' Thea gave him a sad smile, remembering that night eight years ago and knowing with absolute certainty, for the first time, that she could never have gone with him even if Helena hadn't needed her. She wasn't built for Zeke's kind of life.

She just hoped he realised that, too.

Zeke watched Thea walk back inside, her hair no longer so groomed and her make-up long gone. Would she go and fix herself up first? What was the point, if she was just going to tell Flynn that she couldn't marry him? Sure, Flynn would know exactly what they'd been doing, but was that such a bad thing? It gave a point-of-no-return sort of feel to things.

Settling back against the swing seat, Zeke pushed aside the guilt that flooded him at the thought of his brother. It wasn't a love match; he knew that. And this wasn't like when they were kids. He wasn't taking Thea just so that Flynn couldn't have her. She belonged with him—always had. Surely Flynn would understand that?

He hoped so. With conscious effort Zeke relaxed his muscles, feeling the happy thrumming that buzzed through his blood, the reminder of everything the evening had brought him. Who would have thought, when she'd dumped him on the roadside that afternoon, that the day would end here?

He should have known that appealing to her reasonable side wouldn't work. Thea wasn't like other people.

She needed to see the truth, *feel* it, not just be told it. Why hadn't he remembered that?

It didn't matter now. He'd shown her they belonged together. Even her most conservative, analytical, risk-averse side couldn't deny that now. She wanted a place to belong? He could give her that. He could give her everything she needed if she let him. Finally they'd get the life they'd been denied eight years ago, and he was going to make it so good for her. Make her loosen up a bit, reveal the Thea he knew was hiding in there somewhere.

Once the sale of This Minute went through to Glasshouse they could go anywhere, do anything. Maybe they'd just travel for a bit, see the world, get to know one another again as adults. He'd have to take things slowly, so as not to scare her. He knew Thea: even after the jump forward their relationship had taken this evening she was bound to scuttle a few paces back. But Zeke didn't care how slowly it went, how much he had to gentle her along. He'd have Thea in his arms every night, just as he'd always wanted. This time *he* was her choice. Not Flynn, not Helena, not the business, not her father or his. *Him*. Zeke. And he could live with everything in their past as long as he was her last choice.

Zeke smiled to himself as he listened to the sounds of the dinner finishing up and people starting to leave inside. He'd go back in soon, find Thea when she was ready for him.

Sure, there was a lot to figure out first—starting with calling off the wedding tomorrow. But once that was done there was a whole new future out there for them.

He was sure of it.

The sounds of the rehearsal dinner were fading. How many people must have left already without even seeing her? She should have been there, playing hostess, saying goodbye to people, looking excited about tomorrow. If Isabella would let her, of course. She had to start reclaiming that role if she was going to be Flynn's wife. People needed to see that she belonged there, at the head of table, running things.

Image was everything; she was the PR face of Morrison-Ashton and, however much this should have been a private event, it wasn't. These were clients, associates, investors, and she should have been there, working the room. Putting on a show.

And instead she'd been outside on the terrace, sleeping with the best man in the open air.

A shudder ran through her. What had she been thinking? Anyone could have walked out and seen them, and then everything would have been destroyed.

Of course, she reminded herself, it might still be once she told Flynn.

'Thea?' Helena clattered into the hall on her high heels. 'Are you okay? I kept everyone else off the terrace and they're all starting to leave now. Do you want to say goodbye? If not I can cover for you if you want to just go to bed?'

Thea gave her sister a half-smile. 'You take such good care of me.'

Helena shook her head and stepped forward to wrap her arms around Thea's waist. 'Not nearly as good as you take of me.'

Was that true? Thea wasn't sure. She'd stayed, yes, when Helena had needed her, and she'd done the best she could to help her. But she'd never pressed her sister to talk about what had happened, never pushed her to get counselling or other help. Whereas ever since she'd come back, thinner and paler, with her stomach still slightly rounded and hidden under baggy jumpers, Helena had made look-

ing out for Thea a priority. She'd been there when her engagements had gone bad, she'd helped Isabella look after
the house and Dad while Thea got on with climbing the
corporate ladder, she'd smoothed out every difficult conversation, every awkward dinner party between the Morrisons and the Ashtons.

And tonight she'd protected Thea's privacy while she
made another huge mistake.

'I need to talk to Flynn.'

Helena pulled back, frowning. 'Are you sure? Now?'

'Yes. Before I lose my nerve.'

'What are you going to tell him?' Helena asked.

Thea wondered how much her sister knew about her
and Zeke. What Zeke had told her. What she imagined
had happened out on the terrace.

Thea took a breath. 'Everything.'

Helena studied her for a long moment, then nodded.
'Okay, then. I'll fetch him. You go and wait in the library,
yeah?'

'Okay.'

The library was shaded and dark, the tiny haloes of light
around the table lamps barely enough to illuminate the
chairs beside them, let alone the bookcases. Thea trailed
her fingers across the shelves, waiting for Flynn, trying
not to listen to the sounds of the guests leaving.

Helena's tinkling laugh caught her attention, though.
'She's been up since dawn! She's so excited about tomorrow. I think she's just crashed! I sent her to bed when she
couldn't stop yawning. Can't have the bride looking anything but well rested on her wedding day, can we?'

Murmurs of amused agreement from the departing
guests made Thea wince. How many lies had Helena told
for her tonight?

The library door cracked open, and Thea spun away from the bookshelf.

'Thea?' Flynn asked, his voice as calm and even as it always was. 'Are you in here?'

Stepping into the light, Thea tried to smile. 'I'm here.'

Flynn closed the door carefully behind him with a click, then turned to her. 'Are you okay? Helena said you wanted to talk to me. I'd have come sooner, but our guests...'

Thea winced again. 'Yeah, sorry. I should have been there to talk with them. To say goodbye, at least.'

'Where were you?' Flynn asked. 'Helena's telling everyone you went to bed, but to be honest you don't look that tired. You look... I don't know...'

But Thea did. Her jaw tightened as she imagined what she must look like. Her hair would be rumpled, her dress creased, her make-up faded. She wished the library had a mirror for her to assess the damage. And maybe, a small part of her insisted, to see if she had that same glow, same radiance, that truly great sex with Zeke had always given her.

She kind of hoped not. She couldn't imagine that was something any man would want to see on his fiancée's face if he hadn't put it there. Even someone as affable and not in love with her as Flynn.

'I was on the terrace,' Thea said. 'With Zeke.'

'But Helena said...' Flynn's face hardened. 'Helena lied. What's going on, Thea?'

'I...I need to tell you some things.' Pacing over to the reading area, Thea placed her hands on the back of one leather wingback chair, her fingernails pressing into the leather. 'Perhaps you should sit.'

'You too, then,' Flynn said, motioning at her chair. When she hesitated, he added, 'Come on, Thea, you look like you're about to fall over.'

Thea slipped around and sat down, instantly regretting it as the stupid table lamp that gave only a glow to the rest of the room illuminated her completely. She could feel the light on her face and see the lamp opposite doing the same to Flynn's as he took his seat. It felt as if she was sitting in an interrogation room, which really didn't give her a good feeling about how the rest of this conversation was going to go.

'So…' Flynn said. 'Talk.'

She should have asked for a drink. Should have stolen the rest of the champagne she'd left outside with Zeke. Should have stayed at her rehearsal dinner if she was going to rewrite the evening.

Instead she took a breath and searched her mind for where to begin.

'Eight years ago,' she said—because wasn't that when everything had started?—'when Zeke left…he asked me to go with him.'

'Why?'

'Because we were in love.' Facts, even painful ones, were the only way to do this. The only way to make Flynn understand what had happened tonight.

Flynn shifted in his chair. 'I should have brought whisky.'

'Yeah. Sorry.'

'So. You didn't go with him. Why?'

'Because…' Could she tell him? It was Helena's secret. She'd told Zeke, but that had been her choice. Flynn deserved the truth… In the end she plumped for the simplified version. 'Helena needed me. She was sixteen, and she had a lot of stuff going on in her life. Our mother had died…she needed me. I couldn't leave her.'

'But if it hadn't been for Helena?'

The million-dollar question. 'I don't know.' Except she

did—in her heart. 'Zeke and I…we're very different people. Especially these days.'

'Okay. So what does this all have to do with tonight?'

Heat flooded Thea's cheeks as the shame of her actions hit home. 'I slept with Zeke tonight.'

'On the terrace? Where anyone could see?' Flynn's eyebrows shot up. 'That…doesn't sound very like you.'

Thea blinked at him. '*That's* your concern?'

Flynn sighed. 'Thea, I'm not an idiot. I knew the moment Zeke came back that there was unfinished business between you. I guess I was away at university when he left, so maybe I didn't know the ins and outs of it then. But seeing the two of you together this week, seeing how you act around me when he's there…neither of you are exactly subtle, Thea.'

'Oh. Okay.' Thea swallowed around the lump that had formed in her throat. 'Do you…do you hate me?'

Flynn's smile was gentle, far gentler than she deserved, and tears stung at Thea's eyes. 'Of course I don't hate you, Thea…' He sighed. 'Look. We know this isn't a love match. We're not married yet, so the fidelity clause isn't in effect.'

She'd forgotten all about that clause. One moment of Zeke's hands on her skin and she'd lost all reason.

'Quite honestly, if you have doubts like this and things you need to resolve, I'd far rather them happen now than in a year's time.'

'So…what happens now?'

'Well, that's up to you.' Flynn sat back in his chair and studied her. 'You need to decide what you want, Thea. If you think you could be truly happy with Zeke, that he can give you everything you need, then we'll go and talk to our parents and call the wedding off right now. But if you want the life we have planned—the business, the family support, kids, everything—if you still want that, then you need to forget about Zeke and marry me tomorrow.'

Thea stared at him, waiting for something more—something to make the choice for her, to make sure she made the right one. To tell her the right answer to this test.

But Flynn didn't offer advice. Didn't counsel…didn't help her reason it out. He just sat there and watched her. How could he be so impassive? But then, she'd wanted businesslike, detached, practical. She hadn't wanted Flynn to love her. He was giving her exactly what she'd always said she needed. And, against all the odds, she was still enough for him. She could still give him what he wanted, too, even knowing how much she'd messed up.

'It has to be your choice, Thea,' he said.

And, worst of all, she knew he was right.

CHAPTER TEN

'ARE YOU OKAY out here?'

Zeke turned at the sound of Helena's voice and saw the concerned crumple of her forehead as she stood in the door, watching him.

'I'm fine.' He patted the swing seat beside him. 'Wanna sit? Your sister has left us a little of the champagne.' He thought it wise not to mention exactly how Thea had been distracted from the champagne, right there on that very swing.

But Helena didn't sit anyway. Instead she leant against the railing opposite and reached out a hand for the bottle. Her high heels had been discarded, Zeke realised, and she seemed far smaller than the loss of a few inches should achieve.

'Everything okay in there?' he asked as Helena lifted the bottle to her lips. Of course what he really wanted to ask was, *Where's Thea? How did Flynn take it? When is she coming back?*

'Fine,' Helena said, passing the bottle back. 'The guests have all gone, or retired to their rooms. Thea and Flynn are in the library, talking. Your dad's in the study, and Isabella and Dad are sipping brandy in the back parlour, I think.'

That strange split again, Zeke thought. Everyone with the wrong person. Mum with Thomas, Thea with Flynn, and him out here with Helena.

'Do you know what they're talking about?' he asked.

Helena raised her eyebrows. 'Dad and Isabella? I dread to think.'

'I meant Thea and Flynn.' Zeke paused. 'And why dread to think?'

'Who knows what those two find to talk about?' Helena shrugged, but the look in her eyes told him there was more to it than a weird choice of phrase.

'Helena. What am I missing here?'

She tilted her head to look at him. '*Are* you missing it, though? Or just pretending you don't see it, like Thea?'

'I've been gone for eight years, Helena. I might have missed some stuff.' But he suspected. Always had. And the horrible certainty was already rising up in his gut.

'I knew when I was fourteen,' she replied.

How much more of life had Helena seen before she was an adult? What else had she been doing while Flynn had been at university and he and Thea had been sneaking around thinking that they were being so clever that no one knew about them?

'Knew what?' Zeke asked, even though he was sure he didn't want to know the answer.

'That my father and your mother were having an affair.'

Zeke grabbed the champagne bottle and drank deeply. 'Knew or suspected?' he asked, after wiping his mouth. Because *he'd* suspected, even when he hadn't wanted to. And he'd been very careful not to look any closer just in case he was proved right.

'Knew.'

Helena looked him straight in the eye, as if she wanted to prove the truth of her words.

'I saw them once. And once I'd seen…it was so obvious. I saw the proof of it in every single thing they did. It was a relief, in a way. At least I understood at last why Isabella was so determined to try and be my mother.'

'Yeah.' It explained a lot, even while Zeke wished that it didn't. What a mess. Tipping his head back against the wall behind the swing, he let his mind rerun the memories of twenty-one years of watching them but not seeing. Helena was right. Once you knew it was impossible not to see.

Was that how people had been with him and Thea?

The thought made him sit bolt-upright. 'Why are you telling me this now? I mean, there's no chance that I'm...' He couldn't even finish the sentence.

Helena's eyes widened. 'Our half-brother? God, no! That's...' She shuddered. 'No. Mum was still alive then, and I'm pretty sure it didn't start until after her death. Besides, Zeke, you look exactly like Ezekiel Senior. I don't think there's ever been any doubt about who your father is.'

'True.' Zeke's muscles relaxed just a little. 'Funny. For years I hated how much of him I saw when I looked in the mirror. Now...I'm profoundly grateful.'

'Hell, yes.'

'So why tell me now?'

Helena paused, her lower lip caught between her teeth. Suddenly she looked like the naughty schoolgirl he remembered, not the poised, sophisticated woman he'd found when he returned. Where had she gone, that Helena? Had all her rough edges and inappropriate comments been smoothed out by the things that had happened to her? By all the secrets she'd had to keep buried? He'd seen a glimpse of her at dinner, though, winding his mother up about the pearls. Maybe she wasn't gone for ever. He hoped not.

'Did you ever wonder why Isabella stayed with your dad?'

Zeke blinked. He hadn't, he realised. But he should have. 'I guess the money. The family. The business.'

'But if she'd left him for *my* dad…'

'They'd have had all of that, to some degree.' And Zeke would have grown up with Thomas Morrison as his step-father. He really couldn't be sure if that would have been an improvement, or not.

'Yeah.'

'So why?'

Helena shrugged. 'I don't know. I never asked. But maybe somebody should.'

'Why?' What did it matter now, anyway? He'd be gone tomorrow—leaving all this behind for his future with Thea.

'Because…' Helena took a deep breath. 'Because I think Thea is about to make the same mistake.'

Zeke's world froze. 'No. She's not. She's in there right now, telling Flynn she can't marry him.'

Helena's gaze was sad and sympathetic. 'Are you sure?'

'Yes,' Zeke lied. 'I'm absolutely sure.'

Isabella was waiting for her outside the library when Thea finally left Flynn alone with the books and headed for bed. It wouldn't do for the bride to look tired and distraught on her wedding day, after all. Just as Helena had said.

'Oh, my dear,' Isabella said, clasping her hands together at the sight of her. 'Come on. We'll go and have some tea.'

'Really, Isabella, I'm fine.' The last thing she wanted after the surrealism of her evening so far was to sit and sip tea with her future mother-in-law. 'I just need to get some sleep. It's been a long day.'

But Isabella wasn't taking no for an answer. 'You'll never sleep like this. Come on. Tea.'

Dutifully Thea trailed behind her, wondering how much longer this day could feasibly get. It had to be past midnight already. Even if the wedding wasn't until tomorrow afternoon she couldn't imagine she'd actually get a lie-in, whatever happened. Apart from anything else she still had to talk to Zeke. Flynn had insisted she did, before making any final decisions.

The kitchens were in darkness, the last of the staff having gone home at last. The dishwashers were still running, though, so Thea suspected it had been a late night for all concerned. Isabella found the light switch without difficulty and flicked it on, before heading unerringly for a cupboard which, when opened, revealed a stock of different varieties of tea.

'Camomile?' she asked, glancing back at Thea. Then she frowned. 'Or maybe peppermint. Good for soothing the stomach.'

'My stomach is fine,' Thea replied. It was just her mind that was spinning and her heart that was breaking.

'As you say.' Isabella selected a tin then, opening another cupboard, pulled out a small silver teapot and two fragile-looking cups and saucers. 'I always make it my first priority to locate the teapot, wherever I'm staying. I just can't sleep without a soothing cup of something before bed.'

'I didn't know that.' Thea watched Isabella as she pottered over to the sink to fill the kettle then, while it was boiling, selected a couple of teaspoons and a tea strainer and stand from another drawer.

'Now, Thea…' Isabella placed the tea tray, complete with lace cloth, onto the kitchen table and took a chair opposite her. 'I want to talk to you about Zeke.'

'About Zeke?' Thea's fingers slipped on the handle of the teapot and she pulled back. She should let Isabella pour, anyway.

'Yes. I know you've always been…close to my son.'

'Your husband already asked me to talk to him about

This Minute,' Thea interjected, wishing she didn't sound as if she was babbling so much. 'And I tried—I did—but no dice. I think tomorrow he plans to leave and sell to Glasshouse, regardless of what we offer.'

'That's interesting,' Isabella said. 'But not what I wanted to talk about.'

'Then…what? Did you want to know where he's been? Because I have a pretty good idea, I think. Or what his plans are now? Because you'd really have to ask him, except…'

Except he was probably still waiting for her on the terrace. Did he know what she'd planned to tell Flynn? Or did he hope…? No. She couldn't think about it.

'I wanted to talk about your relationship with him. And my relationship with your father.'

Thea blinked. 'I don't understand.'

'Then you haven't been paying very close attention.' Isabella reached for the teapot and, placing the strainer over Thea's cup, started to pour. 'This should be brewed by now.'

'What exactly *is* your relationship with my father?' Thea asked, even though she suspected she already knew the answer. Should have known it for years.

'What exactly is *your* relationship with my youngest son?' Isabella didn't even look up from pouring the tea into her own cup as she turned the question round on Thea.

'I haven't seen him in eight years,' Thea said. 'I think that any relationship we did have will have been legally declared dead by now.'

'Except he was the one who came after you when you were upset tonight. And I suspect he's the one who's left you looking like your whole world is upside down.'

'Tell me about you and Dad.'

Placing the pot back on the tray, Isabella picked up her

teacup and saucer and sat back, surveying Thea over the rim of her steaming cup. 'I think, in some ways, our situation is very similar, you know.'

'I *don't* know,' Thea said. 'I don't know what you're talking about.'

'After your mother died your father was a wreck. I tried to help out where I could. And then, after that nastiness with Helena…'

'You saw your chance and pushed me out,' Thea said, her hackles rising. But Isabella merely raised her eyebrows a few millimetres as she sipped her tea.

'I did what was needed to keep things…settled.'

Sending Helena away and taking over Thea's home. Smoothing over the rough edges of the actual truth and providing a glossy finish. Thea shook her head. 'I don't see how this applies to me and Zeke.'

'Wait,' Isabella said. 'Drink your tea and listen. Over time, your father and I grew close. We talked a lot. We listened a lot. That was something we both needed. You might not have noticed, but my husband is not one of the world's great listeners and his only subject of conversation is the company. It was…different with Thomas.'

Thea's hands tightened around the warmth of her teacup. 'You fell in love.'

'We did. Very deeply.'

No wonder her father had chosen Isabella over her. For the first time Thea saw her past through new eyes. No, she hadn't been up to the job her father had thrown her into. But maybe that had been because it was a role that was never meant to be hers. Maybe he'd wanted Isabella there at his side all along.

Except he'd never got all of her, had he?

'You never left Ezekiel.'

'I never even considered it,' Isabella said without pause. 'And your father never asked me to.'

'Why?'

Isabella sighed. 'Because I was old enough and wise enough, by the time I fell in love for real, to know that love isn't everything. Thea, we all need different things in this life. Yes, we need someone to listen to us, to laugh with, to love. But we need other things, too.'

'Like money,' Thea guessed, not hiding the bitterness in her voice. How different might her life have been with Isabella as a real stepmother rather than someone who had to help out because Thea couldn't manage things on her own? 'Dad could have given you that, too, you know.'

'Not just money. Yes, Thomas could have given me that—and stability, and lots of other things. But what about the business? What about our social standing? My place in the world? What about Ezekiel and the vows I made?'

'You mean, what about the scandal?' Thea shook her head. 'Is that what it's always about with you? Was this just Helena all over again?'

'All I am saying is there are many aspects of a woman's life for which she has needs. You need to look at your requirements over the course of a lifetime when you're making a decision about whom to marry.'

'And Ezekiel gave you what you needed over the course of your lifetime? Because, if so, why did you feel the need to have an affair with my father?'

Isabella sipped at her tea delicately before responding. 'That's what I'm saying. Did it ever occur to you that perhaps it is unreasonable to expect one person to fulfil your every need?'

'No.' The response was instinctive, automatic. Even if she were willing to contemplate such a thing, neither Zeke nor Flynn was the sort of man who liked to share.

Isabella gave her a sad smile. 'You're young. You're still holding out for the dream. So, which of my sons do you think can give you that?'

Thea had no answer to that at all.

'If that's the way you feel you have only two options,' Isabella said. 'One: you marry Flynn as planned. Everyone is happy and no one needs to be any the wiser about your…indiscretion. You go about your life and probably never see Zeke again.'

'What's option two?' Thea asked, her mouth dry.

'You call off the wedding and leave with Zeke. You leave behind your career, your family and reputation, your chance at a stable and loving future, for a man who has already left you behind once. In an effort to put a good face on the company my husband will probably marry Flynn off to someone else pretty quickly. Helena, I imagine, would be the best candidate.'

'No.' The very idea chilled Thea's core. 'She wouldn't.'

'She would,' Isabella replied, with certainty in her voice. 'She couldn't bear to let everyone down *again*. Besides, surely you've noticed the way she looks at him.'

'No.'

Was Isabella just saying that to convince her to marry Flynn? Didn't she know that if she'd thought Helena wanted him she'd step aside in an instant? Probably not. Isabella had spent so many years watching Ezekiel drive a wedge between her sons she probably believed everyone wanted what their sibling had.

'I'd look closer, then.'

Thea shook her head. 'You're imagining things, Isabella. And it doesn't matter anyway.'

'Oh? Have you found a magical third path, then? Other than my original suggestion?'

'No.' Thea stared down into her teacup. If she was hon-

est, she'd known all along what she really had to do. For
her future and for her family. 'I'll marry Flynn, just as
we've always planned.'

Isabella watched her for a long moment, then nodded.
'Good. Now, more tea?'

'No. Thank you.' Thea pushed her chair away from the
table and stood. 'I need to go to bed. Lots to do tomorrow.'

Starting with explaining her decision to the one person
in the world who would never, ever understand it.

Zeke woke early the next morning. He'd waited up for
Thea on the terrace until he'd realised all the lights inside
had been turned off. Helena had kept vigil with him for
a while, before patting him on the shoulder and bidding
him goodnight. When he'd finally given up and gone to
bed he'd lingered outside Thea's door for long moments,
contemplating knocking and going in. But Thea had to
make this decision for herself—even he knew that much.

In the end he'd headed to bed alone, for a night of rest-
less dreams and uncertainty. And now it was the morning of Thea and Flynn's wedding, and he still didn't know
her decision.

From the moment he woke he felt panic surge through
him at the realisation that he was alone again. Why hadn't
she come? He'd been so sure… Flynn must have said something. Threatened her, perhaps… Except that wasn't his
style. No, he'd have baffled her with logic. Probably had a
spreadsheet of reasons they should get married as planned.

Just what Thea didn't need.

Sitting up in bed, Zeke stamped down on the fear creep-
ing across his brain and contemplated his next move. He
could still fix this, still win, if he played the right hand.
Did he wait for Thea to come to him, or did he seek her
out? There was always the chance that she might not come

at all. If she'd made her decision—the wrong decision—what would be the point? But Zeke knew he couldn't live with the not knowing.

So what other choice did he have? He could just cut his losses now. He could go and say goodbye to Thea, give her one last chance to go with him, then leave if she said no.

In the end the choice wasn't his or Thea's. As he exited his bedroom, freshly showered and casually dressed—no way was he getting stuck in a tux this early in the day, even if the wedding went ahead and he actually attended—he saw Flynn, marching towards him.

'You and I need to talk,' his adopted brother said, face solemn. 'And then you need to talk to Thea.'

'Okay.' Zeke fell into step with Flynn, his heart rising slightly in his chest. Maybe he wouldn't need to convince Thea again after all. If Flynn wanted him to talk to her surely that meant he didn't approve of her decision. Well, he was damned if he thought Zeke would try to persuade her otherwise. 'What exactly do we need to talk about?'

Flynn gave him an exasperated look. 'Thea, of course.'

'Right.'

Zeke waited until Flynn had yanked open the door to the library and impatiently motioned him in before asking any more questions. Settling down into a wingback chair, he suddenly remembered Helena's words from the night before. This was where Flynn and Thea had talked after the interlude on the terrace. How he wished he could have heard what they'd said…

Maybe Flynn would tell him. If he asked right.

'So,' Zeke said, folding one leg up to rest his ankle on the opposite knee. 'What's up? Last-minute nerves?'

Flynn glared at him. 'In precisely six hours I'm supposed to marry Thea. If you have any interest at all in that event, however twisted, you need to stop playing *now*. I need you to be my brother, for once, and I need you to be honest with me.'

Zeke flinched under his brother's gaze. How had he become the kid brother again, the screw-up, the one who couldn't be serious about anything that mattered? Especially when he'd worked so hard to get away from that. Away from the bitter rivalry for something that had turned out not to matter at all—their father's approval.

'Fine. Then talk.'

'Thea told me that she slept with you last night.'

'She said she was going to.' Zeke looked Flynn right in the eye as he talked. He wasn't ashamed, even if he should be. Thea belonged with *him*, not in some soulless, loveless marriage of convenience. Getting her out of that was not a sin. Trapping her was.

'I still plan to marry her.'

'For the love of God, *why*?' Zeke grabbed the arms of the chair and sat forward. What else did he have to *do*? 'You don't love her—I know you don't. You couldn't be this calm right now if you did. And she doesn't love you!'

'Do you think she's still in love with you?'

'I know she is. And I know she deserves a lot better than what you have to offer.'

'And what, exactly, are *you* offering?' Flynn asked, staring at Zeke. 'The chance to say *screw you* to our father?'

'That's not...' Zeke sank back down into his chair. 'That's not why.'

'Are you sure?' Flynn tilted his head as he considered his brother. 'It's been eight years, Zeke. Why come back now, if not to prove a point?'

'Oh, I don't know—maybe to stop Thea making a huge mistake.'

'And you think you're the best judge of Thea's mistakes?'

'Better than her, at least,' Zeke said, thinking about Helena and all the guilt Thea carried on her behalf.

Flynn shook his head. 'You're wrong. But I told Thea last night she had to decide for herself what to do. I told her to think about it overnight, then talk to us both this morning. She'll be here any minute.'

And just like that the decision about how to approach Thea was taken away from him.

'Good,' Zeke said, hoping his surprise didn't show on his face.

He didn't want to have this conversation in front of his brother. Flynn made him a different person even now, after all these years. He needed it to be just him and Thea, so they could just be themselves, the people he remembered so well. But apparently his love life was now in the public domain. And before he could even object the library door opened and Thea was standing there, looking pale and lovely—and determined.

Zeke stood up. Time to win this.

CHAPTER ELEVEN

THEA SUCKED IN a breath as she opened the library door and saw Zeke and Flynn waiting for her. This was it. The moment that decided the rest of her life. Whatever she'd told Isabella, whatever she'd told herself in the dark of the night, her decision couldn't be final until she'd told the two men in this room. This might be the biggest choice and possibly the biggest mistake she'd ever made as an adult. So of course it involved Zeke Ashton.

'Thea, you're here. Good.'

Flynn gave her a gentle smile that made Thea's insides tie up in knots. She didn't want to be there *so much*.

But she was, and she was out of other options, so she moved to the centre of the room and took the chair Flynn indicated. This was his condition: he'd marry her today if she talked things through with both of them and still decided it was the best option. Since she'd slept with someone else the night before their wedding, Thea had to admit that this was more than fair. That was the thing about Flynn. He was always scrupulously fair. Even when she wanted him to just yell, or walk out, or make a decision for her.

'Okay, so here's what I'm thinking.' Flynn settled into his own chair, looking for all the world as if this was an everyday meeting or discussion. As if they weren't debating whether or not to get *married* that afternoon. 'We all know the situation. And we all agree that Thea has to be the one to make a decision about what happens next—correct?'

He glanced between them, focussing first on Zeke, who eventually nodded in a way that made it very clear he was doing so under duress, and then at Thea, who whispered, 'Yes,' even though she didn't want to.

'So... I think the best way to proceed is—'

'Oh, for God's sake!' Zeke interrupted. 'This isn't a board meeting, Flynn.'

'No,' Flynn replied, his voice calm and even. 'It's a meeting about my future. And since you're the one who's put that into the realm of uncertainty, I think you should just let me deal with it my own way, don't you?'

Zeke settled back into his chair at that, and Thea risked a glance over at him. His eyes were dark and angry, and she could see the tension in his hands, in the way they gripped the arms of the chair, even if his posture was re-laxed. How he must hate this—must hate waiting to see if Flynn was going to beat him again. Because of course that was how Zeke would see it, even if it wasn't true. This wasn't about either of them, really, even if only Flynn seemed to realise that.

It was about Thea. About her making the right decision for once. Whatever that might be.

'So, here's what I propose,' Flynn said, and Thea tried to concentrate on listening to him instead of watching the way Zeke's jaw tightened with every word. 'Zeke and I will both lay out our arguments for why we feel you should choose our proposed course of action. You can listen, ask questions, and then we'll leave you alone to make your decision. The only thing I ask is that you decide quickly; once guests start arriving it will be a lot harder to cancel this thing, if you choose to.'

Thea nodded, and stopped looking at Zeke altogether.

'Okay. Shall I go first?' Flynn asked, and when no one answered he continued, 'Right. Thea, obviously I want to marry you today. I understand what happened last night, and I think, after talking with you yesterday, I can see why. But I don't believe that one impulsive action has to change the course of your whole life. We agreed to a contract—a marriage between us based on very sound reasoning and mutual desires. Everything we discussed and decided still stands. I can give you the security, the business, the future that you want. And marriage is only a small part of our lives; we have to consider the other people we love— what *they* want. I think we both know that everyone in this villa except Zeke wants a future with us as a couple in it. We can do so much together, Thea. And, quite honestly, I'd worry about your future if you left with Zeke today.'

He got up from the chair and came to stand by her side, gently taking her hand in his.

'Because, Thea, I care about you. Maybe we don't have that grand passion. But we have more. Mutual respect, caring, common interests and values. They matter too. And I suggest to you, right here, that they matter more for what we want to achieve in life.'

He wasn't just thinking about the business, Thea realised. He was talking about kids. Flynn would be a great father—calm and fair. And she was pretty sure he wouldn't ever sleep with his best friend's wife. Unlike her own father. Unlike Zeke, she thought, stealing a glance at him. Hell, he'd slept with her the night before her wedding. Morality had never been a strong motivation for him.

Or for her this week, it seemed.

Flynn seemed to be waiting for an answer, so Thea nodded and said, 'That all makes a lot of sense,' even though her poor muddled brain could barely remember what he'd said.

Maybe it didn't matter, she realised. Maybe, whatever they each had to say, it all meant nothing in the end. She couldn't weigh up the pros and cons of two people, could she?

Except she had to. And not just of the two men in front of her but of the whole lives they represented. She could see two futures for herself, branching off from this moment, and she simply didn't know which one was more terrifying.

But she still had to decide.

Flynn gave a sharp nod, then moved away to his own chair, yielding the floor to his brother. 'Zeke. Your turn.'

Zeke looked up slowly, his dark gaze finally meeting hers. 'I don't know what you want me to say.'

'Neither do I,' Thea admitted. Did she want him to talk her out of marrying Flynn—really? Or did she want him to say something so awful that she stopped feeling guilty about marrying Zeke's brother in the first place? She wasn't sure.

He blew out a long breath. 'Okay. I don't want you to marry Flynn. I think it's a mistake.'

Thea flinched at the word, even though she tried not to. 'It's mine to make, though.'

'It is,' Zeke conceded. 'I just… I really don't want to do this with him in the room.'

'He's your brother. And he's right—he does have kind of a big stake in this conversation.'

'I know.' Zeke took another breath. 'Okay, fine. I know you think you're doing this for the family, to prove yourself to them somehow. And I know you believe that everyone will be happy if you just go along with their plans. But you're wrong.'

'And our happiness is suddenly of such importance to you? Zeke, you haven't cared about us for the last eight years. I find it hard to believe that we suddenly matter that much to you.'

'Of course I've cared!' Zeke yelled, and Flynn's gaze shot to the door, as if he was worrying about who might be listening. It was a fear that seemed all the more reasonable when Zeke's words were followed by a knock on the library door a moment later.

'Ah, here you all are,' Isabella said, giving them all her best hostess smile. 'Thea, darling, there's a small question about the table settings that we could use your input on, if you have a moment.'

Isabella's eyes were knowing, but Thea refused to meet them.

'I'll deal with it,' Flynn said, getting to his feet. 'Thea and Zeke are just reminiscing about old times, Mother. Something they won't have much of a chance to do once we're married.'

She had to know it was a lie, but Isabella let it go nonetheless. 'Come on, then. And once this is sorted, perhaps you can help me with the question of the gift table.'

Flynn shut the door firmly behind them, and Thea felt as if he'd taken all the air in the room with him. Now it was just her and Zeke and every moment of their history, weighing down on them like the books on the shelves.

'That's better,' Zeke said. 'Now we can do this properly.'

How could she look so poised and calm, when he felt as if his insides were about to combust? For Thea this might as well be just another business meeting. Maybe she was a perfect match for Flynn after all.

No. If this was his last chance to try and uncover the Thea he'd known and loved, the one he'd glimpsed again as he'd made love to her on the terrace last night, then he was grasping it with both hands. He had to make her see sense.

'Maybe we should wait until Flynn gets back,' Thea said, as if she truly believed that any part of this discussion really did involve his brother.

'This isn't about Flynn,' Zeke said. 'He could be anyone. Any poor bloke you'd roped in to try and make your life safe and predictable. Just like the last two. No, this is about you and me, and it always has been.'

Thea's gaze shot up to meet his, dark and heated. 'You mean it's all about *you*. You proving a point to your father. Just like it always is.'

'Last night wasn't just about me,' Zeke replied, enjoying the flush of red that ran up her neck to her cheeks. 'In fact I distinctly remember it being all about you more than once.'

'This isn't about sex, Zeke,' Thea snapped. 'This is my future you're playing with.'

'Who said I'm playing?' Because he wasn't—not one bit. He knew exactly how important this moment was. But with Thea sometimes you had to get her mad to see the truth. To let her true self break out from all the rules and restrictions she'd tucked herself in with like a safety blanket.

Thea gave a bitter laugh. 'It's always been a game to you—all of it. You've always cared more about beating your father and Flynn than anything else. If you'd paid any attention at all you'd know that Flynn isn't even competing. He's just getting on with his life, like an ordinary, good man.'

'And that's what you want, is it? Ordinary?' If she thought it was, she was wrong. Thea deserved much, much more than ordinary.

'I want to not be a trophy! I want to not be one more

thing you can use against your family for some misguided slight almost a decade ago!'

The words hit him hard in the chest. 'That's not what I'm doing.'

'Isn't it? Are you sure? Because it seems to me that coming back here—right when you're about to sell your company to our competitor, just when I'm about to get on and make a success of my life—is far more about you and your need to win than anything else.'

'You're wrong.'

'Prove it.'

'How?'

'I don't know, Zeke! But if you really want me to throw over all my plans for the future, to upset both our families, probably damage the company's reputation…you need to offer me a little more than a cheap victory over your father and one night on a terrace.'

One night. Was that what it was to her? Was that all he'd ever been? A bit of fun, but never the one you chose for the long haul. No wonder she'd stayed eight years ago.

'Helena must have been a real handy excuse that night,' he said, letting the bitterness creep into his voice.

Thea blinked. 'What?'

'Tell me honestly. If it hadn't been for Helena would you have come with me when I asked, that night of your birthday party?'

The colour faded from Thea's cheeks and he knew the answer before she even spoke the word.

'No.'

Zeke tightened his muscles against the pain, stiffening into strength and resolve. With a sharp nod, he said, 'That's what I thought.'

'I just… I wanted…'

'You don't need to justify yourself to me.' A strange

calm had settled over him now. At last he knew, and to his surprise the truth made all the difference. 'I understand.'

'No! You don't,' Thea said, but Zeke just shook his head.

'Sure I do. You want a safe and predictable life, even if it makes you miserable.' How had he thought for so many years that Thea was different from the rest of them? He should have known that they were all the same at heart. More concerned with the appearance of the thing than the substance. Better that he realised that now, however belatedly, than go on believing she was something more than she was.

'That's not... It's not just that,' Thea said unconvincingly.

'Yeah, Thea, it is. Deny it all you want, but I know what's going on here. You're doing exactly what Daddy wants, as usual. You're going to marry Flynn to buy yourself the place you think you deserve.'

She looked away, but Zeke wasn't looking for shame in her expression. It was too late for that now, anyway. She'd made her choice and he knew his future now. But that didn't mean he couldn't open her eyes to a few home truths before he left.

'You realise you could be pregnant with my child already?' They hadn't used protection last night. Had been too caught up in the moment even to think of it.

'I know.'

'Does Flynn?'

'Yes.' A whisper...barely even a word.

'And he's happy to marry you anyway?' Of course he was. In fact he probably hoped that she was. 'Because that would give him the one thing he's never had, wouldn't it? Legitimacy. Raising a true Ashton blood heir with the Morrison heiress. Perfect.'

Thea sprang to her feet to defend her fiancé. 'You don't

have a clue what you're talking about! And anyway Flynn *is* the Ashton heir, remember? You gave it all up to run away and seek revenge.'

'Because my father chose him over me!' Zeke couldn't keep the anger from his voice this time. However far he moved past the pain, the sting of unfairness still caught him unawares sometimes.

'Your father made a business choice, not a personal one.'

Zeke flinched at her words. 'You're wrong there,' he said.

'Am I?'

He knew she was, but couldn't bring himself to explain, to argue. To revisit in glorious Technicolor the night he'd left. The things he'd heard his father say. What had really driven him away. Why he'd had to go even when Thea wouldn't leave with him. Why her rejection had been just one more slam to the heart.

What was wrong with him? He'd moved past this years ago. Wasn't that one of the reasons he'd come back in the first place? To prove that he'd moved on, that he had his own life now, that he didn't need his family or the business? So why was he letting her arguments get to him?

Was it the idea of a possible baby? The thought that *his child* might be brought up in the Morrison-Ashton clan, living its whole life waiting to see if it would be deemed *worthy enough* to inherit everything that Zeke had walked away from…? It made him sick to his stomach. No child— no person—deserved to go through that. But what were the honest chances that Thea was pregnant? Slim, he'd imagine. And she'd tell him, he knew. Thea might not be everything he'd thought she was, but she was honest. She'd told Flynn about sleeping with him, hadn't she? She'd tell Zeke if he were a father.

And then he'd be tied into this accursed family for ever. Perfect.

What had he been thinking, sleeping with her last night? Zeke wanted to beat himself up for it, except he knew exactly what he'd been thinking—that he might be able to save Thea from herself this time.

But Thea didn't want to be saved. She'd rejected him again, and this time it cut even deeper. She'd chosen Flynn. She wanted Flynn.

Fine. She could have him. But Zeke was making sure she knew exactly what she was letting herself in for first.

CHAPTER TWELVE

THEA THOUGHT SHE could bear anything except sitting one moment longer under Zeke's too knowing gaze. Who was he to judge her, to condemn her? To think he knew her better than she knew herself?

Except he just might.

No. She couldn't let herself believe that. After a sleepless night, spent with Flynn and Isabella's words resounding in her brain while her memories ran one long, sensual video of her evening with Zeke, she knew only one thing for certain: she was done with doing what other people said she should. Everyone in the whole villa thought they knew what was best for her, and Zeke was just the latest in a long line.

Well, she was done with it.

'You realise that you're choosing what other people expect of you over what you really want, right?' Zeke said, and she glared at him.

'How would you know what I want? And if you make one single innuendo or reference to last night after that comment I'm walking out right now.'

The smirk on his face told her that was exactly what Zeke had been about to do, but instead he said, 'Because I've seen you do it before, far too many times. You admitted you wouldn't have come with me even if Helena hadn't needed you. But why? I can tell you, even if you don't know yourself.'

Thea rolled her eyes. 'Enlighten me, oh, wise one,' she said, as sarcastically as she could manage.

'Because you're scared. Because you've spent your whole life doing what other people think is best for you and you don't even know how to stop. You can't make peace with your own desires because you think they might upset someone.'

'They upset *me*!' Thea yelled. 'Zeke! Do you think I want to be this person? The sort of woman who sleeps with the best man the night before her wedding? I hate myself right now! The best thing I can do is try and get back to my regularly scheduled life, without the chaos you bring into it. Is that so bad?'

'Not if the regularly scheduled life is what you really want.'

Zeke moved closer, and Thea's body started to hum at his nearness.

'But I don't think it is. I think that you want more. You want a life that makes your heart sing. You want it all.'

He swayed closer again, and before she knew it his hand was at her waist, pulling her towards him, and his lips were dipping towards hers…

She wanted this so badly. Wanted his mouth on hers, his body against her. But she couldn't have it. Not if she wanted all the other things she'd promised herself—her family, security, her work. This was her last chance to get things right—and she had to take it. However tempted she was to give in to desire over sense.

'No, Zeke.' She pushed him away, not letting her palms linger on his chest for a moment longer than necessary. 'I'm marrying Flynn.'

'Then you're a fool.'

Zeke stepped away, turning his back on her, but not before she saw the flash in his eyes of—what? Anger? Frustration? She couldn't be sure.

'I'm making the sensible decision,' Thea said, even though it felt as if her heart might force its way out of her sensible ribcage at any moment to fight its own case.

'You're making a mistake.'

'Am I?' Thea shook her head. This was going to hurt. And this was going to make him angry. But she needed to say it. Hell, she'd been waiting eight years to tell him this. It was past due. 'What about you? You say I'm relying on other people to tell me how to live, but how are you any better?'

'I live my life exactly the way I want.' Zeke ran his hand through his messy hair as he turned back towards her. 'By my own judgement. No archaic family loyalty rules or duty to manipulative men.'

'Really? Seems to me that everything you've done since you left—hell, even leaving in the first place—has all been more about your father than you.'

Zeke shook his head. 'You don't know what you're talking about.'

'I do,' Thea said firmly. 'Because I know you, Zeke. You said you wanted to leave Morrison-Ashton and everything it represented behind when you left. But what did you do? You went and worked for another media conglomerate and then set up your own rival company, for heaven's sake!'

'Stick with what you know, and all that,' Zeke said with a shrug, but Thea wasn't listening.

'And now you're here, still trying to prove to everyone that you don't need them. You're still so bitter about your father giving Flynn the job you wanted—'

'It's not just that!'

'You're so bitter,' Thea carried on, 'that you can't move

on. I bet even when you were away you were still checking up on your family. People keep saying that you walked out and left us, but you didn't. You've carried us with you every step of the way and, Zeke, that chip on your shoulder is only getting bigger and heavier. And until you let it go you're never going to be happy. Not even if I left with you right now.'

'You're wrong,' Zeke said, but even as he spoke he could feel the truth of her words resonating through his body. 'I'm done with the lot of you for good this time.'

Her smile was sad, but it enraged him. Who was she to tell him the mistakes he was making in his life? Thea Morrison—the queen of bad decisions. And, even if she didn't know it yet, this was the worst one. Well, she'd have a long, miserable marriage during which to regret it.

Zeke might have been willing to take a lot from Thea Morrison, but this was the last. The last rejection he'd ever face from anyone with the surname Morrison or Ashton.

He was done.

His chest ached as he realised this might be the last time he ever saw her. That he was walking away again and she wouldn't be coming with him this time, either. He choked back a laugh as he realised the awful truth. She'd been right all along. She'd been right not to leave with him eight years ago. They *had* been kids. And he knew now that he hadn't even understood what love was then.

He couldn't have loved Thea at eighteen—not really. He hadn't known her the way he did now, for a start. But mostly he knew it had to be true because, however much he'd thought it had hurt to leave her last time, it didn't come close to the pain searing through his body at the thought of leaving her now..

He loved Thea Morrison, the woman she'd grown up

to be, more than he'd ever believed possible. And it didn't make a bit of difference.

None of it mattered now. Not their past, not this horrific week in Tuscany, and certainly not their impossible future. When he left this time he wouldn't be coming back. And he knew just how to make sure that every atom of his relationship with these people was left behind too.

'Maybe you don't know it yet,' he said, keeping his voice calm and even, 'but you're going to make yourself, my brother, and everyone else around you desperately unhappy if you go through with this wedding. I love you. And I would have done anything to make you happy. Anything except stay here and live this safe life you think you want. But it will end up driving you mad. One day you're going to wake up and realise all that, and know what a mistake you've made. But, like you say, it's your mistake to make.'

He didn't look back as he walked to the door. He didn't want to see her standing there, beautiful, sad and resolved. She loved him—he knew it. But she wasn't going to let herself have the one thing that could make her happy.

Fine. It was her mistake, as she'd said.

But she couldn't make him watch.

'Goodbye, Thea,' he said as he walked out through the door.

The door shut behind him with a click, although it felt like an earth-shattering slam to Thea. She'd done it. She'd really done it. She'd sent him away, made the right decision for once. Avoided the oh, so tempting mistake she'd made so many times before. She'd won.

So why did she feel so broken?

Sinking into the chair, Thea sat very still and waited for whatever would happen next. The stylist would be here soon, she vaguely remembered, to do her hair and make-up. Helena would come and find her when it was time, wouldn't she? And in the meantime…she'd just wait for someone to tell her what she was supposed to do.

The irony of her thoughts surprised a laugh from her, and she buried her face in her hands before her laughter turned to tears. The decision was made and Zeke would leave now. She could get back to that regularly scheduled life she'd been hankering after for the past three days.

It was over at last.

Hearing a click, she looked up again in time to see the door open. For one fleeting moment her heart jumped at the thought that it might be Zeke, coming back to try and win her one last time. But, really, what else was there to say? They'd both said everything they needed to, everything they'd been holding in for the last eight years. That moment had passed. *Their* moment.

Flynn stuck his head around the door and, seeing she was alone, came in, shutting it behind him.

'Everything okay?' he asked, hovering nervously at a distance.

Poor Flynn. The things she'd put him through this week… He was such a good man. He didn't deserve it.

So she tried very hard to smile as she looked up at him, to make him feel wanted and loved. To feel like the winner he'd turned out to be. Her man, her choice, her future. Now and always.

'Fine,' she said, her cheeks aching. 'But I'm afraid you're going to need a new best man.'

The look of relief on his face was almost reward enough. 'I think I can arrange that.'

He moved towards her, settling on the arm of her chair, one hand at her shoulder in a comforting fatherly gesture. He'd be a brilliant dad, Thea thought again. It was important to focus on all the excellent reasons she had for marrying him, rather than the one uncertain and confusing reason not to.

'Are you okay?' Flynn asked, and Thea nodded.

'I'm fine. It was…a little difficult, that's all.'

'And you're sure you want to go through with this today? I mean, I appreciate you choosing me, Thea, I really do. And I think it's the right decision. We're going to have a great future together, I know. But it doesn't have to start today—not if you don't want. We could postpone—'

'No,' Thea interrupted. 'I've made my choice. I want to do this.'

Before she changed her mind.

Zeke didn't knock on his father's office door. He didn't need permission or approval from his father for what was going to happen next. In fact he didn't need anything from him. That was sort of the point.

Ezekiel Ashton looked up as Zeke walked in, and his eyebrows rose in amused interest. 'Zeke. Shouldn't you be off practising your best man's speech somewhere?'

'I believe that by now Flynn will have chosen a better man.' Zeke dropped into the visitor's chair, slouching casually. 'I'll be leaving as soon as I'm packed.'

Guests would start arriving soon, he was sure, for the pre-wedding drinks reception that Isabella had insisted on when she'd discovered that Thea planned a late afternoon wedding. He could probably grab one of the taxis bringing people up from the hotel to get him to the airport. He'd call his assistant while he packed and get her to book a flight.

This time tomorrow he'd be in another country. Another life.

'You're not staying, then.' Ezekiel shook his head sadly and turned his attention back to his paperwork. 'I don't know why I'm surprised.'

He doesn't matter. Nothing he thinks or does matters to me any more.

'I have one piece of business to conclude with you before I go,' Zeke said, watching in amusement as he became of interest to his father again.

'Oh, yes? I was under the impression that the very idea of doing business with your own father was distasteful to you.'

'It is,' Zeke said bluntly. 'But it has come to my attention that it may be the only way to sever my ties with you for good.'

'You make it sound so violent,' Ezekiel said. 'When really all you're doing is running away from your responsibilities. And, Zeke, we all know that you'll come back again eventually. We're family. That's what you do for family.'

Zeke shook his head. 'Not this one. Do you know why I left eight years ago?'

'Because you felt slighted that I'd given a position you considered rightfully yours to your brother.'

'No.' Zeke thought back to that horrible day and for the first time felt a strange detachment from the events. 'Because I finally understood why you'd done it. I heard you that day, talking to Thomas about us. I'd come to talk to you about you giving Flynn my job—the one I'd always been promised. I had all these arguments ready...' He shook his head at the memory of his righteous younger self. 'I heard you laugh and say that you realised now that perhaps it wasn't such a misfortune that Mum had fallen pregnant twenty-one years ago, just as Flynn's adoption was confirmed. That while you hadn't planned for two children perhaps it had all been for the best after all.'

He'd stood frozen outside his father's office door, Zeke remembered, his hand half raised to knock. And he'd listened as his father had ruined his relationship with his brother for good.

'This way,' Ezekiel had said, 'they have built-in competition. In some ways it's better, having two sons. Flynn has always felt he has to earn his place, so he fights for it—he fights to belong every day. And as long as I let Zeke feel that he's the disappointment, the second son, he'll keep fighting to best his brother. It's a perfect set-up.'

"'I've told Zeke I've given Flynn the position as my right-hand man,"' you said.' Zeke watched the memory dawning in his father's eyes. "'Of course Zeke will get the company one day. But I want him to fight his brother for it, first."'

The words still echoed in Zeke's skull—the moment his whole life had made horrifying, unbelievable sense, and everything he'd ever thought he wanted had ceased to matter. He'd had to leave—had to get away. And so he'd run straight to Thea and asked her to go with him, only to have his world, his expectations, damned again. That one night had changed his whole life.

'Do you remember saying that, *Dad*?'

Ezekiel nodded. 'Of course I do. And what of it? Healthy competition is good for the soul.'

'That wasn't healthy. Nothing you did to us was *healthy*.'

Zeke leant forward in his chair, gripping the armrests tightly to stop himself standing and pacing. He wanted to look his father in the eye as he told him this.

'What you did to us was unfair at best, cruel at worst. You pitted two people who should have been friends, brothers, against each other. You drove a wedge between us from the moment we were born. You made me feel rejected, inadequate. And you made Flynn believe that he had to fight for every scrap from the table. You drove your wife into the arms of your best friend, you drove me to the other end of the country, and you drove Flynn and Thea to believe that marrying each other is the only way to serve the family business, to earn their place in the family. You are a manipulative, cold, uncaring man and *I am done with you.*'

Ezekiel was silent at his words, but Zeke didn't bother looking for remorse in his expression. He wouldn't find it, and even if by some miracle he did it didn't matter now.

'I am here today to undertake my final act of business with you, old man,' Zeke said, relaxing back in the chair. 'I am going to sell you This Minute, for twice what Glasshouse were offering.' He scribbled down the figure and pushed the scrap of paper across the table.

Ezekiel read it and nodded. 'I knew you'd see sense about this in the end.'

'I'm not done,' Zeke said. 'That's just the financial cost. I want something more.'

'A position at the company?' Ezekiel guessed. 'Would Director of Digital Media suffice for now?'

'I don't want a job. I never wanted to work for you in the first place. I want you to give Thea that role. I want you to make sure she has the freedom to run it her way, and to make her own mistakes. You cannot interfere one iota.'

Ezekiel gave a slow nod. 'That should be possible. As her father always says, her business decisions are far more credible than her personal ones. And she's due a promotion once the wedding is over.'

Zeke knew this game. By the time he left Ezekiel would have convinced himself that Thea's new job had been all his idea in the first place.

He'd have a harder time doing that with his second demand, Zeke wagered.

'One more thing,' Zeke said, and waited until he had his father's full attention before he continued. 'I want you to step down and appoint Flynn as the CEO of Morrison-Ashton. You can take a year for the handover,' he said, talking over his father's objections. 'But no more. By his first wedding anniversary Flynn will be in charge.'

'The company is supposed to come to you,' Ezekiel said.

Zeke shook his head. 'I don't want it. Flynn does. He's your son, as much as I am, and he's earned it a lot more than I have. It's his.'

Ezekiel watched him for a long moment, obviously weighing up how much he wanted This Minute against how much he hated his son right then. Zeke waited. He knew that his father's pride wouldn't allow him to let This Minute go to his main rival. Plus he probably thought he'd be able to get out of stepping down somehow.

He wouldn't. Zeke's lawyers were very, very good at what they did, and they would make sure the contract was watertight. But he'd let the old man hope for now.

'Fine,' Ezekiel said eventually.

Zeke jumped to his feet. 'I'll have my team draw up the papers. They'll be with you by next week.'

'And what about you? What are you going to do?'

Zeke paused in the doorway and smiled at his father. 'I'm going to go and live my own life at last.'

CHAPTER THIRTEEN

ISABELLA WAS WAITING for her in the hallway with the stylist when Thea finally pulled herself together for long enough to make it out of the library. Flynn still hovered nervously at her shoulder, but she tried to give him reassuring smiles when she could, in the hope that he might leave her alone for a few minutes.

'Thea! We're running behind schedule already, you know. And you look dreadful!'

'Thanks,' Thea said, even though she knew her mother-in-law-to-be was probably completely correct.

'Sorry. But...well, you do. Now, come with me and Sheila, here, will get you sorted out. Flynn, I think your father is looking for you. I saw Zeke come out of his office a few moments ago, so God only knows what that is about. Why don't you go and find out?'

Was Isabella just trying to get rid of Flynn for a moment? Thea wondered. Or did Ezekiel really want him? And, if so, why? Had Zeke finally agreed to sell This Minute to them?

And why did she still care?

It was business, that was all, Thea told herself. It was all business from here on in.

'Will you be okay?' Flynn asked.

'Oh, Flynn, don't be ridiculous. Of course she will! It's her wedding day.'

But Flynn was still looking at Thea, and ignoring his mother, so she nodded. 'I'll be fine. Go.'

Flynn gave her an uncertain smile. 'Okay. I'll see you at the church.'

'At the church,' Thea agreed weakly.

Sheila had set up in Thea's bedroom, so she followed the stylist and Isabella up the stairs, trying to focus on what happened next. One foot in front of the other—that was the way. One small step at a time until she was married and safe. Easy.

'So, what are we doing with your hair, then?' Sheila asked. 'Did you decide? I think all the styles we tried looked good on you, so really it's up to you.'

Thea tried and failed to remember what any of the practice styles had looked like. It had been days ago, before Zeke arrived. And everything before then was rapidly fading into a blur.

'I liked the curls,' Isabella said. 'With the front pinned up and the veil over the ringlets. It looked so dramatic with your dark hair. Don't you think, Thea?'

'Uh, sure. Sounds good.'

'Great!' Sheila said brightly, obviously used to brides almost comatose on their wedding day. Did everyone feel like this? Shell-shocked? Even if they hadn't been through the sort of drama Thea had in the last few days, did every bride have this moment of disbelief? This suspended reality?

Maybe it was just her.

Sheila started fussing with her hair and Thea sat back and let it happen, focussing on the feel of the strands as they were pinned, the warmth of the straighteners as the stylist used them to form ringlets. There was a strange calm in the room as Isabella flicked through a magazine and Sheila got to work, but still Thea had the feeling that she was being watched by her jailer as she was restrained.

Crazy. She'd shake her head to dispel the notion, but Sheila might burn her with the straighteners.

'Thea!'

The door burst open at the same time as Helena's shout came, and Sheila wisely stepped back before Thea spun round.

'What's happened?' Thea asked. Even Isabella closed her magazine for the moment.

'Zeke's leaving!'

Oh. That. 'I know.'

'He's supposed to be the best man!'

'Daniel's going to stand in, I think.'

'Right.' Helena leant back against the door. 'And… you're okay with this?'

'Helena,' Isabella said, putting her magazine aside and getting to her feet. 'Why don't we let your sister finish getting ready? Go and check on the centrepieces and the bouquets. Then you can come and have your hair done next. Okay?'

'Right. Sure.' Helena's brow crinkled as she looked at Thea. 'Unless you need me for…anything?'

Thea gave her a faint smile. 'I'm fine,' she lied. 'You'll come and help me get into my dress later, though, yeah?'

'Of course,' Helena promised as Isabella ushered her out of the door—presumably in case her little sister gave her the chance to reconsider her decision to marry Flynn.

Thea settled back into her chair, feeling comfortably numb and barely noticing that Isabella had left with Helena. It was almost time, and Zeke was almost gone.

There was nothing to reconsider.

Zeke had almost expected the knock at his door. Placing a roughly folded shirt on top of the clothes already in his case, he turned and called, 'Come in.'

His mother looked older, somehow, than she had since his return. Maybe it was just that she'd let the perma-smile drop for a moment.

'You're leaving me again, then?'

'Not just you,' Zeke pointed out, turning back to his wardrobe to retrieve the last of his shirts.

'I don't imagine you were planning on saying goodbye this time, either.'

Isabella moved to sit on the bed, to one side of his suitcase. The one place in the room he couldn't hope to ignore her.

'I wasn't sure you'd miss me any more this time than last,' he said, dropping another shirt into the case. 'What with the wedding to focus on. And I'm sure you have plans for marrying Helena off to someone convenient next.'

Picking up the shirt, Isabella smoothed out the creases as she folded it perfectly. 'I suppose I should be grateful that you're not staying to ruin Thea's wedding.'

Zeke stopped, turned, and stared. 'Thea's wedding? Not Flynn's?' He shook his head. 'You know, for years I never understood why you cared so much more about someone else's children than your own. I guess I thought it must be because they were girls, or because you felt sorry for them after their mother died. I can't believe it took me until now to realise it was because you thought they should have been yours.'

'I don't know what you're talking about,' Isabelle said, her gaze firmly fixed on the shirt. 'I loved all four of you equally. Even Flynn.'

'Ha! *That*, right there, shows me what a lie that is.' Grabbing the shirt from her, he shoved it into the case, making her look up at him. 'Why didn't you just leave, Mum? And marry Thomas? It can't have been for our sakes. We'd have been downright grateful!'

'My place is at my husband's side.' She folded her hands in her lap and met his eyes at last. 'Whatever else, I am his wife first and foremost.'

Zeke stared at her in amazement. 'You're wrong. You're *yourself* first.'

She gave him a sad smile. 'No, Zeke. That's just you.'

Zeke grabbed his case, tugging the zip roughly round it. He'd probably forgotten something, but he could live without it. He had his passport and his wallet. Everything else was replaceable. *Except Thea.*

'Do you even know how you made us feel all those years?' He wasn't coming back again. He could afford to tell her the truth. 'You let our father pit us against each other like it was a sport, and you ran off to another man's family whenever we weren't enough for you. For years I felt like an unwanted accident, every bit as much as Flynn felt like the outsider.'

'That's not…that's not how it was.'

'It's how it felt,' Zeke told her, pressing the truth home. 'And when I left… Thomas says that you missed me. That I broke your heart. But, Mum, how would I even know?'

'Of course I missed you. You're my son.'

'But you never thought to contact me. I wasn't hiding, Mum. I was right there if you needed me.'

'You made your feelings about our family very clear when you left.'

She still sounded so stiff, so unyielding. Zeke shook his head. Maybe her pride would always be too much for her to get over. Maybe his had been too, until now. But he'd already cut all ties with his father—could he really afford to do the same with his mother?

'I'm going now, Mum. And to be honest I'm not going to be coming back in a hurry. Maybe not ever. But if you mean it—about missing me—call me some time.' He lifted his carry-on bag onto his shoulder. 'Goodbye, Mum.'

But she was already looking away.

Outside his room, the corridors were cool and empty. He supposed most people would be in their rooms, getting ready for the wedding. A few were probably already down at the church, making sure they got a good seat for the wedding of the year. If he was quick he could grab one of the taxis milling about and be on his way to the airport before anyone even said 'I do'.

'Dad says that you're leaving.'

Zeke stopped at the top of the stairs at the sound of his brother's voice ahead of him. So close. And now he'd have to deal with all three family members in the space of an hour. At least it was the last time.

'Well, yeah,' he said, turning slowly and leaning his case against the wall. 'Not a lot of reason to stay now.'

'Is that truly the only reason you came back? For Thea?' Flynn asked. 'To try and win her back, I mean.'

'No. I thought…' With a sigh, Zeke jogged down a few steps to meet his brother in the middle of the staircase. 'I thought I'd moved on. From her, from the family, from everything. I came back to prove that to myself, I guess.'

'Did it work?'

Zeke smiled ruefully. 'Not entirely as planned, no. Turns out I was a little more tied in to things here than I thought.'

'And now?'

'Now I'm done,' Zeke said firmly. 'Ask our father.'

'I did.' Hitching his trousers, Flynn sat on the step, right in the middle of the stairs.

After a moment Zeke followed suit. 'I feel about five, sitting on the stairs,' he said.

Flynn laughed. 'We used to—do you remember? When

Mum and Dad had parties, when we were really little, we'd sneak out of bed and sit on the stairs, watching and listening.'

'I remember,' Zeke said. He must have been no more than four or five then. Had he known, or sensed, even then that he and Flynn were different? Or rather that their father believed they were?

'Dad told me your terms for selling This Minute to Morrison-Ashton.'

Zeke glanced up at his brother. 'All of them?'

Flynn ticked them off on his fingers. 'No role for you, Director of Digital Media for Thea, and...' Flynn caught Zeke's gaze and held it. 'CEO for me.'

'That's right.' Zeke dipped his head to avoid his brother's eyes.

'It was yours, you know,' Flynn said. 'I always knew that in the end Dad would give it to you. You're Ashton blood, after all.'

'I don't want it,' Zeke said. 'And you deserve it.'

'I'll do a better job at it, too.'

Zeke laughed. 'You will. I want to build things, then move on. You want to make things run smoothly. You're the best choice for it.'

'Was that the only reason?'

Zeke stared out over the hallway of the villa, all decked out in greenery and white flowers, with satin ribbons tied in bows to everything that stayed still long enough for the wedding planner to attack. 'No. I wanted to show Dad that his plan hadn't worked.'

'His plan? You mean, the way he always pitted us against each other?'

'Yeah. I wanted him to know that despite everything, all his best efforts, you were still my brother. Blood or not.'

Flynn stretched his legs out down the stairs and leant

back on his elbows. 'You know, that would sound a whole lot more sincere and meaningful if you hadn't slept with my fiancée last night.'

Zeke winced. 'Yeah, I guess so. Look, I'm...' He trailed off. He wasn't sorry—not really. He hadn't done it to hurt his brother, but he couldn't regret having one more night with Thea. 'That wasn't about you. It was about Thea and I saying goodbye to each other.'

'That's not what you wanted it to be, though, is it?'

'Maybe not.' Zeke shrugged. 'But it's the way it is. She wants a different life to the one I'm offering. And I need to live my life away from the bitterness this family brings out in me.'

'She told you that, huh?'

'Yeah.'

'So I guess I have her to thank for my promotion, really?'

'Hey! I played my part, too.'

'Let's just agree to call it quits, then, yeah?'

'Sounds like a plan.' Although Zeke had to think that all Flynn had got out of that deal was a company. He'd got to sleep with Thea. Clearly he was winning.

Except after today Flynn would get to sleep with Thea whenever he wanted. And Zeke would be alone.

Maybe Flynn was winning after all, even if he *did* have to deal with their parents and Morrison-Ashton for the rest of time.

'But, Zeke, after today... She's off-limits, yeah?'

'I know.' Zeke grabbed hold of the banister and pulled himself up. 'It's not going to be a problem. As soon as I'm packed I'll grab a cab to the airport and leave you guys to get on with your happy-ever-after.'

'You're not coming back?' Flynn asked.

Zeke shook his head. 'Not for a good while, at least. I

need to…I need to find something else to make my life about, you know?'

'Not really,' Flynn said with a half-smile. 'I've spent my whole life trying to get in to this family, while you've spent it trying to get out.'

'I guess so.' Zeke wondered how it would feel to finally get the one thing you'd always wanted. Maybe he'd never know. 'Something you and Thea have in common.'

Flynn tilted his head as he stared up at him. 'You really love her, don't you?'

Zeke shrugged, and stepped past his brother to climb the stairs to retrieve his suitcase. 'Love doesn't matter now.'

CHAPTER FOURTEEN

'WOW,' HELENA SAID as Thea stepped out from behind the
screen. 'Maybe you should just walk down the aisle like
that. I'm sure Flynn wouldn't complain. Or any of the
male guests.'

Thea pulled a face at her sister in the mirror. She wasn't
even sure she looked like herself. From the ringlets and
veil, to the excess layers of make-up Sheila had assured
her were necessary to 'last through the day'—despite the
fact the wedding was at four in the afternoon—she looked
like someone else. A bride, she supposed.

She let her gaze drop lower in the mirror, just long
enough to take in the white satin basque that pushed her
breasts up into realms they'd never seen before and the
sheer white stockings that clipped onto the suspenders
dangling from the basque. She looked like a stripper bride.
She hoped Flynn would appreciate it.

Zeke would have.

Not thinking about that.

'Help me into the dress?' Thea said, turning away from
the mirror. 'We're late already, and I think the wedding
planner is about to have a heart attack. She's been calling from the church every five minutes to check where
we are.'

Helena reached up to take the heavy ivory silk concoction from its hanger, then paused, biting her lip as she looked back at Thea.

'Don't, Helena,' Thea said, forestalling whatever objection her sister was about to raise. 'Just pass me the dress, yeah?'

Helena unhooked the dress and held it up for Thea to step into. Then, as Thea wriggled it over her hips, pulling it up over the basque, Helena said, 'Are you sure about this? I mean, really, *really* sure?'

Thea sighed. 'Trust me, Helena. You are not the only person to ask me that today. But I've made my decision. I'm marrying Flynn.'

'I'm glad to hear it.'

Thea spun around at the words, to see Flynn leaning against the doorframe.

'What are you *doing here*?' The last couple of words came out as a shriek, but Thea didn't care.

'I need to tell you something,' Flynn said, perfectly reasonably. 'It's important.'

'Not *now*!'

'You look beautiful, by the way,' Flynn added, as if that meant anything. The groom wasn't allowed to see the bride in her wedding dress before the wedding! It was terrible, *terrible* luck!

'Flynn, why don't you tell her what you came to tell her so she can stop freaking out?' Helena suggested. 'Plus, you should be down at the church already.'

Flynn nodded his agreement. 'Zeke has agreed to sell This Minute to Morrison-Ashton.'

Thea stopped trying to cover up her dress with her arms and stared at him. 'Seriously? *Why*?'

'Probably because someone convinced him he had to leave everything here behind and find his own path in life.'

'Ah,' Helena said, eyes wide. 'Thea, what—?'

'It doesn't matter.' Thea cut her off. 'Does that mean he's not taking the director job?'

'No. He insisted that Dad give that to you.'

Thea started to shake. Just a tremor in her hands and arms to start with, but she could feel it spreading.

'And he's made Dad agree to step down within the next year and pass the company to me,' Flynn finished. Even he looked a little shell shocked at that bit.

Thea dropped into the nearest chair as the tremors hit her knees. 'Why? Why would he do that?'

But she already knew. He'd given in. He'd given his father exactly what he wanted so he could walk away clear and free. Just as she'd told him he'd never be able to do.

'I think he wanted to make things right,' Flynn said, and Thea felt the first tear hit her cheek.

Zeke was free of them all at last. Even her. And she was being left behind again, still trying to prove she was good enough to belong. After today she'd be tied in for ever, never able to walk away.

Was she *jealous*?

'Thea? Are you okay?' Helena asked.

'No!' Thea sobbed, the word a violent burst of sound. 'I'm a mess. I'm a mistake.'

'That's not true,' Helena said soothingly, and Thea could see her giving Flynn looks of wide-eyed concern. 'What would make you think that?'

Thea gave a watery chuckle. 'Oh, I don't know. Maybe sleeping with the best man the night before my wedding? Perhaps having to have an intervention with my almost-mother-in-law about how it was better to have an affair than marry an inappropriate guy?'

Flynn swore at that, Thea was pleased to note.

'Or maybe sending away the guy I love so I can marry the guy I'm supposed to? And now, on top of everything else, Flynn's seen me in my wedding dress. That's not just like pearls! Everyone knows that's *absolute* bad luck! It's against all the rules!'

With another glance back at Flynn—who, Thea was frustrated to note, was still standing perfectly calmly in the doorway, with just a slight look of discomfort on his face—Helena knelt down beside her.

'Thea. I don't think this is about rules any more.'

'No. It's about me messing up again. I was so close to being happy here! And now I'm making a mess of everything.'

Helena shook her head. 'No, you're not. And today's not about family, or business, or any of the other things you seem to think this wedding should be about.'

Thea looked up at her sister. 'Then what *is* it about?'

'It's about love,' Helena said. 'It's about trusting your heart to know the right thing to do. And, since you're sitting here sobbing in a designer wedding dress, I think your heart is trying to tell you something.'

It couldn't, Thea wanted to say, because it had stopped. Her heart had stopped still in her chest the moment Zeke had walked out of the library that morning, so it couldn't tell her anything.

But her head could. And it was screaming at her right now that she was an idiot. She'd spent so long trying to find her place in the world, trying to force her way into a role that had never been right for her, she'd ignored the one place she truly belonged all along.

She looked up at Flynn, still so calm and serene and perfect—but not perfect for her.

'Go,' he said, a faint smile playing on his lips. 'You might still catch him.'

'But…but what about the wedding? Everyone's here, and our parents are waiting, and—'

'We'll take care of it,' Helena promised, glancing over at Flynn.

Was there something in that look? Had Isabella been right? Thea couldn't be sure.

'Won't we?'

'We will,' Flynn agreed. 'All you have to do now is run.'

Somewhere in the villa a door slammed, and Thea knew it had to be Zeke, leaving her again. But this time she was going with him.

Shoving the heavy wedding dress back down over her hips, Thea stepped out of it and dashed for the door, pausing only for a second to kiss Flynn lightly on the cheek. 'Thanks,' she said.

And then she ran.

Zeke shut the front door to the villa behind him and walked out into the late-afternoon Tuscan sun. Everyone must have already headed down to the little chapel at the bottom of the hill, ready for the wedding. His talk with Flynn had delayed him, and now there were no taxis hanging around. He might be able to find one down at the church, but he didn't want to get that close to the main event. Not with Thea due to make her grand entrance any time now. The wedding planner's schedule had her down there already, he remembered, unless they were running late.

No, he'd call for a cab and sit out here in the sunshine while he waited. One last glimpse of his old life before he started his new one.

Phone call made, he settled onto the terrace, sitting on the edge of the warm stone steps rather than the swing seat round at the side. Too many memories. Besides, he wouldn't see the cab arrive.

He heard a car in the distance and stood, hefting his carry-on bag onto his shoulder and tugging up the pull-along handle of his case. No car appeared, though, and he started to think it must have been another guest heading for the chapel. But he made his way down the driveway anyway, just in case.

'Zeke!'

Behind him the door to the villa flew open, and by the time he could turn Thea was halfway down the stairs and racing down the drive towards him.

He blinked in disbelief as she got closer, sunlight glowing behind her, making the white of her outfit shine.

White. But not her wedding dress.

'Isn't this where I came in?' he asked, waving a hand towards her to indicate the rather skimpy lingerie that was doing wonderful things for her heaving cleavage as she tried to get her breath back.

'Don't,' she said, scowling.

'Don't what?' Zeke asked. 'You're the one chasing me in your underwear. Five more minutes and my cab would have been here and I'd have been out of your life, just as you wanted.'

'Don't joke. Don't mock. I need you to…' She took a deep breath. 'I need you to stop being…you know…*you* for a moment. Because I need to tell you something.'

'What?' Zeke dropped his bag to the ground again. Apparently this was going to take a while.

'I don't want you out of my life.'

Zeke's breath caught in his chest—until he realised what she was *actually* saying. 'Thea, I can't. I can't just stick around and be Uncle Zeke for Christmas and birthdays. You were right; I need a fresh start. A clean break. Besides…' *I can't watch you live happily ever after with my brother when I'm totally in love with you myself.*

But Thea was shaking her head. 'That's not what I mean.'

'Then *what*, Thea?' Zeke asked, exasperated. He'd so

nearly been done. So nearly broken free for good. And here he was, having this ridiculous conversation with Thea in her underwear, when she was supposed to be getting married *right now*.

Unless…

'I've spent all day listening to people tell me what I should do. What's best for me. Where my place is. And I'm done. You were right—but don't let it go to your head. I need to make my own decisions. So I'm making one right now. I'm choosing my home, my place in the world. And it's the only choice that's going to matter ever again.'

She stepped closer, and Zeke's hands itched to take hold of her, to pull her close. But this was her decision, and she had to make it all on her own. And he had to let her.

'I'm choosing you,' she whispered, so close that he could feel the words against his lips. 'For better or worse, for mistake or for happily-ever-after, for ever and ever.'

Zeke stared into her soft blue eyes and saw no doubt hiding there. No uncertainty, no fear. She meant this.

'You're sure,' he said, but it wasn't a question. He knew.

'I'm certain. I love you. More than anything.'

Thea's hands wrapped around him to run up his back, and the feel of her through his shirt made him warmer.

'I should have known it sooner. *You're* my place. *You're* where I belong.'

'I can't stay here, Thea,' he said. 'Maybe we can come back, but I need some time away. I'm done obsessing about the past. It's time to start my own life.'

'I know.' Thea smiled. 'I'm the one who told you that, remember?'

'I remember.' Unable to resist any longer, Zeke dipped his head and kissed her, long and sweet and perfect. 'I love you. I thought when I came back that I was looking for the girl I'd known—the one I loved as a boy. But I couldn't have imagined the woman you'd become, Thea. Or how much more I'd love you now.'

Thea buried her laugh in his chest. 'I'm the same. I thought it would kill me, saying goodbye to you last time. But the thought of living the rest of my life without you…' She shook her head and reached up to kiss him again.

'Unacceptable.' Zeke finished the thought for her. And then he asked the question that had echoed through his mind for eight long years, hoping he'd get a different answer this time. 'Will you come with me?'

Thea smiled up at him and said, 'Always.'

And Zeke knew, at last, that it didn't matter where they went, or who led and who followed. They'd always be together, and that was all he needed.

* * * * *

Lorenzo's eyes were very dark. Beautiful.

He reached over and wound one of her curls round the end of his finger.

Oh, help. That sensual awareness of him over dinner had just gone up several notches. It would be so easy to tip her head back and invite him to kiss her…but that would be such a stupid thing to do.

Indigo was about to take a step backwards. Just to be safe. But then Lorenzo leaned closer and brushed his mouth against hers.

His kiss was sweet and almost shy at first, a gentle brush of his mouth against hers that made every single one of her nerve-ends tingle. And then he did it again. And again, teasing her and coaxing her into sliding her hands into his hair and letting him deepen the kiss.

Indigo had had her fair share of kisses in the past, but nothing like this.

CROWN PRINCE, PREGNANT BRIDE

BY
KATE HARDY

Published in Great Britain 2014
by Mills & Boon, an imprint of Harlequin (UK) Limited,
Eton House, 18-24 Paradise Road, Richmond, Surrey, TW9 1SR

© 2014 Pamela Brooks

ISBN: 978-0-263-91308-8

23-0814

Harlequin (UK) Limited's policy is to use papers that are natural, renewable and recyclable products and made from wood grown in sustainable forests. The logging and manufacturing processes conform to the legal environmental regulations of the country of origin.

Printed and bound in Spain
by Blackprint CPI, Barcelona

Kate Hardy lives in Norwich, in the east of England, with her husband, two young children, one bouncy spaniel, and too many books to count! When she's not busy writing romance or researching local history she helps out at her children's schools. She also loves cooking—spot the recipes sneaked into her books! (They're also on her website, along with extracts and stories behind the books.) Writing for Mills & Boon has been a dream come true for Kate—something she wanted to do ever since she was twelve. She also writes for Medical™ romance.

Kate's always delighted to hear from readers, so do drop in to her website at www.katehardy.com.

With special thanks to Mike Scogings for sharing
his expertise on stained glass, and to C.C. Coburn
for the lightbulb about the mermaid.

CHAPTER ONE

She wasn't supposed to be there.

OK, Lorenzo knew that tourists were important. Without the income they brought when they visited the house and gardens of Edensfield Hall, his old school friend Gus would never have been able to keep his family's ancient estate going. Even keeping the roof of the house in good repair ate up huge chunks of the annual budget, let alone anything else.

But there were set times when the estate was open to the public. Right now wasn't one of them; the house and gardens were supposed to be completely private. Yet the woman in the shapeless black trousers and tunic top was brazenly walking through the grounds with a camera slung round her neck, stopping every so often to take a picture of something that had caught her eye. At that precise moment she was photographing the lake.

Strictly speaking, this was none of his business and he should just let it go.

But then the woman turned round, saw him staring at her, and snapped his photograph.

Enough was enough. He'd insist that she delete the file— or, if the camera was an old-fashioned one, hand over the film. He was damned if he was going to let a complete stranger make money out of photographing him in the grounds of Edensfield, on what was supposed to be private time. A couple of weeks to get his head together and prepare himself for the coronation.

Lorenzo walked straight over to her. 'Excuse me. You just took my photograph,' he said, not smiling.

'Yes.'

At least she wasn't denying it. That would make things easier. 'Would you mind deleting the file from your camera?'

She looked surprised. 'What's the problem?'

As *if* she didn't know. Lorenzo Torelli—strictly speaking, His Royal Highness Prince Lorenzo Torelli of the principality of Melvante, on the border between Italy and France—was about to inherit the throne and start governing the kingdom next month, when his grandfather planned to abdicate. There had been plenty of stories about it in all the big European papers, all illustrated with his photograph, so no way could she claim she didn't know who he was. 'Your camera, please,' he said, holding his hand out.

'Afraid not,' she said coolly. 'I don't let people touch the tools of my trade.'

That surprised him. 'You're actually admitting you're a paparazzo?'

She scoffed. 'Of course I'm not. Why would the paparazzi want to take pictures of you?'

She had to be kidding. Did she *really* not know who he was? Did she live in some kind of bubble and avoid the news?

'I don't like my photograph being taken,' he said carefully. 'Besides, the estate isn't open to the public until this afternoon. If you'll kindly delete the file—and show me that you've deleted it—then I'll be happy to help you find your way safely out of the grounds until the staff are ready to welcome visitors.'

She looked at him and rolled her eyes. 'I'm not doing any harm.'

Lorenzo was used to people doing what he asked. The fact that she was being so stubborn about this when she was so clearly in the wrong annoyed him, and it was an effort for him to remain polite. Though he let his tone cool by twenty degrees. 'Madam, I'm afraid the house and grounds simply aren't open to visitors until this afternoon. Which means that right now you're trespassing.'

'Am I, now?' Those sharp blue eyes were filled with insolence.

'The file, please?' he prompted.

She rolled her eyes, took the camera strap from round her neck, changed the camera settings and showed the screen to him so that he could first of all see the photograph she'd taken, and then see her press the button to delete the file from her camera's storage card. 'OK. One deleted picture. Happy, now?'

'Yes. Thank you.'

'Right.' She inclined her head. 'Little tip from me: try smiling in future, sweetie. Because you catch an awful lot more flies with honey than you do with vinegar.'

And then she simply walked away.

Leaving Lorenzo feeling as if he was the one in the wrong.

The man was probably one of Gus's friends; he looked as if he was about the same age as Lottie's elder brother. And maybe he'd meant to be helpful; he'd clearly been trying to protect the family's privacy. Indigo knew she should probably have explained to him that she was a family friend who happened to be working on the house's restoration, not a trespassing tourist. Then again, it was none of his business what she was doing there, and his stick-in-the-mud attitude had annoyed her—especially when he'd accused her of being a paparazzo.

She'd only taken his photograph because she'd seen him striding around the grounds, scowling, and he'd looked like a dark angel. Something she could've used for work. It had been a moment's impulse. An expression on his face that had interested her. Attracted her. Made her wonder what he'd look like if he smiled.

But the way he'd reacted to her taking that photograph, snarling about people taking his photo without permission… Anyone would think he was an A-list celeb on vacation instead of some dull City banker.

What an idiot.

Indigo rolled her eyes again and headed for the house. Right now, work was more important. They were taking the window out of the library today and setting it in the workroom Gus had put aside for her in Edensfield Hall. Indigo had already made a short video for the hall's website to explain what was happening with the window, and she'd promised to write a daily blog with shots of the work in progress so the tourists could feel that they were part of the restoration process. And she didn't mind people coming over and asking her questions while she was working. She loved sharing her passion for stained glass.

And the stranger with the face of a fallen angel—well, he could do whatever he liked.

Lorenzo was still slightly out of sorts from his encounter with the paparazzo-who-claimed-she-wasn't by the time he went downstairs for dinner. When he walked into the drawing room, he was shocked to see her there among the guests. Except this time she wasn't wearing a shapeless black top and trousers: she was wearing a bright scarlet shift dress, shorter than anyone else's in the room. And they were teamed with red shoes that were glossier, strappier and had a higher heel than anyone else's in the room.

Look at me, her outfit screamed.

As if anyone would be able to draw their eyes away from her.

Especially as her hair was no longer pulled back in the severe hairdo of this afternoon; now, it was loose and cascaded over her shoulders in a mass of ebony ringlets. All she needed was a floor-length green velvet and silk dress, and she would've been the perfect model for a Rossetti painting.

Lorenzo was cross with himself for being so shallow; but at the same time the photographer was also one of the most beautiful women he'd ever met. He couldn't help acting on the need to know who she was and what she was doing here.

He just about managed a few polite words with Gus before drawling, 'So who's the girl in the red dress?' and inclining his head over towards the trespasser, as if he wasn't really that interested in the answer.

'Who?' Gus followed his glance and smiled. 'Oh, that's Indigo.'

How could Gus be so cool and calm around her? Lorenzo wondered. The woman made him feel hot under the collar, and he hadn't even spoken to her yet this evening.

'A friend of the family?' Lorenzo guessed.

'She's one of Lottie's best friends from school.'

Which was surprising; Indigo didn't look as if she came from the same kind of titled background that Gus and his sister did.

'Actually, she's here on business, too; she's restoring the stained glass in the library for us,' Gus explained. 'My mother's asked her to work up some ideas for a new stained-glass window, so she's been taking photographs of bits of the estate.'

Which explained why she saw her camera as one of the tools of her trade. Lorenzo felt the colour wash into his face. 'I see.'

'What did you do, Lorenzo?' Gus asked, looking amused.

'I saw her taking photos this afternoon and I thought she was a trespasser. I, um, offered to help her find her way out of the grounds,' Lorenzo admitted.

Gus laughed. 'I bet she gave you a flea in your ear. Our Indi's pretty much a free spirit. And she really doesn't like being ordered about.'

He grimaced. 'I think I'd better go and apologise.'

'Good idea. Otherwise you might be in danger of getting an Indi Special.'

'An Indi Special?' Lorenzo asked, mystified.

'Indi. Short for Indigo, not for independent. Though she's that, too.' Gus raised an eyebrow. 'Let's just say she's an original. I'll let Lottie introduce you.' He caught his sister's eye and beckoned her over. 'Lottie, be a darling and introduce Lorenzo to Indi, will you?'

'Sure. Have you two not met, yet?' Lottie tucked her arm into Lorenzo's and led him over to Indigo to introduce them. 'Indi, this is Lorenzo Torelli, a very old friend of the family.' She smiled. 'Lorenzo, this is Indigo Moran, who's just about the coolest person I know.'

Indigo laughed. 'That's only because you live in a world full of stuffed shirts, Lottie. I'm perfectly normal.'

Lorenzo looked at her and thought, no, you're not in the slightest bit normal—there's something different about you. Something *special*. 'Gus said you were at school with Lottie,' he said.

'Until she escaped at fourteen, lucky thing.' Lottie patted Indigo's arm. 'Indi was brilliant. She drew caricatures of the girls who bullied me and plastered them over the school. It's a bit hard to be mean when everyone's pointing at you and laughing at your picture.'

Indigo shrugged. 'Well, they say the pen is mightier than the sword.'

'Your pen was sharper as well as mightier,' Lottie said feelingly.

Now Lorenzo understood what an 'Indi Special' was. A personal, public and very pointed cartoon. And he had a nasty feeling what she'd make of him, given what she'd said to Lottie about coming from a world full of stuffed shirts.

'Can I be terribly rude and leave you two to introduce yourselves to each other properly?' Lottie asked.

'Of course,' Indigo said.

Her smile took his breath away. And Lorenzo was surprised to find himself feeling like a nervous schoolboy. 'I, um, need to apologise,' he said.

She raised an eyebrow. 'For what?'

'The way I behaved towards you earlier today.'

She shrugged. 'Don't worry about it.'

But he did worry about it. Good manners had been instilled into him virtually from when he was in the pram. He was always polite. And he'd been rude to her. 'I didn't realise you were a friend of the family, too.' He looked at her. 'Though you could have explained.'

'Why? For all I knew, you could've been a trespasser, too.'

'Touché.' He enjoyed the fact that she was back-chatting him. After all the people who agreed with everything he said and metaphorically tugged their forelocks at him, he found her free-spirited attitude refreshing. 'Gus says you're restoring the glass in the library.'

'Yes.'

'Forgive me for saying so, but you don't look like…' He

stopped. 'Actually, no. Just ignore me. I'm digging myself a huge hole here.'

She grinned, and the sparkle in her eyes made his pulse speed up a notch. 'I don't look like a glass restorer, you mean? Or I don't look the type to have been at school with Lottie?'

Both. Ouch. He grimaced. 'Um. Do I have to answer that?'

She looked delighted. 'So, let me see. Which shall we do first? School, I think.' Her voice dropped into the same kind of posh drawl as Lottie's. 'I met her when we were eleven. We were in the same dorm. And unfortunately we shared it with Lolly and Livvy. I suppose we could've been the four musketeers—except obviously I don't have an L in my name.'

'And it sounds as if you wouldn't have wanted to fight on the same side as Lolly and Livvy.'

'Absolutely not.' Her eyes glittered and her accent reverted back to what he guessed was normal for her. 'I don't have any time for spitefulness and bullying.'

'Good.' He paused. 'And I hope you didn't think I was bullying you, this morning.'

'If you'll kindly delete the file,' she mimicked.

He grimaced. How prissy she'd made him sound. 'I did apologise for that.'

'So are you a film star, or something?'

'No.'

'Well, you were acting pretty much like a D-list celeb, trying to be important,' she pointed out.

Should he tell her?

No. Because he didn't want her to lose that irreverence when she talked to him. He didn't think that Indigo Moran would bow and scrape to him; but he didn't want to take that risk. 'Guilty, m'lady,' he said lightly. 'Are you quite sure you're a glass restorer and not a barrister?'

She laughed. And, oh, her mouth was beautiful. He had the maddest urge to pull her into his arms and find out for himself whether her mouth tasted as good as it looked. Which was so not how he usually reacted to women. Lorenzo Torelli was always cool, calm and measured. He acted with his head rather than his heart, as he'd always been brought up to do. If you stuck to rigid formality, you always knew exactly where you were.

What was it about Indigo Moran that made him itch to break all his rules? And it was even crazier, because now absolutely wasn't the time to rebel against his upbringing. Not when he was about to become King of Melvante.

'I'm quite sure I'm a glass restorer. So were you expecting me to be about forty years older than I am, with a beard, John Lennon glasses, a bad haircut and sandals?'

Lorenzo couldn't help laughing. And then he realised that everyone in the room was staring at them.

'Sorry. I'm in the middle of making a fool of myself,' he said. 'Not to mention insulting Ms Moran here at least twice.'

'Call me Indigo,' she corrected quietly, and patted his shoulder. 'And he's making a great job of it,' she cooed.

'I, for one,' Gus's mother said with a chuckle, 'will look forward to seeing the drawing pinned up in the breakfast room.'

Indigo grinned. 'He hasn't earned one. Yet.'

'I'm working on it,' he said, enjoying the banter. How long had it been since he'd been treated with such irreverence?

Though a nasty thought whispered in his head: once he'd been crowned, would anyone ever treat him like this again, as if he was just an ordinary man? Would this be the last time?

'Indigo, may I sit with you at dinner?' he asked.

She spread her hands. 'Do what you like.'

Ironic. That was precisely what he couldn't do, from next month. He had expectations to fulfil. Schedules to meet. A country to run. Doing what he liked simply wasn't on the agenda. He would do what was expected of him. His duty.

CHAPTER TWO

WHEN THEY WERE called to dinner, Lorenzo switched the
place settings so he was seated next to Indigo.

'Nicely finessed, Mr Torelli,' she said as he held her
chair out for her.

Actually, he wasn't a Mr, but he had no intention of
correcting her. 'Thank you,' he said. 'Your name's very
appropriate for a stained-glass restorer.' Not to mention
pretty. And memorable.

'Thank you.' She accepted the compliment gracefully.

'So how long have you been working with glass?'

'Since I was sixteen. I took some evening classes along
with my A levels, and then I went to art college,' she explained.

Very focused for someone in her mid-teens. And hadn't
Lottie said something about Indigo leaving their school
at the age of fourteen? 'So you always knew what you
wanted to do?'

She wrinkled her nose. 'It's a dreadfully pathetic story.'

'Tell me anyway,' he invited. 'It'll make me feel better
when you savage me in one of your cartoons.'

'I was sent away to boarding school at the age of six.'

Lorenzo had been five years older than that when he'd
been sent away, but he remembered the feeling. Leaving
home, the place where you'd grown up and every centi-

metre was familiar, to live among strangers. In his case, it had been in a different country, too. With a child's perception, at the time he'd thought maybe he was being sent away as a punishment—that somehow he'd been to blame for his parents' fatal accident. Now he knew the whole truth, and realised it had been his grandparents' way of giving him some stability and protecting him from the potential fallout if the press had found out what had really happened. But it had still hurt back then to be torn away from his home.

'I hated it,' she said softly.

So had he.

'I cried myself to sleep every night.'

He would've done that, except boys weren't allowed to cry. They were supposed to keep a stiff upper lip. Even if they weren't English.

'The only thing that made school bearable was the chapel,' she said. 'It had these amazing stained-glass windows, and I loved the patterns that the light made on the floor when it shone through. I could just lose myself in that.'

For him, it had been music. The piano in one of the practice rooms in the music department. Where he could close his eyes and pretend he was playing Bach at home in the library. 'It helps if you can find something to get you through the hard times,' he said softly.

'I, um, tended to disappear a bit. One of my teachers found me in the chapel—they'd been looking for me for almost an hour. I thought she'd be angry with me, but she seemed to understand. She bought me some colouring pencils and a pad, and I found that I liked drawing. It made things better.'

He found himself wanting to give Indigo a hug. Not out of pity, but out of empathy. He'd been there, too. 'Why did you decide to work with glass instead of being a satirical cartoonist?' he asked.

'Drawings are *flat*.' She wrinkled her nose. 'But glass… It's the way the colour works with the light. The way it can make you feel.'

Passion sparkled in her dark blue eyes; and Lorenzo suddenly wanted to see her eyes sparkle with passion for something else.

Which was crazy.

He wasn't in the market for a relationship. He had more than enough going on in his life, right now. And, even if he had been thinking about starting a relationship, a glass artist with a penchant for skewering people in satirical cartoons would be very far from the most sensible person he could choose to date.

Besides, for all he knew, she could already be involved with someone. A woman as beautiful as Indigo Moran would have men queuing up to date her.

'You really love your job, don't you?' he asked.

'Of course. Don't you?'

'I guess so,' he prevaricated. He'd never known anything else. He'd always grown up knowing that one day he'd become king. There wasn't an option not to love it. It was his duty. His destiny. No arguments.

'So what do you do?' she asked.

She really wasn't teasing him, then; she actually didn't know who he was. And he wasn't going to make things awkward or embarrass her by telling her. 'Family business,' he said. 'My grandfather's retiring, next month, so I'm taking over running things.' It was true. Just not the whole truth.

'Workaholic, hmm?'

He would be. But that was fine. He'd accepted that a long time ago. 'Yes.' Not wanting her to get too close to the subject, he switched the topic back to her work with glass.

* * *

When he smiled, Lorenzo Torelli was completely different. He wasn't the pompous idiot he'd been in the garden; he was beautiful, Indigo thought.

And she was seriously tempted to ask him to sit for her. He would be the perfect model for the window she was planning.

'If you're really interested in the glass,' she said, 'come and have a look at my temporary workshop after dinner.'

'I'd like that,' he said.

They continued chatting over dinner, and Indigo found her awareness of Lorenzo growing by the second. It wasn't just that she wanted to sketch him and paint him into glass; she also wanted to touch him.

Which was crazy.

Lorenzo Torelli was a total stranger. Although he seemed to be here on his own, for all she knew he could be married. And her radar to warn her that a man was married or totally wrong for her hadn't exactly worked in the past, had it? She'd made the biggest mistake of her life where Nigel was concerned.

Though at the same time she knew it wasn't fair to think that all men were liars and cheats who just abandoned people, like her ex and her father. Her grandfather hadn't been. Gus wasn't. And, from what Lottie had told her, their father had been a total sweetheart and had never even as much as looked at another woman. Though Indigo still found it hard to trust. Which was why she hadn't even flirted since Nigel, much less dated.

'Penny for them?' Lorenzo asked.

No way. She fell back on an old standby. 'When I'm about to start work on a new piece, I tend to be pretty much in another world.'

'There's nothing wrong with being focused on your work.'

Good. She was glad he understood that.

After coffee, he asked, 'Did you mean it about showing me your work?'

'Sure.' She took him through to the library. 'I guess it starts here. We took the window out this afternoon.'

'There's a facsimile of the window on the boards,' he said, sounding surprised.

'People come especially to Edensfield to see the mermaid window. I don't want to disappoint them by hiding everything behind scaffolding,' she explained. 'I went to Venice when they were doing some work on the Bridge of Sighs, and they'd put a facsimile of the bridge on the advertising hoardings. I thought that was a brilliant idea and I've tried to do something like that with my own work, ever since.'

'Good idea,' he said.

'Come and see the mermaid up close. She's gorgeous. Victorian—very much in the style of Burne-Jones, though she isn't actually one of his.'

He smiled. 'I was thinking earlier, if you'd been wearing a green velvet dress, you would look like a PRB model.'

'Thank you for the compliment.' She blushed, looking pleased. 'That's my favourite art movement.'

'Mine, too.' He almost told her that his family had a collection and that Burne-Jones had sketched his great-great-grandmother. But then he'd have to explain who he was, and he wasn't ready to do that yet.

'I'd love the chance to work on some PRB glass.' She gave a wistful smile. 'Maybe one day.' She led him into a room further down the corridor. 'Gus set up this room as my workshop. Obviously we've had to rope off my table for health and safety purposes—I work with dangerous substances—but people can still talk to me and see what I'm doing. I have a camera on my desk and the picture feeds through to that screen over there, so they can see the close-up work in total safety.'

She was so matter-of-fact about it. 'Don't you mind working with an audience?' he asked. 'Doesn't it get in your way?'

'The house is only open for a few hours, four days a week,' she said with a shrug. 'The visitors won't be that much of a distraction.'

The window from the library had already been dismantled into frames; the one containing the mermaid was in the centre of her table.

'I took close-ups of the panel this afternoon so I have a complete photographic record,' she said. 'Next I'm going to take it apart, clean it all and start the repairs.'

'Which is why the camera's one of the tools of your trade.' He understood that now. 'I'm sorry I accused you of being a pap.'

'You've apologised—and nicely—so consider it forgotten.' She looked at him. 'Though if you really want to make it up to me, there is something you could do.'

Quid pro quo. It was a standard part of diplomacy. Though part of Lorenzo was disappointed that she'd asked. He'd thought that Indigo might be different. But maybe everyone had their price, after all. 'Which is?'

'Would you sit for me?'

He blinked. 'Sit for you?'

'So I can draw you.'

He'd already worked that out. 'Why?'

She spread her hands. 'Because you look like an angel.'

Heat spread through him. Was this her way of telling him that she was attracted to him? Did she feel the same weird pull that he did? 'An angel?' He knew he was parroting what she said, but he didn't care if he sounded dim. He needed to find out where this was going.

'Or a medieval prince.'

That was rather closer to home. Though he thought her ignorance about his identity was totally genuine. 'And what would sitting for you involve?' he asked.

'Literally just sitting still while I sketch you. Though modelling is a bit hard on the muscles—having to sit perfectly still and keep the same expression for a minimum of ten minutes is a lot more difficult than most people think. So I'd be happy to compromise with taking photographs and working from them, if that makes it easier for you.'

Which was where this had all started. 'Is that why you took my photograph?'

She nodded. 'You were scowling like a dark angel. You were going to be perfect for Lucifer.'

'Why, thank you, Ms Moran,' he said dryly.

She grinned. 'It's meant as a compliment. Or you could be Gabriel, if you'd rather.'

'Didn't Gabriel have blond hair?'

'In the carol,' she said thoughtfully, 'his wings were drifts of snow, his eyes of flame.'

On impulse, he sang a snatch of the carol.

Her eyes widened. 'I wasn't expecting that. You have a lovely voice, Mr Torelli.'

'Thank you.' He bowed slightly in acknowledgement of the compliment.

'So will you sit for me?'

He was tempted. Seriously tempted. But it was all too complicated. 'Ask me another time,' he said softly. When he'd worked out how to say no while letting her down gently. 'Tell me about your work here. The mermaid's face is damaged, so are you going to replace that bit of the glass with a copy?'

'I could do, but that would be a last resort. I want to keep as much of the original glass as possible.' She grimaced. 'I'd better shut up. I can bore for England on this subject.'

'No, I'm interested. Really.'

'Trust me, you don't want to hear me drone on about the merits of epoxy, silicon and copper foil,' she said dryly.

He smiled. 'OK. Tell me something else. What's the story behind the mermaid?'

She raised an eyebrow. 'Gus hasn't told you?'

'It's not exactly the kind of thing that comes up when you're a schoolboy,' he said, 'and since we left school I guess we've had other things to talk about.'

'Rebuke acknowledged,' she said.

He wrinkled his nose. 'That wasn't a rebuke.'

Maybe not. It hadn't been quite like the way he'd spoken to her in the garden, when he'd been all stuffy and pompous.

'Tell me about the mermaid,' he invited.

He really meant it, she realised in wonder. He actually wanted to hear what she had to say. 'So the story goes, many years ago the Earl was a keen card-player. He won against almost everyone—except one night, when he played against a tall, dark stranger. It turned out that the stranger was the devil, and his price for letting the earl keep the house and the money he'd wagered and lost was marriage to the earl's daughter. The earl agreed, but his daughter wasn't too happy about it and threw herself into the lake. She was transformed into a mermaid and lived happily ever after.'

'I thought mermaids were supposed to live in the sea,' Lorenzo said.

She grinned. 'Tut, Mr Torelli. Hasn't anyone told you that mermaids don't actually exist? Lottie says there's a version of the story that has the mermaid rescued by a handsome prince, but that might be a bit of a mix-up with the Hans Christian Andersen story.'

'I hope not, because if I remember rightly that doesn't have a very happy ending.'

Lorenzo's eyes were very dark. Beautiful. She itched to paint him, to capture that expression. If only he hadn't said no. Or maybe she could paint him from memory.

He reached over and wound one of her curls round the end of his finger. 'I can see you as a mermaid, with this amazing hair floating out behind you,' he said softly.

Oh, help. That sensual awareness of him over dinner had just gone up several notches. It would be so easy to tip her head back and invite him to kiss her...but that would be such a stupid thing to do.

Indigo was about to take a step backwards. Just to be safe. But then Lorenzo leaned closer and brushed his mouth against hers.

His kiss was sweet and almost shy at first, a gentle brush of his mouth against hers that made every single one of her nerve-ends tingle. And then he did it again. And again, teasing her and coaxing her into sliding her hands into his hair and letting him deepen the kiss.

Indigo had had her fair share of kisses in the past, but nothing like this. Even Nigel, the man she'd once believed was the love of her life, hadn't been able to make her feel like this—drowsy and sensual, and as if her knees were going to give way at any second.

When Lorenzo stopped kissing her, she held on to him, not trusting her knees to hold her up. The last thing she wanted to do was fall at his feet and make an idiot of herself.

Though she had a nasty feeling that she'd already done that.

'We really ought to get back to the others,' she said.

'Are you worried that they'll think you lured me here for other reasons than to talk about glass?'

'No.' She could feel the colour seeping into her face. 'Don't be ridiculous. They all know how I am about my work. They probably think I'm boring the pants off you right now.'

He gave her a slow and very insolent smile. 'Interesting choice of phrase, Ms Moran.'

Her face heated even more. Because now she could see herself taking his clothes off. Very, very slowly. And not because she wanted to paint him naked: because she wanted to touch him. Skin to skin. Very, very slowly. Until he was begging her for more.

Oh, for pity's sake. She'd only just been introduced to him. Insta-lust wasn't the way she did things. Why was she reacting to him like this? 'Let's go back,' she said, hoping she didn't sound as flustered as she felt.

'Has Indi been showing you what she's doing with the mermaid?' Gus asked Lorenzo when they rejoined the others in the drawing room.

'Yes.'

'She's brilliant. Maybe you ought to commission her to do you a portrait for the coronation. Glass instead of oils,' Gus suggested.

Indigo frowned. 'Coronation? Whose coronation?'

Gus looked embarrassed. 'Whoops. I think I might have just put my foot in it.'

'It's fine,' Lorenzo said.

Oh, no, it wasn't, Indigo thought. There was a lot more to this than met the eye. Especially as Lorenzo looked shifty, all of a sudden.

They chatted for a few moments more; when they were alone again, Indigo narrowed her eyes at him. 'What's this about a coronation?'

'The King of Melvante is abdicating next month and handing over to his grandson,' Lorenzo said.

She still didn't get it. Why had Gus suggested that Indigo should do Lorenzo's portrait in glass? 'And?' she prompted.

He wrinkled his nose. 'That would be, um, me.'

'You're going to be the King of Melvante?'

He nodded. 'Nonno's already passed on a lot of his duties to me. And he's going to be eighty, next month. I want him to enjoy his old age, not have the burden of the crown.'

'So that's what you meant about the family business. Being king.'

He shrugged. 'Running a country isn't so different from running a business.'

Even so, she was hurt that nobody had told her. Lottie was her closest friend, and she'd known the family for years. Lorenzo obviously thought that she'd tell tales to the media, but surely Lottie's family knew otherwise?

A king-to-be.

No wonder he'd been sensitive about having his photo taken, and no wonder he hadn't wanted to sit for her.

This changed everything.

When he'd kissed her, only minutes before, she'd thought this just might be the start of something. How stupid of her. No way could a king-to-be have a fling with someone like her. OK, so strictly speaking Indigo's father was an earl, so it wasn't so much the noble and commoner thing; but he'd been married to his countess when Indigo was born and not to Indigo's mother. The press would drag that up if they found out she was even vaguely involved with Lorenzo. Plus there was the whole mess of her relationship with Nigel and the way he'd let her down. That would look bad, too. A king couldn't afford to be touched by scandal.

So her common sense needed to kick back in, and fast. Absolutely nothing was going to happen between them now.

It *couldn't*.

'I'll make sure I address you properly in future, Your Highness,' she said coolly. 'It's a pity you didn't bother to tell me before.'

'It wasn't relevant. You're a friend of the family and so am I. Who we are outside Edensfield isn't important.'

'You still could've told me.'

'How? Was I supposed to correct you and tell you that, actually, no I'm not *Mr* Torelli, and it should be "Your Royal Highness Prince Lorenzo" to you?' He grimaced. 'Talk about an arrogant show-off.'

She blew out a breath. 'I guess you have a point. I understand now why you were annoyed with me for taking your photograph.'

'Because I try to protect my privacy—not because I think I'm a celeb or a special snowflake who deserves red carpet treatment,' he said.

Her frown deepened. 'What about your bodyguards? I assume you have them, and they're so discreet that I haven't noticed them yet.'

'I get a little bit more liberty than usual from my security team because I'm staying in the house of a family friend,' he said.

'But you still can't do anything spontaneous or even go for a walk without telling half a dozen people where you're going. Your life must be scheduled out down to the millisecond.'

'Most of the time, yes,' he admitted. 'But I'm officially

on leave at the moment. Taking a bit of time to get my head in the right place, so to speak.'

'Before you're crowned king.'

'Yes. Obviously I'm not entirely neglecting my duties while I'm here—I can do a lot of things through the internet and the phone—but Nonno thought I needed a bit of time out to prepare myself.'

'Your grandfather,' she said, 'sounds very sensible.' Like hers had been. 'But forgive me for being dim. I don't tend to read the society pages, so I really had absolutely no idea who you were.'

'You,' he said, 'are the last person I'd accuse of being dim.'

'You only met me today. I could be an airhead.'

He raised an eyebrow. 'Give me some credit for being able to judge someone's character quickly and accurately.'

'I guess in your position you have to do that all the time.' She paused. 'So how come you're taking over, and not your father?'

'He died in a car crash when I was ten,' Lorenzo said. 'Along with my mother.'

She could see the pain in his eyes, and then he was all urbane and charming again. Behind a mask. Clearly it hurt too much to talk about. She could understand that; there were certain bits of her own past that she didn't talk about.

'I'm sorry,' she said softly. 'That must've been hard for you. And for your grandparents.'

'It was a long time ago, now,' he said. 'You get used to it.'

'Yes, you do.'

'That sounds like experience talking,' he said.

She nodded. 'My grandparents brought me up.' She couldn't quite bring herself to tell him of the circumstances, not wanting him to pity her.

'Something we have in common,' he said.

Not quite. She didn't think that Lorenzo's parents were

like hers, choosing to abandon their child. In his case, his parents had been taken from him in an accident. In hers, her father had chosen to distance himself before she was born—his only contribution to her life had been to pay for part of her education—and her mother had been more focused on her own love-life than family life. 'Just about the only thing.'

He smiled. 'Sometimes that makes life more interesting.'

And more complicated, she thought. Lorenzo Torelli was gorgeous. The way he'd kissed her earlier had made her bones melt. Which meant she needed to keep a safe distance between them until he left Edensfield for his kingdom. 'I guess I ought to stop monopolising you and let you chat to everyone else. And I have a few things I need to do for work, so I'd better get a move on. Nice to have met you. Good evening,' she said.

He gave her a tiny little smile that very clearly called her a chicken. Guilty as charged, she thought—because he scared her as much as he drew her. She couldn't afford to let him matter to her.

Besides, a man destined to be king would've been taught how to be charming from when he was in the cradle. The attention he'd paid her had been flattery. And she already knew the dark side of flattery—the last time she'd let herself fall for a spiel, it had ended in tears. She'd learned the hard way that relationships let her down, but her work never did.

'Good evening, Indigo,' he said softly, and she fled.

CHAPTER THREE

INDIGO WASN'T IN the breakfast room when Lorenzo came downstairs, the next morning. And when he casually mentioned her name, Gus just smiled. 'She's even more of a workaholic than you are. She'll have been in her workroom since the crack of dawn.'

Lorenzo knew that he ought to be sensible and avoid Indigo. But the attraction from last night hadn't gone away. So he couldn't resist taking a detour to the kitchen, making her a mug of coffee and wandering casually into her workroom. Just to say hello, he told himself. There couldn't be any harm in that. Could there?

Today Indigo was back to wearing shapeless clothes and having her hair pinned back, and she was also wearing a pair of safety goggles. This had to be the most unsexy outfit in the world. And yet Lorenzo was aware of every drop of blood thrumming through his veins when she glanced up from her work and saw him.

'I thought you might like this,' he said, and handed her the mug. 'Milk, no sugar.'

'Thank you.' She pushed the goggles up on top of her head. 'How do you know how I like my coffee?'

'I noticed yesterday at dinner,' he said. He'd been taught from an early age to notice the details. 'Do you need a hand with anything?' It was a stupid question, and he knew it even as the words came out.

'Thank you,' she said, 'but, apart from the fact that my work needs specialist training, I work with acids, flux, a hot soldering iron, sharp blades and glass—all things that could do serious damage to you.'

'I guess so.'

'Even if I didn't have bad intentions towards you—and, just for the record if you happen to be wired and your security team's listening, I don't—there's still the risk of an accident. My insurance company would have a hissy fit at the idea.'

He liked the fact that she'd clearly thought this through. Though it also surprised him that Indigo Moran had such a deeply conventional side, given the dress she'd worn last night. 'And that bothers you? I thought you had a reputation for being a free spirit.'

'Which isn't the same as being reckless and stupid,' she said. 'What do you expect me to do—jump into a lake and pull you in with me?'

He laughed. 'Point taken. No, I don't think you're stupid.' He paused. 'So can I watch you work, today?' he asked.

She looked surprised. 'Are you really interested in glass, are you being polite, or are you just bored and at a bit of a loose end?'

He liked her plain speaking. But either they could spend all day fencing, or he could come clean. Given how little time he had left here, he chose the latter option. 'It's an excuse to spend time with you. And I have a feeling it might be the same for you, too.'

She looked wary. 'I'm not so sure that it's a good idea.'

At least she hadn't denied that she wanted to spend time with him. So he could be just as honest with her. 'I *know* it isn't a good idea,' he said softly.

She said nothing, just looked even warier.

'If I wasn't who I am, would your answer be different?'

'Probably,' she admitted.

'Do you have any idea how refreshing it was yesterday,' he said, 'to have someone backchat me and treat me like a normal person, for once?'

'Poor little rich boy,' she said, folding her arms and giving him a pointed look.

He grinned. 'And you're still doing it. I like you, Indigo. I think you like me. What's the harm in two people getting to know each other?'

'As you pointed out yesterday, you're used to the paparazzi following you. You have a security team looking after you. You're not just a normal person. If anyone wants to get to know you, or you want to get to know someone, then the whole world will know about it.'

'This is a private house,' he said.

'Which is open to the public,' she reminded him.

'Who won't be expecting to see me—they might think, oh, that man sitting by the table over there looks a bit like that Prince Lorenzo guy, but they'll think no more than that.'

'What if they do recognise you?'

'They won't,' he said confidently. 'It's like when that famous violin player busked on the metro in Washington DC a few years ago, playing a Stradivarius. People weren't expecting a famous musician to be busking on the metro with one of the most expensive instruments in the world, so they didn't recognise him and hardly anyone stopped to listen to what he was playing. It's all about context.'

'You,' she said, 'are just used to getting your own way all the time.'

'Not *all* the time.'

'Did you get an A star in persistence lessons at prince school?' she asked.

He laughed. 'There isn't such a thing as prince school. Besides, you know very well I went to the same school as Gus.'

'In a different country, and when you were still very young,' she said thoughtfully.

'Not as young as you were when you went to boarding school—I was eleven.' And how he'd missed his family. Thought it had been good practice for his stiff upper lip. 'I know this is crazy,' he said. 'I just want to spend a bit of time with you. I have a free day, but I know you're working, so maybe I could make myself useful. Kind of multi-tasking.'

She scoffed. 'You're telling me that a man can multi-task?'

'Don't be sexist.' He grinned at her. 'I learned how to multi-task at prince school.'

She laughed, then. 'Says the man who claims that prince school doesn't exist.'

'They're not formal lessons, exactly, but over the years I've been taught about the importance of diplomacy and how to...' He wrinkled his nose. 'I was going to say, how to handle people, but I think you might take that the wrong way.'

Her blush was gratifying. 'Yes. I would.'

'I don't mean manhandle,' he said softly. 'That's not who I am. I'm not expecting you to fall into my arms because I'm about to become the King of Melvante. But I can't stop thinking about you. And I think it's the same for you, too. That kiss, last night...' He paused. 'I don't behave like that. I don't usually act on impulse and I definitely don't do insta-lust. I'm pretty sure you don't, either.'

'No.' Again, she blushed. Telling him that maybe, just maybe, it was different with him.

'It would be sensible if we just stayed out of each other's way. But I can't do that. Something about you…' He blew out a breath. 'OK. I'll shut up and stop distracting you now.'

'Maybe,' she said quietly, 'if you wear goggles, that'll be enough to disguise you. And you need to wear goggles anyway if you're going to be on this side of the rope. I don't want you to get a glass splinter or dust in your eye. And you need gloves, too, if you're going to work with me.' She reached under her table and rummaged around in a box. 'Try these.'

They fitted perfectly. Which was a sign, of sorts, he thought. 'They're fine.'

'OK.' She handed him a pair of protective glasses, and he put them on.

'What do you need me to do?' he asked.

'Help me clean the lead cames. That'd be easy to teach you.'

'I'd like that,' he said. It was so far away from his normal life that it really was like having a rest.

He watched her work, fascinated by how neatly and quickly she worked to remove the stained glass from the leads without damaging the fragile glass or the soft metal. And he noticed how she labelled everything before putting it in a specific place and then photographing it.

'I assume that's to be sure everything goes back in the right place?' he asked.

She nodded. 'Plus I'm documenting everything that I do, so the next time the glass needs work the restorer will know exactly what I've done and how.'

Her work was methodical, neat and efficient. She was good at giving instructions, too; when she showed him how to clean the leads, she gave him an old piece of lead from her box of tricks under her desk so he could practise first, and corrected his technique without making him feel stupid. Lorenzo liked the fact that she was so direct and clear.

And when the house opened to the public, he discovered that Indigo was far from being the socially inept nerd she'd claimed to be. She was seriously good with people; she was patient, charming, and he noticed that she assessed them swiftly so she could work out whether they wanted a quick and simple answer, or if they'd prefer a longer and more detailed explanation.

Lorenzo noticed how patient Indigo was, never once making her questioners feel stupid or a nuisance. If anything, she went out of her way to make them feel appreciated.

Funny, all the formal training he'd had in diplomacy didn't even begin to approach this. Indigo was a natural with people, warm and open, and the rigidity of boarding school clearly hadn't left its mark on her. Lorenzo knew that she could teach him a lot, just by letting him shadow her. And maybe if he could focus on that, on the way that Indigo could help him prepare for his new role, it would stop him thinking of her in a different context. One that would cause too many problems for both of them.

Once the crowds had left, Lorenzo fetched them both some more coffee.

She looked up at him and smiled. 'Thank you—that's really kind of you. Sorry, I'm afraid I've rather ignored you this afternoon.'

'You were busy working and talking to visitors,' he said. 'And I have to say, I'm impressed by how at ease you are with people.'

She looked surprised. 'But you're a prince. You have to talk to people all the time. Aren't you at ease with them?'

'Not in the same way that you are,' he admitted. 'You

have this natural empathy.' And, because he was so used to formality, he had to work at being at ease with people. Which pretty much negated the point.

'I'm surprised they didn't teach you that sort of thing at prince school.'

He rolled his eyes. 'Very funny.'

'I still think you'd make an awesome model for a stained-glass angel,' she said. 'Though I can understand why you don't want to sit for me.'

'It's not that I don't want to. I *can't*. In another life,' he said softly, 'I'd sit for you with pleasure.' And he'd enjoy watching her sketch him, seeing the way she caught the tip of her tongue between her teeth when she was concentrating. And then maybe afterwards…

'But in this life it'd be a PR nightmare,' she said, going straight to the root of the matter. 'The new King of Melvante has to be squeaky clean.'

'Yes.' Until he'd met Indigo, that hadn't been a problem. But Indigo Moran made him want to break every single one of his rules and then some. To stop himself thinking about it, and to distract her from probing his thoughts too deeply, he made an exaggerated squeaking noise. 'Like this.'

She laughed. And, to his relief, everything felt smooth and light and sparkly again.

'I'd better let you get on. You've had enough distractions for today.'

She smiled at him again. 'You can stay if you want to.'

Tempting. So very, very tempting. And he wanted to spend more time with Indigo. He liked this side of her, the fun and the carefree feeling he didn't normally have time for.

But he really needed to let his common sense get back in charge. Preferably right now. He was supposed to be preparing for his new role, not acting on impulse and indulging himself. 'Thanks, but I'll see you later, OK?' And then, hopefully, the next time he saw her he'd be back in sensible mode and he'd be able to treat her as just another acquaintance. He could be charming and witty, but he could keep his emotions totally in check.

And what he needed more than anything else, right now, was a little time at the ancient grand piano in the library.

Now the visitors had gone and the house was back to being fully private, the family dogs had the free run of the place again, so a couple of minutes after Lorenzo had settled at the piano he discovered that Toto, an elderly golden Labrador he'd known since puppyhood, was leaning against his leg. Just like home, except with a bigger dog, he thought with a smile, and reached down to ruffle the dog's fur. And then he lost himself in the music.

Indigo could hear piano music. Which was odd, because she had a very quiet cello concerto playing on her iPod. She reached over and paused the track, and listened again. Definitely a piano, but not something she recognised.

The piece stopped, and there was silence for a moment, before a snatch of something, and then a pause and a few bars of something else, as if someone was trying to decide what to play next.

Curious, Indigo made sure that all her electrical equipment was turned off and her pots of acid all had lids on, and went in search of the music. As she neared the library, the music got louder. She paused in the doorway of the library. Lorenzo was sitting at the piano; from her vantage point, she could see that his eyes were closed as he was playing.

In another life, she thought, this could've been his career. Though he didn't have the luxury of choice.

When he'd finished, she clapped softly, and Lorenzo opened his eyes and stared at her in surprise.

'What are you doing here?' he asked.

'I heard the music,' she said simply.

He grimaced. 'Sorry. I didn't mean to disturb you.'

'I was going to have a break anyway.' She paused. 'You're very good.'

'Thank you.'

Lorenzo accepted the compliment gracefully, even a little bit shyly. Indigo had the strongest feeling that this was a part of himself that he normally kept hidden. She couldn't resist asking, 'Would you play some more for me?'

'I...' He gave her another of those shy smiles that made her heart contract. 'Sure, if you want. Take a seat.'

She heeled off her shoes and curled up on a corner of the battered leather chesterfield sofa. The Labrador came over and put a paw on one of the cushions, clearly intending to lever himself up next to her.

'Toto, you bad hound, you know you're not allowed on the furniture,' she scolded him.

The dog gave her a mournful look and she sighed and slid off the chesterfield onto the floor. 'All right, then, I'll come down and sit with you.'

He wagged his tail, licked her face and then sprawled over her.

'And you're much too big to be a lapdog,' she said, but she rubbed the dog's tummy anyway and he gave her a look of absolute bliss.

'You like dogs?' Lorenzo asked. Then he rolled his eyes. 'That was a stupid question, because the answer's obvious.'

'I love them. But my work takes me all over the place and not everyone's comfortable with dogs, so I can't have one of my own. I come and borrow Lottie and Gus's every so often.' She paused. 'I see you didn't mind Toto leaning against your leg while you were playing. I take it you like dogs, too?'

He nodded. 'I have dogs at home, but mine are a little smaller than Toto.'

She grinned. 'Prince Lorenzo, please don't tell me you have a Chihuahua.'

'And carry it around with me in a basket?' He laughed. 'No. We have various spaniels. And although they're nearly as old as Toto, they're not quite as well behaved. They sneak up onto the furniture as soon as you've looked away. Especially Caesar. He's my shadow when I'm at home.'

And she could tell that he didn't really mind. Which made him seem so much more human. A king who didn't necessarily expect all his subjects to obey him and would indulge an elderly and much-loved dog.

'What do you want me to play?' he asked.

'Anything you like,' she said, and listened intently as he ran through several pieces.

'That was fabulous,' she said when he'd finished. 'When you said last night that it helped to get through tough times if you had something... It was music for you, wasn't it?'

He nodded, and she had to stop herself from walking over to the piano and hugging him. She didn't want him to think she was pitying him; but she could understand how a lonely little boy, far from his home and his family, needed to take refuge in something. She'd been there herself. 'Did you ever think about being a musician?'

He shrugged. 'It wasn't exactly an option. My job's been mapped out for me pretty much since I was born.'

She frowned. 'Doesn't that make you feel trapped?'

'It's my duty and I'm not going to let anyone down.'

She noticed that he hadn't actually answered the question. Which told her far more than if he'd tried to bluff his way out of it. She knew she'd feel trapped, in his shoes.

Stuck in a formal, rigid culture where you were expected to know every single rule off by heart and abide by them all. Stifling. She'd hate it even more than she'd hated the rigidity of boarding school.

'If you could do whatever you wanted, what would you do?' she asked softly.

'Anything I wanted?' His eyes were very, very dark.

'Uh-huh.'

'Right here and right now?'

She nodded.

'I'd do this.' He got up from the piano stool, walked over to her, drew her to her feet, wrapped her in his arms and kissed her.

Just like last night. Except it was more intense because, this time, she knew how perfectly his mouth fitted against hers. How his touch made her pulse beat faster. How *right* it felt.

Oh, help.

She really didn't want Lorenzo to know how much he affected her. After the way Nigel had betrayed her trust and abandoned her, she didn't want to be that vulnerable ever again. Hopefully being a little sarcastic with him would defuse the situation and make her feel more in control again.

She fanned herself with one hand. 'You're not too shabby at this, Your Royal Highness,' she drawled. 'Did they teach you this at prince school, too?'

He narrowed his eyes at her. 'Indigo, will you please shut up about prince school?'

But her idea of a defence mechanism turned out to be a total failure, because then he kissed her again, tiny nibbling kisses that inflamed her senses and left her breathless. And she ended up kissing him right back.

This had to stop. Now. 'Had a lot of practice, have we?'

It didn't seem to faze him in the slightest. 'That'd be

telling, and a prince should never kiss and tell,' he shot back. 'You talk way too much, Indigo Moran.' He caught her lower lip between his, sending her pulse skyrocketing again. 'But, since you clearly want to talk—let's talk about last night,' he said. 'At dinner. That dress.'

She frowned. 'What was wrong with my dress?'

'Nothing.' He sighed. 'Apart from the fact that it made me want to pick you up, haul you over my shoulder in a fireman's lift, and carry you to my bed.'

Which put another set of pictures in her head.

If he carried on like this, she was going to do something seriously stupid.

'Droit de seigneur?' she asked.

'No.' He kissed her again. 'For the record, I don't believe in forcing anyone to do anything they don't want to do. Being a troglodyte and carrying you off to my bed is—' he licked his lower lip '—well, a fantasy. Which I would only do if you liked the idea, too.'

Now he'd said it like that, she could really picture it. And what would come after, too...

She shivered.

'What's the matter, Indigo?' he asked softly.

'You've just made it hard for me to breathe,' she admitted.

'Good. Now you know how that dress made me feel last night. And your shoes. I noticed just how long your legs are. And if you'd had any idea how much I wanted to touch you...' He traced the outline of her mouth with the tip of his forefinger. It made her tingle all over and she couldn't help parting her lips in response.

And then he actually grinned.

Oh, *really*? she thought. He honestly believed he had more self-control than she did? Well, two could play at that. She held his gaze, then sucked the tip of his finger into her mouth.

Instantly his pupils dilated and there was a slash of colour in his cheeks.

'Touché,' he whispered. 'Indigo, we need to stop this. Now.' He dragged in a breath. 'It wouldn't be fair or honourable of me to lead you on. I'm going back to Melvante soon. My life's going to change out of all recognition.'

Of course it was.

He looked tortured. 'I can't offer you a future.'

'I know. And even if you could, I'd be the worst person you could ask,' she said. What with the scandal surrounding her birth, and the fact that she'd been naive enough to trust Nigel and not work out for herself that he was already married, she was totally unsuitable even to be a king's mistress. 'I take it you need to find yourself a princess.' Which would put her totally out of the running. Not that she wanted the formal, rigid life of a royal family.

He rolled his eyes. 'I probably do have to choose a bride within the next six months, yes. And she probably has to be from a noble family. Though, just for the record, I don't care if your parents aren't aristocrats. It's how you treat other people that matters to me, not how many coronets are in your family tree.'

'Actually, my father's an earl.' He looked surprised, and honesty made Indigo add, 'The problem is, though, he was still married to his countess when he had a fling with my mother and she fell pregnant with me.'

'So that's why you ended up at the same school as Lottie?' he asked.

'It was my father's idea of providing for me,' she said dryly.

'Money instead of attention?'

He'd hit the nail right on the head. 'My father and I are never quite sure if we ought to acknowledge each other or not,' she said. 'I don't want to hurt his family by claiming him as kin—I mean, I'm the child of an affair, and it'd be horrible to rub their noses in that. It wasn't their fault that he behaved badly. So it's easier…' She sighed. 'Well, for me not to acknowledge him and for him to pretend that I don't really exist.'

'But that hurts you.'

Did it still show? Or was Lorenzo just particularly perceptive? She shrugged. 'I'm lucky: my grandparents loved me. I was never deprived of love, if that's what you're thinking.'

'But your grandparents let you go to boarding school at such a young age?'

'They didn't exactly have a lot of choice. My grandmother wasn't very well at the time—they had enough on their plates without having to look after a small child.'

He frowned. 'What about your mother? Why didn't she look after you?'

She blew out a breath. 'You might as well know the worst. When it was obvious that the earl wasn't going to leave his wife for my mother, she left me with her parents and bolted.' She looked away. 'With someone else's husband.'

Lorenzo knew first-hand what kind of damage affairs could cause. Collateral damage, too. His own mother's affair had blown his whole world apart. If she'd been able to cope with life in the royal family, then she wouldn't have had the affair—and his father wouldn't have reacted by driving their car into a wall. And just maybe he would've grown up with both his parents, in a happy family, and it would've been another thirty years before he'd had to think about becoming king.

Or maybe it would've been a different kind of unhappy childhood, with his parents always arguing in private and pretending everything was just fine and dandy where the public was concerned.

Not that he was going to tell Indigo about that. He didn't talk about the scars on his heart to anyone. Ever. 'That's tough on you.'

She shrugged. 'As I said, my grandparents loved me.'

The implication was clear: her mother hadn't. 'Do you see your mother now?'

Indigo shook her head. 'She ended up in a yachting accident with Married Man Number Four. She drowned. All I have of my mother are photographs and some very fleeting memories.'

It was the same for Lorenzo. Photographs and fleeting memories. Except nobody knew the true circumstances of his parents' accident. Nobody except his grandfather and their legal adviser. They wouldn't have told him the truth, except some papers had been misfiled and he'd come across them when he was eighteen and discovered the truth for himself. He'd gone off the rails for a week, shocked to the core that his father could've done something so terrible. The paparazzi had taken a picture of him looking haggard and with the worst hangover in the history of the universe; and then his grandfather had hauled him back to the palace, had a very honest and frank discussion with him, and Lorenzo had reassumed his stiff upper lip.

'That's tough on you,' he said again.

'It was tougher,' she said, 'proving to everyone that I wasn't like my mother.'

Yeah. He knew all about that, too—having to convince his grandfather that he wasn't like his father.

'Especially when I wanted to leave boarding school. But I hated the rigidity of the place, and the sense of entitlement that so many of the girls had.'

'What did you do?' he asked.

'Gave my father a business plan,' she said. 'If I went to a normal state school at the age of fourteen, he'd save four years of fees—which would be enough to buy my grandparents' cottage. If he let them live there rent-free for the rest of their lives, then he'd get his investment back when he sold the cottage. Win-win. He got money, and I got freedom.'

Lorenzo's heart bled for her. How could her father have been so cold-blooded that she had to offer him a business plan as a way out of a school that she hated? 'And he agreed to it?'

'Yes.'

For a second, he saw pain in her eyes.

And then she grinned. 'I told him the alternative was that I'd behave so badly, I'd get thrown out of every boarding school in England. But he knew I was right. And I proved to my grandparents that I wasn't like my mother. I wasn't running away, I was making the right choice. I got a weekend job in the local supermarket as soon as I was old enough, and a bar job to keep me going through art college until I graduated.'

'And you got a First?' he asked.

She inclined her head. 'I made my grandparents proud of me before they died.'

Though her father had obviously not acknowledged her achievements. 'Indi. I'm not pitying you, but right now I want to hug you,' he said.

'It's OK. I'm a big girl. I learned to deal with it years ago.' She shrugged. 'It's the earl's loss, not mine.'

And what an idiot the man was, not realising what a treasure he had in Indigo.

Lorenzo stole another kiss. 'Indigo. Will you please tell me to stop this?'

She kissed him back. 'Colour me bad, Your Royal Highness, but what's the alternative to stopping?'

His breath hitched. 'I think you've just spiked my blood pressure. Are you suggesting…?'

'We both know where we stand. You're about to take over from your grandfather and become king. You don't have time for a relationship. I have an empire to build with my business—I don't have time for a relationship, either.' She paused. This was crazy. But, at the same time, it was safe, because what she was proposing involved a time limit. Which meant she wouldn't get involved with him. 'I'm here until the end of the month. You said you don't have to go back to Melvante for a little while. Are you staying here until you go back?'

'Yes.'

'So we're in a private house. Among friends who would never rat us out to the press. Lottie's my oldest friend, and I'm guessing that Gus is one of your oldest friends, too.'

'He is. And I trust him totally.' He lifted her hand to his face and pressed his lips against her wrist, feeling the way her pulse beat hard against his mouth. Indigo Moran was everything he couldn't have. A breath of fresh air. Vibrant and lively. Totally unsuitable. And he knew without having to ask that she'd hate his world just as much as his mother had. This was never going to work.

Yet, at the same time, neither of them could deny the attraction between them.

'So you're suggesting we have a fling,' he said slowly.

'A *mad* fling,' she corrected. 'Because we both know that, although we're attracted to each other, in the real world we're not remotely suitable for each other. So we go into this with our eyes open. And we both walk away at the end of it. Intact.'

Which told him someone had walked away from her before, and left her very far from intact. 'It feels a bit—well, dishonourable. To offer you just a fling.' Especially now he knew about her background. She was the child of a fling, and she'd paid the price by losing a whole generation of her family.

'Lorenzo, I'm not suitable marriage material for you, so you're not in a position to offer me anything else,' she pointed out. 'Which means either we have to spend the next couple of weeks having a lot of cold showers and trying to avoid each other, or...' Her breath caught. 'Just for the record, I don't normally proposition men.'

He stole another kiss. 'I already know that. Despite that dress you were wearing last night, you're not the type. And I'm very flattered that you should proposition me.'

Her eyes narrowed. 'But you're going to say no.'

'My head's telling me that this is a bad idea,' he said. 'But...' He blew out a breath. 'I don't do this sort of thing, either. I'm just a boring businessman.'

'You're a king in waiting,' she corrected.

'Same difference. Running a country's the same as running a business. It's just a slightly different scale.' He shrugged. 'Indigo, I always act with my head. I think things through and I look at all the options. I never do anything on impulse.' Not since that week of getting seriously drunk—and he hadn't touched brandy ever again after that. 'Yet I can't stop thinking about you. And kissing you just now was more impulsive than I've been in years.' He leaned his forehead against hers. 'Have you ever wanted something so much, you feel as if you're going to implode?'

She didn't answer; and he was pretty sure it had something to do with the man who'd walked away from her.

Which was precisely what he was going to have to do.

And he didn't want to hurt her. Though he had a feeling that it might already be too late for that. She'd been rejected by her father, dumped at boarding school, and left in pieces when someone she loved had walked away from her. The fact that she'd been brave enough to suggest a fling also meant she'd made herself vulnerable.

He pulled back just enough to drop a kiss on her forehead. 'Cold showers and avoidance it is.'

'I'm not so sure that's going to work. I have pictures in my head. And I think you do, too.' She moistened her lower lip with the tip of her tongue, and he was near to hyperventilating. He really wanted to kiss her again.

'Indigo, I'm trying really hard to maintain control, here.'

'What if you didn't have to?' She stroked his face, and he turned his head to press a kiss into her palm. 'What if you could be whoever you wanted to be, just for, say, one night?'

'What scares me,' he admitted, 'is that I don't think one night with you would be enough.'

'A week, then. A fortnight. Maybe until you go back to Melvante. Look, you can still do whatever it is you planned to do here—spending time with Gus, thinking things through, sorting out kingly strategies. And I have work to do on the window. I'm not going to back out of my business commitments.' She paused. 'But, in between the business stuff, there are spaces.'

He could see what she meant. 'Spaces where we can just be.'

'Together,' she confirmed softly.

He sat down on the chesterfield and pulled her onto his lap. 'Your arguments are very persuasive, Ms Moran.'

She inclined her head. 'Why, thank you, Your Royal Highness.'

'Though I still feel dishonourable, offering you nothing but a fling.'

'They're the only kind of terms that either of us is in a position to offer,' she pointed out. 'So it's your choice,

Lorenzo. Cold showers—or this.' She cupped his face in her hands and skimmed her mouth against his.

His lips tingled where her skin touched his, and he couldn't help tightening his arms round her and responding to her kiss in kind.

'This,' he said when he could finally drag his mouth away from hers. *'This.'*

CHAPTER FOUR

ALTHOUGH INDIGO WENT back to her work when she left the library, she found herself stopping often to think about Lorenzo. She still couldn't quite believe what they'd agreed to. Since when did she do anything crazy like this? After Nigel's betrayal and the way her life had collapsed, two years ago, she'd kept all her relationships strictly platonic.

And now she was about to have a mad fling with a man who was about to become king.

Mad being the operative word, she thought wryly.

It took her ages to choose what to wear for dinner. At home, Indigo didn't bother changing for dinner—there wasn't much point when her meal was a hastily grabbed snack and she was going straight back to work for the rest of the evening. But she knew that Lottie's family always dressed for dinner, and when she stayed at Edensfield she always tried to fit in, so as not to embarrass her friend.

Last night's dress had made Lorenzo want to be a troglodyte and carry her off to his room.

Tonight, then, she'd wear something more demure. Something that would give him the chance to change his mind, maybe. Because she was pretty sure that one of them needed a dose of common sense, and right at that moment she didn't think she was the one who'd get it. So she picked a dress that one of her friends from art college had made as a prototype Edwardian costume and then presented to her because it practically had her name written over it: a midnight-blue velvet creation with a high scooped neck and cap sleeves, which came down to her ankles and was teamed with a silk sash in the same colour, a chunky faux-pearl necklace and a matching bracelet.

And hopefully seeing Lorenzo in a dinner jacket— looking a bit too much like the actor who played James Bond for her comfort—wouldn't make her do anything rash…

Lorenzo knew the second that Indigo walked into the room, but he forced himself not to turn round and stare at her.

They hadn't yet discussed whether they were keeping their mad fling just between themselves, so for now he was going to err on the side of caution. Besides, what if she'd come to her senses during the afternoon and had changed her mind?

He played it as cool as he could when Gus beckoned her over to join them. He couldn't read her expression at all. But then, just for a second, she dropped the guard on her gaze and he could see the heat in her eyes. He returned the glance, hoping that she could read exactly the same thing in his eyes, and then they went back to polite, neutral conversation.

Except inside he was far from feeling polite and neutral.

Last night's dress had been the equivalent of a cheeky come-hither whistle.

Tonight's was clearly meant to be demure. Except it wasn't. The velvet dress skimmed her curves and just made him want to see more. And he wanted to undo every single one of the tiny buttons on the back of her dress and kiss each millimetre of skin as he bared it.

Not to mention seeing that glorious hair spread all over his skin.

Right now, he could really do with a cold shower to shock some common sense back into him.

For all he knew, he was speaking utter gibberish and he could barely concentrate on the people he was speaking to. This was insane. He never lost it like this. What was it about Indigo Moran that made him react like this?

It made it worse that he was seated opposite her at the dining table. So near, and so out of reach. He knew it was appallingly rude of him, but he just wanted dinner and all the social chit-chat to be over, so he could be on his own with Indigo and kiss her until they were both dizzy.

'And she drags me off to the most obscure little churches,' Lottie was saying, but her tone was so indulgent that Lorenzo could tell she wasn't really complaining.

'And you love it, because it always means finding a nice little tea-shop nearby afterwards,' Indigo teased back.

'Exactly. It's so civilised. Where would we be without afternoon tea?' Lottie asked. She ruffled Indigo's hair. 'Actually, it's lovely to know someone who can find beauty so easily and help others see it. I'm so going to get you that "vitrearum inconcinna" T-shirt we saw at the stained glass museum that time.'

'Glass geek,' Lorenzo translated with a smile. That would be just about perfect for Indigo.

Indigo gave him a sassy look. 'I'm glad to see that prince school didn't skimp on your education in Latin, Your Royal Highness.'

He coughed. 'Given my native language, it'd be pretty embarrassing if I didn't know any Latin.'

'Though I guess you'd call it *il vetro antico*.'

He inclined his head. 'Or maybe *il vetro artistico*, depending on how old it was.'

Gus topped up their glasses. 'We really should've introduced you two *years* ago. You could've had so much fun out-geeking each other.'

Indigo laughed. 'I'm not that competitive.'

'Yeah, right,' Lorenzo drawled, and she just laughed again.

From the chatter over the dinner table, Lorenzo could see how well Indigo fitted in at Edensfield; she was clearly loved by all the family, not just Lottie, and it sounded as if she was a regular visitor to the estate. He wondered why they'd never met before, given how long they'd both been friends with the family. Maybe they'd just visited the house at different times. But surely she'd been invited to Gus's wedding to Maisie two years ago, when he'd been Gus's best man? Though he didn't remember meeting her then, and he was pretty sure that he would've remembered.

And then he looked up to discover that she was watching him. He raised his glass casually, as if to take a sip of wine, then held her gaze and gave her the tiniest, most discreet toast.

She smiled, and copied his actions.

So she hadn't had second thoughts about their mad fling, then. Good. And funny how it made him feel so warm inside. To the point that, after dinner, Lorenzo let Gus coax him into playing the piano for them. They all crowded into the library round the baby grand, and Lorenzo played the slow bit of Beethoven he'd played for Indigo that afternoon. He hoped she'd work out that he was playing it for her. Would it make her think of the way he'd kissed her afterwards in this very same room? He sneaked a discreet glance in her direction, and the slight wash of colour in her face was gratifying in the extreme. Yup. She was thinking about that kiss, too.

And then he switched to pop, choosing songs that he

knew would get everyone singing. Then he discovered something else about Indigo. Her singing was *terrible*.

But he liked the fact that nobody called her on it. She was just—well, part of the family and accepted as one of them. Something he had a feeling she hadn't experienced that much.

He saw her expression change from pleasure to utter horror, the moment she realised that she was singing aloud, and he had to fight back a smile. Did she really have no idea how cute she was?

'I'm afraid I'm going to be a bit of a party pooper,' she said, when he stopped playing. 'I need to load the photographs I took this afternoon and finish off the restoration blog post for tomorrow morning.'

In other words, she was embarrassed about her singing and was desperate to escape, he thought. How could he tell her that it didn't matter, without bringing up the very subject she wanted to avoid? And if he asked her to stay, he might as well be wearing a T-shirt emblazoned with 'Hey, everyone, I'm interested in Indigo'. Or worse.

Lottie gave her a hug. 'Don't work too hard, Indi. You're not here as our slave, you know. You're here as our friend.'

'I know,' Indigo said. 'But I'm also here to do a job.'

'And you love your job more than anything else.' Lottie ruffled her hair. 'Go be a glass geek, then. See you later.'

According to Lottie, Indigo loved her job more than anything else. Which made Lorenzo wonder again about the man who'd clearly hurt her in the past. Was she using work to block it out? Then again, he didn't have much room to talk. He'd always had workaholic tendencies, too, trying to make up for the way his father had disappointed his grandfather. Which was stupid, because you couldn't make up for someone else. He knew that. But he still couldn't seem to stop himself trying. And Indi had already admitted that she did the same. She was the first person he'd met who really understood what made him tick. Was it the same for her, too?

He stayed at the piano for just long enough to be polite and make it seem that he wasn't following Indigo, and then he headed over to her workroom and leaned against the doorway. To his surprise, she really was typing away on her laptop; so maybe her swift exit hadn't just been an excuse because she'd been embarrassed by her voice.

She looked up and saw him, then gave him a sheepish smile. 'Sorry. I'm an awful singer.'

'Don't apologise,' he said. 'Actually, it was nice that the music carried you away. And you don't have to be perfect at everything, every second of the day.'

'Uh-huh.' But she didn't sound convinced.

Why was she so hard on herself? Was it something to do with the strained relationship with her father? But he had a feeling that Indigo's flaw was the same as his own: she tried to be perfect. When she wasn't, she covered it up by being boho and arty. When he wasn't...well, that didn't happen. He always did the right thing.

Except for this mad fling with her. Which he wasn't going to let himself think about.

'You're busy,' he said. 'I'll leave you be.' He paused. 'Unless you want some coffee.'

'Coffee would be very nice,' she said softly. Then she looked him straight in the eye. 'But you would be better.'

His common sense vanished entirely. 'I'm giving you fair warning that I'm about to switch to troglodyte mode,' he said.

She blushed, just a tiny bit. 'Good. Though you should have noticed that I dressed demurely tonight.'

'I beg to differ.'

'High neckline, low hem.' She gestured to her dress.

'An indigo dress for Indigo.'

'That's what Sally said when she gave it to me. My friend from art school—she was studying textiles. We shared a flat and I sometimes used to model for her.' She smiled. 'It's a copy of an Edwardian design. What's not demure about it?'

'The buttons,' he said succinctly.

'The buttons?'

'The ones down the back of your dress. They make me want to undo them.'

'Oh, really?' She gave him a slow, insolent smile. 'Give me ten minutes to check this and upload it. My room?' Then she paused and looked awkward. 'Wait. Your security team.' She bit her lip.

'Bruno and Sergio? They're discreet. Totally and utterly.'

'It still feels a bit…' She grimaced. 'Well. As if we have an audience.'

'We don't,' he reassured her. 'This afternoon, when I was playing the piano, they knew I was in the library and they left me to it because they knew I needed some space. They didn't see me kiss you then, or the evening before.' He paused. 'I take it you want to keep this just between us?'

She nodded. 'It's a temporary thing,' she said softly, 'and we both know nothing can ever come of it, plus we're both staying at a friend's home. We're not in our own space.'

'If you're worrying about what people might think of you,' he said equally softly, 'I'd say the corridors of this house have seen plenty of people quietly slipping through them in the dead of night to a different bedroom, over the years.'

'I know.' She sighed. 'Sorry, I'm being silly. Not to mention very unsophisticated.'

'No, I know what you mean.' He smiled at her. 'I did wonder if you'd changed your mind.'

'I thought you might've changed yours.'

He shook his head. 'Every time I remember that I'm this sober, sensible and ever so slightly *boring* man, I look at you. And then all I can think is how much I want to kiss you.'

'In that case, it would be terribly rude of me not to let you,' she said.

'I'll see you in ten minutes,' he said. He checked which room was hers and was pleased to find that they were at least on the same corridor. There would be nothing more embarrassing for both of them than for him to be found wandering around on the wrong side of the house—because then Gus and his family would guess exactly what was going on.

Ten minutes later, Indigo was in her room. Adrenalin was fizzing through her veins, and she couldn't sit still; she couldn't even concentrate on browsing through the latest textbook on glass she'd bought before coming to Edensfield, planning to study it in her free time. Instead, she found herself pacing the room and looking at her watch every two seconds.

All she could think about was Lorenzo. The fact that he'd be coming to her room. The fact that they'd be starting their mad fling. And it made her feel like a teenager after her first kiss, light-headed and giddy with desire.

Well, the giddiness had to stop. She was going to enjoy every second of this, but she was also going to keep remembering that this was temporary. No promises on either side. And then they'd both be able to walk away with their hearts intact. She wouldn't be broken and helpless and hurting, the way she'd been after Nigel. She'd be strong and happy and absolutely fine.

There was a soft rap on the door.

Lorenzo.

She could barely get the words out. 'Come in.'

He walked in looking even more like James Bond, still wearing his dinner jacket but with his shirt collar open and his bow tie untied. And he had both hands behind his back, just as you always saw royal men walking. It brought it home to her that she was having a mad fling *with a king-to-be*. How crazy was that?

But then he lifted her up and swung her round before setting her back on her feet. 'Indigo Moran, I've wanted to kiss you all evening.'

'I've wanted that, too,' she admitted. 'A lot.'

'Good.' He traced the edge of her face with a finger-tip. The feel of his skin gliding against hers made every nerve-ending fizz.

'Kiss me, Lorenzo,' she whispered.

He did.

Slowly. Taking his own sweet time about it and heating her blood to fever pitch until she forgot everything else except him.

He removed the sash, spun her round so her back was to him, scooped her hair over her shoulder to bare her nape to him, and then traced the edge of her dress with one fin-gertip. 'I like this, Indi,' he said. 'The softest velvet. Except your skin's even softer. Though I need to prove that theory. Empirical evidence is very important.' He undid the first button, then the next, and stroked every centimetre of skin as he uncovered it.

And then she felt his lips brushing her skin very lightly. She shivered. 'Lorenzo.'

'You're beautiful,' he said softly. 'And you smell of roses.'

She smiled. 'It's my favourite scent. I love the garden here in summer because it's like drinking roses when you breathe.'

'I'm going to think of you every time I smell roses,' he said, and traced a path with his mouth all the way down her spine.

Then he turned her to face him again, slid the dress off her shoulders, and scooped it up from the floor when she'd stepped out of it. To her amusement, he hung her dress neatly over the back of the rococo chair next to the matching dressing table. 'Details?' she asked. 'Or are you just a buttoned-up neat freak?'

'Details,' he said. 'Attention to them is...' His gaze heated. 'Essential.'

Meaning that he intended to pay very close attention to her? Her knees went weak at the thought.

'You're wearing too much,' she said, aware that she was only wearing skimpy, lacy underwear and the only thing out of place for him was his bow tie. 'I think we need to even this up slightly.'

'What do you suggest?' he asked.

The choice was too delicious. 'I'm not sure whether I want you to strip for me, or whether I want to undress you myself,' she confessed.

'I have a practical solution. Pick one,' he said, 'and you can do the other next time.'

There was definitely going to be a next time?

'Then right now I get to undress you,' she whispered. And she did it very slowly, helping him shrug out of his jacket and then enjoying discovering the texture of his skin as she unbuttoned his shirt. 'I've changed my mind about you being James Bond. I think you're Mr Darcy.'

'Are you suggesting skinny-dipping in the lake, Ms Moran?'

'No. It's like the director said—it's better when something's left to the imagination.' She smiled. 'But you in a

white shirt, rising out of the lake and looking all sexy—
yes, that would be very nice. Very nice indeed.'

'I'll see what I can do,' he promised. 'You'd make a rubbish valet, by the way.'

'How?'

'You're much too slow. I've lost patience.'

'Pulling rank, are we?' she teased. The king-to-be and
the commoner.

'Totally.' He kissed her, and swiftly finished stripping.
Then he placed his hands on her shoulders, holding her at
a distance so he could look his fill. 'Indigo Moran,' he said
huskily, 'you are totally luscious.' With that, he picked her
up and carried her over to the bed.

And after that neither of them spoke for a long, long
time.

CHAPTER FIVE

THE NEXT MORNING, Indigo woke, her head pillowed on Lorenzo's shoulder and his arms wrapped round her.

For a moment, she felt cherished and safe.

And then she shook herself. That wasn't the deal.

Even so, she couldn't help wondering: how long had it been since she'd woken like this, wrapped in a man's arms?

She really couldn't remember.

She'd dated men before Nigel, but she'd been more focused on her work than on relationships in art college. She'd wanted to prove to her grandparents that she'd done the right thing in rebelling against the education her father had planned, and that she wasn't flighty like her mother. She'd always put her studies first. And it had paid off, because she'd ended up with a first-class degree and a job working for a very prestigious glass studio.

Though Indigo hadn't been one for all work and no play. She'd attended plenty of parties, dated whoever she wanted to see, and when it had suited her she'd let things go further than a chaste kiss good-night at the door of her flat. But committing to a relationship, putting herself in a position where her heart could be broken—she'd avoided that as much as possible, keeping her relationships light and fun through college and most of her working life.

Until Nigel.

And that had been the biggest mistake of her life. She'd fallen in love with him and got her heart well and truly stomped on in the process. And, with Nigel, she'd never actually woken in his arms. He'd never stayed overnight in the six months they'd been together and he'd never invited her back to his place, saying that he lived and worked on the other side of London from her and the extra commute would be a nuisance for both of them.

Why had she never questioned that? Why had she just accepted it?

But there was no point in beating herself up about the past. Indigo knew she wasn't going to make the same mistake again. This time, she was protected against heartbreak. Right from the start she and Lorenzo had agreed that this was just a mad fling. One with a time limit. She wasn't going to fall in love with His Royal Highness Prince Lorenzo Torelli. This was going to be light and sweet and fun, a kind of respite for both of them. And she was going to enjoy every second of their fling.

It was still very early in the morning, and the summer sunlight was just seeping around the edges of the curtains. She shifted slightly so she could lie on her side and watch him sleeping.

In repose, Lorenzo was truly beautiful. He had a perfect bone structure and long, long lashes that made her itch to sketch him. And the way his mouth turned up at the corners naturally made it look as if he was smiling in his sleep. Or maybe he *was* smiling in his sleep. Dreaming of her, perhaps, and the way they'd made love in the ancient four-poster bed?

She smiled. Lorenzo had proved himself a spectacular lover, too. He'd paid attention to detail, noticed where she liked being touched and how she liked being kissed. The first time they'd made love should've been awkward and ever so slightly embarrassing, but it hadn't been that way. It had felt so natural, so right: unexpectedly and wonderfully perfect.

She couldn't resist leaning over and kissing his mouth, very lightly.

His eyes opened. She saw the second that he focused and realised where he was. And then he smiled. The kind of smile that could melt the most frozen heart.

'Good morning, Indi,' he said softly.

Her heart did a backflip. 'Good morning, Lorenzo.'

He moved slightly closer. 'Was that my imagination, or did you just kiss me awake?'

She wrinkled her nose. 'Sorry. I didn't mean to wake you. But you looked like Sleeping Beauty, and I'm afraid it was a bit too much to resist.'

He coughed. 'I hate to tell you this, Indi, but Sleeping Beauty was a girl. And I'm not a girl.'

No. He was all man. And the thought of how they'd made love last night, how his body had felt inside hers, sent a warm glow through her. 'Hey, there's no reason why a man can't be beautiful.' She spread her hands. 'I mean, "Sleeping Handsome" doesn't sound right, does it?'

'Is that how you see me?' he asked.

'Kind of yes and kind of no.' She thought about it. 'I like the idea of playing around with fairy tales, seeing what happens if you change an element.'

He looked at her and sighed. 'I have a nasty feeling I know where this is going. Please tell me you're not planning to do a series of stained-glass windows with all the fairy tale roles reversed—and with me as the model.'

'If things were different,' she said, 'I'd talk you into that, because it's a *brilliant* idea. But it's not going to happen,' she reassured him, stroking his hair back from his forehead. 'That's why I said yes, that's kind of how I see you—because you're from a different world. And being here with me is almost like a temporary enchantment. Except in this case it doesn't involve spinning wheels and pricking your finger, you're not going to sleep for a hundred years—oh, and a kiss isn't supposed to break the spell,' she added hastily.

'I'm glad to hear it.' He shifted so that he could pull her back into his arms. 'Well, now you've woken the sleeping prince, I think there's only one thing to do.'

And he kissed her until they were both dizzy.

'Now that's a way to start a morning,' she said with a smile.

He smiled back. 'My thoughts exactly. But I'd better go back to my own room before everyone else in the house wakes up. Do you always wake at the crack of dawn, Indi?'

'Not always, but I'm not actually that used to sharing my sleeping space,' she admitted.

He stroked her face. 'Good. Just for the record, neither am I.'

'Good.' She kissed him. 'Now disappear before you bump into Gus's mum, still wearing last night's clothes, and embarrass everyone.'

'Yes, ma'am,' he teased, and climbed out of bed. He gave her a sidelong glance. 'Shouldn't you be looking away while I get dressed?'

'My degree's in art. I've taken enough life drawing classes that I'm very comfortable with people being naked in front of me.' She raised an eyebrow. 'Has anyone told you that your posterior view is nicer than that of Michelangelo's David?'

To her delight, he actually blushed. 'No. But thank you for the compliment.' He finished dressing—though he left his shirt collar open and didn't bother with the bow tie—

then came to sit beside her on the bed. 'When will you be free today?'

'After the house and garden are closed, late this afternoon.' Much as she wanted to spend time with him, enjoy every precious second, she had commitments and it wouldn't be fair to back out. Though she knew he understood; he was busy, too, and they'd agreed to see each other in the spaces between each other's work.

'Maybe we could take a walk in the grounds when you're free.'

'I'd like that,' she said. 'Maybe I could text you when my workroom's clear, and you can text me back to let me know where and when to meet you.'

'Good idea.' He fished his mobile phone from his pocket. 'What's your number?'

She told him. A couple of moments later, her mobile beeped. She opened the text. 'A smile and a kiss. Works for me,' she said, smiling and kissing him. 'See you later, Lorenzo.'

She didn't see him at breakfast, because she ate a hasty bowl of granola, yoghurt and fruit in the kitchen rather than the breakfast room and she took her coffee through to her workroom. Lorenzo didn't come to see her while she was working on the glass in the morning; no doubt he had king-in-waiting stuff to do, she thought. And then the house opened for visitors, and she was busy talking to people and showing them what she was doing.

Once the last visitor had left, she sent a quick text to Lorenzo, letting him know that she was free.

See you in the rose garden in half an hour, was his reply.

When she walked into the rose garden, he was sitting on one of the wrought iron benches beneath a bower of roses. Again, she thought of the Sleeping Beauty story and how she'd love to paint Lorenzo in a stained-glass window. And she smiled when she realised that Toto, the elderly golden Labrador, was sitting patiently next to him, his chin on Lorenzo's knee.

'I hope you don't mind us having a companion. Toto rather insisted on coming along,' Lorenzo said wryly.

She laughed and made a fuss of the dog. 'No, it's nice having a dog around. Especially in a garden as gorgeous as this one.'

'Did you have a good day?' he asked.

She nodded. 'I made quite a lot of progress on the mermaid and had some interesting chats with the visitors. You?'

'I worked through some files for my grandfather.'

'And you need some downtime?' she guessed.

'Just a little,' he admitted.

She heeled off her shoes, and sighed in bliss as her feet sank into the soft lawn. 'Ah, that's better. The only thing I don't like about my job is that you need to wear shoes all the time.'

'In case of splinters?' he asked.

She nodded. 'And this is bliss. The softest grass in the world.'

The way she'd just pushed off her shoes and was walking barefoot on the lawn... Lorenzo envied the way that Indigo could just act on impulse. It was something he never did; he was always aware of the consequences of his actions. Which was a good thing, but it also meant that he missed out on the joy that Indigo seemed to find so easily in things. 'Don't you worry about getting a thorn in your feet?'

'Hardly. Roses drop petals rather than thorns,' she pointed out.

'Even so. Sometimes they drop branches.'

'Which I can see and avoid.' She laughed. 'Though I admit I wouldn't walk barefoot by the lake. The ducks are a bit indiscriminate about where they have a toilet break and it's annoying having to watch where you put your feet instead of being able to watch the water and the sky.' She looked at him. 'Why don't you take your shoes off?'

'What, now?'

'Yes, now. Feel the grass under your feet. It's cool and springy and lovely.'

When was the last time he'd walked barefoot on the grass? Probably not since he was a small child. But, not wanting to appear a total stick-in-the-mud, he complied. He tucked his socks into his shoes and let his shoes dangle from one hand, just as she was doing.

'You're right,' he said, when he'd taken a couple of steps on the cool, soft grass. 'It's wonderful.'

'When was the last time you walked barefoot on a beach?' she asked.

He shrugged. 'I really can't remember.'

'Is there some rule at prince school that you should always be fully, impeccably dressed unless you're in the shower?'

He knew she was teasing him, but at the same time she had a point. As a prince, he always had to look the part. Not that he was going to let himself dwell on that side of things. 'Or swimming,' he said lightly. 'Unless of course you're dressed in Regency costume and want to turn some heads. Then you're allowed to be partially undressed. Especially in a lake,' he added, knowing that it would amuse her.

She laughed, and he loved the way she tipped her head back, her face up towards the sunlight and her face full of smiles. 'You half promised me that before, Lorenzo. I am *so* holding you to that Mr Darcy moment.'

'Talking about holding...' He brushed his free hand against hers.

'Would that be a hint, Your Royal Highness?' she teased.

He rolled his eyes. 'Are you saying that I have to give you an official royal order?'

'No. I probably wouldn't obey an order. But I can take a hint.' She smiled again and twined her fingers through his.

Walking through the rose garden with her, hand in hand, with the dog pattering along beside them, felt like being in another world. An enchanted bubble. Maybe she was right when she said he reminded her of Sleeping Beauty, Lorenzo thought, because this was like a dream. It wasn't real. They couldn't have a future. He needed to find a future queen for Melvante, someone his grandfather and his political advisers would approve of—and they definitely wouldn't approve of Indigo, despite her charm and her work ethic. And he already knew that Indigo hated his world; she'd escaped it before and wouldn't want to go back.

So he was going to enjoy every second of their fling together and take it for what it was: a beautiful interlude, a few moments out of time.

'So why do you have a thing about roses?' he asked.

'They're beautiful, they smell nice, and they look stunning in a stained-glass window. They're probably the perfect flower,' she said.

He smiled. 'My grandfather would agree with you. He has a rose garden.'

'One he tends himself?'

'When he gets the chance, yes. I'll know exactly where to find him when he's retired.' Lorenzo was surprised by her perception. She'd clearly worked out that what music did for him, roses did for his grandfather. 'So do roses figure much in stained glass?'

'Quite a bit,' she said. 'I'm trying to talk Syb into letting me do a window of roses for the library. Well, I know technically Gus should make the final decision, but he wants it done as a birthday present for his mum and he says it's her choice.' She looked wistful. 'I'd love to make a window full of roses. I'd have one myself if I had the right house.'

'And your house isn't right?'

'It's a modern bijou flat. Rented.' She gave a half-shrug. 'I'm not there very much, so it doesn't make sense to have a large place. I'm either at my studio, or working on location somewhere.'

'I guess,' he said. But still he wondered, if what Indigo really wanted was to have roots? She'd grown up with her grandparents; deep down, did she want a space of her own?

'So what about you? I assume as the prince you have to live in the castle?'

'I have an apartment in the castle,' he said. 'I can be independent if I choose and cook my own meals.'

She smiled at him. 'As *if* a prince is going to cook for himself. I bet you have a team of chefs who pamper you to within a millimetre of your life.'

That was a little too close to home. When was the last time he'd cooked for himself? Normally, he was so busy that it was easier to eat something prepared by the castle chefs when he was in Melvante, and to get takeout if he was in London. 'I make an excellent chilli, I'll have you know,' he protested. 'I learned to cook when I was a student—and, actually, I like cooking.' He just didn't do it that often, any more.

She raised her eyebrows at him. 'Is that a cue for a challenge, Your Royal Highness?'

'Maybe.' He knew he'd enjoy cooking for her; he could imagine her sitting at his kitchen table in bare feet, chatting and maybe sketching as he cooked. Then he shook himself. Such domestic scenes weren't going to happen, however much he might like them to. She wasn't going to be in his apartment at the castle and he was hardly ever going to get the time to cook or play the piano. He definitely wasn't going to have much time to do ordinary things like this—walking hand in hand with a pretty girl in a rose garden.

He pushed the thought away.

As if she noticed that he'd gone quiet and brooding, and she wanted to change the subject to something that would be less painful for him, she asked, 'So what's your castle like?'

That was an easier topic to talk about. 'It's pretty much your standard picture-postcard European castle. White stone, lots of turrets with pointed tiled roofs, a drawbridge and a moat.'

'That sounds nice. What about inside?'

'Red carpets, oak panelling and suits of armour—and there's a gallery with pictures of every King of Melvante since Carlo the First.'

'Will you be the first Lorenzo?' she asked.

'The third—my grandfather's the second.' His father had been supposed to be the third, with himself as the fourth. How different his life would've been, had his father lived.

'So you were named after your grandfather?'

He nodded. 'How about you?'

She looked rueful. 'I think my mum just picked the most unusual name she could think of. And possibly something that would annoy my father, because it's not very traditional.'

He thought of the traditional royal English names. 'I can't see you as an Elizabeth, a Mary or an Anne.'

'Maybe if I'd been Elizabeth, I would've fitted in at

school. I could've been Lizzie in the four musketeers of our dorm,' she mused.

He shook his head. 'Even if you'd had an L in your name, you wouldn't have been part of those girls. Besides, if you'd really hated your name, you could've used your middle name. Or any other name you liked, for that matter.'

'I hated my name when I was really small—in the days when I needed to feel I fitted in,' she admitted, 'and back then some of the girls weren't very nice, saying it wasn't a proper name for a girl because it was a colour.'

'There are plenty of colours used as names. Ruby, Jade and Amber,' he said, taking the first three that came into his head.

'They're gemstones,' she corrected.

'How about Violet and Rose?'

She shook her head. 'Flowers.'

'Scarlet,' he said. 'Even you can't argue against *that* one.'

'I guess not.' She grinned. 'Nowadays, I like my name.'

'So,' he said, 'do I. It suits you and it suits your job.'

She gave him a half-bow. 'Why, thank you, Your Royal Highness. Anyway, before I sidetracked you, you were telling me about your art collection. Lots of portraits of kings.'

'My great-grandfather collected art. You'd like what he bought.' He smiled at her. 'And there's a picture of my great-great-grandmother you'd really love. She sat for Burne-Jones when she was a child.'

'How fantastic. I hope you know I'm horribly envious.'

'Maybe you can come and see it.' The offer was out before he could stop it.

'Maybe.' She gave him the sweetest, sweetest smile.

And he knew without having to ask that it was a polite way of saying no.

She paused. 'OK. You like the building and you like the art. But is it home?'

He thought about it. 'Yes, it is. I have a lot of happy memories there.' Despite his parents' early deaths, the lies he'd been told to spare him from the truth and the shock of discovering that his father had had such a dark side.

'I'm glad.' Her fingers tightened briefly round his. 'So what are you going to do when you're king?'

'Build on the work of my grandfather and make my people proud of me,' he said promptly.

'Good goals,' she said approvingly. 'How do you plan to get there?'

Lorenzo found himself talking seriously to Indigo about Melvante, about his people and what he wanted to do for his country. Whenever he stopped, thinking that maybe he was being too boring and ought to change the subject, she drew him out a little more, asking questions that showed she'd been paying attention to what he'd said and coming up with ideas that really made him think. And he was oddly pleased that she was showing as much of an interest in his job as he had in hers.

Toto flopped down with a grunt; she stopped, and made a fuss of the old dog. 'I think we've tired him out, poor old boy.' She glanced back at the house. 'Look how far we've walked. I don't think he's going to find the return walk very easy.'

'Then I'll carry him back.' Lorenzo put his shoes back on, preparing to pick up the dog. Toto was slightly overweight and a bit on the heavy side, but no way was Lorenzo going to abandon the old dog. He'd allowed Toto to join them for a walk and he hadn't thought enough of the fact that the dog was elderly now and couldn't walk as far as he'd been able to run alongside them when Lorenzo and Gus had been students and Toto had been a boisterous pup.

'Lorenzo, you ca–'

Her protest died as he picked up the dog.

'You're an elephant, Toto. You need to go on a doggy diet,' he informed the dog, who licked his nose gratefully.

When he glanced at Indigo, he was surprised to see a film of tears in her eyes. 'What's wrong, Indi?' he asked gently.

'You're going to be a king next month. And there you are, carrying an old dog home.'

'Toto and I go back a long way. And you always look after your own, don't you?' He smiled at her. 'Strictly speaking, he's Gus's dog. But I spent enough time here as a student to think of him as at least partly mine.'

'Even so. A lot of people would…' She swallowed hard. 'Well, just leave him.'

'Until he'd had a rest and could find his own way back to the house? No way.' He grimaced. 'I suppose we could've gone to find a wheelbarrow and a blanket for him, but I wouldn't abandon him just because he's old and tired and needs a break.'

'I guess.'

She was quiet until they got to the house, where he gently set Toto back on to his feet.

'You're a good man, Lorenzo Torelli,' she said softly. 'And you're going to make an awesome king.'

'I hope so,' he said, equally softly. 'I really hope so.'

CHAPTER SIX

OVER THE NEXT WEEK, Lorenzo and Indigo spent as much time together as they could, while trying to be discreet and not flaunt their affair in everyone's faces. Every sneaked moment was precious.

'I'm still thinking about how you carried Toto back to the house. He weighs a ton, and you carried him for ages. Do you do weight training or something?' Indigo asked when they were curled up on Lorenzo's bed together.

'Or something.'

'Which is?'

'Come and train with me in Gus's fitness room, and I'll show you,' Lorenzo said.

The fitness room? It was one of the rooms at Edensfield Indigo had never set foot in; she'd never been remotely interested in running on a treadmill or picking up weights. 'But I'm not sporty. I was always the last one picked for the team at lacrosse. And even when I moved to the local secondary school, I was never any good at netball, hockey or rounders. I used to get an A for effort and a D for achievement.'

'The trick is to find something that you enjoy doing.'

'I didn't enjoy team sports. At all,' she said with a grimace. 'I don't mind going for a long walk—I'm not a total couch potato—but I'm really not sporty.' She stroked his pectorals and his abs. 'You have muscles—a proper six-pack. So I guess that means you're really sporty.'

'Mens sana in corpore sano,' he intoned.

'A healthy mind in a healthy body,' she translated. 'More prince school stuff?'

He laughed. 'You translated it, so I thought you'd know where it comes from.'

'I only studied Latin to help me with the glass—sometimes you get wills or what have you to help you with the provenance of the glass. People donating particular windows to a church, that kind of thing.'

'It's Juvenal, from the *Satires*. And it doesn't just apply to princes—it's a list of what he thinks you should ask for in life. I can't remember the whole lot, but it includes a stout heart, one that's not scared of hard work and isn't angry or lustful…' He leaned over to kiss her. 'Most of that works for me. Except the lustful bit. Because you're incredibly desirable, Indigo Moran, and you make me feel lustful. Very lustful indeed.'

'Why, thank you, Your Royal Highness. I would curtsey in gratitude—'

'Would you, hell.' He stole another kiss.

'Let me finish. I would curtsey in gratitude for the compliment, but…' She laughed. 'Well, I'm comfortable and I don't want to move.'

'I don't want you to move, either.' He tightened his arms round her.

'So what sport do you do?' She thought for a moment. 'You promised me a Mr Darcy moment, so I'm guessing swimming.'

'I can swim, but it's not my favourite.'

'Rowing, then?' She looked at him. 'And I bet you got a Blue for it at Oxford.'

'Well, yes,' he admitted. 'But rowing isn't my favourite, either.'

She was intrigued. 'Tennis? Cricket? Rugby?'

'That's three more guesses—and all wrong. Forfeits are due,' he said, claiming a kiss for each.

'OK. I give up. Tell me.'

'Sparring.'

'*Boxing?* No way.' She shook her head. 'They'd never let a king-to-be take a risk like that. Boxing's dangerous. People get seriously hurt.'

'Sparring just means padwork. So I get all the fun of boxing but without the risk of being hurt,' he said. 'Come and spar with me.'

'I hate to point this out, Your Royal Highness, but you're six inches taller than I am and I'm not exactly muscle-bound. I'm not going to be a very good sparring partner, am I?'

'Sure you are. You'll work with the gloves, not the pads.'

'And I don't have any workout gear.'

'Borrow some from Lottie or Maisie. They're both about your size, so one of them is bound to have something she can lend you.'

He clearly wasn't going to let this go. 'So when are we doing this training, then?'

'Tomorrow morning. I was thinking the crack of dawn, given that you always seem to wake so early.'

It really wasn't her idea of fun, but she'd indulge him. 'OK.'

'Good.' He nuzzled the hollows of her collarbones. 'So, where were we?'

Later that day, Indigo borrowed a T-shirt and a pair of shorts from Lottie—at least she had a pair of training shoes with her—and the next morning she followed Lorenzo to the fitness room.

He handed her a skipping rope. 'This is a speed rope. It's weighted so you can skip properly.'

'Skipping?' She looked at him, mystified. 'I thought we were doing boxing stuff?'

'We are. This is to warm up your muscles.'

She managed five skips before she tripped over the rope.

'You need to jump over the rope with both feet together,' he explained, 'not one foot at a time as if you're a rocking horse.'

She spread her hands. 'That's the way I learned to skip at school.'

'This is boxing skipping. It's much more effective at getting your heart rate up and warming up your muscles.'

'What's the difference?'

'Watch.' He skipped slowly, jumping over the rope; then he quickened his pace and it was as if he were floating on air. His feet didn't even seem to touch the ground—he just seemed to be hovering mid-air.

'Now that's just showing off,' she grumbled, wanting to hide just how impressed she was.

He laughed. 'No, that's practice. Do a little bit every day and eventually you'll be able to do this.'

She didn't think so. 'Show me again.'

He coughed. 'You're trying to wriggle out of doing it.'

'All right.' She rolled her eyes. 'I admit that was seriously impressive, Your Royal Highness, and I'd like to see you do it again.'

He laughed. 'OK. I'll skip for you again. But you have to earn it.'

'That's mean,' she said.

'It's a carrot for a reward,' he corrected. 'If you want to see me skip, you have to do some skipping yourself, first. OK. Let's work on your technique.' He walked her over towards the mirror. 'Now, watch yourself in the mirror.'

'Haven't we just proved that I can't skip?'

'We've just proved that you panicked and you need to change your technique,' he corrected. 'Remember what I said: jump over the rope with both feet together, and watch your feet in the mirror. Focus on lifting your feet.'

She tried again, and this time managed a few more skips before she tripped over the rope and had to stop.

'See? You're getting better. Now do it again. Watch your feet in the mirror and focus on the rhythm. Jump, jump, jump.'

She was hot and breathless by the time he finally let her stop. 'This is vile. I'm all sweaty and disgusting.'

He just grinned and kissed the tip of her nose. 'Tut, Ms Moran. Didn't your teachers tell you that horses sweat, men perspire and ladies glow?'

She glowered at him. 'I'm not a lady.'

He brushed his mouth against hers. 'I beg to differ. You're all woman, Indigo Moran, and right now you look as sexy as hell.'

And how was she supposed to concentrate, when he was looking at her like *that*?

He took the skipping rope from her and put the gloves on her. 'Right—now you need to keep your knees soft, crouch slightly, and keep your hands up to guard your face.'

He talked her through doing a jab and a cross, then put his hands into two pads and held them up. 'OK, now jab the pad to your right, then punch the one on your left. Remember to keep the hand you're not using up by your face.'

She hit the pads as he directed. This was surreal: *she was throwing punches at a king-to-be.* Surely there had to be laws against this.

'Harder,' he said.

She shook her head. 'But I might hurt you, Lorenzo.'

He smiled. 'Indi, my sweet, you're not going to hurt me. I wouldn't get you to hold the pads for me because I'm used to this and I'd hit too hard for you, but this is new to you and I assure you that you won't hurt me, however hard you hit. Now punch.'

By the time he called a halt, Indigo was breathing hard—and she was full of exhilaration. 'That was amazing! I get why you love it.'

'It's a great cardio workout, plus it's good for your arms and your abs. We're going to stop now or you'll be really sore tomorrow—actually, you might be sore anyway.' He looked faintly guilty. 'Sorry. I was enjoying that and I probably should've stopped earlier.'

'It's fine. I enjoyed it, too, even though I thought I'd hate it,' she said. 'And if anyone told me that a king-to-be would love putting on a pair of boxing gloves...'

He kissed her lightly. 'I'm a man first, Indi. Remember that.'

And the heat in his gaze sent a shiver of pure lust all the way from the top of her spine down to her toes.

'So now what?' she asked, her voice ever so slightly shaky.

'Now,' he said, 'we go and shower.' He bent down so he could whisper in her ear, 'And my vote is for us to do that together.'

'No arguments from me,' she said, feeling breathless.

He took off the gloves, and kissed the back of her hand. 'You did really well.'

'Because you're a good teacher.' She smiled at him.

'So were you, when you talked me through cleaning the lead cames.'

'It's just a matter of being clear with your instructions, paying attention and adapting things to suit the person you're teaching.'

'It's the same with this,' he said, and kissed her again. 'Right. Shower. Now.'

'Yes, Your Royal Highness,' she said, and kissed him back.

The following morning, Lorenzo walked in to Indigo's workroom at half past eleven. 'Time for lunch.'

'Lunch?' She glanced at her watch. 'Isn't it a bit early?'

'No. It means we'll be finished before the house and grounds open at one.'

'Fair enough.' She made sure that all her electrical equipment was switched off and all the liquids were safely in sealed containers, and followed him out of the house.

He was carrying a wicker basket, she noticed. They found a nice spot on the lawn outside the hothouses with a view of the lake. Lorenzo produced a rug for them to sit on and shook it out. Then he spread out a red and white checked tablecloth next to the rug and set out plates, cutlery and two champagne flutes.

So much more stylish than the plastic box of food and slightly scuffed plastic cups she was used to on a picnic.

'So you talked someone in the kitchen into making all this for you?' she asked.

'Actually, no. I sent one of my team into the local town with a very specific list. And I put this together with my own fair hands.'

'Resourceful and able to delegate. Good combination,' she said. Though part of her wondered, did he ever yearn to be just an ordinary man who could nip out to the shops himself on the spur of the moment without it having to be planned like a military operation, complete with security detail, or having to send someone else out with his list?

The first box contained watercress, baby plum tomatoes, strips of yellow pepper and slices of mango. Then there was a box of sliced chicken, which he arranged on top. He added a pot of dressing. 'Creamy chilli and coconut. I forgot to ask if you liked spicy food,' he said.

'I do.'

He brought out some rich seeded bread, which he carved into chunks, and his next foray into the picnic hamper was for a pot containing a red purée. She sniffed as he took the lid off. 'It smells like strawberries.'

'Pureéd,' he said, and deftly put some in each champagne flute, which he topped off from a tiny bottle of champagne. 'I thought we'd have just enough for one glass each, so it won't make you drowsy or affect your work,' he said.

She took a sip. 'This is fabulous—what is it, a kind of strawberry Bellini?'

'Yes. It's called a Rossini.'

'Where did you discover these?'

He laughed. 'Elementary class at prince school?'

'Yeah, yeah.' She raised her glass in a toast to him. 'To you. And thank you so much for spoiling me so delightfully.'

'My pleasure.' He leaned over and kissed her lightly.

Indigo enjoyed the food and the sunshine; and she especially enjoyed the company.

When they'd finished the salad, Lorenzo fed her more strawberries and miniature macaroons the colour of pistachio that tasted of coconut.

'They're perfect,' she said blissfully.

He smiled. 'We aim to please.' He reached over and kissed the corner of her mouth. 'Crumb,' he said.

Two could play at that game, she thought, amused. She kissed the corner of his mouth. 'Smear of sugar.'

He just laughed, and kissed her until she was dizzy. Finally, he settled back with his head in her lap, looking pensive. She stroked his hair away from his forehead. 'What are you thinking?'

'Sometimes I wish I could keep a moment in time,' he said.

'You can. In here.' She rested one hand over his heart. 'And in here.' She stroked his forehead.

'I'd keep this moment,' he said softly. 'A perfect English summer afternoon.'

She knew exactly what he meant. Sunshine glinting on the lake, birds singing, the scent of roses, strawberries and champagne... There was really only one thing missing. She reached over to pick some daisies.

'What are you doing?' he asked.

'Nothing. Just close your eyes and chill out,' she said, and proceeded to make a daisy chain. When she'd finished, she made it into a crown. 'For you,' she said, and he opened his eyes to see the crown just before she draped it over his head.

He looked unutterably sad for a moment, as if she'd just reminded him that he'd be wearing a much heavier crown in a few short weeks.

'Actually, I was thinking Oberon,' she said softly.

'"Ill met by moonlight, proud Titania"?'

'I hope we're not ill met.' She smiled at him. 'Trust you to know Shakespeare—or was your degree in English?'

'Economics. But I had friends who read English.'

'Did you not think about studying music?' she asked. Surely that had been the subject of his heart?

He shrugged. 'Economics was more practical.'

'But if you'd had a choice?'

'Then, yes, I probably would've studied music,' he admitted.

'I was lucky,' she said softly. 'I got to do what I love.'

'I love what I'm going to do,' he said, though his words

sounded a little hollow to her, and just for a second he looked so very, very lonely.

The only way she could think of to make it better was to kiss him.

His arms tightened around her as if he really needed her. When he broke the kiss, he said, 'I guess we'd better get back.'

She helped him clear away the picnic. 'Thank you for spoiling me, Lorenzo. I really enjoyed this.'

'My pleasure.' He stroked her face. 'I'm glad I could share it with you.'

And she was glad, too.

Later in the week, Indigo woke to find herself alone.

Lorenzo hadn't said anything to her about needing an early start or going up to London.

Or had he changed his mind about their fling?

Hurt, she got up and slipped her dressing gown on. Then she saw a note next to the bed. A 'Dear Jane' letter? she wondered.

Well, they'd agreed it was a fling. The fact that she was falling for him—more fool her.

Steeling herself, she picked up the note and read it.

Meet you at the lake, by the boathouse.

Not a 'Dear Jane' letter, then. He'd clearly left the note on his pillow and it had fallen off. And they'd had those conversations about Mr Darcy. Was he really going to do that? Or was he doing something crazy and spontaneous, like planning to row her across the lake to watch the sunrise?

She smiled, dressed swiftly and headed out to the lake.

Lorenzo was sitting there on the steps of the boat-house, wearing full Regency dress—including knee-length leather boots. He looked utterly fantastic and her heart did a backflip.

He sketched a salute to her as she neared him, then took off his boots.

She stopped. Was he really going to do what she thought he was about to do?

She watched as he shed his dark jacket, his cravat and finally his silk waistcoat, leaving them on the steps of the boathouse. And then he gave her the most sensual smile ever and dived into the lake, still wearing the cream-coloured breeches and loose white shirt.

'Oh, my God,' she said softly. 'Mr Darcy in the flesh.'

She watched him swim, his arms moving powerfully through the water. And then he emerged from the lake, the white cotton of his shirt plastered to his skin.

It was the sexiest thing she'd ever seen.

'Did I get it right?' he asked as she walked over to join him.

'Oh, yeah, you got it right.' And how embarrassing was it that her voice had practically dropped an octave, going all husky? 'And your hair goes slightly curly when it's wet. I never really noticed that before—and you've got those lovely huge dark eyes, just like Colin Firth...'

Lorenzo gave her a pained look. 'Oh, please. Don't go all fan-girly on me.'

'Hey, you ask Lottie—she'll say the same,' she protested. 'Mind you, I'm sure I read somewhere that Jane Austen based Mr Darcy on Byron.'

'I'm not sure about that. But even so I'm not mad, bad or dangerous to know,' he said.

She laughed and thought, actually, you are dangerous to know, because I could so easily fall in love with you, and that would be the most stupid thing ever—because I wouldn't fit into your world and you couldn't leave yours and join mine. Instead, she said more prosaically, 'I hope you brought some dry clothes.'

'Of course. Just as well, actually, because the lake was a bit colder than I thought it was going to be.' He took her hand and led her into the boating house, then stripped off and towelled himself dry.

'I'm pretty sure Mr Darcy didn't have a spare set of clothes nearby,' she commented, hoping that he couldn't hear how hard her heart was beating.

'But I didn't want to meet you in the garden and make small talk. Or drip water all over the carpets at Edensfield. Besides, Darcy would've needed a valet,' he pointed out.

She grinned. 'I would offer, but I've been told I'm a rubbish valet.'

He gave her a smouldering look. 'This could be your chance to prove me wrong.'

'I'd rather sketch you than dress you.'

He groaned. 'Don't tell me you've got pencils and a sketchpad with you.'

'No. But I do have this.' She tapped her head.

'You're wired with a hidden camera? Female James Bond, so there's a microphone in your lipstick and a camera in your contact lenses?'

'Very funny. You know what I meant.' Her memory.

And that was what they were doing, wasn't it? Making the most of their fling and making wonderful memories in their brief time together. Memories that were going a long, long way to wiping out some of the heartache Nigel had caused her.

He kissed her lingeringly. 'Come on. I need a hot shower. Preferably with you.'

'If that's a royal order,' she said with a grin, 'then it's one I'm quite happy to obey.'

'Good.'

This time, when he undressed her, he just let everything

drop to the floor in a crumpled heap—so different from the way he'd hung her velvet dress so neatly over the chair.

She laughed and kissed him. 'I'm glad you're losing your neat-freak ways.'

'You've taught me that spontaneous can be good,' he said.

She loved the fact that he was trying. For her. 'Planning can be good, too,' she said. It had definitely taken planning to sort out the picnic and that Mr Darcy moment, and she'd loved every second of them.

'Indi, you talk too much,' Lorenzo said, and proceeded to kiss her.

CHAPTER SEVEN

'ARE YOU BUSY tomorrow morning?' Indigo asked Lorenzo on the Friday morning.

He shrugged. 'I can move things if you want to do something.'

'Some of my favourite bits of glass in the country aren't very far from here. I thought I could take you to see them.'

He looked thoughtful. 'I'd like that. Bruno can drive us.'

'In your official car?' She hadn't really considered it before, but of course Lorenzo probably didn't drive himself very often. He couldn't go out without his security team being nearby, so everything he did had to be planned. 'But if people see a big black car in the car park, they'll immediately think there's a celeb in the church and rush in to see who it is. If they see my slightly battered van with "I Moran, Glass Restoration" on the side, they'll guess we're there to see the glass, so we won't be interrupted.'

'Is there room for my security team to sit in your van?' he asked.

She shook her head. 'There aren't any seats in the back—it's where I keep my tools or transport frames.'

'Much as I'd like to go—and I know your intentions are good,' he said softly, 'it wouldn't be fair on you or on my grandfather to leave here without my security team.'

'Sorry. I didn't think it through.' Whereas Lorenzo was

used to having to plan everything with military precision. And how awful it must be for him, she thought, never being able to do things on impulse and always having people watching his back. When did he ever get space just to *be*?

He leaned forward and kissed her lightly. 'We could compromise. There's always a way.'

Was there? She wasn't so sure.

'Your van isn't suitable and neither's my car. But maybe we can borrow a car from Gus that's a little more subtle. Bruno can drive us, and he and Sergio will give us space in the church to look around.'

'I'd like that,' she said.

'Good.' He kissed her lightly. 'I'll go and see Gus.'

'She's talked you into doing glass geek stuff with her?' Gus laughed. 'Lottie's going to be most put out at missing coffee and pastries.'

'I'll grovel and I'll promise to bring back some pastries for her,' Lorenzo said, laughing back.

'Of course you can borrow a car, idiot. Indi's right—if you take that huge black monster of yours, everyone's going to know there's a celeb about.'

'I'm not a *celeb*,' Lorenzo said, his voice pained.

'You are, where the papers are concerned.' Gus paused. 'This thing between you and Indi—are you sure it's a good idea?'

Lorenzo felt the colour seep into his face. 'We know what we're doing. It's temporary.'

'You've got the same look on your face as I'm sure there was on mine when I met Maisie,' Gus pointed out. 'And I've never seen you like this before.'

'It's temporary,' Lorenzo repeated. 'We'll both walk away when I go back to Melvante. And we'll part as friends.'

Gus raised an eyebrow. 'She's a lot more vulnerable

than she makes out, you know. If you hurt her, Lottie will fillet you.' He paused. 'Actually, no, I'll be first in line to call you out and I'll fillet you myself.'

'I'm not going to hurt her.' Lorenzo placed his hand briefly on Gus's shoulder. 'Though I'm glad she has someone to look out for her.'

'She's had a rough deal where her family's concerned.'

'I know. She told me.'

'She told you?' Gus looked surprised. 'Then it's worse than I thought. She never talks about her family.'

'I'm not going to hurt her,' Lorenzo repeated.

'This is going to end in tears,' Gus warned, shaking his head.

'No, it's not. I'll make sure of that,' Lorenzo said.

Though he thought about Gus's words all afternoon. His best friend had fallen for Maisie and married her within six months. Two years later, they were still deliriously happy.

But the difference was, Gus and Maisie came from the same world. He and Indigo didn't. Well, they'd both been born to noble fathers, but that was as far as it went. Indigo had escaped from that world as soon as she possibly could, and no way would she ever go back to it. And she loved her job; she wouldn't be prepared to give that up for what she'd see as life in a goldfish bowl.

He shook himself. He wasn't in love with Indigo Moran, and she wasn't in love with him. They weren't planning a happy-ever-after. They were having fun and enjoying each other's company—taking a moment out of their usual lives. Gus was just seeing things through the rosy-tinted glasses of a happy marriage and impending fatherhood. Everything was going to be just fine.

On Saturday morning, Lorenzo breakfasted quickly with Indigo in the kitchen, then met his security team as arranged next to the car Gus was lending them. Bruno tapped the details of the church into the satnav system and drove them through narrow country lanes into a pretty little village. The flint-built church was set high on a mound at the edge of the village and, as Indigo had predicted, when Lorenzo twisted the huge iron ring in the heavy oak door the latch clicked up and allowed him to push the door open and follow her inside.

The church was beautiful; with two storeys of windows, it was full of light.

'Come and see my centaur. He's my favourite piece of glass in the world,' she said, and drew him over to one of the windows.

There was a circle of glass set into the diamond-paned window. The outside of the circle had a thick border of purple glass, and in the middle was a black and white picture highlighted with bright yellow, of a centaur playing a violin with a little dog running round his feet.

'And then there's this.' She turned him round and pointed at an angel.

He smiled. 'Trust you.'

'OK, so I have a thing for angels.' She smiled back. 'I just love Gabriel's feathery trousers. Did you know that when they did the medieval Mystery Plays, this is the sort of costume the angels wore?'

Her love for her subject was infectious as well as endearing. He loved her enthusiasm, and the fact that she had the scholarly information to back it up.

Just then, a woman walked in carrying an armful of flowers. She smiled at them. 'Oh, sorry, don't mind me. I'm just sorting out the flowers. We have a wedding here this afternoon,' she confided.

Lorenzo and Indigo exchanged a glance.

Weddings.

For one crazy moment, Lorenzo could imagine standing there in front of the altar, the church filled with roses and crammed with people wanting to share the moment, waiting for Indigo to walk down the aisle towards him.

Oh, help. Maybe Gus had had a point, because Lorenzo had never, ever visualised something like that before. He hadn't even thought about his future wedding, knowing that it would be more or less an arranged marriage for diplomatic purposes because the needs of his country had to come before his personal desires.

But, now the idea was in his head, he couldn't shift it: Indigo in a wedding dress and a veil, carrying a simple bouquet, walking down the carpeted aisle towards him.

'This would be the perfect place to get married,' Indigo said softly.

Was she thinking it, too? Imagining herself walking down the aisle...towards him?

As they moved away from the woman arranging the flowers, he couldn't help asking, 'Is this where you want to get married?'

'I'm never getting married.' She lifted her chin. 'Marriage is just a piece of paper, and it doesn't stop people lying or cheating.'

The hurt was obvious in her voice. Was she thinking about her parents' situation, he wondered, or had she been married before and been hurt by someone who'd cheated on her?

Her face twisted. 'Besides, marriage is an institution and I'm not very good at institutions.'

How he wanted to hold her. Tell her that everything would be OK and he'd never let anything hurt her again.

But it was a promise he knew he wouldn't be able to keep. Short of keeping Indigo wrapped in cotton wool, he couldn't guarantee to protect her from everything. And if she was wrapped in cotton wool, she'd lose her freedom. She'd suffocate. Just as his mother had.

How could he turn this round?

'If you ever did change your mind and get married, I bet it would be in a church with amazing glass,' he said. 'And I bet you'd have a really untraditional wedding dress and outrageous shoes.'

She smiled. 'I'd get my friend Sally to design it for me—the one who made the indigo dress. But I'm not getting married.' She took a deep breath. 'And you'll get married to someone wearing a specially made, hugely elegant and very traditional dress with lots of handmade lace. In a cathedral.'

'I guess.' Let it go, he told himself. *Let it go.* But his mouth had other ideas. 'You'd like the cathedral in Melvante. It's very gothic.'

'Good glass?'

'You'd be a better judge of that than I would.' He paused. 'Come and see for yourself.'

She shook her head, looking sad. 'We both know that when you go back, we won't see each other again. So let's not talk about this. We were talking about cathedrals.' She smiled. 'I love the cathedral in Norwich. There's a Burne-Jones window there and it's absolutely beautiful. I remember going Christmas shopping with Lottie one year, and we went to the carol service at the cathedral. There was a huge Christmas tree and lots of candles. It was totally magical, with the scent of the tree, the singing of the choir and the glass. We went to a patisserie afterwards, and it was just starting to snow, making it feel even more Christmassy. We had hot chocolate and the nicest coffee cake I've ever tasted.'

'Maybe we could go there now,' he suggested.

She shook her head. 'We're taking enough of a risk visiting a tiny country church. Bruno and Sergio would definitely not be happy with an unscheduled visit to the city.'

'I guess,' he said.

She looked at him and thought, there were so many things he couldn't do. She was so lucky to have her freedom and not be in his world.

She put some money in the church collection box; then they said goodbye to the flower-arranger and headed back outside into the bright sunlight.

'We need to go to the patisserie on the way back,' he said.

'Why?'

'Because I owe Lottie nice pastries. For coming out here with you in her place,' he explained.

She looked at Sergio. 'Are we allowed to visit a patisserie? Or maybe if I go in while His Royal Highness waits here in the car with you and Bruno?'

Lorenzo coughed. 'My life's not *that* restricted.'

Oh, yes, it was, she thought.

'We can all go to the patisserie, if His Royal Highness wishes,' Sergio said.

Indigo smiled. 'So I get to have morning coffee with three handsome men? Cool. That works for me.' She nudged Lorenzo. 'And would I be right in thinking that, being royal, you're like the Queen and you don't carry money, so this will be my treat?'

'No, you would not.' He looked offended. 'I can pay for coffee.'

She smiled. 'I was teasing. And offering. I'd like to buy you a coffee. Especially as you spoiled me with that picnic.'

'I'll pay,' Lorenzo said.

'You're not listening. I'm independent, Lorenzo. I've paid my own way since I got my first Saturday job at the age of fourteen. And I want to buy you coffee. I'd like to do something nice for you. So just shut up and let me do it, OK?'

* * *

For a moment, Lorenzo wondered if her ex had tried to take away her independence. Was that why she guarded it so very fiercely now?

He took her hand and squeezed it. 'Then thank you. Coffee would be very nice.'

The patisserie was crowded, but nobody seemed to pay much attention to the four newcomers. They were just part of the crowd. How long had it been since he'd managed that? he wondered.

Indigo ordered coffee and pastries for four, and Lorenzo was surprised to discover that the coffee was every bit as good as what he was used to in Melvante, and the pastries were delicate and delicious. And all the time, she chatted easily to Bruno and Sergio. He'd never known them so talkative, ever, even if one of them was training with him or sparring in the gym. Indigo had a gift for drawing people out. She could teach him so much. But what could he offer her, in return?

Indigo bought a box of treats for Gus, Lottie, Syb and Maisie before they left. And then she noticed a box of home-baked dog treats on the counter, so she bought some for all the dogs, too.

Lorenzo went quiet on the way back to Edensfield, but he held her hand all the way. And Indigo was aware that she was getting way too close to him. If this carried on, she'd get hurt. She really had to keep her heart protected and remember who he was. He could be her Mr Right Now, but not her Prince Happy-Ever-After. Much as she'd like him to be.

CHAPTER EIGHT

LORENZO'S LAST WEEK at Edensfield was idyllic. By day, he worked on official court business; his nights were spent making love with Indigo and sleeping with her wrapped in his arms; and in the spaces between they found time to go for long walks, hand in hand, or he'd play the piano for her, or she'd read to him with his head resting in her lap. Sometimes they watched the sun set over the lake; sometimes they lay on the damp grass and watched the stars. All the sweet, simple things that lovers did.

And he actually found himself writing music again—something he hadn't done in a long, long time. He knew he'd been inspired by Indigo and the way she acted on impulse and saw joy in everything.

Each day grew more bittersweet, because each day was nearer to the moment when he'd have to leave her.

And then it hit him.

He didn't want to leave her. He liked having Indigo in his life, and he was pretty sure she liked having him in her life. OK, so they'd agreed this would be a fling and it would end when he left for Melvante. But there was no reason why they couldn't renegotiate that agreement.

'Indi—I've been thinking,' he said, when they were lying on a blanket by the summer house, looking up at the stars.

'Should I be worried?' she teased.

'I leave in three days.'

'I know.' She stroked his face. 'I'll miss you.'

'I'll miss you, too.' He shifted so that he was facing her and could look into her eyes. 'That's why I've been thinking. It doesn't have to be like this.'

'Yes, it does. You're going off to be King of Melvante, and I'm staying here at Edensfield to finish my work on the library windows.'

'You've made a business commitment, and of course you want to honour that. But when you've finished here, there's nothing to stop you coming to Melvante and being with me.' He stole a kiss. 'Between-times, we're going to have to be pretty much long-distance, but we're only a couple of hours apart by plane. We can work something out.'

'Hang on. Are you saying you want to make this thing between us...?' She looked at him, wide-eyed.

'Official and no longer temporary. Yes.'

He wanted to be with her. In public as well as in private. And she wouldn't be Indigo Moran, stained-glass restorer, any more. She'd be the equivalent of a royal WAG, living her life on a public stage, hobbled by rules and regulations.

Yes, she'd be with Lorenzo. She wouldn't have to give him up.

But the misery of his lifestyle would eat into their relationship, sucking up all the love and leaving nothing but emptiness and hurt.

And she really, really didn't want that. She wanted to keep these memories intact. Perfect.

'Indi?' he asked.

Telling him the truth would hurt him. But going along with what he wanted would hurt him more, in the end. 'No, we couldn't,' she said softly. 'I wouldn't fit into your world, Lorenzo.'

'How do you know?'

'I just do.'

Which gave him nothing to argue against. He needed to know why she was so set against it. So he asked her straight out. 'Indi, what's so bad about my world?'

'It's full of rules and regulations. You're stuck in a box and you're expected to stay there. And you have to watch what you do, the whole time. Especially now there's social media—it means you can never switch off. You're being watched every second of the day. One accidental slip, and suddenly you've told the whole world something that maybe you would rather have kept private. It's like talking with a megaphone in the middle of a plinth on Trafalgar Square. And it gets passed on within seconds—juicy gossip.' She shuddered.

'And then someone else does something, and what you said or did is forgotten about.'

'Until the next time. Then it's dragged up again. Every little mistake is catalogued and held against you.'

'You'd be in a different position, as my partner,' he said. 'Nobody would try to put you down.'

She could see in his expression that he really believed it. For someone so clever, she thought, sometimes he just didn't have a clue what it was like in the real world. 'Maybe not to my face, but behind my back they would. Everyone expects you to marry a princess. And the press would be merciless. They'd want to know what you see in me. They'd dig up all the stuff about my parents.' And about Nigel—and she really didn't want to tell Lorenzo about that. She was too ashamed of how naive and stupid she'd been, having a relationship with a man who'd turned out to be married. And it still hurt to think about the miscarriage; talking about it was next to impossible.

'You can't be held to ransom by the choices your parents made,' he said.

'I can't fit into your world, Lorenzo. Don't ask me. I don't want to be the stick that the press uses to beat you. And we only have a few days left together. Please don't spoil it.'

What could he say to that?

All he could do was hold her.

And, that night, his lovemaking was much more intense. Yearning. If only she'd give them a chance, he was sure they could make it work.

But stubborn was definitely her middle name, and he didn't have a clue where to start convincing her that life with him wouldn't be anywhere near as scary as she feared.

On Lorenzo's last night, he fell asleep in Indigo's arms. She lay there, unable to sleep and wishing that she could somehow freeze time.

He'd asked her to make their relationship permanent. But how could she? She'd expose him to the kind of scandal he really didn't need, especially as he was just going to start ruling Melvante. She didn't want that tarnished.

'You're going to be a brilliant king,' she whispered, holding him close. 'Go with my love, always, and I wish things could've been different.'

Now, she knew she was always going to be on her own, because Lorenzo had spoiled her for other men. Nobody would ever match up to him, and it wouldn't be fair to get involved with someone else, knowing that he'd always be second best to Lorenzo. But being single was fine. She had good friends and her job. They'd see her through.

Though, when Lorenzo did marry his suitable princess, Indigo definitely wasn't going to tune in to the televised broadcast. She'd wish him luck, but she couldn't watch him marry someone else.

'I wish we'd met in another life,' she said softly. 'When things could have worked. But it wasn't to be, and we're going to be grown up about it. We're going to shake hands, say goodbye, and walk away from each other with our hearts intact.'

Even though she knew she was lying to herself.

When Lorenzo woke, the next morning, Indigo was still asleep. Her mermaid hair was spread all over the pillow, and her eyelashes were so long. So cute.

'If only you weren't so stubborn,' he said softly. Why couldn't she see that they could make it work? This was the twenty-first century, and a lot of the old social taboos had been broken. It didn't matter that she wasn't a princess. It didn't matter that her parents hadn't been married and that she was the child of an affair—it wasn't her fault. And he knew that Indigo was strong enough to hold her own in any social situation; she had a genuine warmth and enthusiasm that would draw people to her. Even those who maybe wouldn't want to accept her at first would come round, once they'd met her.

But the main stumbling block was Indigo herself.

If she didn't believe in herself—in their relationship— then it couldn't work.

How could he get her to believe?

He held her until she woke, then made love to her one last time. And he knew his own eyelashes were as wet as hers.

'We don't have to say goodbye,' he said, holding her close. 'We can make this work.'

She simply shook her head, as if not trusting herself to speak.

He sighed, and reached for his wallet. 'Here.'

She looked at the storage card. 'What's this?'

'For you. I wrote a song. Well, there aren't any words. But it's called "Indigo".'

'You wrote a song for me?'

'About how you make me feel.'

'Nobody's ever written a song for me before.' She stared at him in wonder. 'Thank you.'

'You might hate it.'

'I won't.'

Funny how she could be so sure of that, and yet she didn't have that same belief in *them*.

'Actually, I have something for you.' She slid out of bed and rummaged in a drawer, then handed him a cardboard tube. 'Don't look at it now. Later.'

She'd drawn something for him?

'Thank you,' he said softly.

She swallowed hard. 'I guess this is goodbye. I don't... not in front of everyone else.'

She'd be working when he left, he guessed. So she could hide behind her glass.

'I know,' he said softly. 'I'm not going to say the words.'

'Be happy,' she said. 'And you're going to be an awesome king.'

There was a lump in his throat and it was hard to get the words out. 'You be happy, too. And I hope you find someone who can give you what I can't.' Freedom. But he was pretty sure that she wouldn't find someone who loved her the way he'd grown to love her.

Later, on the plane back to Melvante, he opened the cardboard tube and took out the piece of cartridge paper. She'd drawn an angel in a rose bower—and the angel had his face.

Indigo and her angels. He smiled fondly, remembering

the church they'd visited together and the joy in her face as she'd shown him the glass.

Then he looked closer. Was it his imagination, or were those roses covering the bars of a cage?

That was how she saw his life. Trapped in a cage.

But it didn't have to be that way. It could be just roses. Somehow, he was going to have to convince her. And not just her: he also had to convince his grandfather that he'd found the woman who would be right for him and right for Melvante.

And maybe a little space between them—space where she had time to think and time to miss him—would help him do that.

CHAPTER NINE

THE BED WAS too wide, the days were too long and everything felt muted.

So much for being able to walk away intact at the end of their affair, Indigo thought. She'd really been deluding herself.

Still. Lorenzo had gone back to Melvante, where he belonged, and that was that. She still had the job she loved, and some good friends who were every bit as good as family. So she'd be just fine, she told herself sternly. Crying herself to sleep was pointless and ridiculous.

But she found it really hard to face breakfast in the mornings.

And she kept waking up at night. Which was ridiculous. At her age, she shouldn't need to get up in the middle of the night to go to the loo.

And maybe it was time she started watching what she ate, because her bra was feeling too tight.

A nasty, insidious thought wormed its way into her brain. Wonky appetite, tight bra, needing the loo in the middle of the night…She'd been there before, a couple of years ago. When her life had imploded.

No. Of course not. She was being paranoid. She and Lorenzo had always been careful about contraception. The last thing a king-to-be needed was an accidental baby, particularly when there was no way he could marry the baby's mother. And she had seriously unhappy memories from her miscarriage, two years ago.

But, now she thought about it, her period *was* a few days late. And she was usually regular down to the hour.

Maybe her period was late because she was stressed and upset about Lorenzo leaving. She hoped so. Because the alternative—that somehow their contraception had failed—would make life way, way too complicated.

Toto had taken to following Indigo about since Lorenzo had left, and tended to stay by her side in the workroom. The Labrador thumped his tail against the floor and nuzzled her knee, as if to say that he could tell she was upset and he was there.

'Lovely boy.' Indigo bent to make a fuss of him. 'I'm being stupid. Of course I'm not pregnant. I can't be.'

Though being pregnant would also explain why she kept crying. The tears could be due to her hormones running amok, not just because she missed the man she loved but knew she couldn't have.

'I can't be pregnant,' she said again.

Though she knew she wouldn't be able to settle until she knew the truth.

After the visitors had left Edensfield and her workroom was silent again, she drove to the nearest large town where she knew she'd be anonymous and bought a pregnancy test from the supermarket.

'Indigo Moran, you're being totally ridiculous. Of course you're not pregnant, and this is going to prove it once and for all,' she told herself sternly.

Back in her bathroom at Edensfield, she did the test, and watched the windows. One to show that she'd performed the test properly, and one that could turn her life upside down.

The last time she'd done a pregnancy test, she'd cried with joy, thinking that although the baby wasn't planned it would give Nigel the excuse he needed to commit properly to her. That she'd have their baby. That once again in her life she'd have someone who was related to her by blood, someone she could love and who'd love her back.

Nigel's reaction to the news had shocked her to the core. But she'd decided to keep the baby; after all, it wasn't the baby's fault that its father had turned out to be a cheat and a liar.

And then, six weeks later, she'd felt the drag low in her belly as she'd miscarried.

She sucked in a breath. This wasn't going to be like that. At all. Because she wasn't pregnant. She wasn't. She couldn't be.

Shaking herself mentally, she glanced at the test stick again.

And then she saw the result.

Positive.

Melvante might be his home, but it wasn't where his heart was, Lorenzo thought.

Being without Indigo for the last few days had crystallised for him exactly what he wanted in a life partner—someone who was bright and sparkly in her own right, who would support him and help him think straight by asking awkward questions, and who would keep her own interests in life, too. He loved her free-spiritedness.

Except he knew she was right about the sticking point. She'd hate what his lifestyle would become, once he was crowned king.

But there had to be a middle way. There had to be space for compromise. And hopefully, if she missed him as much as he missed her, she'd help him work out a compromise to suit them both.

He lasted two more days before he tackled his grandfather at the breakfast table.

'Nonno, you know you said I should think about marriage?'

'Yes.' His grandfather poured them both more coffee. 'So you're ready to discuss it? Good. I've drawn up a list of suitable brides.' He smiled at Lorenzo. 'Just as my father did for me.'

'That's the point, Nonno. I've already met the woman I want to marry,' Lorenzo said. 'Her name's Indigo Moran, she's a stained-glass restoration specialist, and she's—well, she makes me a better man. And I know I'll be a better king if I marry for love rather than duty.'

'I've had this conversation before.' His grandfather grimaced. 'With your father. He married for love, and look what happened.'

He'd ended up driving his car into a brick wall, with Lorenzo's mother by his side, killing them both. The rest of the world thought it was a tragic accident, but Lorenzo and his grandfather knew the truth: it had been a deliberate act, because Lorenzo's father couldn't bear the idea of his wife leaving him.

Lorenzo looked his grandfather straight in the eye. 'Nonno, I've spent most of my life trying to show you that I'm not my father. Indigo is nothing like my mother.'

'Your father married for love and it went wrong,' his grandfather pointed out. 'I married for duty, and your grandmother and I were happy together. We both knew what was expected of us.'

'I want to marry someone who understands my work and supports me,' Lorenzo said.

'Which your grandmother did for me.'

'Did you love Nonna?' Lorenzo asked.

'I respected her and I admired her,' his grandfather said. 'So, yes, I loved her.'

'Whenever you saw her, did your heart beat faster and the world seem a little brighter?'

His grandfather smiled ruefully. 'Lorenzo, you're confusing passion with love. Love is something that grows out of respect and mutual understanding. Something solid. Passion…that never lasts. It's like a firework—it burns brightly, it feels spectacular, and it's over almost immediately. Take my advice, and marry for sense—don't marry for passion. Your father married for passion, and he regretted it.'

'I'm not my father,' Lorenzo said again. 'I was thinking—you wanted to do something to mark the coronation. We could commission a rose window for the castle.'

'And you just *happen* to know a glass specialist,' his grandfather said wryly.

Lorenzo smiled. 'OK, so that was a little unsubtle. But it's a good way for you to meet Indi without raising any expectations on either side.'

'How does she feel about you?' his grandfather asked.

'That's tricky,' Lorenzo said. 'She has doubts about the world we live in. She thinks it's like a goldfish bowl.'

'It is, and she's right to have doubts. Our world isn't an easy one.' His grandfather sighed. 'You need to understand that you and I have responsibilities that other people don't. We have to put the needs of our country before our own needs. Which is why you need to marry someone who can cope with our world. Someone who's been brought up in it. Someone who doesn't have doubts.'

'Just meet her,' Lorenzo said. 'Give her a chance. And maybe she can give our world a chance.'

'And then?'

'We'll play it by ear,' Lorenzo said decisively.

'You've changed,' his grandfather said. 'The Lorenzo I know plans everything a long way in advance.'

Which was how he'd been brought up. Formal and rigid and disconnected from people. 'I still do,' Lorenzo said. 'But I've learned a lot from Indi. Sometimes, to really connect with people and make a difference, you have to be a bit more flexible.'

'She taught you that?' His grandfather looked thoughtful. 'She sounds an intriguing young woman.'

'She is.' Lorenzo smiled. 'I'll call her and arrange it.'

There was a gentle but insistent rap on the door. 'Indi? Indi, are you all right? Can I come in?'

Lottie.

Should she lie and pretend that she had a crashing headache?

But Lottie was perceptive. Even if Indigo could stall her for now, Lottie would notice that something was up. And she was a close enough and old enough friend to ask what was wrong.

'Come in,' she croaked.

'Indi, you've been crying,' Lottie said as she walked in and closed the door behind her.

Indigo felt the tears well up and forced them back.

'Sweetie, what's wrong?' Lottie asked. 'Is this to do with Lorenzo?'

'Sort of,' she hedged.

Lottie hugged her. 'I know you're missing him. Look, do you want Gus to have a word with him?'

'No, I'll be fine.' Indigo shook her head. 'I'll pull myself together.'

'Why don't you go to Melvante and see him?'

She blew out a breath. 'I can't do that. He's busy preparing to be king.'

'But you're missing him, and I bet he's missing you just as much.'

'We agreed it was just a fling and we were both going to walk away at the end.'

Lottie raised her eyebrows. 'I think it was more than just a fling. You fell for him, didn't you?'

Indigo bit her lip. 'Is it that obvious?'

'Sweetie, you two might have thought you were being discreet, but it was obvious to everyone,' Lottie said, squeezing her hand. 'You both always seemed to disappear at the same time, so we knew you were together—and the way you looked at each other across a room was, well…' She fanned herself. 'Scorching.'

'Oh.' Indigo felt the colour flood into her face. 'Sorry. We didn't mean to—' Then, to her horror, she burst into tears.

Lottie held her close and let her cry.

'Sorry. I'm being really wet,' she apologised.

'No, you've been alone for a long time and you just fell in love with Lorenzo.'

'He's the worst person I could fall in love with.'

'I can think of worse,' Lottie said darkly. 'Besides, Lorenzo's one of the good guys. Actually, Gus has already had the big-brother talk with him about you.'

Indigo scrubbed away the tears. 'That's so sweet of him.'

'Gus thinks of you as his other little sister. Actually, you're the sister I would've chosen, if I'd been able to.'

Indigo sniffed. 'Don't, Lottie, you'll make me cry even more.'

'What is it, Indi?'

She dragged in a breath. 'I don't know where to start.'

'Try the beginning—or the middle, if it's easier. Or just cut to the difficult bit and come straight out with it,' Lottie suggested.

'The difficult bit.' Indigo raked a hand through her hair. Well, she'd been here before. And Lottie had listened before. She was a safe person to tell. 'I'm pregnant.'

Lottie placed a hand on her shoulder. 'Indi, are you sure? You're not just late because you're stressed about Lorenzo going back to Melvante?'

'I'm sure.' Her breath hitched. 'I did a test. Three days ago.'

'You've known about this for *three days* and you didn't tell me?' Lottie looked hurt.

'I didn't want to dump it on you like I did last time, and I'm—I'm—oh, God, I'm so sorry.' She felt her face crumple again.

'Stop apologising. You're not dumping it on me. That's what friends are for, and I know you'd be there for me if it was the other way round.' Lottie hugged her again. 'So what do you want to do?'

'I don't know what to do for the best.' Three sleepless nights hadn't helped her decide a single thing. 'I mean, I have to tell Lorenzo—of course I do, it wouldn't be fair to keep the news to myself—but I'm not expecting anything from him.'

'He's not Nigel the Scumbag. He's an honourable man.'

'That's the point, Lottie. He's about to become the King of Melvante. Having an illegitimate child just isn't going to work for him.'

Lottie spread her hands. 'So make the child legitimate and marry the man. You and Lorenzo are crazy about each other.'

'But I won't fit into his world.' Indigo sighed. 'And it'll be like living in a goldfish bowl, with everyone watching what I do all the time. I can't just decide to go to the park or the beach because it's a glorious day. His schedules are mapped out months in advance and there are security people everywhere. I don't want that kind of life for me or for my baby.'

'What about what Lorenzo wants?' Lottie asked.

'He's got enough on his plate without having to deal with a baby.'

'Indi…you're not thinking…?' Lottie looked horrified.

Indigo shook her head. 'I haven't exactly slept well for the last three nights. I've had time to think about it. And I'm going to make the same decision as I made last time.' She dragged in a breath. '*Last time.* And we both know what happened then. Who's to say this won't resolve itself in the same way?'

'You lost the baby then, but it doesn't mean to say you're going to lose this baby. Right now, what you need,' Lottie said, 'is to see a doctor and get checked over. Get all the blood tests done and what have you. And I'll come with you to hold your hand.'

'I can't ask you to do that.'

'You're not asking—I'm telling you,' Lottie said. 'And, for once, that independent streak of yours is going to have to shut up and listen. Right?'

Indigo gave her a watery smile. 'Right.'

When Indigo came out of the doctor's surgery—with her pregnancy confirmed and a dating scan booked in at the hospital—she switched on her phone.

The message flashed up onto the screen: two missed calls. Both from Lorenzo. And there was a voicemail from him asking if she could give him a call.

She swallowed hard. How stupid to find herself almost in tears just at hearing his voice. That had to be the hormones whizzing round her system. She really wasn't that pathetic and needy.

Why did he want her to call him? Surely he didn't…?

She shook herself. No. Of *course* he didn't have any idea about the situation she was in right now. He couldn't read her mind, and she knew that Lottie wouldn't have betrayed her confidence.

Returning his call would at least give her the chance to talk to him. Maybe she'd get an opening to broach the subject of the baby. Not that telling him on the phone was ideal, but talking to him would be a start. She could see how he sounded and play it by ear.

Once back in the privacy of her car, she rang Lorenzo. Although she'd half expected to end up leaving a message on his voicemail, he answered immediately. 'Indi. Hello. Thanks for calling back.'

'You're welcome.' And she was *not* going to burst into tears. She played it as cool as she could. 'What can I do for you?'

'I have a commission for you. In Melvante. I was thinking maybe a rose window.'

Her dream job. She'd talked to him about what she'd love to create, given the chance. And he was offering her that chance—albeit in his home, rather than her own.

'Would this be in the palace?' she asked tentatively.

'Yes. It's for the coronation. I know it's ridiculously short notice, but do you think you could fit it in?'

So he wanted her to work for him?

How naive she'd been, thinking that he might've wanted just to talk to her. After all, he'd asked her to make their fling permanent and she'd turned him down. He had no reason to think she might have changed her mind or regretted the decision. Their affair was over and life had moved on; he was about to become king. And he even sounded different—slightly more formal and a little distant. Which made what she needed to tell him even more difficult. Just how was she going to bring up something so emotional, when all he wanted to talk to her about was work?

'I could look at where you want to site it and come up with some designs, yes,' she said carefully. She had some more projects scheduled in for when she'd finished at Edensfield, but she was pretty sure that her clients would be flexible about the timescales if she asked them nicely. 'When were you thinking?'

'Tomorrow?' he suggested.

'Sorry, I really can't. I'm fitting the mermaid window back into place at Edensfield tomorrow.'

'How about the day after?'

'The day after is fine,' she said. Though he'd forgotten one crucial little detail. 'Provided I can book a flight. If there isn't one available, it might have to be later.'

'You don't need to book a flight.'

'As a mere mortal,' she said crisply, 'I don't actually have wings to get me to Melvante under my own steam.'

'I didn't mean that. I meant, I'll get it arranged for you.' He laughed. 'Oh, Indi. I've missed your straight talking.'

Maybe. But he clearly didn't miss *her*.

As if he could read her thoughts, he said softly, 'But not as much as I've missed you.'

She had to swallow really, really hard. Because right then she really, really missed him. Talking to him and knowing that he was hundreds of miles away was sheer torture.

'Come to Melvante,' he said, his voice as warm and tempting as melted chocolate.

'Because you want me to design some glass for you?'

She regretted the words as soon as they were out, knowing how needy they made her sound. And she didn't want Lorenzo to think she was pathetic.

'The commission's genuine,' he said, 'and I'll pay the going rate—I'm not expecting you to give me some ridiculously huge discount. But I guess it's also an excuse to see you.'

And she really needed to see him. Oh, God. The idea of Lorenzo wrapping his arms round her and holding her close, telling her not to worry and that everything would be OK because he loved her...

But how could he possibly do that? He was about to become the King of Melvante. She knew Lorenzo was attracted to her, and she knew he liked her. Maybe the two together made up love. Though Indigo had learned not to trust love, because in her experience it just ended in heartache. Nigel had dumped her as soon as he'd discovered that she was pregnant, and then she'd found out how deep his betrayal had been. OK, so Lorenzo wasn't a cheat and a liar—but, even so, how could he possibly support her and the baby, with all that he had going on in his life right now? Plus the press would have a field day if they found out that the new King of Melvante was going to have a love-child with a woman who was the illegitimate daughter of an earl...

She couldn't see any way out of it. Lorenzo had to follow his duty, and that would mean dumping her because she was totally unsuitable to be a queen. And, even if her life hadn't been so tarnished in the past, there was the fact that he'd live the rest of his life in the glare of the public eye—which wasn't what she wanted for herself or for the baby.

'Indi? Are you still there?' he asked.

'It's a bad connection,' she lied.

'OK. I'll get Salvatore to call you with the flight details and an agenda.'

'Who's Salvatore?'

'My assistant. I'll see you the day after tomorrow. *Ciao.*'

He hung up, and Indi stared at her phone. This didn't seem real. She'd just agreed to go to Melvante and see him. And the way he'd dropped so easily into speaking Italian at the end of their conversation... Well, it wasn't surprising. He was right where he belonged, in his European kingdom. While she belonged here in England. And she had a nasty feeling that the distance between them now wasn't just geographical.

CHAPTER TEN

LATER THAT AFTERNOON, Indigo's phone rang. She didn't recognise the number on the screen and almost didn't answer it, assuming it was some cold-caller; then again, Lorenzo had said that his assistant would contact her about the flights. Maybe it was him.

She answered the phone warily. 'Hello?'

'Signorina Moran?' The stranger's voice had a very slight accent, something which sounded as if it came from the southern Mediterranean.

'Yes,' she said. 'Who's calling?'

'My name is Salvatore Pozzi. I'm the personal assistant to His Royal Highness Prince Lorenzo of Melvante. He asked me to get in touch with you with the details of your flight.'

'Thank you.' Oh, and how formal was this guy? No wonder Lorenzo was so buttoned up if this was the way things were in Melvante. The chances were that she wouldn't fit into his private world, either, she thought with a sinking heart.

'Do you have an email address so I can send you the information and the agenda for meeting His Royal Highness?' Salvatore asked.

Agenda? Meeting?

It all felt very cool, very brisk—and it was the total opposite to what she'd shared with Lorenzo here in England.

Well, it was her own fault for blurring the lines between business and personal stuff. Here at Edensfield, they'd been in a bubble, protected from the rest of the world. In Melvante, Lorenzo was in the full glare of the public eye. A business meeting with him was the best she could hope for. And what he'd said about missing her—maybe he did, but things were different now and she knew he couldn't afford to act on those feelings.

'Yes, I have an email address.' She dictated it coolly and professionally. Because, after all, this was a job. She was planning to meet her client, not her lover. And she'd better keep that in mind if she wanted to keep what was left of her heart intact.

'*Bene.* Good. I'll email you now. If there are any problems or you have any questions when you've read through the details, please call me.'

'I will. And thank you for your help,' she said.

'My pleasure, Signorina Moran.' Though there wasn't really any warmth in his voice. It was just politeness.

By the time she'd powered up her laptop, the email from Salvatore was waiting in her in-box. Her flight was at ten a.m. the day after tomorrow—from the local airport rather than one of the larger London airports, so she guessed there would probably be a connecting flight somewhere in Europe. And there was an agenda giving her times when the prince would be meeting her over the next few days. A briefing meeting. A tour of the castle. A tour of the cathedral. A status update. A meeting with His Majesty King Lorenzo II and His Royal Highness Prince Lorenzo to discuss final details—*oh, help.* Not just Lorenzo, then. His grandfather as well. And his grandfather definitely wouldn't approve of her.

Everything was tightly scheduled, she noticed, down to the minute. Well, obviously Lorenzo had a thousand and one demands on his time right now. She was lucky he was giving her this much time.

But just when was she going to get the chance to tell him about the baby?

She blew out a breath. She'd definitely have to play that one by ear. But at least she had enough time in between those meetings to work on the designs and come up with something she hoped would do him justice.

She finished scanning the list. Charity ball? What? Why on earth did he want her to go to that? Oh, for pity's sake. He must know she wasn't the kind of person who went to glamorous events like charity balls. She was a glass geek who was more likely to go to an exhibition or find the nearest art gallery or medieval church.

Apart from the fact that Lorenzo had made it very clear he was busy—otherwise he would've called her himself with the flight details and he wouldn't have asked his assistant to send her an agenda—Indigo didn't trust her voice not to wobble when she spoke to him. Salvatore had said to call him with any queries, but this one was a little bit too personal. So she sent Salvatore a brief, polite email thanking him for the information, then texted Lorenzo. *Why is there a charity ball on the agenda?*

t took him a while to respond. Probably, she thought, because he was in a meeting and there would be tons of other messages on his phone. Assuming he didn't just forward everything to his assistant to deal with; and then the fact that she'd texted the prince instead of contacting his assistant wouldn't go down too well.

Too late, now. She couldn't recall the message.

She was just finishing up a last piece of work on the mermaid window when her phone beeped to signal a text. She made herself wait to read it and not rush straight to it. So you can meet some of the people of my country, get more of a feel for the background. Are you worried about it?

Trust him to pick up on that. Of course not. she lied.

Of course she was worried about attending a charity ball in Melvante. Even though she'd be there as a business associate, there was still a chance that people might guess that her relationship with Lorenzo hadn't been strictly business in England.

Just checking the dress code, she typed.even though she was pretty sure she knew what it was already.

Black tie, he responded.

Which meant a ball gown. Something she didn't own. Luckily, she knew two people who did and who'd be prepared to lend her one—and they were both here in this house, which would save her a rushed journey. OK. Thanks.

He didn't text her back, this time. Super-busy, she guessed. Still. At least she was going to see him. And she would have plenty of time in Melvante to think, to work out how to tell him about the baby.

Funny how just talking to Indigo had made him antsy, Lorenzo thought. It brought home to him how much he'd missed her. How much he wanted to see her.

But she'd sounded very cool, calm and businesslike on the phone. So was she going to treat this as just another commission, or was she using it as an excuse to see him— the way he was using it as an excuse to see her?

He really couldn't tell.

So he'd just have to compartmentalise things and

keep his feelings separate. Maybe he'd be able to tell more when he saw her.

Work kept Indigo occupied for the rest of the day; she spent the evening looking up everything she could about Melvante and making notes. The next day was spent putting the mermaid window in place; and then it was time to pack. Just as well, she thought, that she had her passport with her; she and Lottie had spent a girly weekend in Paris just before she'd started work on the window, and she'd gone to Edensfield from Paris rather than via her flat in London.

'I'll drive you to the airport—I've got stuff to do in town anyway, so it's not very far out of my way. And you can leave all your stuff here while you're in Melvante. You need to be back here for the official unveiling of the window, in any case,' Lottie told her.

'Thanks.' She paused. 'Lottie, I meant to ask you last night—can I borrow a ball gown, please?'

'A ball gown?' Lottie looked surprised.

'Lorenzo wants me to attend a charity ball. He says it's good background for designing his window.'

Lottie raised an eyebrow. 'He must live on a different planet.'

One where Indigo knew she wouldn't fit in. 'I guess.'

'Of course you can borrow a ball gown. Come and raid my wardrobe.'

Doing something girly helped to occupy Indigo's mind for a little while, but once she'd chosen a plain black ball gown—one she intended to wear with her red strappy shoes, to give her a bit of courage—and packed some business suits, her mind went back to Lorenzo. How was he going to react to her? And how would he react to the news about the baby?

Worry kept her awake for most of the night, having end-less conversations in her head with him. And she couldn't even drink coffee to keep her awake, the next morning—apart from the fact that it wouldn't be good for the baby, the smell of it made her feel queasy. Maybe she could have a nap on the plane or something.

She didn't say much on the way to the airport; her stom-ach felt as if it was tied in knots and panic rather than blood was flowing through her veins. But she made an effort when Lottie dropped her off.

'Thanks, Lottie.' Indigo hugged her. 'I'll text you when I get there.'

'Good. And remember, Indi, Lorenzo's not Nigel. He's not going to abandon you.'

'I know.' Though he might not actually have a choice in the matter, Indigo thought. He might *have* to abandon her.

Why couldn't she have fallen for a man who didn't come with complications?

At the customer services desk, she said to the assistant, 'I think I have a ticket to pick up?' She gave her name and the flight number.

'Of course, Madam. This way.'

To Indigo's surprise, she was waved straight through Customs. There were none of the usual checks she was used to—not even her passport, much less having her bag X-rayed and walking through a scanner. What was going on?

When she was escorted out to the runway, she saw a small private jet.

What?

'Is there—well—some mistake?' she asked. 'I was ex-pecting a connecting flight to Melvante.'

'There's no connection needed, Madam,' the attendant told her. 'This is the Melvante royal plane.'

Lorenzo had sent the royal plane for her? But…

'I—um—thank you,' she said, flustered. No wonder he'd said that she wouldn't need to sort out a flight. This one was just for her. Which was crazy. She barely even travelled first class, let alone in super-luxury. This wasn't the kind of life she was used to.

Clutching her suitcase, she walked up the steps to the door of the plane, where a woman in a smart navy suit greeted her.

'Good morning, *signorina*. My name is Maria, and I'm your flight attendant today. Let me take your luggage.'

Indigo had to blink twice as she stepped into the aisle. This was nothing like the kind of planes she'd flown in before, with slightly cramped seats and a narrow aisle. This was more like a hotel business suite than a plane. There were cream leather sofas at one end, and a table at the other end which looked as if it belonged in a board room together with the deeply padded chairs. There was even an arrangement of fresh flowers on a coffee table.

'His Royal Highness asked us to make sure you were comfortable on your journey, *signorina*,' Maria said, ushering her over to one of the sofas. 'May I get you something to eat or drink?'

'A glass of water would be lovely, please, Maria,' Indigo said, summoning a smile. Right at that moment she felt very much out of her depth. Lorenzo hadn't sent her a plane ticket—he'd sent her a *plane*. How unreal was that?

'Can I offer you a magazine?'

Indigo shook her head. 'That's very kind of you, but I was actually planning to do some work.'

'Of course. You're very welcome to use the table, if you prefer it to the sofas. There are plugs if you need them to charge a laptop.'

'Thank you, Maria,' she said, and settled herself at the table.

When Maria returned with a glass of water, Indigo noticed that it had ice and a slice of lime too. And the glass was lead crystal rather than the disposable plastic cups she was used to seeing on a plane.

'If you wish for anything, please ring the bell and I'll come straight away,' Maria said.

'Thank you, Maria.' Indigo tried out some of the Italian she'd learned over the last day or so. *'Mille grazie.'*

Maria's smile showed her how much the gesture was appreciated.

So this was what a royal lifestyle meant. The ultimate in comfort and convenience. And yet it wasn't super-flashy; the room had a businesslike air.

And she'd better remember that she was going to be in Melvante on business, first and foremost.

She read through the file she'd made on Melvante, the day before, and made some more notes for possible designs. The flight went incredibly quickly; at the airport in Melvante, she was also waved straight through Customs with no passport check. Then again, she supposed, if you were travelling on the king's private plane, that kind of guaranteed you were expected and welcome in the country.

There was a car waiting for her; she recognised the chauffeur standing outside. 'Bruno! How lovely to see you.'

'And you, too, Signorina Moran,' he said with a formal little bow.

'It's Indi to you, as you know very well,' she said with a smile, and gave him a hug that made him blush.

When Bruno opened the rear door for her, she asked, 'Can I be cheeky and ask if I can sit in the front with you, please, Bruno? All this…' She grimaced. 'It's a little bit overwhelming.'

'Of course, *signo*—' he began, then with a smile corrected himself. 'Indi.' He opened the door for her and waited for her to settle before closing it again and going round to the driver's side.

Indigo had seen a similar large black diplomatic car with tinted windows at Edensfield, but Bruno hadn't been in livery there. Here, he wore a smart uniform with gold braid and a cap, and he looked every inch a royal chauffeur. This was feeling more and more unreal with every second.

In a different life, Lorenzo might have met her at the airport himself. He might have run towards her, lifted her off her feet, swung her round, and kissed her until they were both dizzy.

But Lorenzo in England wasn't the same as Lorenzo in Melvante. Here, he was about to become the king. And it most definitely wasn't suitable for a king to meet a contractor at the airport, much less greet her with such warmth.

How would he greet her when the schedule said he'd meet her? Would he be cool, calm, collected and distant? Or would he still be the man he'd been in England, passionate once his defences were down?

She damped down the panic. 'I assume His Royal Highness is in a meeting?'

'He's always in meetings,' Bruno said. 'He works harder than anyone I know.'

That didn't surprise her. She knew that Lorenzo had a strong sense of duty, and she respected that. 'Uh-huh,' she said.

Although Indigo could normally chat to anyone, and she'd chatted quite happily to Bruno at Edensfield, right now she was feeling ever so slightly intimidated. As they drove through the city towards the castle, she could see that it was just as Lorenzo had said: a picture-postcard style white stone castle with turrets and pointy tiled roofs. Had she been visiting the place on holiday, she would have thought it pretty. But, at that moment, it felt as if it towered over her disapprovingly.

Bruno parked the car on the gravel outside the castle, opened the door for her and took her bag, then ushered her in to the castle through what she guessed was the equivalent of the tradesman's entrance.

He took her through to an office; as she stepped onto the carpet, her feet sank into it. Everywhere was polished wood and gilt—like the office of a CEO in a major company. Which, Indigo supposed, was effectively Lorenzo's position. Only his 'company' happened to be a country.

A middle-aged man in a three-piece suit looked up from behind his mahogany desk as the door opened, and stood up. He said something swiftly in Italian to Bruno—too fast for Indigo to translate, with her meagre stock of tourist vocabulary—and inclined his head at her. 'Good afternoon, Signorina Moran. I am Salvatore Pozzi.'

'Good afternoon, Signor Pozzi.' She stepped forward and offered her hand; and when he took it she made sure that her handshake was firm and businesslike. 'Thank you for arranging my flight and the car here.'

'No problem.' Though he still wasn't smiling.

'Bye, Bruno,' she said as the chauffeur left, sketching her a salute. It felt as if her only friend in the place had gone. Salvatore was perfectly polite, but his expression was inscrutable. Indigo had no idea what Lorenzo had told him about her, or if he knew about their fling back in England.

The only thing she could think to talk about was business. 'The agenda says that I am to meet—' Hmm, so how did she refer to the prince in front of his assistant? She could hardly call him by his first name—not in such formal surroundings. 'His Royal Highness,' she finished, 'at three.'

'I am afraid His Royal Highness's meeting is running a little late. But if you would care to wait in the sitting room, *signorina*, I can arrange for some tea to be brought to you.'

'Thank you, but I'm fine. Please don't feel you have to order tea.'

'As you wish, *signorina*.' Salvatore led her through to another room. There was still the same deep carpet, exquisite furnishings and silk drapes at the window. It really brought it home to Indigo that she was in a palace, not just a normal office or home.

'Please sit down.' Salvatore indicated the sofa.

Just then a dog burst through the doorway, trotted over to them with his tail a wagging blur, and sniffed at her.

'Caesar!' Salvatore scolded. 'Bad dog—you shouldn't be in here.'

'Lorenzo's favourite spaniel. The one who sneaks onto sofas.' Indigo smiled, remembering what he'd told her about the palace dogs.

Salvatore looked surprised, and she realised what she'd just said. 'I mean, um, His Royal Highness's spaniel,' she corrected herself swiftly.

He looked slightly less disapproving now she'd remembered her place and resumed formal protocol. 'Yes.'

'I like dogs,' she offered. And at least having a dog to make a fuss of would give her something else to think about instead of worrying how it would be when Lorenzo finally came out of his meeting to see her again. 'I don't mind if he stays.'

Again, that cool inscrutable expression. 'If you're sure, *signorina.*'

'I'm sure.' She sat down. 'Come and sit with me, Caesar.'

The dog gave a happy wriggle at the sound of his name and trotted over to the sofa.

Salvatore gave a brief nod. 'I will call you as soon as His Royal Highness Prince Lorenzo is ready to see you.'

'Mille grazie,' she said, but Salvatore didn't seem as impressed as Maria had been by her effort to speak Italian. He just gave another of those curt little nods and left.

'So it's just you and me, Caesar,' she said.

The dog wagged his tail and put his paws on her knee.

'I'm really glad you're here,' she said. 'Because I have no idea how your master's going to react to me. Whether he meant it about missing me, or whether he just wants me to design a window for him—I haven't a clue.' Lottie had said that Lorenzo wasn't like Nigel, and Indigo knew that was true; at least his first words when she told him about the baby wouldn't be to demand that she had a termination.

But as to how he'd really feel, what he'd say...

She swallowed hard. 'And how he's going to react to my news—that scares me even more. I don't fit in here. I might be the daughter of an earl, but I didn't grow up in his world and I'm no Cinderella. I'd be much happier in the kitchen, chatting to the cooks and swapping recipes for cake.'

Caesar licked her hand.

'I guess it's a matter of wait and see,' she said, and leaned back against the back of the sofa.

Twenty minutes later, Lorenzo walked into the sitting room to discover Indigo fast asleep on the sofa, with Caesar curled up on the sofa in the space behind her knees. She looked exhausted, with dark hollows under her eyes.

Clearly she'd been pushing herself as hard as he'd been pushing himself.

Part of him really wanted to wake her with a kiss, to see those gorgeous blue eyes open and see her smile at him. But part of him thought it would be kinder just to let her rest. He found a blanket and tucked it round her.

'Keep an eye on her, Caesar,' he said softly, and the dog wagged his tail ever so gently, as if trying not to wake her.

'Your Royal Highness, would you like me to—?' Salvatore began.

'No, let her sleep for a bit longer,' Lorenzo said quietly. 'I'll work on my laptop in here for a while.'

CHAPTER ELEVEN

INDIGO WOKE WITH a start, and realised that there was a blanket tucked round her and Lorenzo's spaniel was curled into the crook of her knees. The dog stretched and yawned as she struggled to a sitting position, trying to get her head straight. There definitely hadn't been a blanket anywhere near her. Who had tucked her in like that? She didn't think it would've been Salvatore, who had been cool with her to the point of disapproval. And she was probably late for her meeting with Lorenzo now.

Oh, great. Her first day at the palace, and it had been a total disaster so far.

She glanced at her watch. Not just late—she'd missed the entire meeting.

'Oh, you *idiot*,' she groaned.

'Why am I an idiot?'

She looked over to where the voice had come from.

Lorenzo was sitting in the chair opposite, working on his laptop.

For a second, the world spun. Was this the man who'd been so passionate in England, or was this the king-to-be? She erred on the side of caution. 'Your Royal Highness. I'm so sorry.'

He smiled. 'Don't be. You clearly needed that nap. Been working stupid hours, have we?'

'Pots and kettles. You have bags under your—' She stopped abruptly. This wasn't Edensfield, where they'd both been friends of the family and on an equal footing—where he'd been her lover and she could tease him with impunity. This was Melvante, where he was her client and he was also about to become the head of the country. Which meant she had to deal with him in a completely different way. 'Sorry, Your Royal Highness,' she muttered.

'You really are different, out of England.' His eyes crinkled at the corners. 'Do you think I'm going to have you thrown into the palace dungeons for insubordination, or something?'

'Are there palace dungeons?'

He laughed. 'Yes, but they're not used. We have a progressive judicial system. Lighten up, Indi. I was teasing you.' He smiled. 'Besides, it was cute when you snored in tandem with Caesar.'

He was still teasing her. Which ought to be a good sign. But Indigo was still feeling groggy from her nap, and the secret she had to tell him felt as if it was gripping her in a vice. She had to tell him the truth—but not until she'd worked out the right words to use and the right time to say them.

'I'm sorry,' she said again. 'It was totally unprofessional of me to fall asleep like that.'

'You'd been travelling, and I'd guess you've been working nonstop over the last few days.'

'I have,' she admitted. And she'd missed him, so much. Part of her really wanted to walk over to him, wrap her arms round him, kiss him and tell him how glad she was to see him. Yet, despite the fact that they were in the same room, there was still a huge gulf between them. She couldn't even call him by his given name, because she was too aware of who he was: the future King of Melvante.

What a mess.

'Have I made you late for your next appointment?' she asked.

'No. Salvatore has rearranged my diary slightly.'

Which made her feel even more guilty. And it was another reason for Lorenzo's assistant to disapprove of her. 'Why didn't you just wake me up?'

'Because you looked comfortable.'

'Did you tuck me in?'

He nodded. 'And Caesar was happy to keep you company.'

'He's a nice dog.'

'He's horribly spoiled,' Lorenzo said, but his tone was indulgent.

If only he'd just come over to her and hold her close. How could they be in the same room and yet the gap between them feel wider than the geographical distance when they'd been in different countries?

'I, um, forgot to ask Salvatore which hotel he'd booked me into,' she said. And she really hoped it was one with a reasonable tariff, rather than a super-luxury one with an astronomical room rate. Her finances wouldn't run to the kind of places that Lorenzo would stay.

'You're not. You're staying at the palace.'

Staying with him?

For one mad moment, she thought he was telling her that this was going to be just like Edensfield, and they'd spend their nights curled up together and wake in each other's arms. Then common sense kicked in as he began speaking.

'We have several apartments for guests.'

'I'm not really a guest,' she said. 'I'm here to work.'

'Maybe a bit of both,' he said. 'Come on, I'll take you to your suite.'

And maybe there, in private, he'd be different with her.

She damped down the flicker of hope before she got too carried away. Of course he wouldn't. He was about to be the king. He didn't have time for this.

'Where's your suitcase?'

A prince most definitely couldn't wait on her. 'It's light. I'll carry it myself.' And she gave him a look just to make quite sure he knew she meant it; she was used to relying on herself, and that was the way it would continue to be.

'As you wish,' he said coolly, and she wished she hadn't been quite so quick to knock back his offer. He came from such a formal, restricted world. How would he know how to be anything else?

She still felt faintly groggy, but she followed him through the corridors with the little dog trotting along beside them. Lorenzo stopped by a door and opened it. 'Your suite. I'll let you freshen up.'

So he wasn't planning to spend too much time in private with her, then. She was really in danger of misreading everything. Best to keep it cool, calm and super-professional. 'Thank you very much. Perhaps we can reschedule our briefing meeting.'

'Of course. You still have my mobile phone number, yes?' At her nod, he said, 'Call me when you're ready and I'll come and collect you. Not because you're a prisoner, but because the castle's a bit of a maze and until you know your way around it can be a bit daunting.'

'Thank you.' Not that she was ever going to get to know her way around this castle.

He kissed her lightly on the cheek. 'Come on, Caesar. We need to let Indi settle in,' he told the spaniel, who gave Indigo a mournful look, but followed him down the corridor.

When he'd left, Indigo explored the suite. The sitting room was huge, with a sofa, coffee table and a couple of armchairs. There was a shelf of books in a variety of languages, a television and a state of the art music system. The bathroom was just acres of marble, with the most enormous walk-in shower, a deep bath and thick fluffy towels. The bedroom held a huge oak four-poster bed, with a wardrobe running the length of the room, a cheval mirror and a chest of drawers. She opened the wardrobe doors and hung up her clothes neatly. A couple of business suits, a couple of pairs of jeans, and Lottie's ball gown; and how meagre her outfits looked in that enormous space. Even if she'd had her entire wardrobe with her, her clothes wouldn't have made much impression.

The pillows looked deep and soft and inviting; she glanced longingly at them, then shook herself. She'd already made enough of a fool of herself, falling asleep on Lorenzo's sofa while she was waiting for his meeting to finish. If she let herself give in to the demands of her pregnancy now and slept again… Well. Lorenzo was sharp. He noticed little details. And she wasn't ready for him to put them all together and work it out for himself. She wanted to tell him the news herself.

Just not quite yet.

She showered and freshened up, then called Lorenzo's mobile.

It went straight to voicemail. Which wasn't so surprising.

'It's Indi. The time's four-thirty in the afternoon. I'm ready whenever you are,' she said, then hung up. She had no idea how long he'd be. But, given that she'd slept straight through their meeting, she was hardly in a position to demand anything.

She worked on her laptop for a while, until there was a knock at the door.

'Come in,' she called.

Lorenzo walked in, with Caesar at his heels. 'Sorry to keep you waiting.'

'No problem. I know you're busy.'

He inclined his head in acknowledgement. 'I meant to ask you, is there anything you'd like for dinner tonight so I can tell chef?'

'Anything, really,' she said, not wanting to be difficult. As long as it didn't have a strong smell. Not that she could explain to him why she wanted bland food without opening up a conversation at totally the wrong time. 'I wasn't expecting you to feed me.'

He smiled at her. 'We're not going to starve you, Indi. I wish I had time to have dinner with you tonight myself, but something's cropped up.'

'It's fine,' she said. Of course he wouldn't have dinner with any of his contractors. Not unless it was scheduled in and rubber-stamped by Salvatore.

'I would have asked you to come with me this evening, but it's state business and it'll be horribly dull.'

At least she would still have been with him, but never mind. She damped down the hurt. 'I know you're up to your eyes,' she said softly. 'It's OK.'

Just for a second, the formality in his face vanished and he looked lonely and lost, as if she was the first person who'd actually noticed that he was struggling to deal with everything. And, after all, it was a huge weight he was about to shoulder, becoming the state leader of his country.

Then the moment passed and Lorenzo was back to being His Royal Highness, ever so slightly remote and aloof. 'Is there anything else you need?'

Only for you to hold me and tell me that everything's going to be all right, she thought. But she knew she couldn't ask for that. Better to stick to business. 'It'd be useful to see the room where the window will be sited.'

'Of course. I can take you there now.'

'That would be good. I'll bring my equipment so I can measure up and take photographs.' Then she grimaced, remembering how he'd been about photographs at Edensfield. 'That is allowed, yes?'

'I'm not going to make you hand over your camera or delete the files,' he said with a smile, clearly remembering their first meeting too.

'And they won't go anywhere but my computer—I won't download them anywhere,' she said.

'I know. But thank you for the reassurance.'

Once she'd gathered her camera, notepad and laptop together, Lorenzo ushered her down the corridor.

Everywhere there were thick carpets and wood panelling; and all the surfaces were so shiny that it was clear there must be a huge number of staff all dusting and polishing the castle to perfection.

'State dining room,' he said, opening one door and letting her peek inside.

Solid gold cutlery, was Indigo's first thought. Followed by *solid gold candelabra.*

She was used to opulence, from her visits to Edensfield, but this was another world entirely. And she'd just bet the crystal glasses were antique, just as any meal served at that table would be presented on antique porcelain.

'Drawing room,' he said, showing her the next room. She glanced at the comfortable upholstered chairs, antique occasional tables and arrangements of fresh flowers—and then stopped dead. 'Is that a Burne-Jones over there on the wall?'

He nodded. 'It's the portrait of my great-great-grandmother I told you about.'

'May I?'

'Of course.'

She walked over to it and studied it for a while. 'It's beautiful—you're very lucky.'

'Salvatore knows a lot about our art collection. Talk to him tomorrow. He'll show you round when he has a moment.'

She didn't think that Salvatore would unbend enough with her to do that, but smiled politely. 'Thank you.'

Finally Lorenzo led her to a room at the very end of a corridor. 'This is where we thought the window could be sited—in the library.'

Like the mermaid window at Edensfield, she thought, and was filled with wistfulness. She would love to have the Lorenzo from Edensfield back rather than the formal, very polite and very guarded stranger walking next to her.

'This is one of my favourite rooms in the house,' he said as he ushered her into a long room.

The two longest walls were lined with books in dark wooden cases with glass fronts and a sliding wooden ladder, so anyone who wanted a book from the upper shelves could reach them. But there were also a couple of leather chesterfields and a low coffee table with a chessboard on it. There was a desk sited in front of a large window with a number of gold-framed photographs—and she'd bet it was solid gold, not gilt framing—and a grand piano in the centre of the room.

And that, she thought, was why it was Lorenzo's favourite room. No doubt he spent as much time at that piano as he could. Which wouldn't be very much, now.

The spaniel pattered over to the fireplace and stretched out on the rug, clearly used to being there.

There were some stained-glass windows at the far end of the room. 'Is that where you want the new window?' she asked.

'Yes.'

As they passed the desk, she glanced out of the window and saw the rose garden. 'Oh, that's gorgeous,' she said, noting the way the colours of the roses blended. 'It's like a rainbow of roses.'

He looked out. 'I've never really noticed that before, but you're right.' He smiled at her. 'Funny, I thought I knew everything about the castle, but you're making me see it with new eyes.'

There wasn't much she could say to that. She distracted herself by taking a couple of photographs and making a couple of sketches. And, unsurprisingly, he had half a dozen messages on his phone that he needed to answer.

He'd just finished with them when she took out her tape measure. 'Need a hand measuring?' he asked.

'If you don't mind,' she said. 'That would be helpful.'

But, as she finished the last section, his hand touched hers briefly, and it felt like electricity coursing through her veins.

'Indi,' he whispered.

She looked up at him and he dipped his head, brushing his mouth against hers. She closed her eyes as he deepened the kiss.

God, she'd missed this so much. Missed *him* so much that she felt the tears stinging her eyelids.

And then she dropped the tape measure.

On his foot.

He broke the kiss and retrieved her tape measure. 'I'm sorry,' he said. 'I probably shouldn't have done that.'

She knew what he meant. The attraction was still there. The same feelings they'd had for each other back at Edensfield. But this was a different world and he just wasn't free to give in to those feelings.

Which made it even harder for her to tell him about the baby; she knew he had such a strong sense of duty and he'd want to marry her for the baby's sake. But she most definitely wasn't a suitable royal bride, so marriage was out of the question.

Time to back off—and to change the subject, before she said something stupid.

Be professional, she reminded herself. This is about your job.

'Would you mind sitting for a couple of portraits?' she asked. 'Photographs, I mean. I'm not going to make you sit for hours while I sketch you.'

He raised an eyebrow, as if remembering their conversation about the fairy tales with a twist. 'You really need to do that?'

'If I'm putting you in a stained-glass window, then the portrait needs to look like you,' she pointed out.

'I guess so.'

'And it would be useful to see your robes of state, or whatever it is that kings wear.' Not just because she could use them in a pose, but because it would remind her of who he was. That he was out of reach.

'Ceremonial robes,' he said.

'And a crown.' Just to hammer it home.

'We can do a crown,' he said, looking thoughtful.

'And where does all this happen? The cathedral?' She forced herself not to think about the fact that the cathedral would also be where he would eventually get married. To a suitable princess.

'Yes—and there's a special coronation chair. I'm scheduled to show you round tomorrow.' He met her gaze. 'Or Salvatore can, if you'd rather.'

It would probably be easier if Salvatore showed her round, she thought. Then she wouldn't slip up and say something inappropriate, because she'd remember who she was talking to and why she was here in Melvante. She'd have it at the front of her mind that this was strictly business and not because Lorenzo wanted her there.

But, to do her job fully, she needed to understand what was in his head. How did he feel about becoming king? And she'd slept through the briefing meeting, so she still had a dozen or more questions. She needed to know if they wanted him to look serene, statesmanlike, or what.

'I'd rather you showed me round, if you don't mind—that means we can catch up with the briefing meeting I missed, too. If you're sure you can spare the time,' she added quickly.

'I'll make sure I do.' His phone shrilled; he glanced at the screen and sighed. 'I'm sorry. I need to take this.'

'Don't worry, I'll find my own way back to my quarters.'

'Are you sure?'

She smiled, giving him her bravest face. 'If I get lost, I can always ask someone for directions.'

'OK. We'll talk later,' he said.

It was weird to be wandering through the palace on her own, Indigo thought as she left the library. She felt like a trespasser; she really didn't belong here. Lorenzo had said that the castle was home and he had happy memories of the place, but to her he looked tired and slightly strained. He'd retreated behind formality, apart from that brief kiss—and he'd apologised for that straight away, telling her outright that it had been a mistake.

Right at that moment, she couldn't see any common ground between them. It underlined how sensible she'd been to say no when he'd suggested continuing their affair. Lorenzo as a man—yes, she could trust him enough to fall in love with him. She already had. But His Royal Highness Lorenzo had so many walls up that it could never work.

She still had to tell him about the baby. It wouldn't be fair either to him or to the baby to keep that quiet. But no way was her baby growing up inside the walls of this quiet, formal, over-restrained palace. She wanted a home where a child could laugh and shout with joy—not an old-fashioned place where children were shut away in a nursery and should be seen and not heard.

CHAPTER TWELVE

THIS REALLY WASN'T going how Lorenzo had expected. Indigo was completely different, out here; she seemed nervous and quiet, not like the independent, sparky woman he'd fallen for in England.

He wanted to hold her and tell her how much he'd missed her. He wanted to kiss her again and feel her warmth seeping through him. But he also knew how his mother had felt so trapped at the palace, and he didn't want that for Indigo. No way would he push her into something that would make her unhappy.

And that was the final proof that he wasn't his father—because, if he had to, he was prepared to let Indi leave.

But first he was going to do his utmost to persuade her that sharing his life here wouldn't be so bad.

He raided the palace gardens before his meeting; afterwards, he grabbed a quick sandwich, then dropped in on Indigo. 'Sorry,' he said, handing her the flowers. 'I've been a rubbish host so far.'

She looked surprised. 'You didn't need to do that, but they're lovely. Thank you.' She breathed in their scent. 'And I understand that you're busy. The coronation's very soon and you have tons to do.'

'Yes, and Nonno's away for a few days—that's why I haven't introduced you to him yet.'

'I'm kind of nervous about meeting your grandfather,' she admitted.

'There's no need.' He spread his hands. 'Nonno's a pussycat.'

'He's a king,' she corrected.

'He's a man first,' Lorenzo said softly. Just as he was. But could Indigo learn to see that?

Indigo didn't want to fight with Lorenzo, so she said nothing, but she disagreed with him completely. If you were in that position, no matter how much you wanted to be seen as a person first, you'd always be seen as what you were rather than who you were. 'I'd better put these in water.'

He followed her into the kitchen and helped her find a couple of glasses to contain the flowers. 'Sorry. I didn't think this through properly. I should've brought you a vase as well.'

'No, I like that you were spontaneous. It's sweet,' she said.

'Just so you know, I wanted to meet you at the airport,' he said softly.

'It's fine. Bruno was there.' Though it warmed her that he *had* wanted to be with her. 'Besides, I'm here as a consultant, so people would think it strange if you met me at the airport.'

He shrugged. 'I guess.'

'Come and sit down—can I make you a drink or something?' She'd checked out the kitchenette and seen that there was a selection of tea and coffee, plus a supply of fresh milk in the small fridge.

He smiled. 'How come you manage to be a good hostess when you've only been here a few hours?'

She shrugged. 'It's just how I was brought up. You always offer someone a hot drink the second they walk through your door. Well, strictly speaking this is your door, not mine,' she amended, 'but you know what I mean.'

'Do you know what I want more than coffee, right now?' he asked.

'Mind-reading isn't one of my special skills,' she said.

'I know.' He laughed. 'OK. I'll tell you. I just want to hold you.'

'That isn't such a good idea,' she said. 'I'm here on business.'

'You're here because I wanted to see you, and right now I can't come to England, so bringing you here seemed like the best solution.'

'You sent a plane for me, Lorenzo. Don't you think that's a little bit flashy?' she asked.

'Probably,' he admitted, 'and it's bad for the environment as well. But, given that you're a mere mortal and don't possess wings…'

When he was like this, it would be so easy to give in and just be with him. He was adorable—sweet and funny, Lorenzo the man and not Lorenzo the Crown Prince.

'Hello, Indi,' he said softly, and kissed her.

She managed to stand her ground. Just. 'We can't do this, Lorenzo. We're not in England any more. You're about to become king.'

'And you're putting obstacles in the way. Why are you so scared?'

'Because,' she said, 'you're not going to be allowed to be with me. No matter what our personal views on the matter might be, you have to think as a king first and a man second. You can't just do what you want.'

'You,' he said with a sigh, 'sound like my grandfather.'

'And he won't think I'm remotely suitable for you. So it's better not to start something we can't finish.'

'What if the barriers were all taken away?' he asked.

If only, she thought. 'And how are you going to do that? There isn't anyone else who can take over from you, is there?'

'No,' he admitted. 'But I think you could be suitable, Indi, if you give yourself a chance.'

'If I change, you mean?'

He shook his head. 'Don't ever change. You're warm and honest and a breath of fresh air. You make things sparkle.'

She stroked his face. 'Lorenzo, don't make this any more difficult than it already is.'

He moved his head so he could press a kiss into her palm. 'You're so stubborn.'

'If the press drag up my past...'

'Then it'll be a two-day wonder, they'll find someone else to gossip about pretty soon after, and nobody's going to judge you on your parents' mistakes.'

'Not just my parents,' she said softly. 'I made a really bad mistake myself.'

Maybe telling him would go some way to making him understand why this couldn't ever work. And it would make him agree with her decision when she found the right words to tell him about the baby.

'Three years ago, my grandfather died.'

'Meaning you were on your own in the world?' Lorenzo asked. 'Well, except your father, and he doesn't count.'

She gave him a wry smile. 'Pretty much, on both counts. Anyway, not long after that I was dragged off to some party. I didn't really want to be there.' She sighed. 'And I met Nigel. He asked me out. I said no, but he was persistent, and I guess... It's weak of me, but...' She stopped, unable to frame the words.

'You were still grieving for someone you loved very much,' Lorenzo said softly. 'It's only natural that you wanted to try and fill some of the hole your grandfather's death had left in your life.'

'I guess.' She stared miserably at the table. 'So I started seeing him. And I was busy sorting out my grandfather's estate and finding a new studio and somewhere else to live, so that kind of distracted me from the things I should've noticed.'

'Why did you have to move?' he asked.

'Because my deal with the earl was that the cottage was my grandparents' for life. After they died, it reverted to him.'

'And he didn't offer to let you stay, at least until you'd found your feet?' Lorenzo looked shocked. 'How mean can you get?'

'That's possibly a bit unfair. I didn't actually give him the chance to offer,' she admitted. 'I moved straight out.'

'Stubborn.'

'Too much so for my own good, sometimes.' She gave him a wry smile. 'So I guess I had enough going on in my life not to notice that Nigel was sometimes a bit cagey when he answered his mobile phone. Or that he only ever visited me—he never invited me back to his place. When we went out, it was always to obscure places—the kind of places I like, because I'd prefer to go somewhere for dinner because the food is amazing rather than because it's trendy. I thought that was why he chose the restaurants.' She shook her head in frustration. 'But I guess he picked them because he wouldn't know anyone there. I never met any of his friends, and he didn't seem interested in meeting mine. It never *occurred* to me that he might be married. I mean, when I look at it now, the signs were all there and it's blindingly obvious, but I was too stupid and naive to read them at the time.'

'It's easy to see things in hindsight. No, you were busy

and you were grieving and you put your trust in the wrong person,' Lorenzo said.

'Yeah.' She couldn't quite bring herself to tell him about the miscarriage. 'Anyway, then I found out he was married. And that he had a baby. He cheated on his wife when she was pregnant, Lorenzo. And he cheated on her with *me*. I can't forgive myself for that.'

He frowned. 'If you'd known he was married, you would've kept turning him down.'

She stared at him. 'Of course I would. I'd seen the damage my mother did. I didn't want to follow in her footsteps.'

'You don't have to tell me that, Indi,' he said softly. 'I already know that you're not your mother.'

'But don't you see? If the press find out...' She bit her lip.

'You met Nigel when you were vulnerable, and he took advantage of that. It isn't your fault.'

'I could have said no.'

'You were grieving and lonely. Anyone else would've done the same, in your shoes.'

'Lorenzo, I've just told you that I had an affair with a married man. Doesn't that...?' She shook her head, frustrated that she couldn't find the right words to make him see her point.

'No, it doesn't make any difference. And if the press does manage to drag it up, then my press team will make sure they're aware of your side of the story to balance things out. You're human, Indi.'

'And you need someone who's perfect.'

'No. Right now,' he said softly, 'I just need you.'

And she could see in his eyes that he meant it.

Even though her common sense knew that this was a huge mistake, how could she push him away when he'd let his barriers down with her like this?

She opened her arms; he held her close, then picked her up and carried her to the sofa in her living room. He settled down with her half lying across his lap. 'Right now,' he whispered, 'I just want to be with you. No talking, no nothing—I just want to *be*.'

That was just fine by her. Back in their bubble, where they had the chance to be together. Warm and comfortable and cosy and...

Indigo had no idea when she fell asleep—or when he did—but she woke when Lorenzo carried her into her bedroom and laid her on the bed, then tucked a duvet round her.

'Lorenzo?' she asked sleepily. 'What time is it?'

'Three in the morning. I'm sorry. I guess I relaxed with you so much that I dozed off,' he said softly. 'I'd better go.'

'You could stay,' she said.

He shook his head. 'I can't. But I'll see you in the morning.' He kissed her lightly. 'I'll take you round the cathedral.'

'And I promise not to be late. Or sleep through the meeting.'

The next morning, Indigo was in Salvatore's office ten minutes before she was due to meet Lorenzo.

'You look up to your eyes in work, Signor Pozzi,' she said.

He shrugged. 'It's a busy time, Signorina Moran. It's the same for everyone.'

'Can I fetch you a cup of coffee or something?' she asked.

He looked at her in surprise. 'Why would you do that?'

'Because you're very busy, and I have ten minutes before His Royal Highness is expecting me, so I have the time to make you some coffee,' she said. 'Do you take milk or sugar?'

'I...' And then he gave her the first real smile she'd seen

since she'd come to the castle. 'Thank you very much. That would be lovely. No milk or sugar, thank you.'

'Just very strong, the way His Royal Highness drinks it?' she asked dryly.

Salvatore spread his hands. 'What can I say?'

'You're from Melvante. Which isn't quite Italian, but pretty near it,' she said with a smile.

She made coffee in the small kitchen next to the of-fice—just about managing not to gag at the scent—and took the mug through to Lorenzo's assistant along with a glass of water. He was on the phone when she got back, so she just placed the mug and glass on a coaster within his reach, and sat quietly in the corner of the office, sketch-ing out some ideas for the window.

Dead on time, Lorenzo came through into his assistant's office. 'Good morning, Signorina Moran. Are you ready to go to the cathedral?'

She put her sketchbook away. 'Of course, Your Royal Highness.'

'You'll like the glass,' Salvatore said. 'Don't let the prince rush you past the rose window.'

'I won't,' she said with a smile.

'What did you do to Salvatore?' Lorenzo asked when they'd left the office.

She shrugged. 'Nothing. Why?'

'Because his job is to be a dragon and protect my time, and there he was telling you not to rush.'

'I made him a mug of coffee, that's all.'

Lorenzo raised an eyebrow. 'I don't think anyone due in a meeting with me has ever done that before.'

'The poor man's up to his eyes, fielding calls and organ-ising things for you. It was the least I could do.'

'Typical you,' Lorenzo said, but his gaze was warm rather than full of censure.

Even from the outside, the cathedral was stunning, all white stone and Gothic arches. Inside, it was even more grand, with soaring arches everywhere and tall, narrow windows—and then a window that made Indigo stop and gasp in pleasure.

'It's beautiful. Like the rose window at York Minster. Why didn't you tell me it was this good?'

He smiled. 'I did tell you to come and see the glass for yourself.' He added softly, 'Remember when you took me to see your angel and the centaur?'

And they'd talked about weddings.

This was where Lorenzo would get married.

Not to her, because she wasn't suitable. But Indigo hoped that Lorenzo would find a royal bride who really loved him—a woman who felt the same way about him that she did.

And then it hit her that she really was in love with him. Bone deep in love with the father of her unborn child. The one man she knew had integrity and she could trust with her heart. Except…they came from different worlds, and she just couldn't see how they'd ever get past that.

'It's beautiful,' she said, forcing herself to focus on the glass.

She enjoyed the rest of the tour of the building, and seeing the ancient throne on which Lorenzo would be seated during the coronation; but all the time she was aware of the widening gulf between them. Just how was she going to be able to tell him about the baby?

They were walking back down the aisle when a small girl came running towards them, tripped on one of the flagstones and fell flat on her face. Indigo scanned the area quickly but couldn't immediately see anyone who looked like a concerned parent or nanny rushing to the child's aid.

The little girl was crying and holding her knee. Indigo went over to her. 'It's all right, we'll find your mummy for you.'

She was rewarded with a blank stare and more tears.

Of course—the little girl didn't speak English. And Indigo knew that her Italian was too scrappy to be useful right now. 'Lorenzo, can you translate for me?' she asked swiftly. 'Tell her that it's OK, and we'll find her mummy for her.'

The little girl was still crying, but she listened to Lorenzo and nodded.

'I've got something in my bag that will stop her knee feeling sore,' Indigo said, taking the small first aid kit out of her bag and finding the antiseptic wipes and a sticking plaster. 'Can you distract her—get her to find something in one of the windows?'

If Lorenzo had been faced with a crying child on his own, he wouldn't have been quite sure what to do or say. But, with Indigo by his side, it was surprisingly easy. 'It's all right, little one. We'll make your knee better and find your mummy,' he said. 'Can you see all the pretty colours in the windows?'

She nodded.

'What's your favourite colour?' he asked as Indigo wiped her knee clean.

'Pink,' she said, and he couldn't help smiling.

He kept her talking while Indigo ministered to her knee and put a sticking plaster over the cut. They'd just finished when a woman ran up to them.

'Melissa! What happened? Are you all right?' She scooped the little girl into her arms. 'I looked round, and you'd gone.' And then she looked at Lorenzo and did a double-take. 'Your Royal Highness! I'm—oh—um...'

'It's all right,' he said, smiling at her to put her at her

ease. 'Your little girl fell over and cut her knee. My friend's just cleaned the cut and put a sticking plaster on it. I hope that's OK.'

'I—oh, yes, thank you so much. But you're…you're… Your Royal Highness,' she blurted out, clearly still flustered.

'We just did what anyone else would've done,' he said.

'Thank you so much, Your Royal Highness. Melissa, you must always hold Mummy's hand when we're out and never, ever go off without Mummy,' the woman said to her little girl. 'Now, curtsey to the prince and say thank you.'

'Mille grazie,' the little girl said, her lower lip wobbling slightly as she tried to do a graceful curtsey.

'Very nice to meet you, Melissa,' Lorenzo said solemnly.

She looked almost as overawed as her mother.

'I'm afraid I'm expected elsewhere now, but do enjoy the rest of your time here,' Lorenzo said.

'Thank you, Your Royal Highness.'

The woman was about to curtsey, but he placed his hand lightly on her arm. 'You really don't need to curtsey to me.' He smiled. 'Have a nice day.'

'I think you just made a hit,' Indigo said as they left the cathedral.

'Only because you were with me. I wouldn't have had a clue what to say otherwise,' he said.

'You would've improvised,' she said, giving him a cheeky wink. 'And you would've been fine.'

Funny how her belief in him warmed him so much.

All he needed now was to get her to believe in *them*.

Ha. All.

Back at the castle, Lorenzo had a swift conversation with Salvatore, then checked his schedule. 'I'm doing a photo shoot with Indigo for the window, so she can see the state robes,' he said. 'We'll be in my apartment if there's anything urgent, but I'm going to switch my mobile off during the shoot so we don't get constant interruptions.'

'Very good, Your Royal Highness,' Salvatore said. 'Did you enjoy the cathedral, Signorina Moran?'

'I did, Signor Pozzi—the rose window is stunning,' Indigo said. 'And please call me Indi. I prefer being on first-name terms with my clients and their colleagues.'

'Then you shall call me Sal,' he said with a smile.

Lorenzo led her off to his apartment. 'Salvatore has really taken a shine to you,' he said. 'I wish I could make people warm to me so quickly.'

'You can,' she said. 'Just be yourself, and don't put all the formal barriers up.' She wrinkled her nose. 'Though I guess that's easier said than done, when you have to deal with protocol all the time.'

'Protocol,' he said, 'maybe needs to learn to change with the times.'

'Dat's ma boy,' she said with a grin. 'You're learning.'

'Give me ten minutes to change. Be as nosey as you like,' he invited.

'Thank you. I will.'

Lorenzo's apartment was at the opposite end of the castle to hers. It had a view of what looked like a format knot garden; but the interior was lovely, with simple furnishings rather than the ornate Louis XIV tables and chairs she'd seen in the rest of the castle. And she loved the artwork on the walls.

There was a piano in his sitting room, along with a bed for the dog that looked as if it were rarely used—from what she'd seen of Caesar, the spaniel would head straight for the rug in front of the fire or a comfortable corner of the sofa. Bookshelves, containing a mixture of biographies, historical tomes and some very geeky science fiction; no music, she noticed, but knowing Lorenzo his collection was probably digital and centrally organised in a system so that he could access it anywhere in his apartment. There was a television, so obviously he watched the occasional programme, but there were no films on the shelves; she assumed that again he used a digital cloud-based service.

The kitchen was all clean lines. His fridge wasn't that well stocked, so she guessed that most of the time he was served by the palace kitchens rather than cooking for himself. There was a table so he could eat in the kitchen if he wanted to, but this was very much a bachelor apartment, she thought, rather than a family one.

She didn't quite have the nerve to explore his bathroom—a bit too personal, she thought, and his bedroom was definitely out of bounds. He'd made it clear that he wanted to change into his robes without an audience.

The sitting room would be the best place to take the photographs, she decided, when he emerged from his room in a dress uniform with a dark blue floor-length cloak trimmed with gold and ermine.

'Very nice, Your Royal Highness,' she said.

'Hmm. Have a nice snoop, did we?'

'Pretty much. You don't have any cake in your kitchen,' she said, teasing him a little to cover the fact that she felt just a little bit out of her depth. 'And I couldn't find your music or films.'

'They're all cloud-based,' he explained. 'Except the cake. Which is an omission I clearly need to remedy.'

'Uh-huh. Well, let's get this shoot sorted.' It didn't take long for her to get the shots she needed. Or, rather, most of them. 'It won't kill you to smile, you know,' she said.

He gave her a formal smile—one that didn't reach his eyes and made him look totally unreachable.

How could she make him take those barriers down?

She knew it was crazy—totally crazy—but she went with the impulse. She walked over to him, slid her arms round his neck and kissed him.

And then she took a step back. 'Lorenzo,' she said softly.

And he smiled at her.

A real smile, full of warmth. The look she loved most on him, all soft and sweet and touchable.

She took the shot, and he grimaced. 'Do you use that strategy with all your models?'

'I don't usually have models,' she said. But she knew he knew the answer. Of course she didn't. She didn't react to anyone the same way she reacted to Lorenzo.

'You kissed me just to get a photograph.'

He looked thoroughly put out, and she couldn't help smiling. 'Not just to get the photo. I kissed you because right now you look like Prince Hottie. Sexy as hell.'

The light came back into his eyes. 'Put the camera down, Indi.'

'Can't.' She shook her head. 'I'm working.'

'That's a royal command, I'll have you know. Put the camera down.'

She lifted her chin. 'Or what, Your Royal Highness?'

'Or face the consequences.'

She smiled. 'Bring it on, Lorenzo.'

'You asked for it,' he said, and took the camera gently from her hand, placing it safely out of the way. And then he kissed her until her knees were on the point of buckling.

'That has consequences, too, you know,' she said, and undid the clasp of his robe before sliding it off his shoulders. She folded it neatly and placed it over the back of the chair.

'Interesting,' he commented, but his voice was full of warmth. 'You've turned into a neat freak, Indi.'

'No chance.' She spread her hands. 'But this is your coronation robe. I don't want you to get into trouble with your wardrobe people.'

He laughed. 'This is the twenty-first century. It's not how things were a hundred years ago, when people with titles still employed valets and ladies' maids.'

'Even so, I don't want to crumple your robes.' She stroked them, enjoying the softness under her fingertips. 'I have to say, Your Royal Highness, you look mighty fine in navy.' She looked at him. 'And even better without your robes.'

'Was that a hint?' He stripped out of his uniform, laying it neatly on top of his robes, and maintaining eye contact with her the entire time. By the time he'd stripped down to his underwear, Indigo felt as if she was about to spontaneously combust.

And then he simply picked her up and carried her into his bedroom. When he set her down on her feet again, he made sure that her body was in close contact to his, so she was left fully aware of how much he wanted her. And then he proceeded to make love to her until she felt as if her bones had melted.

Later, lying curled in his arms, Indigo thought how this was every bit as good as their time spent in England. The physical attraction between them was still strong.

But would it be enough to help them keep the world at bay?

And how would he cope when she told him her news?

'Penny for them?' he asked, stroking her hair away from his forehead.

No. Now wasn't the right time. 'Just worrying that I've made you late for something.'

He glanced at his watch. 'Um.'

'Sorry. You're going to be up to your eyes, now.'

'Yes,' he said regretfully, and switched on his phone. Immediately his phone started beeping with a barrage of incoming messages.

'Go and do whatever you need to do,' she said, 'and I'll sort things out here.'

'Are you sure?'

'I'm sure,' she confirmed. 'Go and do all your prince stuff.'

'You're wonderful.' He dressed swiftly, kissed her again, and vanished. She took her time, and made sure she hung up his uniform and his robes properly before putting his bed to rights, then took her work things back to her apartment and went back to sketching out designs.

Later that afternoon, Lorenzo came by her apartment. 'We forgot the crown.'

She raised an eyebrow. 'Aren't you supposed to be in a meeting?'

'I can afford to be spontaneous,' he said.

Hmm. She remembered just how spontaneous he'd been in his apartment, and warmth spread through her. 'So where do I get to see you model the crown?' she asked.

'In the vaults. Bring your camera.' He waved a key at her.

She laughed. 'You're telling me that, in this day and age, you're using old-fashioned technology?'

'A little more than that. There are layers.' He took her hand as they walked down the corridor. Even though Indigo was pretty sure that it was going to cause a mad rush of gossip once it was spotted on the palace CCTV, she couldn't quite bring herself to pull away. It felt good, having her fingers tangled with Lorenzo's. She'd loved walking hand in hand with him in the gardens at Edensfield, and this wasn't so very different.

To get to the vaults, they had to pass through a series of doors and use a series of different things to unlock them—codes, fingerprints and even iris recognition.

'I take it back. You're in full James Bond mode,' she teased.

'Which means I get to dally with the beautiful girl.' He stole a kiss, shocking her.

'Lorenzo—was that just caught on CCTV?'

'Probably.'

'But...'

'I don't care. And, for someone who's supposed to be a free spirit, you worry far too much,' Lorenzo said and kissed her again.

Inside the vaults, he took out a box and unlocked it.

'Oh, my.' Indigo had never seen so many jewels in one place—or such large ones.

He took the crown out of the box. 'I can remember my grandfather placing this on my head.'

'When you were little—like dressing up?' she asked.

He shook his head. 'When I was eighteen. I'd just spent a week going off the rails, and he wanted me to understand that I had a commitment. That I needed to—well, strengthen myself so I could carry the burden.' He handed her the crown.

'It's really heavy,' she said, shocked and also a little afraid of dropping it and denting it.

She handed it back to him. 'So why did you go off the rails?'

He was silent for a long, long time. And then he sighed. 'I'm going to tell you something now that maybe half a dozen people know, and they're all sworn to secrecy. Everyone thought my parents died in a car accident when I was ten. But it wasn't an accident.' He blew out a breath. 'My mother was having an affair. She was planning to leave my father, and my father found out. He drove their car into a wall with her beside him, deliberately, because he couldn't bear to be without her and he couldn't bear the idea of her being with anyone else. My grandparents told everyone that it was a tragic accident—but then I found some papers when I was eighteen. Papers that my grandfather had thought were destroyed. And that's when I learned the truth.'

Indigo looked at him, shocked. 'Your father killed himself and your mother? But that meant he'd be leaving you on your own. How—' She shook her head, completely not understanding. 'How could he do that?'

'It's not a choice that I would make,' Lorenzo said. 'If I married someone who hated the world I lived in, I'd find a compromise.'

Was this his way of telling her that that was what he was trying to do, right now? Find a compromise so they could be together?

'I'd love my wife enough to let her go, if I had to. I'd want her to be happy. And if that meant not being with me—well, so be it. I wouldn't stop her,' Lorenzo said. 'But I'd try my hardest to find a way round it, so we could be together.'

She stroked his face. 'And the accident—' she couldn't bear to think of what it really was '—happened not long before you were sent away to school. That's so hard, Lorenzo.' And she could understand now why he'd been brought up in such a rigid, formal way. His grandparents had tried to protect him from the truth.

'I've had a long time to get used to it,' he said softly. 'Take the pictures, Indi. I wasn't intending to be maudlin. I just wanted you to understand.'

'I do. And I promise you it won't go any further than me. Ever.' She kissed him swiftly on the lips. 'And I get now why you keep everyone at a distance. It stops you getting hurt. But if you let people close, Lorenzo—the whole world will love you.' Just as she loved him.

Perhaps, he thought. But there was only one person he wanted to love him.

And he thought that maybe, just maybe, she might feel the same way about him as he felt about her.

But would they be able to find a compromise so she could feel comfortable in his world?

He placed the crown on his head. 'OK. Do what you need to for the designs.'

She took several photographs. And then he placed the crown back in the box, locked it again, and returned it to its place in the vault.

CHAPTER THIRTEEN

THE NEXT DAY, there was a story in the newspapers about the Prince of Hearts, with a photograph of Lorenzo and another of the little girl they'd rescued in the cathedral, standing with her mother.

'I've never had anything like this before,' Lorenzo said, handing her a translated version of the story on a tablet. 'People have always seen me as—well, a bit remote.'

'Low-key's fine. But let them get to know you,' she said, 'and they'll see you're not in the slightest bit remote.'

She scanned through the text. 'Oh, no. They're talking about a mystery woman being with you.' She swallowed hard. 'That means they're going to dig up what they can about me.' Panic flooded through her.

'Stop worrying. For now, the press office will handle it. They'll explain that you're a glass specialist and I was briefing you in the cathedral.'

'But what if…?'

He kissed the tip of her nose. 'Then I'll deal with it. I promise you, there's nothing to worry about.' His voice was very calm. 'And I don't break my promises, Indi. I don't tell lies.'

Whereas she was telling him a lie, sort of. A lie of omission. She was going to have to tell him the truth, very soon. She just needed to work out how.

* * *

He took her through to the palace gardens, that morning. What she'd thought was a formal knot garden turned out to be a series of concentric circles made from stone slabs.

'What's this—some kind of sculpture?' she asked.

'A water maze. If you stand on the wrong slab, it tilts and you get sprayed.'

How come a stuffy, formal palace would have something as crazy and fun as this in the garden?

The question must have been written all over her face, because he said, 'It was my grandmother's idea. She grew up in a house with a hedge maze and she liked the idea of having something fun in the garden. I remember when I was small, I loved the mazes here. I used to spend all day playing here and in the hedge maze.' He looked slightly wistful. 'Life was a bit simpler, back then.'

Before his parents had died? Or before he'd realised what being king would mean?

'OK. So the idea is that you reach the middle without getting wet.' He spread his hands. 'Your challenge, should you wish to accept it…'

'But what,' she asked, 'is my reward, should I beat the challenge?'

He leaned forward. 'Spontaneous inventiveness on my part.'

And, oh, the picture that put in her head.

'You're on,' she said, and picked her way through the first ring.

'Four more to go,' he said.

One and a half rings later, she stepped on the wrong stone. It tilted, and a fountain of water sprayed over her.

She just laughed. 'When you were a kid, I bet you jumped on every stone to make sure you got soaked every single time.'

'I might've done,' he said with a grin.

'Which makes you the expert on how to do it without getting wet, because you know where the tilting slabs are. Show me how it's done,' she said.

He picked his way round the circles until he reached her, then took her hand and showed her which stones to leap over.

Until they were about to reach the centre of the maze, and she jumped on the slab that he was clearly about to avoid. Water sprayed up and over him. 'Gotcha,' she said, laughing.

He laughed back, and jumped onto the same stone, pulling her into his arms at the same time so that the water sprayed over both of them. And while the droplets were still falling, he kissed her stupid.

This was the Lorenzo she'd fallen in love with back at Edensfield. The Lorenzo who'd dressed up in Regency clothing and copied the Mr Darcy scene from the movie, just for her. The Lorenzo who'd carried a tired, elderly dog home through the gardens.

'Lorenzo,' she whispered.

Now was the right time to tell him. When they were laughing in his garden, enjoying some harmless fun. When he was reliving some of the fun of his own childhood. When he could see how it might be for his own child. He'd told her his deepest, darkest secret in the castle vault; and now it was time for her to tell him the truth about the baby.

'Indi.' He kissed her again, and she could see the passion in his eyes.

'There's something I—'

Her words were cut off by his phone shrilling.

He made a nose of frustration. 'Sorry. I'm expecting this.'

And he'd already taken time out to spend with her. Time

he couldn't really afford. 'Go,' she said. 'Is it OK for me to walk in the gardens for a bit longer?'

'Sure. Go where you like. I'll see you later.' He kissed her again, then took the call.

Indigo went back to her room for her camera and sketchbook, then headed out to find the rose garden. Up close, she might get the last ideas she needed for the window design.

And, up close, it was even better than she'd hoped. She closed her eyes and breathed in the scent. The essence of summer, she thought.

Then she became aware of someone speaking to her in rapid Italian. She opened her eyes to see an elderly man carrying secateurs. He was probably one of the palace gardeners, she thought, and he probably thought she was a trespasser.

She dredged up her limited Italian. 'Um, *mi scusi—parla inglese*?'

The man smiled. 'Yes, I speak English.'

And very well, too, she thought; he had only the slightest trace of an accent.

'Can I help you? Are you lost?' he asked.

How ironic that she'd met Lorenzo at her best friend's house and he'd thought she was a trespasser—and now she was in Lorenzo's home and being mistaken for a trespasser again.

'I'm not trespassing,' she said hastily, 'I'm working on some designs for a glass window for the palace, and I wanted a closer look at the roses—is that all right?'

'Of course, *signorina*.' He paused. 'May I ask, why the roses?'

'Because they're beautiful and they remind me of home,' she said wistfully. 'My grandparents had a rose garden—nothing on the scale of this, of course, but I love the scent of roses. And I saw the garden from the library window the other day. It's like a rainbow of roses, with the way the colours shade from white to yellow to peach, pink and red. How could I resist coming to see them?'

He looked pleased. 'You like our roses here at the palace?'

She nodded. 'And I like that they're not all the same type—you have floribundas here, mixed with hybrid teas and Bourbons and ramblers.'

He inclined his head. 'So you know your roses.'

'I'm not an expert, by any means,' she said, 'but I know what I like.'

'You grow them yourself?'

She shook her head. 'I only have a windowsill in my flat, so I have a couple of pots of miniature roses. But if I ever move to a place with a garden, I'll have a bower of roses just like we used to have at home.' She smiled back at him and held her hand out for him to shake. 'Sorry, I've been very rude—I should have introduced myself. I'm Indigo Moran.'

'Enzo,' he returned. 'You have a very pretty name.'

'Thank you.'

'Would you like me to show you round?'

'If that's not going to interfere with your job or make you late for something, then yes, please, Enzo. That would be really kind of you.'

She spent the next half hour wandering through the garden with him, learning about the oldest roses in the garden and taking some photographs. 'I really love this one. It's so pretty,' she said, pointing out a crimson rose with pink and white stripes. She leaned over. 'Oh, and the scent's amazing.'

'*Rosa mundi*,' he said. 'It's one of the oldest striped roses known, nearly a thousand years old.'

'It's beautiful,' she said.

'It was the favourite rose of my wife,' he said quietly.

'Oh, I'm sorry—I didn't mean to bring up something that would hurt you.' In impulse, she took his hand and squeezed it.

'They're good memories,' he said. He glanced at her sketchbook. 'May I see?'

'They're just scraps of ideas,' she said.

He flicked through it until he came to a sketch of Lorenzo. 'The young prince.'

'Yes—it's one of the ideas I'm working on.'

'So you've met the prince?'

She nodded. 'Actually, his best friend is the brother of my best friend. He came to stay with them while I was restoring their mermaid window. He liked my work and asked if I would do some designs for a window.'

'For the coronation?' Enzo asked.

'Yes, so I want to make sure I get it right and come up with a design to do him justice. He's a good man and I think he'll make an excellent king.' She grimaced. 'Sorry, I'm not from Melvante and it isn't my place to comment. I don't mean to be rude.'

'But you say things how you see them.'

'Honesty,' Indigo said, 'is always the best policy. Then everyone knows where they are.' She smiled. 'Which isn't an excuse for being rude. You can still be tactful and kind.'

'True.'

They chatted for a bit longer, then Enzo cut half a dozen of the *rosa mundi* roses and gave them to her.

She gasped. 'Is this going to get you into trouble with the king?'

'No. I'm the head gardener, so I can cut any roses I choose,' he said. 'If anyone asks you, say Enzo gave them to you and you're using them to help design your window.'

'I will—and thank you for being so kind and spending so much time with me. *Mille, mille grazie*,' she added.

'My pleasure, child,' he said with a smile, seeming touched that she'd bothered thanking him in his own language.

That evening, it never seemed to be the right time for Indigo to tell Lorenzo what she'd tried to tell him at the water maze. And, the next morning, she had an email from Lottie telling her that she needed to look at the newspapers.

When she did, she discovered a buzz of media speculation. A paparazzo had managed to capture a photograph of her with Lorenzo in the water maze, her hand on his arm, with them looking at each other. And they both looked as if they'd just been thoroughly kissed.

Is our prince falling in love?

Oh, no. She tried to get hold of Lorenzo, but his phone was switched off. In the end, she went to the office to talk to Salvatore. 'When His Royal Highness is free, please can you apologise to him for me?'

'About the papers this morning, you mean?' Salvatore asked.

She nodded. 'That wasn't meant to happen.'

To her relief, he didn't look angry. 'There's nothing you can do about the media, Indi. And it wasn't just you in the photograph, remember. Don't worry. The press office will handle it.'

'They already have enough on their plates, with the coronation.' And she dreaded to think of the media reaction to the rest of the news. A baby, and definitely no wedding because she wasn't a suitable princess.

'You look out of sorts,' Salvatore said, 'and would I be right in thinking it's not just the press?'

She sighed. 'I can't get the design for the window right.

I need to do something with my hands. Normally I'd make something in glass so I can let my subconscious work on whatever's blocking me, but I don't have my tools with me. This visit was just to look at the site and present some designs to His Majesty and His Royal Highness.'

'My sister always makes cake when she wants to think,' he said.

'Making cake would work for me. Or cookies.' She wrinkled her nose. 'Except I don't have a proper kitchen in the apartment.'

'You know we have a little kitchen here in the office. You could use that. And I'll arrange that you can borrow whatever you need from the palace kitchen.'

'And in return you get cookies?' she asked with a smile. 'Sal, thank you, that would be wonderful.'

He made a swift call, then smiled at her. 'Go and see Tonia in the kitchen and she'll get you what you need.'

'You,' she said, 'are a wonderful man.' She kissed his cheek, making him blush; then she headed to the palace kitchen and spoke to Tonia to sort out what she needed, carried the lot back to the office kitchen, and lost herself making shortbread biscuits.

She'd just melted some chocolate ready to decorate the top of the shortbread when Lorenzo walked in. 'What's this, commandeering my office kitchen?'

'Yes.'

'I love the smell of vanilla.' He stole one of the warm biscuits and tasted it. 'Mmm. This is good.'

She tapped the back of his hand. 'I don't know about Prince of Hearts—I think you're the knave, stealing shortbread.'

'The knave of hearts,' he said, 'allegedly stole tarts, not shortbread.'

'Same difference.'

He laughed. 'I never get told off in the palace kitchen.'

'Really? Well, you're getting told off in mine.' On impulse, she dipped her finger into the melted chocolate and dabbed a stripe on each cheek.

He looked at her. 'That's war paint. Hmm. Now there's an idea.' He dipped his finger into the melted chocolate, too.

As soon as Indigo realised his intentions, she ran.

Too late. He caught her, and painted her lips with the melted chocolate. And then he kissed it off.

Very, *very* slowly.

'I give in,' she sighed.

'Good.' He paused. 'So why are you baking?'

'I needed time to think about my design—I'm stuck on something, and my subconscious needs to work through it,' she said. She grimaced. 'And then there's that bit in the paper. I'm so sorry.'

'The photograph.' He didn't look in the slightest bit fazed. 'Yes, the press office has been fielding calls all morning.' He shrugged. 'Maybe it's better out in the open.'

'But you—we—we *can't*. You're supposed to marry a princess.'

'This is the twenty-first century. And, apart from the fact that I can marry someone not of royal blood if I choose, you're the daughter of an earl.'

'Illegitimate daughter,' she corrected. 'And my past is messy.' She still hadn't told him quite all of it. Or about their baby. But, the longer she left it, the harder it became, and she didn't want to just blurt it out.

'You're human,' he said. 'And people like you.' He tipped his head slightly to one side. 'People like the man I am, when I'm with you. *I* like the man I am, when I'm with you.'

'But it's not just you. There's your grandfather,' she said.

'I have a feeling he's going to like you.'

'But it's not enough,' she said. 'You have your position to think of.'

He grinned. 'Which is, right now, in my office kitchen, covered in crumbs and with chocolate all over my face. Very princely.'

'Lorenzo, why are you making it so hard?' she asked.

'I'm not,' he said softly. 'From where I'm standing, it's easy. You just have to believe. In *yourself*, as well as in us.'

That, she thought, was the rub. She couldn't believe in them until she believed in herself. And how could she possibly see herself as the wife of a king, having to live up to so many expectations when she'd been found so wanting in the past?

'I believe in you. And in us,' he said softly, and kissed her again. 'I'm stuck in official stuff all evening. But I'll see you tomorrow. We'll talk then.'

And she'd have to tell him then, she thought. She'd really, really have to tell him. She couldn't put it off any longer.

Predictably, Lorenzo was caught up in palace business until just before the time when he was due to introduce Indigo to his grandfather for the presentation of her designs, on the morning of the charity ball.

'Sorry,' he said, and kissed her on the cheek.

'It can't be helped. I know you're busy,' she said. Though inwardly she wondered: just supposing they did manage to make a go of things between them, would he be able to carve out enough time to spend with their baby?

Not that she could ask.

He ushered her in to one of the state rooms. And Indigo froze in horror when she saw the man sitting at the head of the table: the man she chatted to in the garden. She nearly dropped her laptop.

'I—you're Lorenzo's grandfather?' she asked, staring at him.

Lorenzo frowned. 'What's going on? Nonno? Indi?'

'We met in the rose garden, the other day,' Enzo explained. 'I was a little…mendacious, perhaps.'

A little? He could say that again. 'I thought there was something familiar about you, but I told myself I was just being ridiculous,' Indigo said.

Enzo shrugged. 'And when you see an elderly man wearing sensible clothes for gardening, you don't expect him to be the king.'

Even though, she thought, Lorenzo had pretty much warned her back in England. Hadn't he said that he would know exactly where to find his grandfather after he retired—in the rose garden? She really should have thought a little harder.

'You told me you were the head gardener,' she said, forgetting all about protocol and the correct method of addressing the King of Melvante.

'Strictly speaking, I am,' Enzo said.

Indigo blew out a breath. 'Well, I apologise if I was rude or said anything out of line. Your Majesty,' she added belatedly.

'I think,' Lorenzo said, 'Nonno was just as much in the wrong as you were. More so, in fact, because he misled you. And you probably weren't rude.'

'She wasn't. Though she does believe in plain speaking,' Enzo said. 'Which is refreshing. Now, Signorina Moran—Indigo—would you like to show us your designs officially?'

'You saw the rough sketches,' Indigo said. 'These are the proper proposals, Your Majesty. I hope you'll allow me to talk you through my ideas.'

* * *

Lorenzo sat back and watched as Indigo went into professional mode. She had a presentation on her laptop which she'd clearly run through a few times because her words were flawless. Then she gave them both paper copies so they could take a closer look; and she'd also made a rough copy of some of her designs on tracing paper and held it up to the window so they could see the colours.

'So the roses aren't a prison, this time,' Enzo said.

Colour flared in Indigo's cheeks. 'You saw the drawing?'

'It was why I agreed to the commission,' Enzo said. 'I notice my grandson isn't an angel this time.'

'He can hardly be an angel at his coronation,' she pointed out.

He looked more closely at one of the designs. 'Is that Caesar at his feet?'

'Um, yes,' she said. 'I could make the window without the dog, if you prefer. But I thought it might be a nice touch to make Lorenzo seem more human.'

Lorenzo coughed. 'I am still here, you know.'

'I know.' She smiled at him, her expression all warm and soft and sweet. 'Lorenzo, having your dog with you is something your people will be able to relate to—a beloved pet. It'll make them feel closer to you.'

'Good point,' Enzo said, sounding approving. 'I vote to keep him. And I like this one, very much. You've captured something in my grandson, Indigo. Something I never expected to see.' This time, he met Lorenzo's gaze. 'But I'm glad it's there.'

Lorenzo knew exactly what his grandfather was saying, and relief flooded through him. Now all he had to do was convince Indigo.

Once they'd finished their discussion, she curtseyed and left the room.

'Thank you,' Lorenzo said quietly, and hugged his grandfather.

Enzo raised an eyebrow. 'She's changed you. And it's a good change.'

'I need to talk to her.'

'Go, child. With my blessing,' Enzo said softly.

Lorenzo caught up with Indigo just outside her apartment. 'Are you OK?'

'Yes.' She sucked in a breath. 'Just a bit shocked that the man I was chatting to in the garden turned out to be your grandfather. I must've broken all kinds of protocol.'

'Sometimes protocol needs to be broken—and, if you think about it, he broke it as much as you did.' He paused. 'He's on our side, Indi.' When she didn't look convinced, he leaned forward and brushed his mouth against hers. 'Trust me,' he said softly.

That was the rub, Indigo thought. She wanted to trust him. She knew he was an honourable man. But that made everything even more mixed up and harder to say. 'You must have a million and one things to do.'

'I can postpone them, if you need me to.'

No. She was never, ever going to stand in the way of what he had to do for his country. 'I'm fine. I need to work out the glass order for your window. Go and do princely stuff.'

He smiled. 'I'll see you at the ball tonight.'

And then—then, she would definitely tell him. After the ball. 'See you later,' she said, and forced herself to smile as sweetly as she could.

CHAPTER FOURTEEN

IT TOOK INDIGO the second half of the afternoon to get ready for the ball. Lottie's gown was gorgeous—plain black and strapless, with a frothy ankle-length skirt that reminded Indigo of a ballerina's dress. And Lottie had given her an early birthday present to go with the dress— an enamelled pendant in the shape of a butterfly, coloured iridescent green and blue. That was the only jewellery she wore.

She didn't look in the slightest bit like a princess, she thought as she looked in the mirror. She looked like a little girl playing dress-up. This wasn't who she was—but it was who she'd have to be in Lorenzo's world.

He'd said that he liked the man he was when she was with him.

Could she learn to like the woman she'd have to be, by his side?

She shook herself, and marched down to the ballroom— luckily Salvatore had given her directions earlier. Salvatore was at the door of the ballroom, and smiled when he saw her. 'You look enchanting, Indi.'

'*Grazie*, Sal.' Even if he was just being polite and flattering, she'd take it. Because right now she could feel every bit of adrenalin running through her veins and spiralling into panic.

'Let me introduce you to some people.' With relief, she noticed that he introduced her as a professional glass expert. And everyone spoke English, so her limited Italian wasn't stretched too far.

Even so, she was aware of people watching her and she knew they were speculating about the photographs and stories in the press. Who was Indigo Moran—Cinderella, or a gold-digger out for what she could get?

It was worse when Lorenzo walked in, because everyone was watching both of them. And either he wasn't aware of it or he was trying to make a point, because he came straight over to her. 'Come and dance with me?'

'I—haven't you got loads of meeting and greeting to do?' she asked, panicking.

'It's a ball. People are supposed to dance at balls, Indi,' he teased.

'Proper ballroom dancing. I've never done this sort of thing. I'm going to trip over and fall flat on my face.'

'Not if your partner knows how to lead you properly,' he reassured her.

For one horrified moment, she thought he was going to kiss her. *In public.* But, to her relief, he simply smiled. And then he swept her into his arms.

'All you have to do is remember to use alternate legs, and go where I steer you,' he said softly as the waltz began.

She discovered that he was absolutely right. In his arms, and with him guiding her, she couldn't fall and make an idiot of herself. And she found herself relaxing, enjoying being in his arms.

He danced with her twice more during the evening. So did Salvatore, as if he realised she was feeling just a bit unsure of herself and could do with some back-up.

But then she went to the Ladies'. She was adjusting her dress when she heard people talking.

'She's plainer than I thought she'd be,' someone said.

In English. Indigo's skin crawled. Did they know she was here and meant her to overhear every word? Or were they just gossiping and at least one person in the group didn't speak good Italian so they were speaking in English to keep her in the loop?

'Darling, she must have something—the prince seems besotted with her.' This voice was more heavily accented.

'But he can't marry her, surely? She's not blue-blooded,' someone else said.

'She's definitely got her eye on the crown. Lorenzo's easy on the eye, but he's so reserved. He'd be such hard work as a husband. But I guess if you want money, you don't care about that sort of thing.'

Indigo was livid that these women had got Lorenzo so wrong and were being so mean about him. But she also knew that if she stormed out of the cubicle and put them straight, they wouldn't believe her—because they'd already decided that she was a gold-digger and her word wouldn't be accepted

She wouldn't be acceptable as Lorenzo's partner, either.

And although she knew he'd be gallant and fight her corner for her, it would place their relationship under such a strain.

He'd said that he wouldn't be like his father; if the woman he loved was unhappy in his world, he'd let her go because he wanted her to be happy. So now she needed to do exactly the same for him—to let him go, so he could find someone that the world would deem a suitable bride for him and let him be happy.

She stayed in her cubicle until the gossiping women had gone—not because she was a coward and afraid to face them, but because she knew that nothing she said would make a difference so it would be a waste of time and effort to confront them—and then slipped back out into the ballroom and found Salvatore.

'I've got a bit of a headache,' she said. 'I think I'm going to have an early night.'

'Can I get you some painkillers?' he asked.

She shook her head. 'That's really sweet of you, Sal, but a bit of sleep's the best thing for me.' Not that she'd be able to sleep. It'd be another night of lying awake at two a.m., worrying and wondering just how she was going to fix things. 'Can you give my apologies to whoever needs them, please?'

'Of course. Would you like me to walk you back to your apartment?'

'Thanks, but you don't have to do that. Really. I'll be fine.' She kissed his cheek. 'I'll see you later.'

As she headed back to her apartment, her heart was breaking.

She was doing the right thing—she *knew* she was—but why did it have to hurt so much?

Tomorrow morning, she'd tell Lorenzo about the baby, and then she'd get a flight back to England. She could work on the window over there and ship it over to Melvante when it was finished. And maybe they could time it so Lorenzo was away from the palace when she came to put the window in place.

'Where's Indi?' Lorenzo asked Salvatore. 'I can't see her anywhere.'

'She had a headache. She's gone back to her apartment for an early night,' his assistant said.

'Hmm.' Lorenzo frowned. 'Something's wrong.'

'Maybe the ball's a little overwhelming.'

Lorenzo shook his head. 'There's more to it than that. I've got a funny feeling. Cover for me, will you?'

'Are you sure about this?' Salvatore asked.

'More sure than I've been about anything,' Lorenzo said, and left the ballroom.

When he knocked on Indigo's door, she took a while to answer. She'd changed out of the ball gown into jeans and a T-shirt; with no make-up on and her hair pulled back, she looked young and very vulnerable.

'How are you feeling?' he asked.

'I'm OK,' she said, and he knew she was lying. 'You shouldn't be here. You're supposed to be at the ball.'

'You disappeared,' he said.

'I have a headache. An early night will sort me out.'

But he could see through the open door to her bedroom—and to the suitcase on the bed, half packed. 'Indi, I think we need to talk.'

'I…' She sighed and stood aside to let him in.

'Are you planning to leave?' he asked when he'd closed the door behind him.

'Tomorrow. I've finished the design. I'll go back and make the window.'

'Can't you make it here?' he asked.

'Better not.'

He frowned. 'What about us?'

'There can't be an us,' she said softly. 'Lorenzo—sit down. I need to talk to you about something.'

He frowned, but did as she asked and sat on the sofa.

Instead of sitting next to him, she sat on the arm of the chair furthest from him. 'I've been trying to find the right words to tell you, but I can't, so I'm going to have to be blunt about it.' She swallowed hard. 'I'm pregnant.'

'You're…' He couldn't quite take this in. 'How long?'

'About nine weeks.'

'How long have you known?'

'A couple of weeks. I've had a dating scan at the hospital.'

'Why didn't you tell me before?'

'Because I couldn't find the right words—or the right time.'

That was fair comment. He'd been rushing around all over the place and hadn't spent much time with her. Though there had been moments when they'd been close. Why hadn't she trusted him with the news then?

He blew out a breath. 'OK. We'll get married.'

'We will *not*,' she corrected.

'Indi, you're expecting my baby. What do you think I'm going to do, abandon you?'

She flinched.

Which wasn't so surprising. She'd been abandoned by her parents, and then dumped by a man who'd cheated on his wife with her.

'It's kind of traditional in my family to get married before you have a baby,' he said, hoping that he sounded light and gentle enough to ease her worries.

Her face was set. 'That's not going to work, and you know it. We've already talked about why we can't be together. Marriage is *that*—' she gestured wildly '—multiplied by a hundred.'

'We need to talk about this, Indi.' He moved to take her hand, but she pulled away. Hurt, he stared at her. 'Indi?'

'Just—please don't touch me. I need to keep a clear head,' she whispered.

That had to be the most backhanded compliment ever: she didn't want him to touch her because she didn't trust herself to think straight if he held her hand. Or did she not trust him not to bully her? He damped down his feelings. 'OK. Let's cut to the chase. You're expecting my child. Of course I want to be there and support you. And the best way for me to do that is if you marry me.'

'Because a king-to-be can't possibly have an illegitimate child?' she asked.

'I don't want to marry you out of duty or to satisfy any social conventions, if that's what you're thinking.' He blew out a breath. 'Right now, you're upset and you're worried. I don't think you'll believe me if I tell you how I feel about you.' He looked her straight in the eye. 'But I'm going to tell you anyway. I fell in love with you, back in Edensfield. You're a breath of fresh air, Indi. My world's a much better place when you're in it. And I'd like you there permanently. You and our child.'

'That picture I drew for you—did you look at it?' she asked. '*Really* look at it?'

'The prince in a bower of roses. Except the roses don't quite hide the fact that he's actually in a cage. Yes, I noticed,' he said dryly.

'That's your life, Lorenzo. It was what you were born to and you're accustomed to it. But I don't want that kind of life for our child,' she said. 'I don't care how gilded the cage might be, it's still a cage. Our baby won't have the freedom to make mistakes and learn from them.'

'So what's the alternative? Freedom, but not having his or her parents together? Not being part of a family?'

She flinched. 'Plenty of people grow up in single-parent families, and they're just fine. They're still loved and the parent they live with gives their best.'

'You and I,' he said, 'were both brought up by our grandparents. Both of us were sent away to school. I think, if we're both honest about it, we were lonely and we felt pretty much a burden to our grandparents. And I don't want that for my child. I want to live with my child. I want to be there for the first smile and the first tooth and the first word and the first step. I want my child to be part of a family. With *me*.'

Her eyes widened. 'Are you saying you'll fight me for custody?'

'No.' He raked a hand through her hair. 'What kind of monster do you think I am? I'm saying I want to do all that with you *and* our baby. Yes, you're right, as my consort you won't have the kind of freedom you've been used to in your life so far. You'll have a security team and a schedule. But there's room for compromise.'

'Is there? Because it seems as if I'm the one giving up everything.'

'You don't have to give up your friends or your job,' he said. 'OK, I admit, you won't be able to do your work to quite the same extent that you do now, because sometimes I'll need you to support me in state affairs and that means attending functions with me. But you don't have to give it up completely. It's important that you have your own interests.'

She still didn't look convinced.

'I want you in my life, Indi,' he said softly. 'Not because you're carrying my child, and not because I think this is the quick way to get everything a king is supposed to have—a crown, a queen and an heir. I want you for *you*.' He paused. 'You've talked about what you have to give up, but have you thought about what you'd gain if you married me?'

'Marriage to a king, and an unlimited budget. Social status and money might be what some people would want—and it's what people think I want.'

'What people?'

She swallowed hard. 'In the Ladies'. I heard them talking about me. They think I'm after a crown.'

He snorted. 'Like hell you are. That's not what you're about, and if they're too narrow-minded to see that then it's their problem.' He shook his head. 'And, actually, it's not what I meant. I think we can give each other something that neither of us has ever really had. We'll both be the centre of our family, not a burden tagging round the edges. Not someone who's going to be sent away.'

For a second, he saw longing in her eyes. He was pretty sure she wanted this, deep down, just as much as he did. But he knew that if he pushed her too hard, too fast, he'd drive her away. She had to come to terms with her own demons, the things that stopped her from wanting to be with him. Maybe she'd come to trust him enough to help her, but at the end of the day the only person who could really fight her fears was Indigo herself.

'At Edensfield,' he said, 'I asked you to make our relationship permanent. I gave you a choice. I knew what I wanted—just as I know what I want now—but I'm not going to bully you into choosing that. I want you to be with me because you want to be here. I don't want you to stay because you think you ought to for our child's sake or because you feel pressured. I want you to stay because you love me and you want to be with me, the way I want to be with you.'

She bit her lip. 'But how can I ever be acceptable in your world? How, with my past?'

'Everyone makes mistakes. The trick is to learn from them and not repeat them.' He sighed. 'Indi, you're hiding behind an excuse.'

She glowered at him. 'No, I'm not.'

'If I wasn't the heir to Melvante and I asked you to marry me, would it be different?'

She was silent for a long time. Then she sighed. 'Yes.'

'And that's the rub,' he said. 'I can't be someone I'm not, Indi. I'm an only child and so was my father. There's nobody else to take over from me. If I abdicate, so I can be the ordinary man you want, then I'd be letting my family down and I'd be letting my country down. But if I don't abdicate, I don't have you. Either way, I lose.' He looked at her. 'Unless you can be brave enough to believe in yourself and take me for who I am.'

'I'm not sure if I'm brave enough,' she said, biting her lip. 'I'm scared that it's all going to go wrong.'

'You're scared that I'll let you down, the way Nigel did? I'm not your ex, Indi.'

'No. You're an honourable man. You didn't even question whether the baby was yours.'

'Why on earth would I? Of course the baby's mine.' He frowned. 'Did *he* do that?'

She nodded. 'And he wanted me to have a termination.' She dragged in a breath. 'He said he already had one brat and he didn't want another.'

'That's despicable,' Lorenzo said. 'I want him in a boxing ring with me. Right now.'

She shook her head. 'Violence doesn't solve anything.'

'I know, but it'd be very satisfying to bring him to his knees and make him grovel to you.'

'I don't care about Nigel. I stopped loving him when I realised what a louse he was,' she said.

'Good. Because I'd hate to think he could hurt you again.' He stroked her face. 'Indi. I'm not him. I'm not going to abandon you—or our baby. And I'm certainly not going to ask you to have a termination.'

'I lost the baby. At thirteen weeks, I had a miscarriage. I'd already had a scan. I'd seen my baby's heart beating. And I…I…' She looked away.

Lorenzo stood up and went over to her, scooped her up in his arms and sat down, settling her in his lap with his arms wrapped tightly round her. 'I'm so sorry you had to go through all that. And on your own.'

'I wasn't on my own. Lottie held my hand all the way.'

'I'm glad.'

'She nearly missed Gus's wedding. I said she had to go because she was a bridesmaid, and I'd be fine on my own.'

'So that's why I didn't meet you at Gus's wedding. I was the best man,' he said. He kissed her hair. 'I'm sorry you lost the baby. That must've been hard for you. But, Indi, having a miscarriage in the past doesn't mean that you're going to lose our baby this time round.'

'I know. At least, the sensible bit of me knows,' she admitted. 'But there's a bit of me that can't help thinking, what if?'

'Which is only natural. But you'll have the best medical attention, I promise you. I'll look after you.'

'And that scares me, too. I'm used to being independent, Lorenzo. I don't want to be wrapped in cotton wool.'

'Noted,' he said gently, 'but at the same time I hope you'll understand that I want to keep you and the baby safe.'

'Because the baby might be your heir?'

'No. Because the baby's *ours*,' he corrected.

'Thank you. And thank you for believing me.' She hugged him back.

'Indi, you're not a liar and anybody who meets you would know that within about two seconds.' He stroked her hair. 'I can't believe we're going to be parents. It's…' He couldn't find the right words to explain how overwhelmed he felt.

'I'm sorry,' she said, sounding miserable.

'Don't be. It's not a bad thing. I'm terrified—but it's awesome, too, and I want to jump up and down and tell the whole world that I'm going to be a dad.'

She looked panicked. 'I'm not ready to tell the world.'

'Not until at least twelve weeks,' he reassured her. 'And definitely not until you're ready. This one's your call.'

'You're not angry?'

'Of course I'm not.' He smiled and held her closer. 'I'm thrilled. I don't care that our baby wasn't planned. We're going to have a *baby*, Indi. We've made a family. Do you have any idea how amazing that is?'

'Really?' For the first time since she'd told him, she started to look less scared and more like the sparky, independent woman he'd fallen in love with.

'Really,' he confirmed. 'I have no idea what kind of father I'll be, but I hope I'll be like my grandfather, and give love as well as boundaries.' He wrinkled his nose. 'Maybe slightly less rigid boundaries. And I'll have you to help me do that. You've already made a difference to the way people see me. I'm a better man with you by my side, and I want to be the best husband and father I can possibly be. Right by your side, Indi. No compromises.'

'But—those women in the Ladies'...'

'Were having an idle gossip. And, actually, they're totally wrong.' He took his phone out of his pocket and flicked into a social media site. 'Look. You're trending. There are a lot of influential people talking about you.'

'And how unsuitable I am for the King of Melvante,' she said gloomily.

'No. Look.' He showed her the screen. 'How you're warm and natural. How you're the perfect modern royal, low-key and approachable. How you've brought out a different side in me and they think I'm definitely ready to be king, now. How they hope the stories in the paper are true and that we really are having a secret romance.'

She stared at him, eyes wide, and a tear spilled over her eyelashes. He kissed it away. 'But the most important one for me was my grandfather. Yes, he had doubts. Especially when I told him that you had doubts about our lifestyle. He said that was sensible, but you were probably right. Today, he told me you're still sensible, but you're totally wrong about us. He thinks you'll fit in just fine, and that you're exactly what I need. Someone who'll have my back, who'll tell me things straight, and who—most importantly—will love me as much as I love you.' He kissed the tip of her nose. 'Indi, I want to marry you. I brought you over here to introduce you to my country and because I hoped you'd see that, although I have duties, I'm not just a king-to-be. I'm a man. I love you, and I want to be with you. Not because of the baby, but because of *you*.' He shifted so that she was sitting on her own, and dropped to one knee in front of her. 'I don't have a ring, but that's probably a good thing because it means we get the fun of choosing one together. But I'm asking you first and foremost as a man, and only secondly as the future King of Melvante—will you marry me, Indi? Will you love me, and let me love you all the way back? Will you make a real family with me?'

She dropped to her knees next to him and wrapped her arms round him. 'Yes. Most definitely yes.'

EPILOGUE

Two months later, the enormous cathedral at Melvante was standing room only.

The previous month, they'd celebrated the coronation of King Lorenzo the Third.

The PR team at the palace had outdone themselves and organised Lorenzo and Indigo's wedding in the shortest possible time. European royalty and heads of state had managed to switch things round in their diaries, and the streets were packed with people eager to catch a glimpse of the new bride and groom.

'You look amazing,' Lottie said, making a last adjustment to Indigo's veil.

'Thanks to Sally.' Her friend's clever dressmaking had managed to hide the bump of the eighteenth week of Indigo's pregnancy. 'And you look amazing, too.'

'Don't. I'll start crying, and then you will, and Lorenzo will throw me in the dungeons for making you cry on your wedding day.'

'I'm not crying,' Indigo said. 'I've never been happier.'

'I'm so glad.' Lottie hugged her, then made a noise of annoyance and fussed with her dress again. 'That's better.'

A carriage drawn by white horses—or, as King Geek had informed her, 'matched greys'—took Indigo to the cathedral.

'Ready?' Gus asked at the door.

'Ready.' She took his arm. 'This is the best day of my life.'

'Just as it should be.' He smiled at her and guided her through the front door of the cathedral, and the organist began to play the beautiful piece of music that Lorenzo had written for her.

The traditional red carpet led all the way to where Lorenzo was waiting for her at the aisle. And instead of cut flower arrangements on the ends of the pews, there were roses in pots, in a rainbow of colours. Half of them had been given by specialist rose-growers, and the other half had been given by ordinary people from their gardens; after the wedding, the roses were going to make a new garden at the palace. And right at the altar was one grown by Lorenzo's grandfather and named after Lorenzo's grandmother.

As Gus delivered her to the altar, Lorenzo looked at her and mouthed, 'You look amazing and I love you.'

'I love you, too,' she mouthed back.

The bishop smiled at them. 'Dearly beloved, we are gathered here…'

And Indigo knew that from now on, it was going to be just fine.

* * * * *

MILLS & BOON®

Why shop at millsandboon.co.uk?

Each year, thousands of romance readers find their perfect read at millsandboon.co.uk. That's because we're passionate about bringing you the very best romantic fiction. Here are some of the advantages of shopping at www.millsandboon.co.uk:

* **Get new books first**—you'll be able to buy your favourite books one month before they hit the shops

* **Get exclusive discounts**—you'll also be able to buy our specially created monthly collections, with up to 50% off the RRP

* **Find your favourite authors**—latest news, interviews and new releases for all your favourite authors and series on our website, plus ideas for what to try next

* **Join in**—once you've bought your favourite books, don't forget to register with us to rate, review and join in the discussions

Visit **www.millsandboon.co.uk** for all this and more today!